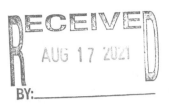

D1011217

CURSES

CURSES

LISH MCBRIDE

G. P. Putnam's Sons

G. P. Putnam's Sons
An imprint of Penguin Random House LLC, New York

Copyright © 2021 by Lish McBride

G. P. Putnam's Sons is a registered trademark of Penguin Random House LLC.

Visit us online at penguinrandomhouse.com

Library of Congress Cataloging-in-Publication Data is available.

Book manufactured in Canada
ISBN 9781984815590

1 3 5 7 9 10 8 6 4 2

Design by Marikka Tamura
Text set in Maxime Std

To Vela Mae McBride—
who, when I was beastly, would tell me
I was breathing a scab on the end of my nose.
I hope this dedication makes your eyes bug out
like a jumped-on frog.
Thanks for giving me the words for Val.
Love you, Grams.

CAST OF CHARACTERS

DuMont Family

Florencia—mother, Pieridaen humanborn

Brouchard—father, Pieridaen humanborn

Tevin—oldest son, Pieridaen humanborn, gifted

Amaury—second son, Pieridaen humanborn, gifted

Kate—only daughter, Pieridaen humanborn, gifted

Val (Valencia) Tern—second in line for the barony of Tern, a rural barony, cousin to the DuMont siblings, Pieridaen fairyborn

The House of Cravan

Merit Cravan—scion of the barony of Cravan, Pieridaen fairyborn, cursed

Lady Zarla Cravan—baroness of Cravan, Merit's mother, Pieridaen fairyborn

Ellery Detante—Merit's healer, sprigganborn

Kaiya DeMarcos—guard for the House of Cravan, Hanian fairyborn

The Royal Family of Huldre

Lady Angelique Latimer—queen of Huldre, mother to Eric, Tiradian fairyborn

King Henrich Latimer—king of Huldre, father to Eric, Tiradian fairyborn

Eric Latimer—crown prince of Huldre and only son, Tiradian fairyborn

Other Characters

Diadora Smythe—stepsister to Wilhelmina, Ivanian fairyborn, gifted

Willa (Wilhelmina) Smythe—heiress, stepsister to Diadora, Pieridaen humanborn, cursed

Glendon DeMarcos—cultural attaché and ambassador from Hane, Kaiya's uncle, Hanian fairyborn

Suitors

Cedric Fedorova—scion of the Fedorova barony, Pieridaen fairyborn

Freddie (Frederick) Dowerglen—second son of the barony of Dowerglen, Pieridaen fairyborn

Fairy Curse—a cruel twist of fate bestowed on someone by a fairy godling, sometimes deserved and sometimes not, but generally unwanted and not well thought out.

Fairy Gift—same as a fairy curse, really, only the fairy in question thinks this one is a *really good idea*.

It is the opinion of the author that both should be avoided if at all possible.

—Excerpt from *Musings: A Personal Look into the Fairy Kissed and Cursed*, author anonymous . . . for reasons

I, for one, would never put my health and safety in the inexpert hands of magecraft. Humans may be enamored with their shiny playthings, but we more enlightened beings know that nothing will ever replace the majesty and stately conveyance that is the horse and carriage.

—Letter to the editor of *The Pieridaen Gazette* in response to the opening of the new train lines, spring 1880

PROLOGUE

House of Cravan Country Seat, 1883

Merit Cravan, only heir to the barony of Cravan and current absentee from her own betrothal ball, locked herself in her room. Then pushed a dresser in front of the door, just in case. The dresser was heavy, and pushing it left her dress askew and her carefully curled and pinned updo a tangled mess by the time she was done.

"You come out this instant, young lady." Lady Zarla punctuated her demand with a moment of consistent but quiet thuds on the stout wooden door.

"No, Mother." Merit started yanking out the hairpins one by one, massaging her scalp. Her hair had a natural wave to it, but the maid had spent so much time heating and curling it that she no longer recognized the texture.

"Stop being such a child!" Her mother's voice through the door was fierce but low, because fairyborn aristocracy wouldn't be so uncouth as to *yell*.

"You stop being such a child!" As a retort, it lacked flair, and in many ways only supported her mother's argument. Merit

1

hadn't considered herself to be a child for several years. As the only heir, she'd had to pack up her childhood early and assume certain responsibilities. And yet, at this exact moment, that was exactly how she felt. Small. Young. *Scared.* "I told you to cancel it." Her words were calm, but the pins in her fist shook. She didn't love him, though that puny fact would not signify with her mother. "He's old enough to be my father." If her betrothed were a few years older, he'd be old enough to be Lady Zarla's father.

"He said he'd wait until you were eighteen. Honestly, Merit. Fairyborn gentlemen of his ilk don't grow on trees."

"He can wait forever!" Merit yelled, throwing her pins at the door. Her mother gasped at the slip in Merit's decorum, and Merit *did not care.* No, she did not. And if she kept saying she didn't care, eventually it would be true, wouldn't it?

"Godling Verity, we are graced with your presence." Lady Zarla's voice had completely altered, her tone now reverent and careful.

Merit put a hand over her mouth, muffling the sound that wanted to come out. In the mess of things, she'd completely forgotten—her mother had hired a fairy godling to gift the union. Godling Verity was temperamental, even for her kind— any perceived slight would be blown entirely out of proportion. Merit slid down the wall, pulled her knees up to her chest, and wrapped her arms around them.

"Is there a problem?" The godling's words held the crisp bite of authority. Merit didn't think anyone had argued with Godling Verity in her entire life. No sane person would.

"Lady Merit is indisposed." Even through the door Merit

2

could tell that Lady Zarla was holding on to her composure by her fingernails. "She'll be back out in a moment."

Fear spiked through Merit, but so did determination. She had already chosen the boy she would marry, and he was most certainly *not* the paunchy, gray-haired baron waiting for her in the ballroom. "I won't," Merit yelled without thinking. "I'm not coming out!"

It was the last straw. Her mother smacked the door with her hand. "You want to wait for your fortune hunter, you beastly girl? Want him to come back and profess his love? Well, he's not coming. Not tonight, not ever. You will grow up and do as I say! Merit!" She banged on the door some more. "Get out here right this minute!"

Merit's fingers slid over the beautiful beading of her skirt. She'd been so excited about this dress when she'd first seen the sketch. The exquisite detail, the sweetheart neckline, the deep purple of the fabric. It was the kind of dress her mother would wear—the dress of a woman, not a girl. Months ago, before she'd actually met her betrothed and the reality had set in, before she'd fallen for Jasper, she'd touched the swatch of fabric the dressmaker had brought and looked forward to this moment. As if donning the dress would wave a magic wand, making her into a sure and steady adult. Now the hem was torn, the beading ruined.

"He *will* come back for me." Merit was no longer sure if she was trying to convince her mother or herself.

A beat of silence then, a hesitation that told her that her mother was struggling with herself. "Fine. *Wonderful.* If he comes back for you—for you, not your money or your title—

you're welcome to him. You'll have my blessings. But he won't come back, Merit."

Her capitulation surprised Merit. It was too easy. "How are you so sure? You don't even know him."

"Because I made him an offer, and he took it. Took the coin and ran. He wanted your family's money. Not you."

Merit choked back a sob. The dull blade of betrayal sliced through her. Her mother was wrong; she had to be wrong. Jasper loved her. He loved her. He'd *promised*.

Lady Zarla smacked the door again. "Merit! You are the heir to one of the oldest and most respected baronies in this land, and you will act like it! Now, come out here before the guests start talking!"

Merit's entire body trembled, but she made no move to open the door. Her mother was lying. She had to be. He would never—only it didn't sound like her mother was lying, did it?

Merit heard a new sound then, the faint buzzing of wings. Her pulse sped up.

"You refuse to honor your mother's choice?" Godling Verity crooned oddly, as though she was pleased by Merit's disobedience.

Merit swallowed her fear. Her doubt. Even if her mother was right, she couldn't marry her betrothed. The thought of his hands on her made her want to curl up and die. "I refuse." The words rasped out of her throat, but the godling heard. There was no doubt about that.

Something tapped against the door—Merit would realize later it was Godling Verity's wand. "Beastly girl is right. You will get your gift from me this night." The hum of wings grew

4

louder. "As you are still young, I will be generous and give you a chance to learn from your folly." Merit could almost see the cold smile on her face. "If love appears, we will bow to your will. If not, it will be as your mother says. You will marry someone of her choosing by your eighteenth birthday."

Merit placed her hands flat on the floor, trying to quiet the trembling of her body. It didn't stop the fear slicing up her spine. For a second, she wavered. But then she thought again of her betrothed—of his greedy eyes on her, his clammy hands when he grasped her fingers and planted a dry kiss on her knuckles. "If I don't?"

"Then you will become a beast in truth. Do you still refuse?"

Merit closed her eyes. "Yes."

There was a flash, then a *whoosh*, and Merit felt like her world tipped sideways and split in half. She didn't remember anything else until one of her mother's footmen removed the door at its hinges. When she opened her eyes, it was to see the footman faint dead away, the heavy door in his hands clattering to the floor.

Then her mother screamed.

CHAPTER 1

A THIEF IN THE GARDEN

Florencia DuMont spit on the ground and cursed.

"There is a chance." From the rolling cadence of her accent, the weather mage was Ivanian, though that wasn't such a leap of logic. Most weather mages were. The woman touched her shoulder, a quick press of warmth, as her fellow mages looked on in sympathy. Or pity. Did it matter? "There is always a chance. Seek the harbormaster—surely they can aid you?"

"My goods were not insured," Florencia said smoothly. She looked down, feigning shame, letting the mage think she was either too poor to pay the dues or too foolish. Both reasons grated, but both were legal. Her cargo was not. Oh, she could petition on behalf of her legitimate goods, but they were cheap baubles and not worth the time and paperwork. Florencia kicked mud off her boot. The salty tang of the breeze off the ocean usually invigorated her. The swarm of humanity on the pier was colorful, bright, and a feast to the eyes, as well as to the pockets if your fingers were deft enough or your tale convincing.

But not today. Today she smelled only salt and dead fish. Everyone's ship had come in.

Hers had not.

"Squalls from the northeast hit the Tirada coast hard," the mage said. "There was nothing to be done." The blue swirl of tattoos on her cheeks, temples, and neck eddied like the wind across her brown skin. Since mages only got tattoos when they reached master status, Florencia had to accept that the harbor mage knew what she was talking about, even if she didn't like the news itself. Her goods were at the bottom of the sea with the fish, and it was impossible to swindle fish.

Florencia thanked the mage, hiding her irritation as she handed over a few small coppers for her to share with the mages behind her. She would get another ship. It never occurred to her to doubt it. Florencia left the docks, absently dodging people and crates of something with wings that hissed as she walked by. Normally she would have taken a peek—who was stupid enough to trade in creatures from the Enchanted Forest?—but her mind was already moving three steps ahead, creating and discarding plans to correct her fortunes.

Florencia fetched her wagon. There would be no staying at an inn tonight. Without the ships, they would need the money to keep their creditors at bay. She could sell the wagon, fattening her purse as best she could. Florencia would keep her horse—it was important to project the image of wealth. No one would do business with a beggar. This was only a momentary upset in their fortunes. They would be back on top again. Florencia clucked at her horse, heading to a nearby inn. The closest one would have a place where she could sit, order a drink, and find a patsy to sell her wagon to.

The Salty Siren was a bare-bones establishment. It wasn't

the kind of place one actually wanted to rent a room from, unless a body loved the company of fleas. The dining room, however, was passably clean, the mediocre ale watered down but cheap, and the clientele diverse. Rich patrons didn't sleep here, but they did come here for business. It was the best place to hire a crew for your ship or to unload your cargo.

Florencia didn't bother cleaning her boots—the boot brush was already stiff with mud, so any effort would have been in vain. She sauntered in, her shoulders back, the tilt of her chin regal. People saw what you showed them, and Florencia Du-Mont had the look of a vengeful goddess made mortal. The haze of cigar smoke was thin, the windows open to catch a late spring breeze. She had to alter her course quickly to avoid kicking over a brimming spittoon resting on the floor next to the bar. With a sneer, she decided that her earlier assessment of "passably clean" had been overly generous. Florencia traded two much-needed coppers for a pint that she wouldn't give to a pig and took a seat at a small round table in the back of the dining room. Now she simply had to wait.

Like any good swindler, Florencia DuMont knew her assets well and traded on them heavily. She knew eyes had followed her confident swagger through the room—tight breeches, expensive boots, and a face wrought of temptation guaranteed it. The Salty Siren was full of hungry patrons, and she was a four-course meal. She sipped and waited and dangled as bait. If she made it to the halfway point of her pint, she'd undo her braids. She usually didn't have to—Florencia was an exceedingly handsome woman—but sometimes people needed a push, and her chestnut locks would do the trick.

She was nowhere near halfway when someone took the seat across from her. Florencia gave her a passing glance, her eyes automatically assessing and cataloguing the woman's worth. Her clothes were shabby, her floppy hat dipping low to obscure blond hair that was almost white and lips that made a dainty bow. An artful smudge of dirt stroked one cheekbone. This woman wanted to appear down on her luck, lowborn, and working class, but the contents didn't match the wrapping. Her skin was porcelain pale, fingernails shaped and clean. Florencia had a hunch, but she needed a little more information, so she stuck her hand out. "Florencia," she said, adopting a local accent she frequently heard around the docks.

The woman took her hand, giving it an awkward shake. "Delilah."

Though she kept her face benignly friendly, inside, Florencia felt a flush of triumph. Delilah, which most certainly was *not* her name, had soft hands. No calluses meant no labor, and the awkward shake implied she wasn't used to that greeting. Between that and her upper-crust accent, Florencia figured that Delilah was the kind of person more used to dropping a curtsey than clasping palms. No, Delilah was fairyborn playing at human.

For a moment, she considered whether Delilah was a godling in disguise—a favorite trick for the capricious creatures, used to catch mortals up so they could bestow their magic upon them. But no, Florencia thought not. When godlings disguised themselves, they used glamour magic to blend, making themselves look human. Away went the tipped ears, the wings, the pearlescent sheen to skin that could be anything from faintly green to blue-black. There was variation on the theme, like any other creatures, depending on ancestry.

The mistake most people made was to trust their eyes, but Florencia knew the secret. Godlings had a way about them, an air of haughty otherness that was hard to explain, but easy for her to identify. She'd made it her mission early in life to learn what she could about them and their fairyborn descendants. Not all of them had deep pockets, but there were other things they could offer, and Florencia had three gifted children to prove it.

The fairy race didn't produce a lot of children, and over the years, they'd intermingled with humans to the point that they were hopelessly enmeshed, producing fairyborn, like Delilah. Oh, Florencia couldn't see any hint of her lineage—the hat covered her ears, skin could be obscured, and very few of the born had wings anymore. But Florencia had spent a lot of her life fleecing those with money or power, and the fairyborn often had both. She was willing to bet her boots that Delilah was one of them, which meant Florencia's luck had turned.

"Delilah, you look like a lass down on your luck," Florencia said, a hint of sympathy honeying her guileless tone. "Care for a drink and a sympathetic ear?" Florencia didn't wait for Delilah to respond before waving at the bar lad for a pint of ale.

"You are too kind." Delilah clasped her hands demurely in her lap. "Am I so transparent?"

Florencia pulled out two more coppers to trade for the horse piss they called ale and smiled. "Only to someone who has been in the same predicament."

The bar lad took the coppers and handed Delilah her glass

with a wink and a friendly smile before scurrying off to the next table.

"I'm afraid I've hit a spot of trouble," Delilah said, her elegant hands fluttering in the air like doves. She was a lovely creature, Florencia thought, and smart enough not to touch her ale. "And, oh, I know it's not your problem, but I needed a friendly face."

Florencia buried a snort. Her face was many things, but "friendly" wasn't on the list. She had the feeling Delilah, or someone in her employ, had witnessed Florencia's problems at the dock. Delilah didn't need a friendly face—she needed a desperate soul.

"Ah, lass, your words land on sympathetic ears," she said, patting the younger woman's hand. "I, too, have had a spot of troubles. I came all this way, only to leave with empty pockets and an emptier cart."

Delilah gasped in dismay, one of those dove-like hands coming to roost on her chest. The motions were perfect, but her eyes gave her away. This was not news to Delilah.

"I'm so sorry," she said.

Florencia shrugged. "The sea is a fickle mistress. She gives and takes, and we love her still, more fools we." For a second Florencia thought she might be laying the folksy sailor routine on a little heavy, but the woman either didn't notice or didn't care.

Delilah tutted, all concern, then leaned back, her face lighting up as if a sudden idea had occurred to her. Florencia wanted to applaud. Someone had given this woman a playbook, and she was following it to the letter. Now she would lean in, clasp

12

Florencia's hand to establish contact and trust, and then offer a proposal that would help them both.

Delilah rested her soft hand on Florencia's, but the eyes shadowed by her hat were intent. "You have a fast horse and know this land well?"

"I do," Florencia supplied. "And once I sell my cart, I'll move faster."

"Oh, this is wonderful! Not your misery," she was quick to add. "But that we may help each other." Delilah spun a tale of a dastardly trader who took her deposit but didn't deliver the goods. "There is a manor close to here, scarcely over the border—a few hours' ride on a good mount and a quick hop on a train, and you'd be there by nightfall. All I would need is a cutting of a plant—a single flower." She held her hands out as if to say, *This is so simple, you should be paying* me *for the opportunity.*

"Why can't you get the cutting yourself?" Florencia asked.

Delilah looked forlornly into her ale. "There was a mix-up with my travel papers. So tedious, but one can't cross the border out of Huldre without them. I'd wait for new papers, but time is a factor, you understand. It seemed better to hire a trader to act as a go-between." She leaned closer, her eyes shifting to the crowd around them. "To be honest, there's some bad blood between the sellers and myself, too. It's all so silly, really."

Silly, but necessary. The kingdom of Huldre may have been as small as some of the baronies under Queen Lucia's thumb, but it was still its own sovereign nation. Slipping across the border between Huldre and Pieridae would be complicated without the right papers.

Delilah pulled a small pouch from under the table. She placed a single golden coin on the scarred table, wing side up. "For the train fare. I can give you five more up front. The other half on delivery."

Florencia picked up the coin. She counted the spots on the wings and the ridged lines. Pretending to consider the deal, Florencia turned the coin in her hand. Her fingers traced the grooved ridges along the thin side of the coin before examining the other side, which held the queen's crown. Forgery was a deadly game, but some people still played. The coin caught the light, a flash of gold. This monarch, at least, was real. Ten of them wouldn't replace what she'd lost today, but it would be a good start. It also tipped Delilah's hand. Five monarchs was more than most people saw in a month. Ten? Ten was mighty desperate.

"That's a lot of money," Florencia said, pretending reluctance. "Is the job dangerous?"

Delilah's hands fluttered again, graceful but with a hint of impatience. "No, it's only that the plant is rare, and I'm in a hurry. I'm already behind schedule as it is."

Florencia didn't ask if the job was illegal. It most certainly was, and though she was curious as to what tales Delilah would spin, the day was wearing on. Time to pluck this errant dove. "Eight now, seven on delivery."

"Six and six," Delilah countered.

"We could spend all day arguing down to the copper," Florencia said, placing the monarch on the table. "Or we can cut to the chase and end on seven and seven."

"Deal," Delilah said, though she wasn't happy about it.

Florencia eased back in her chair, a smile on her face. "Well, then, I think our stars align themselves nicely, don't you?"

• • •

Florencia sold her cart, fattening her purse further. She would need the speed more than the cart. She packed her meager supplies into her saddlebags before swinging smoothly onto her horse and heading inland to catch the train. She'd memorized Delilah's instructions, burning the paper they'd been written down on.

She forked over a half crown for her train ticket to Veritess, grumbling over the extra buckeye she had to add to cover her horse's travel in the livestock car. The line to get on board was slow since everyone had to show not only their tickets but their papers. Florencia's happened to be fake, but her youngest son had made them, so she knew they'd pass scrutiny. His forgeries were impeccable.

On her way off the train, she picked a man's pocket merely to make herself feel better and to make up for the money spent on tickets. She'd long ago graduated past such things, but liked to keep in practice. Her horse was galloping away down the muddy streets before the man even noticed his money was gone.

Night descended, clouds gathered, and a cold, cutting rain fell, turning the road into ruin. Though the woods might offer cover, a hard winter and a cool spring made for desperate wolves and other things. Worse things. She powered through toward the manor. If she could sneak in during the cover of nightfall, all the better.

Florencia thought she was dreaming when she spotted the

golden magework bird roosting on the manor gates. When the bird's beak opened and the crisp voice of one of the staff issued out, offering a warm meal and a dry bed, she knew she'd found the right place. The magework was delicate and so exquisitely done that it looked real. Not a lot of people would be able to afford such a creation, but the kind of person who would have a flower worth fourteen gold pieces *would*. Through the bird the staff offered hospitality without having to slog down to the gates in the rain. Florencia had expected the offer. It wouldn't do to turn down a stranger—a weary traveler might be a godling in disguise.

Florencia was fed, bathed, and tucked into opulent guest quarters in a sprawling mansion set far back from the road. She met no one but the staff, who were faultless in their duties. After she was cared for, Florencia considered sneaking out to look for the flower, but decided to wait until morning. The evening was miserable, the manor lands appeared quite vast, and it would do her no good to get lost in the rain.

In the morning she found her trousers, shirt, and other clothing clean and pressed, smelling faintly of oranges. She put them on, feeling light with possibility, and if a few small, priceless objects found their way into her pockets, who was there to see? No one. The staff had left her to her business after breakfast. Once her horse was saddled, a groom gave directions back to the main road coupled with a warning to stick to the path. She tipped her hat at him, amused by the blush that pinked his ears.

Florencia kept her eyes to the sides of the path as she rode. Delilah had never given her the plant's name, but had described it in detail, so Florencia dawdled, stopping frequently on any pretext to take a moment to search the side of the path. As her horse clopped along, they passed orchards, topiaries, and brightly colored flowers she could not name, all things she'd missed in last night's darkness and rain. She was entranced by their vivid pinks, yellows, and deep, vibrant reds. The road turned, and she saw a small shrub tucked away off the road, the first in a neat series of rows. Triumph bloomed in her.

She urged her horse closer and inspected the flowers. Long, delicate white petals, freckled with a muted gray. The center and stamen were a gentle, blushing pink. She was no botanist, but even she could identify a flower if given enough detail. She didn't hesitate, but swung down, sliding her field knife from the leather sheath attached to her belt. Florencia cut away a small branch with three of the flowers, wrapping the stem in a dampened handkerchief as she'd been instructed. Giddiness filled her, as it always did when a job was going well. Now all she had to do was take the train back over the border and collect.

Florencia turned to grab her horse, but never reached the reins. Metal brambles, their thorns thick and barbed, boiled from the forest floor, trapping her. Up they grew, tangling her in their grip, until her feet left the ground. Her horse shied away from the magecraft, but not fast enough, the reins snagging on the briar, keeping the horse from bolting completely. There Florencia hung, bleeding, fuming, and cursing the magic that held her tight, when a roar cut through the forest.

All bird chatter stopped.

Insects quieted.

Even the sun hid behind a cloud. She reached for her pistol, her fingers barely grazing the grip. Her knife lay on the grass under her, useless.

Florencia's mind tried to make sense of the creature materializing from a copse of woods. Horns spiraled back from an angry brow. Eyes flashed. Fangs snarled. A scaled tail lashed, and a grinding voice of nightmares issued forth from its maw. "How dare you take what's ours?"

Florencia trembled, the brambles digging deeper, and for the first time in her life, she knew real fear.

"You will pay," the creature snarled. "With your life if need be." The creature moved then, all sinuous grace and predatory glide.

"I have no money," Florencia said. She'd sewed her coins into her jacket lining this morning. It was unlikely that the creature would find them. Florencia kept her words calm and even, though her mind spun, looking for an out. There had never, not once, been a situation she couldn't spin, or a deal gone south that she couldn't talk her way out of.

"What you hold is more precious than money. You have taken my hospitality. You've seen my home. Do you think I need something as common as coin?" A chuckle escaped the beast, low and mean.

Only someone born to privilege could be so dismissive of such things. Florencia ignored the voice, the tail, the snarling teeth. Those would only frighten her, and she needed her wits. She looked into its eyes and calmed almost immediately. This beast may snarl and growl, but the eyes glittered with intelligence. She could reason with it. Florencia had spent her entire life fleecing those born to privilege. Whether the creature was hideous and horned didn't signify. Inside, the rich were all the same.

"I'm sure we can come to some sort of understanding."

"Perhaps," the beast said. "I think our trade should be like for like, don't you think? You took several blooms, likely damaging the plant in the meantime. Blooms that could mean someone's life." The creature stalked closer to her now. She could feel its hot breath on the back of her neck.

"You want my life?" Florencia asked.

"I'm not sure it would be worth the trade," the beast snarled. "Caen's bloom is worth more than the life of a dishonorable thief."

"You're right, of course," Florencia said quickly. "I'm hardly worth the trade. What use would I be?"

The beast stopped, eyes narrowing. It hadn't expected her quick agreement.

Florencia licked her lips, the idea barely forming before she spoke it. "I have nothing, am nothing. The only thing I have worth a bean is my son."

The beast crept around her now, staring her in the face. "You wish to trade your son for your freedom?"

"Yes," Florencia said. "As you have pointed out, I have no value. But Tevin? The light of my life? The jewel of the DuMont house? You will find no one more charming or handsome. He would cover my debt, I am certain."

And so Florencia DuMont sang the praises of Tevin to the beast, feeling no guilt whatsoever about trading away her oldest son. After all, it wouldn't be the first time.

CHAPTER 2

GOOD FAMILY ALWAYS BAILS YOU OUT

Tevin DuMont waited at the servants' entrance. Now that the Downings knew the truth, they wouldn't want the likes of him coming in the front door. He spun a bowler hat in his hand, his body relaxed as he leaned against the brick edifice that was the Downing household when they weren't at their country estate. The townhouse was in a fashionable neighborhood off of the market square, nestled right in downtown Grenveil. If that didn't tell Tevin how deep the Downings' pockets were, the bustle of servants going in and out the back and the scale of deliveries being dropped off would have. Out of habit, Tevin counted them up as they went in the door next to him. *Hothouse flowers, sides of venison, a brace of quail, cheeses in thick wax rinds, fresh apples, and cases of sparkling wine.* And more— so much more. It was an embarrassment of supplies, and they weren't even having a party. Well, maybe they were going to have a private one as soon as they got rid of him.

Tevin popped his hat back on and began to whistle. That was usually the last straw for most people. He only managed a few bars before the door snapped open and one of Downing's hired men poked his head out.

"The master will see you." His tone very much implied that he didn't think the master should do any such thing.

"Obliged." Tevin tipped his bowler with a grin, and the man *softened*. That was the best way Tevin could describe it. His gift of charm didn't change people or cloud their minds; it only made them more moldable, like warm wax in skilled hands. The charm might have been a fairy gift, but his looks were his own, and he wielded both with the casual ease of someone long used to a task.

The hired man—probably a butler—led Tevin through the kitchen. "Would you like something? Sandwiches? A fresh apple? The cook makes a lovely raisin bun—"

Tevin patted the man's shoulder genially. "No, thank you. I'm sure the master would like to see me quickly." When the butler looked crestfallen, he added, "Perhaps on the way out." After all, he didn't want to disappoint the man. And he *was* hungry.

The butler nodded. "I'll ask the cook to set one aside for you."

Tevin followed the butler through the obscene wealth that comprised the Downing household. His boots met thick imported carpets. The light that fell on him was filtered through stained-glass windows. The candleholders all had fresh beeswax tapers ready for dusk. Mage light would have been cheaper and more convenient, but Downing had an old fairy lineage and wouldn't want to dirty his home with mage magic. It would be beneath him. To Tevin it seemed senseless to pass up a cheap and useful innovation, but what did he know?

The butler waved him into a study but didn't enter. Tevin almost asked him to wait. Downing wasn't one for power plays, so this meeting would be short, and he would call the butler back to make sure Tevin left immediately.

"Don't sit." Avrel Downing, baron of a small but—unfortunately for him—rich barony in the south, stood up from his desk and glared at Tevin. Well, technically, Avrel thought he was glaring at Tomas. Swindlers never used their real names, and the DuMonts were meticulous with their craft.

"Wouldn't dream of it." Tevin's smile was a sharp blade. It wasn't sporting to kick a man when he was down, but Tevin harbored a dislike for parents who bullied their children. In many ways, Avrel doted on his daughter. She could have anything she wanted, except the one thing that mattered—control over her future.

Avrel sighed as he descended into his chair. The baron likely knew, at least intellectually, that he was angry, but the emotion would be muted while Tevin's gift worked its magic . . . whether Tevin wanted it to or not. He missed a really good argument. Tevin's gift had been bestowed when he was seven. He couldn't charm his family—his parents had made sure that their children wouldn't be able to turn their gifts on them—and every once in a while, he met someone who was immune, but not often. If the charm didn't get them, his looks did.

"You're a monster," Avrel said, dropping his head in his hands.

"I know." Tevin shifted his weight, his feet and calves aching from the lifts he'd shoved into his boots, despite the thick carpet he stood on. Everything in Avrel's office, from his leather chair to the gilded spines of the books lining the shelves, said plainly that this home was full of wealth, comfort, and power.

Tevin's stomach was an empty ache, reminding him he hadn't eaten since last night.

"You played her for a fool, an absolute fool." Avrel's face took on the appearance of a mournful dog.

Tevin kept his mouth shut, though he wondered what bothered Avrel most—the loss of face or his daughter's heartache? It wasn't his place to correct the baron. He was here to get paid. "We could always go through with the engagement—"

Avrel recoiled as if he'd been struck. "My daughter's line is fairy-blessed on both sides."

Whereas Tevin's blood was common as dirt, not a noble speck of magic anywhere in his lineage. This is what they banked on, the parents' aversion to sullying their own bloodlines. Diluting them. Tevin relied on them choosing that over a supposed love match. No one had picked their daughter's wishes over bloodlines, not in the four years he'd been running this particular con for his parents.

Avrel didn't disappoint. With a groan, he handed Tevin a leather pouch. Tevin opened it, counting the coin inside.

"I hope you're proud of yourself, you miscreant." His voice held no heat, though.

Tevin pocketed the leather purse. *Miscreant* was new. He rather liked the stately sound of it. "I am, thank you."

Avrel stared mournfully through the window. "You can let yourself out."

Tevin didn't say anything as he slipped out the office door.

He ran smack-dab into Lydia, who was waiting in the hall. Her big blue eyes were wide, anxious. Tevin opened his coat and showed her the purse. Those big blues lit up, and she danced in place. She threw her arms around Tevin and kissed him on the cheek. He held her for a second before letting her go.

She handed him an embroidered handkerchief, the ends tied up in a small bundle. He didn't count that one out, putting it directly into his pocket with the purse from her father. She gave his shoulders a final squeeze, a grin lighting up her whole face. Tevin shooed her off, sending her back up the stairs to her room. Wouldn't do for her doting papa to come out and find them.

He made his way down the hall and into the kitchen. The cook, a rather fierce-looking woman with apple cheeks, waved a begrudging hand at the bun sitting on the table. "Jennings wanted you to have it."

Tevin picked up the bun and took a bite. He didn't have to feign enthusiasm. It was perfect—raisins and a hint of cinnamon and some sort of honey glaze. "You, madam, have a gift. This is perfection."

The cook wiped her hands on her apron, a flush tinting her cheeks. "It's merely a bun."

He shook his head. "Not to me." He lifted it. "This, madam, is *art*."

She firmed her lips, her eyes getting distant. She held up a finger telling Tevin to wait as she strode briskly to the pantry. Tevin savored his bun, licking each drop of honey off his fingers, and waited to see what else the cook would offer.

• • •

Tevin managed to charm a carriage ride from Downing's stable, making it to his parents' home in short order. His cousin,

24

the esteemed Valencia Tern, second in line to the barony of Tern, sprawled across his porch swing, her boots up on the edge of the railing. Well, technically it was Val's porch swing. The DuMonts had taken up residence two years ago after a swindle had gone sideways and they'd needed fresh territory. The house was on the edge of the respectable part of Grenveil, and though the distance from the Downings' was small, the two homes were worlds apart. The DuMonts were good at making money, but they were good at losing it, too. And spending it. At least his parents were.

"A ride *and* a gift basket?" Val asked, tipping her telescope hat back from her eyes, her country accent giving her a pleasant drawl. "I take it everything went well?" Val took after her mother, fresh faced and girl-next-door pretty, with short copper hair, tipped ears, freckles, and the most adorable button nose this side of the divide. She could also shoot the dots off a domino and didn't like anyone calling her "adorable."

Val opened the door for Tevin, and they went inside, taking off their boots and placing them by the door.

"They home?" Tevin mouthed, scooping up the gift basket.

Val shook her head. "Your mother isn't back yet, and your father drug your sister off to a horse market. No idea where your brother got off to, and with him it's always better not to ask."

Tevin glanced around his house. The DuMont fortune fluctuated like the tides. One week they were eating seven-course meals off fine china. The next week they had to fire the cook and sell the china. More money always came, but the in-between times could be long and uncomfortable. Tevin could do without the creature comforts, but if things got too dire, his parents got desperate. And if they were desperate, they got hasty, taking riskier jobs that weren't always well planned. Last time that happened, they'd barely made it out of town with the clothes on their backs.

Tevin was nineteen, and for the last year or so he'd often spent days, sometimes weeks, on a job and barely been home. He needed to work, to bring in money, but part of him always worried that he'd come back one day to find one of his parents in jail or his siblings thrown into a reckless con. If he was home, he could step in, take the risk himself. Make sure Kate and Amaury had some safety, some stability. But he couldn't always be there, and one of these days, his siblings would fail to talk their parents into being sensible and he wouldn't be there to step in. It was a fear that clawed at his guts whenever he thought about it, which was frequently.

Amaury was six months from his eighteenth birthday, but Kate had three more years at home. Three long years in their parents' tender care, her fate tied to their whims. So Tevin looked around to see the state of things—did they still have the china? the silver? candlesticks? Small things that could be sold quickly would go first. The candlesticks were gone, and so was the dining room rug. It had been there last week when he'd checked in. Things were bad, then.

He peeked into a small room off the hall, relieved to see the ornate silver mirror hanging on the wall. He supposed it was too useful to part with easily. Mirrors were mage magic, not fairy, but his parents didn't care where magic came from as long as it did what they wanted.

Godlings, though powerful, were limited in their magic and

could only gift and curse living things. Mages were the balance, humans born with a trace of magic that, after years of schooling, could work together to enchant objects. They couldn't gift or curse, but they could invent. Some of the fairyborn didn't trust magecraft, and so avoided things like enchanted mirrors, mage lights, and trains. Others embraced these new creations because they made life easier. His parents saw the advantages of both.

"Were they selling or buying at the horse market?" Tevin asked.

"Selling, I think," Val said.

Tevin's father, Brouchard, would have taken Kate to get the best deal possible. His baby sister had been fairy gifted with savvy. Even at fifteen she could negotiate the lifeboat from under a sea captain in the middle of an ocean.

Tevin felt a wave of relief that his parents were out, enabling him to talk freely. "At least we can't lose the house." A little over two years ago, after one particular job had gone disastrously wrong, Tevin's family were forced to flee in the night and find new lodgings—no easy business with a family of five and no money. His father had remembered a rancher cousin in the sticks who'd managed to marry into a fairy line, and decided that now would be a good time to reacquaint themselves. It had been one of the best days of Tevin's life. For the first time in ages, they had a steady home. The three-bedroom house was opulent enough to please Tevin's parents—though he and Val had to bunk in the attic when they were here—and quaint enough that Val's family was letting them live there rent-free as they recovered from the "troubles" that had plagued his family. Tevin tried to remember

27

what web of lies they'd told, what misfortunes they'd spun from nothing, but couldn't. Not that there hadn't been misfortunes, but Val's family wouldn't give them much charity if they told the truth.

Val's family mostly kept to their rural barony, which meant that before the DuMonts, this house often sat vacant. Val's family, being the good, decent sort, didn't seem to know what the DuMonts were capable of and had been happy to loan the house to them long term. They even encouraged Val to stay with them, thinking that the impeccable manners of their refined relatives might rub off on their daughter—an idea so wrongheaded that it made Tevin laugh every time he thought about it. On her end, Val had decided to keep anything she learned about Tevin's family to herself. After all, she didn't want to be called back out to the country. Not when the city offered proper mischief.

The neighborhood they were in was nothing like the Downings', and they didn't have live-in help—only a woman who came to clean in the mornings. It was a far cry from where Tevin had just been, but it was also much better than where they'd been living before. Definitely had fewer people with fire and pitchforks coming after them, which worked in their favor.

"Come see my bounty," Tevin said, holding his basket aloft and making a side trip into the study. He handed Val his basket, smiling as it made her tip forward—it was heavier than it looked. After taking his percentage out of the big purse, he deposited it into the family safe. He put his cut into the knotted handkerchief and saved Val by taking back the basket before leading her upstairs. There he would separate his take into two places. He put a few coppers into the skinny lockbox hidden in the false bottom of his trunk.

"You know they have these things called banks," Val said dryly as he locked the trunk.

"Banks establish a paper trail and make it difficult to grab your money in the middle of the night when trouble arises." With the DuMonts, trouble always seemed to arise.

"Okay, but is *that* necessary?" she asked as she watched Tevin carefully move his nightstand so as not to leave scratches on the floor. Then he pried up the loose board, pulling up a leather purse.

"My parents search my room. They won't believe that I'm not keeping anything for myself, so I have the decoy for them to find." He put the rest of his cut into the dusty leather purse before stashing it back into the floor. The one thing he could always count on was his parents' greed.

Val dug into the basket as Tevin settled in. "I still don't understand why you have to give so much of what you make to your family."

"If I'm turning a profit, I'm left alone, mostly. They're left alone." He didn't have to specify who "they" were. Val would know he meant Amaury and Kate. Tevin didn't keep things from Val if he could help it. He also didn't admit that he liked the look of pride on his father's face when he counted out the coins Tevin brought home. They weren't good people, he *knew* that. But they were still his parents, and he wanted to hoard a few crumbs of their esteem. It was wrongheaded, but there it was.

He stripped off his vest and shirt, making his way to the

pitcher and bowl of water on his dresser. "Besides, the last time I tried to keep a purse, it was . . . bad."

"You can't leave it at 'bad.'"

"I was locked out of our rooms for three days. We lived in a rough area at the time, and it was January." It had taken Tevin a full day to warm up when he'd been let back inside, and a week to get over the fever he'd developed as a result. He'd barely eaten, even with his gift. It was hard to charm food away from people who didn't have any, and their neighbors had precious little. He'd had to be so careful that what he took wasn't stealing food away from younger, weaker children. By the time his parents let him back in, he almost didn't care. He would have snatched a morsel of bread out of the hands of a babe. "I was ten."

Val shook her head. "Okay, but—"

"They said if I did it again, I would have to stay out longer, and take my siblings with me." Tevin kept his voice matter-of-fact while he washed, enjoying the coolness of the water. The room he shared with Val was in the attic, and it was at least ten degrees hotter than the rest of the house on most days.

"If they locked you all out now, you'd probably have a party." Val pointed at the basket. "If you can manage this by yourself, without even trying hard, then imagine all three of you together."

Tevin grabbed a cloth to dry his face. "That was the threat they made when I was ten. I have no idea what they would do *now*." And that was the problem. Florencia and Brouchard were adaptable and cunning, masters at understanding people's weaknesses. Whatever punishment they chose would slip a dagger unerringly into the spot that would hurt their children most.

30

So Tevin worked hard, handing over most of his coin, saving what he didn't. A cushion in case something came up, because something always did. A healer for Kate, food for the larder, the bill for the mage light. He could ignore the thinning soles of his boots and his father's tailor bills, but he couldn't ignore the important things, because his parents *did*.

Tevin dried his face. Val watched in interest as he did his transformation act. Lenses popped out, changing brown eyes to green. False lashes were removed—research had told him that Downing's daughter liked thick-lashed, brown-eyed men with auburn hair. She'd liked them tall and lanky, a description that fit his younger brother, Amaury, better, but you didn't send Amaury out to charm anyone. He generally had the opposite effect. Even though Tevin had already grown into a decent-sized man, he'd added lifts to his boots. Lydia also favored aristocratically thin gentlemen, but he hadn't been able to change his musculature on such short notice, which was good, because Tevin was fair sick of dieting. It was too close to starving, and he'd had his fill of that.

Val shook her head. "It doesn't matter how often I watch that, it's still disturbing. How long will your hair stay auburn?"

"Another good wash should do it." Tevin put on a clean plaid shirt, making quick work of the mother-of-pearl buttons. His hair was usually a golden brown that caught the light, or so one mark had told him. It also took dye well, which worked in their favor. "At least I can eat again."

"You need to find an heiress who likes chubby, lazy men."

"Chubby doesn't mean lazy."

"I know," Val said. "I didn't mean it like that. But this last

31

one had you dancing, horseback riding, and all kinds of social flittering. Wouldn't it be nice to just sit and read a good book once in a while?"

Tevin laughed, rubbing a hand over his mouth. Val could always make him laugh. "That sounds like a lovely dream, cousin."

Val peered into the wicker hamper. "Wow. There's cheese, marmalade, a loaf of bread, roast quail." She dug around inside the basket. "Fresh fruit, honey cakes." Val whipped out a single red rose and bit it between her teeth, waggling her eyebrows. "The cook *really* liked you."

Tevin grabbed a pillow, collapsing back onto his bed, his legs hanging off the side. "They all do." He closed his eyes. "I hope tonight's money holds them until Mother's ship comes in." It may have been two years since the last big disaster, but that didn't mean they were safe. Last time, they'd been lucky Val's family had taken them in. Next time, they might not be so lucky. To Tevin, Val had also been a gift. She had a habit of saying whatever honest thing popped into her head. For a boy raised on half-truths and fabrications, she was a beacon in rough seas. Plus, Val was fun.

Val set the basket aside. "I don't know about you, but I reckon a game of cards and a pretty lady on my knee would feel right welcome."

Tevin grunted. "Val, you always feel that way."

"So?"

"I'm tired. Lots of social flittering, as you put it. And now some pigheaded fool is trying to get me to leave my comfortable bed."

32

She poked him. "Let's hit the kitchen, make a dent in this basket, and pour a pitcher of coffee down your gullet."

"Val." He laughed, but kept his eyes closed. If he could just get a short nap—

"Don't force me to make chicken noises. It's undignified."

He opened one eye. "Well, now I want to see that."

Val cleared her throat. "Boooooooock." She sang the sound, slow and operatic. She thumped a fist against her chest and sped up. "Bock-bock! Squawky-bock bock!"

Tevin laughed, pulling his smaller cousin into his arms and pressing his cheek against the top of her head. "I love you, you addlepated loony."

Val squeezed him back. "Is that a yes?"

"As if I've ever been able to say no to you." He shoved her off the bed. "Let's go put the coffee on."

• • •

"You're a cheat." The man spit on the ground, his saliva and tobacco spattering out in an interesting pattern. If Tevin twisted his head exactly right, it looked like a bunny. He kept this to himself as the man's cronies laughed like he'd said something clever. The man's statement was both right and wrong. Tevin *had* been counting cards, which was technically cheating. They hadn't caught him, though. They were accusing Val, as she was the one with the side irons.

Cards had gone well, Tevin playing and Val chatting up the dancing girls, but the men had lost heavily. They had also drunk heavily, and one of them had noticed the fine pearl-handled side irons that Val carried in the worn leather holster on her

33

hips. Tevin suspected the men weren't overly bright to begin with, but when you added in the rotgut they'd been drinking, they lost all good sense. They'd decided that Val was just another fairyborn noble with more funds than brains, assuming her pistols were just for show. It was when they'd swapped cards for the shooting range that things had gone downhill at a regrettable speed. The men had lost more coin than they could afford to lose, and Val was surly, as she'd lost the pretty girl sitting on her knee, because the girl knew better than to head to the target range in the first place.

Val sighed, popping open the chamber of one of her pistols and slipping new rounds in. Tevin caught the mage script on the copper jacketing—firecracker rounds. Not only would they hit the target, but they'd make quite a ruckus while doing it. Val was annoyed. And from the sneer on the spitting man's face, he wasn't in the mood for words. He was in the mood for fists. Tevin loosened his stance, getting ready for the inevitable.

This wasn't always the way it went—usually Tevin could smooth things over. Val was the talent, he was the charm. Tevin couldn't shoot worth a damn, but his family had spent a lot of time and resources making quite sure that he was charm incarnate. But the spitter was drunk, angry, and not listening, and if he wouldn't listen in the first place, Tevin couldn't use his gift.

Val flicked her wrist, snapping the chamber back into place. She glared at the man and raised the pistol to the side, aiming it at the yellow heart of the bullseye. She fired. The round hit the enchanted target with a loud pop, indicating that she'd hit the blue ring outside of the yellow eye. The man laughed, but Tevin knew that was Val's calibrating round. He slipped his hand into his trouser pocket, grabbing his leather sap. Like Val, his eyes never left the spitting man or his cronies.

Val adjusted and fired. The bang and whistle of the firecracker round rang loud and clear. Bullseye. She stepped forward and fired in rapid succession down the line of targets, each pop of the pistol followed by the staccato sound. Bullseye, bullseye, bullseye, bullseye. She stopped. *Pop.* Then the telltale puff of air as the spent rounds hit the dry earth. Val reloaded and snapped the chamber back in again before holstering it. She tipped back the flat rim of her hat.

"The shooting range is spelled against sharpin', you know that. Or perhaps you don't. I can't tell how deep your ignorance lays. But you accusing me of being a pistol sharp seems mighty convenient, seeing as how you owe us some pretty big coin."

The man's face turned red, and he sneered. "You and pretty boy here accusing me of something?"

She rested her hands on her hips. "I was implying, rather forcefully, that you're a coward of the worst sort trying to escape his debts, so yeah, I suppose I'm accusing you of something."

Her words weren't a surprise, but inwardly Tevin groaned. Another brawl meant pretty soon they wouldn't be allowed at this tavern, either. At least they were outside this time. It also meant bruises, so he would hear about it from his parents. No one wanted damaged goods.

The man swung and Val ducked, Tevin jumping in from behind to hit the back of his head with the sap. He knew already that the fight would be short and brutal, and they likely wouldn't win. Two against five, and the five were grown men well into their thirties. They'd recently celebrated Val's eighteenth two months ago, making her not quite a year younger than him. Technically adults, but hardly filled out like the men in the brawl. Val might be a wicked shot, but she was the size of a minnow. Some of the men were bloated from liquor and slow living, but that didn't mean they couldn't throw a punch. Still, he backed Val automatically. Single-minded undying loyalty will do that to a person.

One of the men grabbed Tevin by the neck, tossing him to the ground and knocking the sap out of his grip. He hit and rolled, getting a mouthful of dry grass for his efforts and barely missing the follow-up kick. Unfortunately, he rolled right into a kick from the other side. It caught him in the ribs, and the pain radiated out. Another boot came his way and he grabbed it, shoving backward until the man lost his balance and fell.

He stood, ducking a punch and slamming his fist into someone's gut before spinning and taking out another man's knee. There was a satisfying grunt of pain, but the movement had left him open, and someone took advantage. A meaty fist grabbed his collar and lifted. A grin split the spitter's face, and it was a right ugly sight. Out of the corner of his eye, Tevin saw Val crawling between one man's legs as he tried to grab her by her belt loops.

Slowly, and with great relish, the spitter drew back his fist. "I'm going to enjoy this."

"I reckon you might," Tevin wheezed, his hands grabbing onto the fist for leverage. "But not nearly as much as I'm going to enjoy this." Tevin swung his legs up, surprising the man holding him. The sudden weight made him drop his arm. Tevin used the distraction to punch the man in the gut. He grunted

36

in pain, his grip going loose, causing Tevin to fall flat on his back, winded.

The crack of a pistol cut through the air, and everyone stopped midswing. Tevin tipped his head back, still trying to breathe, and caught sight of the sheriff and her constable. The sheriff was a tall woman, handsome rather than pretty. Tevin liked her a great deal, despite the fact that they usually met under similar circumstances. The constable was blond and boyish looking, but Tevin knew from experience that he was older and wiser than his looks. It didn't do to discount the constable.

"Sheriff Mulroon," Tevin wheezed. "Constable Wright. Fine weather we're having."

Sheriff Mulroon crossed her arms, but Wright kept his pistol out just in case. Tevin knew from past interactions that Mulroon usually had Wright pack stunning rounds, but there was always a first time for things, and he didn't want to press his luck. They were firm, but fair, and he and Val would simply have to ride this out.

Val offered Tevin a hand, pulling him out of the dust. They all looked a little worse for wear—several bloody noses, bruised faces; one of the men was holding his sides, while another spit out a tooth, the poor bastard.

The spitter started to argue his side, but the sheriff cut him off. "Afraid I don't care much right now why you all saw fit to disturb the peace, just that it stops. Val, Tevin, you know the drill."

Val tapped the rim of her brown telescope hat, which she'd rescued from the dirt, and Tevin did the same with his bowler before dusting himself off and making his way to the jail. He'd lost two buttons off his vest, and his shirtsleeve had a tear in it. Val didn't look much better. The other men started to follow suit, all except the spitter.

"I knew it! I knew they was sharpin'!"

Mulroon tilted her head, a few of the black curls from her ponytail escaping around her face. It made her look soft, which was misleading. Fair, yes. Soft? There was a reason she was sheriff.

"What are you blathering about, Denton?"

Denton, the spitter, puffed out his red cheeks at her tone. He looked like an angry squirrel. "Why else would they know the drill?"

Wright, finally holstering his pistol, snorted. "Because these two draw trouble like flies. Val here is a crack shot. Why would she need to sharp, you big galoot?" He cuffed Denton on the back of the head. "Now, get going. We got a nice, cozy cell with your name on it."

• • •

The prisoners left the jail one by one, either when Mulroon and Wright felt they'd cooled off to a reasonable degree, or when bail was posted, depending on the charges. Val, Tevin, and Denton were last, Denton being kept in a separate cell. He'd blustered and yelled at first, but had settled down during the last hour into a quiet sulk.

Val stretched out over the bench, her hat tipped down to cover her eyes.

"You mirror your parents?" Tevin asked.

Val grunted. "My father asked if he should set up an account here and save himself some time. Wiring funds is a pain. My mother pointed out that the time it took gave me opportunity to reflect on my poor decision-making skills. My sister laughed so hard, I thought she might actually wet herself."

"But they're paying your fine?"

She side-eyed him. "They'd pay your fine too, if you'd let me tell them you were here."

"As long as they see us as good influences, you can stay. If I'm always your jail buddy?" He spun his bowler hat in his hand. "I'd rather not take my chances, thank you."

Val looked like she wanted to argue, but kept her trap shut for once.

Tevin rolled his shoulder, trying to loosen the building ache. The fight had left him sore and stiff, and sitting on the hard plank wasn't helping. "Mine won't get me until they need me. My father probably sees this as a fine way to not pay for my meals and upkeep for a few days." He settled in close to Val. Might as well take advantage of the quiet cell.

Tevin's stomach was grumbling and the sun had dipped on the horizon before the front door to the jailhouse opened and Mulroon walked in, Wright a close shadow behind her. They didn't look happy, which set Tevin's alarm bells ringing. Val's family had already agreed to pay her fines, so either someone awful had come for the spitter, Denton, or—

"Get up, my precious darling." Brouchard had a handkerchief pressed beneath his nose, his eyes wide. The jailhouse didn't smell like roses, but it hardly warranted his father's reaction.

But his peacock of a father was always a little on the dramatic side. Now he was choosing to play the doting papa, which sent Tevin's hackles up.

Tevin and Val rose slowly, a quick exchanged glance telling them they were on the same page. Something was wrong. When the rest of the DuMont clan poured in, Tevin felt a heavy dread settle in his stomach. It didn't take three people to post bail.

"Greetings, Father." Tevin stood up, brushing his vest and pants, straightening out the wrinkles. "Amaury. Kate." Amaury nodded, and Kate smiled, tight-lipped. Only Brouchard carried on like his heart was breaking to see his son in jail.

There was no getting around the fact that his family was handsome. Brouchard was green eyed and trim, his thick lashes casting him into a category labeled as "beautiful" and "pretty." He looked almost unearthly and either inspired glorious sonnets or filthy limericks, depending on the poet.

Amaury stood behind him, several inches taller, lean and tough-looking. He was a specter in black, from his duster to his boots; the only color showing was the dark chestnut of his hair. Amaury didn't care much for hats. Or smiling. His brother absorbed the world through eyes the fierce golden brown of a bird of prey.

Kate had the same wavy chestnut hair and eyes, but lacked her sibling's height and icy façade. Kate hid her thoughts with a lively expression, but a mask was a mask, no matter what it was made from. Pretty and cunning creatures, all, but in features, Tevin had the best of them. It wasn't conceit, simply a fact that his parents had drilled into him since he hit puberty.

His father faked a sob. "My jewel, I cannot stand to see you

40

in such dire circumstances. What would your mother say?"

She would box my ears for getting caught. Tevin kept his mouth shut. His father liked the stage to himself, and Tevin didn't want to ruin his performance.

Val joined him at the bars, her stance wary. She wasn't sure what game was being played yet either, but she didn't care for it. "Uncle. Cousins."

"Sheriff, you must release them at once. Family emergency. My wife—" Brouchard choked on another sob. Kate patted their father's back while Tevin looked at Amaury. Over the years Tevin had become adept at reading his brother. Something in Amaury's eyes spoke of exasperation.

Tevin got it then. They needed Tevin for some reason, but were also trying to get out of paying any bail or fines. Mulroon and Wright weren't stupid. They may not have known Brouchard's past, but they knew on some level he was a criminal, and didn't like him.

Tevin gripped the bars. "Sheriff, I understand that we disrupted the peace and all—brawling in your lovely street. Val and I will both sign a writ conceding guilt. My word of honor that the fines will be paid in due course."

The sheriff snorted. "If I let you out, I also have to let him out." She jerked a thumb at Denton, who was currently snoring away in his cell.

"If we're fast and quiet," Tevin whispered, "we won't even wake him. He was plenty drunk earlier. You might have several peaceful hours."

She grimaced and waved at Wright. He took out his key ring and opened their cell door. Brouchard continued to look like he was a breath away from swooning, but somehow managed to be quiet about it.

Val and Tevin followed the sheriff to her desk, where Wright handed Val a piece of paper and a fountain pen.

"Careful," Mulroon said. "It leaks."

Val quickly dashed off her writ, conceding that they'd disrupted the peace and were woefully sorry for it. She signed it with a flourish, her cursive lettering perfect and looping in a way that told a tale of fine and expensive tutors. When she was finished, she handed it to Tevin, who read it quickly and added his own signature, slightly bolder but no less neat than Val's. Then he handed the pen back to Wright. "Thank you both for your understanding."

Mulroon looked them all over, obviously smelling that something was off about the whole situation, but with nothing to go on, she simply sighed. "Out of my sight, you two. I don't want to see you back in here for at least a month."

Val and Tevin agreed, and the whole family exited with alacrity.

As soon as they were out of the jail, Brouchard waved them into a waiting hack. This hack was large, the carriage big enough to fit all of them. A small steel box sat where a driver would perch in a normal carriage, the mage constructs leashed to the front giving only the barest impression of horses. Brouchard pushed a copper into the opening of the box. "Grenveil train station, please." He glanced at Val. "I assume you're coming?" When Val nodded sharply, he sighed. "Five passengers." Then he added a second copper.

They all piled into the waiting carriage, the hack not pulling into the street until all five of them were seated.

Before Tevin could ask any questions, his father tossed him a small brass object, the light glinting off the metal as it flew. Tevin caught it and waited until Val was looking over his shoulder before he cracked it open. Instead of a normal mirror, an abalone surface greeted him. A magic mirror, then. The surface pulsed, regular as a heartbeat. There was a message waiting for him.

"Speak," Tevin said, tapping the surface and making the abalone shine, a riot of color, before it faded to a flat black. An image appeared, one of his mother in a cell similar to the one he'd just left. Despite her captivity, her hair was braided and pinned up, her appearance immaculate.

"Tevin." Florencia DuMont's voice sliced through the silence of the carriage. "I'll cut to the chase. I'm being held in Veritess. I won't get into the details, but know that I've secured my freedom. I need you to come here immediately."

Her sentence was punctuated by his father handing him a train ticket.

She sniffed. "Don't dally." She snapped her compact shut. Flat black, then the slow shine of abalone. The message was done.

He held tightly to his ticket. Okay, not great, but not the worst thing that could happen. A little train ride—he tried not to think too much on that—and then they'd get their mother and go home. He glanced at the ticket. "Veritess?" What was his mother doing there?

43

"Your mother ran into a spot of trouble at a country estate. Veritess had the closest cell." Brouchard's tone was firm, his words clipped. Everyone in the carriage knew that meant no other information was forthcoming, so they didn't bother to ask. They rode in silence all the way to the train station.

CHAPTER 3

A CONUNDRUM OF CURSES

Merit Cravan was tired, making her an unusually patient beast at the moment. That didn't keep her from growling at her healer. The sitting room they were in might have been Merit's, or at least her mother's, but when it came to the beast's health and curse, Ellery was in charge.

"I'm not shining mage light into your eyes for my own amusement, Merit." Ellery's wry tone didn't fool Merit for one minute. Her personal healer made mules look docile. Of course one couldn't manage the Beast of Cravan and have a retiring nature.

"How long did the episode last?" Ellery let go of Merit's jaw and took off their wire spectacles, cleaning them on a handkerchief. The healer was slim hipped and willowy, and a stranger looking in would be forgiven for assuming that the charming dark-haired person was human.

Merit glanced over at the other occupant of the room, Kaiya, her mother's concession to letting her daughter stay in the country estate without her. Unlike Ellery, Kaiya looked exactly like what she was—a young, Hanian fairyborn, more dangerous rogue than aristocrat. Her trousers, shirt, vest, and even the long fitted coat that was hung up in the front hall were all an unrelieved black. No patterns or accessories except for the fine silver shine of the buttons on the coat, which, when she wore it, hugged her torso tight but flared out at the hips. Silver glittered in her ears and from the thin hoop dangling from her septum, a small moonstone bead making up the bottom curve lying flat against her naturally tan skin. The sides of her head had been shorn close, the long, straight black hair remaining on top braided back into a fishtail.

"Three hours," Kaiya said, her voice still holding the soft accents of her homeland. Concerned brown eyes met Ellery's. "They're getting longer."

Ellery put their glasses back on carefully. "You don't remember any of it?"

"No," Merit said, her claws catching in her skirts. "Kaiya managed to lock me in the study." Merit grimaced. "The door will have to be replaced."

"It doesn't matter, Merit. A door is easily replaced. You are not," Kaiya said.

When Merit caught Ellery looking at her shaking hands, she clasped them together. Ellery already knew she was scared. One of the few things Merit could rely on was her mind, and it was betraying her.

Ellery dug through their leather satchel, extracted a stethoscope, and listened to Merit's heart. Finally, they straightened, made a few notes in their journal, and put everything back into a worn leather travel bag. "Well, you're fit as a fiddle, which is the good news." They leaned back into their chair and sipped the coffee the maid had brought earlier, grimacing when they realized it had gone cold.

"Ellery," Merit said when the healer didn't continue. Though Ellery was a healer, they weren't much older than Merit, and they'd become friends over the duration of her curse. "I need to hear the bad news, too."

Ellery gave up on the coffee and set it aside. "Your curse is escalating, Merit. We knew it would."

Merit frowned at the tray set on the table next to them. Coffee, tea, cakes, and dainty sandwiches she could pierce with one claw and eat like a regular barbarian. Her mother would hate that. Her mother wasn't here. She stabbed the sandwich with a claw and brought it up to her mouth so she could nibble. Kaiya turned her head, trying and failing to hide her smile. The staff at the country house might adore Merit, but at the end of the day, her mother was the one who paid their wages. Which meant everyone had to behave as if Merit *wasn't* a beast. She was a fairyborn lady and would act like it, table manners included.

"You need to tell your mother about your episodes." Ellery crossed their legs, leaning their elbows on the armrests. Since they were at home, their shirtsleeves were rolled up, hat hanging on a hook by the door, though they still had their vest and pocket watch on.

Kaiya examined the food. "I love your country's obsession with tiny sandwiches. They make me feel like a giant." She popped one into her mouth, waiting until she swallowed before continuing. "I can tell you exactly what your mother is going to do—tut in sympathy, remind you that it's your own fault, then present a list of suitors."

Merit picked up Ellery's coffee cup, dumping its cold contents into a nearby potted plant.

"I don't think ferns like coffee," Ellery pointed out.

Merit ignored the comment, using her tail to grasp the handle of the silver coffeepot so she could pour Ellery a fresh cup, freeing her hands to make herself a cup of tea at the same time. The curse had many downsides—delicate china teapots and dishes were hard to keep intact. She was a nightmare to keep clothed. Her claws caught on silk finery, and whether her mother liked it or not, allowances had to be made for her tail. Until now, there had been upsides, too. No one bullied a beast. When she growled, they listened. Before the curse? She'd been quiet, bookish, and plain. Oh, she'd always had someone to dance with at a ball. Her title guaranteed that. But no one wanted to listen to her, least of all her mother. No one wanted her for *her*. Which had left her foolishly open to the first boy who showed her attention. She ignored the stab of pain as she thought of Jasper before firmly closing the door on that particular regret. She couldn't change the past; she could only try to learn from it.

At first her curse, while terrible, had also been a boon. The beast made her feel powerful. No one looked at her beautiful, regal mother and then clucked their tongue, wondering where Merit had gone wrong. Somehow being the beast had made her *right* for once in her life. Even her pushy mother had backed off and given her a little space. Only now . . . now it was falling apart.

"You think the episodes will become more frequent?"

"They already are." Ellery set down their cup and took out a

48

notebook, showing Merit the dates, times, and duration of the "episodes," as they'd been calling them. "Your curse gives you until your next birthday—which is only six weeks away. You need to keep your tincture on hand until then. Manage your episodes until you can break the curse."

Merit used her claw to take another sandwich. "Which means I need to marry."

"Someone of your mother's choosing," Kaiya added with a grimace.

Merit bit the sandwich off her claw. "*Or* someone who truly loves me."

"We love you," Kaiya said, her brows furrowing. "But I suppose we don't count. Do you need to love them back?"

"Godling Verity didn't specify," Merit said, "but I believe it was implied."

Ellery's grin was charmingly lopsided. "At least you have a loophole."

"It's not a loophole," Merit chided, carefully stabbing sandwiches until one tipped each claw at the end of her furred hand, making Kaiya snort. "Not really. I mean, who could fall in love with a beast? And what are the odds I'd love him back?"

"Show them your sandwich-hands trick," Kaiya said, grabbing one of the dainty cakes on the tray. "That would impress anyone."

• • •

After tea, Merit donned her veil and took a carriage to the train station, Ellery and Kaiya at her side. Since her mother preferred to stay in the city when she could, Merit had been slowly

49

taking over some of the business aspects of Cravan, managing them from their country home while her mother handled the rest from the city. They'd never been close, though Merit had tried. Before the curse, Lady Zarla had been frustrated by her daughter's inability to follow exactly in her footsteps—a frustration Merit had shared. Her mother was elegant and fierce, and though Merit wished daily that she could be someone her mother was proud of, it didn't stop her from looking up to her in awe. No one said no to Lady Zarla.

Until Merit had.

Then everything had collapsed. They now existed in a strangely fractured life. When they were together, conversation was polite, but the air around them boiled with everything left unsaid.

Despite all of this, there was one thing Merit did enjoy about the city, and that was the weekly gatherings she attended at a coffee shop called the Dented Crown, in an older section of Veritess. The streets were worn cobblestone, and though workers were starting to install mage light in the area, some of the older brick buildings were soot stained. The streets bustled with all kinds of people, the noise a blend of the clopping of horseshoes, the rumble of hacks, and the shouting of street vendors.

The Dented Crown boasted a dim room in the back built for meetings, and once a week she made the journey there. The coffeehouse was centrally located, which made it perfect for this particular group—fairyborn and human, their common denominator being their afflicted state. They'd tried hosting the meetings at the home of Glendon DeMarcos, since he was the founder of the group and Kaiya's uncle. He was also the ambassador of Hane, which meant he had a lavish home, but it was a bit high in the instep for some, so they moved it to a place where everyone felt comfortable attending.

Merit stepped through the rear entrance, flipping back her veil as she did. Ellery had been given permission to listen in but didn't participate. Instead the healer took a small table off to the side and waited there, available to anyone who had health-related questions. After the meeting, Ellery would dispense free vials of tincture to those who needed it. The healer had been helping Merit set up a program that provided free or heavily subsidized bloom for the cursed who couldn't afford it. Caen's bloom was a difficult plant to grow, sensitive and delicate, which meant it was expensive. Merit's lands happened to have the perfect conditions, and her family had generations of experience with its cultivation. It wasn't bragging to say that the Caen's bloom grown by the Cravans was the best.

Though it had other uses, tincture of bloom was the most vital. Not every cursed person needed it, but for those who did, it was priceless. It wouldn't make the curse go away, but for four precious hours, the physical effects disappeared. For Merit, that meant no horns, fangs, or lashing tail.

The Cravan barony was healthy financially, but even if it hadn't been, Merit didn't feel right making coin off of people who needed medicine and couldn't afford it. After a long discussion with her mother, they came to an agreement—those who could pay did, and handsomely, covering the costs of those who couldn't. No one would do without, not on their lands, where they could give the tincture directly to their people. Not outside their lands, either. The subsidized tincture was offered to heads of other baronies, making sure their poor had access to it . . . as long as that barony didn't turn around and overcharge for the bloom they'd been given. If they were caught doing so, they got a single warning. A second time, and they were fined heavily. Merit wouldn't withhold medicine, but they'd had to put something in place to keep unscrupulous barons from profiteering.

After Kaiya greeted her uncle, she took the seat across from Ellery, aiding the healer until Merit was ready to leave.

There were a lot of familiar faces at the long table, and Merit took a seat next to her friends Diadora and Willa Smythe. The girls were a study in contrasts. Diadora had the tipped ears and pearlescent brown skin of fairy ancestors who'd immigrated from the Ivani Islands. Tight brown ringlets haloed her head, framing an inviting face.

Willa had bobbed black hair with bangs cut straight across. She was several inches shorter than her sister, with the ivory skin and rounded human ears of her father. The stepsisters didn't share a single drop of blood and couldn't have cared less. Merit envied their relationship, though she loved having them as friends.

"It's so good to see you both," Merit said, carefully removing her hat and veil. "How are you faring?"

Diadora smiled warmly, her brown eyes lighting up. "We're well, thank you." As she spoke, two daisies and a small diamond fell from her lips and into her lap unheeded.

Willa rolled her eyes. "Yes, just peachy." A thin emerald-green snake curled past her lips and dropped into her lap, followed by a toad. Willa calmly picked them up and took them to the nearest window, then released them. With a resigned look on her puckish face, she snatched a slate from under her seat and wrote out a message. *The owner of the shop has complained that I'm creating a pest problem.* She erased it after Merit finished reading, then took up her chalk again. *I suggested the judicious use of mongooses. He declined. Writing takes so* bloody *long.* She'd underlined the word *bloody*.

"Wilhelmina!" Diadora tutted, though she grinned at her sister. "You promised Papa to watch your tongue." She squeezed her stepsister's hand fondly. "The owner's not a bad man. He must think of his other patrons." A veritable bouquet fell from her mouth as she spoke, ending in a gladiolus, which brought on a sneeze.

What Papa doesn't know won't hurt him. Willa handed her a tissue.

Diadora grabbed the slate. *How are you?*

Merit wanted to answer with some variation of *oh, I can't complain.* But she looked at her furred hands, clenching them in her lap. Fear clawed at her, and she pushed it down. "My curse is escalating. We knew it would. I kept putting it off—marrying. I guess I hoped for the impossible."

You're very lovable. Willa underlined her statement twice. *It's just that the majority of the men in your class are supercilious dunderheads. I'd rather be left naked in the Enchanted Forest than marry any of them.*

Diadora's laugh was a burst of flower petals, the heady fragrance momentarily overpowering the scent of roasted coffee. "I think there was a nicer way to put that, but I can't argue with the sentiment." She smiled fondly at her stepsister as she brushed more flowers onto the floor. "It's also possible that our own experiences are coloring our vision a bit?"

Willa snorted and pointed at the word *dunderheads*.

The meeting filled up with all sorts. An older barmaid whose hand was stuck to a goose, a formerly frog prince and his fiancée, and even Willa's own groom, Shem. He looked like a normal gawky twelve-year-old until he doffed his hat and you saw Everett, a very large toad. If Shem didn't keep Everett fed, he would eat Shem, starting with his face. You would think this would make Shem hate Everett, but the groom took an oddly protective stance toward his squatter. The groom tipped his hat at Merit, and she smiled. Their curses varied, but all of them had something in common—they'd caught the attention of a godling. Merit often wondered what had caused the godlings to pick out the curses in this room. She couldn't for the life of her figure out what would make someone stick a woman's hand to a goose or a giant carnivorous toad to someone's head, but there had to be some twisted logic there.

Glendon took his seat at the front. When his daughter began suffering from a curse, he'd started hosting these meetings so she wouldn't feel so alone. Even though her curse had been temporary, lasting only a few months, and she'd been cured for years now, he still ran the meetings. "Okay, would anyone like to share—"

"He wants his goose back," the barmaid said, sniffing, her nose red. It took Merit a moment to figure out what she'd said—she was clearly from the eastern part of Veritess, as she had a tendency to drop her *h*'s and *w*'s, so it sounded like, "'E 'ants 'is goose back." The barmaid looked fondly at the goose and sniffed again. Diadora handed her a handkerchief. "Thank you, milady. Awful kind."

"You don't want that?" Glendon asked gently.

"I wouldn't mind," the barmaid said. "Giving it back would break the curse, and I know it's not my goose. I only took it 'cause the gentleman kicked it." She blew her nose into the handkerchief. "But the godling didn't see that part, did she? No, they only see what they want, those godlings, and what she saw was a human snatch a golden goose from a gentleman, so *I'm* the one that's cursed. It ain't right." She sniffed. "I didn't want the gold, I didn't." The last part was muttered almost to herself.

Glendon went to comfort her, only to snatch his hand back when the goose hissed at him.

"I can't buy the goose," the barmaid said. "And I won't give it back to the likes of him."

"You need to talk to our arbitrator," Glendon said gently, stopping her before she interrupted. "Her fees are paid by a trust that's specifically for this group. I know you see it as charity, but if you won't do it for yourself, do it for the goose."

"Oh, for fairy's sake, it's only a goose!" Tatiana interrupted. "I'll buy you a dozen geese!"

Does Tatiana think golden geese grow on trees? Willa wrote on the slate.

Diadora took the chalk, adding, *Yes, she probably does.* Glendon shot them a look, and the sisters set down their chalk, both pretending they hadn't been caught passing notes.

"Tatiana." Glendon kept his voice carefully neutral when Merit knew he wanted to chide. "Please remember that the troubles discussed here are given equal weight."

Tatiana fluttered her hands, dismissing his words. "Ranulf

55

keeps moving the date of the wedding." Her voice was huffy, her hands knotting in her skirts. "It's humiliating."

Ranulf, formerly cursed frog prince, scoffed. At thirty-five, his hair had only recently started to silver, giving him a rather stately look. "You're making too much of it," he said casually.

Tatiana's eyes narrowed. "We've had to redo the invitations three times. The stationer practically cackles when my family comes in."

Ranulf waved his hand. "It's not like you can't afford it."

"That's not the point." Tatiana pushed the words through clenched teeth. Her eyes narrowed. "Is this because of the 'incident'?"

Ranulf turned on her, all casual demeanor dropping, his face flushed. "You threw me against a wall!" Merit shared a glance with Willa, her eyes huge. Tatiana might have been a brat, but she was entertaining. Willa barely held her glee, and Diadora reprimanded them both with a look that said, *Behave*, though she was clearly barely containing her own smile.

Tatiana jutted her chin out stubbornly. "Are you still holding that against me? It broke the curse, did it not? That's because of *me*." She smacked her chest with one hand. "And if I went about it in a less than genteel manner—"

"A *wall*, Tatiana."

"I am the daughter of two fairyborn lines, and I was supposed to share my pillow with a reptile? It was not to be borne!" She paused, her eyes going wide as she looked at Willa.

Willa shrugged. "You get used to it." She carefully scooped up the black garter snakes that fell from her lips. Diadora glared at Tatiana, her mouth pinched. The sisters were very protective of each other, which was how Willa had ended up cursed to begin with.

Ranulf stood. "Frogs are *not* reptiles. They're amphibians. There's a difference. I was amphibian royalty, and you treated me like a common toad." He shook his head. "I can't do this anymore." He gave a curt nod to the group. "My apologies." Then he strode from the room.

"Ranulf!" Tatiana fluttered to her feet. "My love! Don't go!" She dropped a quick curtsey before running after him. "You're not a frog anymore! It doesn't matter! I love you!"

They watched the door until they heard the outer one slam twice.

Glendon cleared his throat. "Anyone else care to jump in?"

• • •

After the meeting, Merit wanted to walk. Her head felt full and her heart heavy, and walking had a way of sorting things out. She left her carriage for Ellery, who planned to stay, as a few of the cursed folk wished to talk to them. Merit had her veil back down before she left, and wasn't too surprised when Glendon jogged to catch up to her, since Kaiya was with her.

He kissed his niece on the cheek. Though the sides of his head were shaved close to the scalp like Kaiya's, he kept the top short in the style currently fashionable in Veritess. "Care for a companion?"

"Of course." Merit put her arm through his elbow. He wouldn't offer an arm to Kaiya—she was on duty and as such needed her arms free. Merit had always liked Glendon—he was a rather dashing older man, kind and calm, something she admired. She found his presence soothing. Because of Kaiya, he often followed them home after a gathering so he could visit. Kaiya said this was more because of his crush on Merit's mother than anything, but Merit knew he was genuinely fond of his niece.

They walked around the building, heading back to the main street. As they passed the back alley, Merit caught sight of Ranulf and Tatiana rather enthusiastically forgiving each other.

"I hope they come up for air soon," Glendon said.

"Do you think they'll actually get married?" Merit asked, stepping around a puddle.

"I wish they would," Kaiya muttered. "So we can all stop hearing about it."

Glendon grinned at Kaiya and squeezed Merit's arm. "You were quiet today. Did you want to talk?"

This was one of the things Merit liked about Glendon—he wouldn't think differently of her if she spoke or if she kept her own counsel. He wouldn't judge her for anything she said. He simply listened, and Merit had realized that was a rare trait. She told him about her recent episode and Ellery's diagnosis.

After she was done, Glendon paused at a food cart, getting them a paper cone of roasted almonds. He handed the cone to Merit after he'd taken a few for himself. "Your mother—" He halted briefly to let a young girl run past, a ragged-looking dog hot on her heels. "Lady Zarla is a complicated woman, and as parents, well, sometimes what you think is best is not what your child actually needs or wants. It's hard to not let our own desires color our vision for our own children, understand?"

Merit nodded thoughtfully as she popped a salted almond into her mouth. Kaiya leaned in and snatched one from the bag,

58

and Merit had no doubt that even in that moment her guard could have told her exactly where everyone on the street was and what they were doing.

"And with your curse . . . There's a lot of guilt wrapped up in that, I think. If you're cured and everything turns out all right, she can stop feeling bad. If she also gets what she wants? Well, what's the harm?" Glendon shook his head. "That makes her sound selfish."

Merit held the almonds out to him. "No, I understand what you mean."

"If I remember correctly, you had to marry someone of your mother's choosing? To break the curse?"

Merit nodded. "Which means he must have a good title, solid fairy lineage, and . . . Well, I think that's it. Or he must love me. There's not much overlap between the two."

"It's not all doom and gloom, Merit. I know your situation isn't ideal, but if you pick someone you can be friends with, someone you can respect, love will come in time."

Kaiya snorted. "You're only saying that because you're not the one in her place."

"I think he's trying to make me feel better," Merit said. "Which I appreciate, even if I don't believe him."

Glendon chuckled. "If you're anything like my daughter, you're going to be dead set against any suitor your mother picks out of principle." He took the paper cone from her, shaking it before choosing another almond. "Let me know if there's anything I can do to help."

She smiled at him fondly. "Thank you." They walked in silence for a few streets, Merit deep in thought. She had frittered away her time, and now she was stuck—she would have to choose soon. The problem was, she didn't trust her judgment. Not after her last heartbreak. What if she chose poorly again, only this time it was for life?

What she needed was a person with a cunning mind who could see past social masks and find her a decent match. Someone entirely on her side. Glendon would do his best to help, but he'd be torn between his friendship to Merit and his affection for her mother.

Her mother's judgment was entirely suspect. Six weeks. She could already feel the moments slipping through her fingers. What was she going to do?

"If you want to assist us, Uncle," Kaiya said, her eyes on a group of children that ran past, chasing the same ragged dog from earlier, "you could distract Lady Zarla. It's going to be difficult enough for Merit to make a decision without her mother hovering every second."

Glendon examined his niece from the corner of his eye, clearly tempted to take her up on the idea, but sensing that it might be a trap. Finally his desire overrode his hesitation. "If you think it will help."

"What would we do without you?" Merit patted his arm before throwing Kaiya a grateful look for solving a problem before Merit even realized it would be one.

Kaiya tapped two fingers to her forehead, flicking them away in a little salute, her hands back at her sides before her uncle turned to look at her.

CHAPTER 4

NOT EVERYTHING THAT GLITTERS IS GOLD

Grenveil station was an overload to the senses. The evening air was hot and sticky, making Tevin's shirt cling to his back. Boots clomped on the boards as people ran to catch their trains, conductors yelling to be heard over the din of food vendors hawking their wares. The delicious smell of roasted meat and candied nuts mixed with the tang of sweat and rotting garbage in the bins and, underneath that, the heady smell of livestock. The layers blended into a miasma Tevin could taste as he breathed, and wished he couldn't.

Their train slid in, heralded by the shouts of the mages controlling it. Three people in the bright blue jumpsuits of the Eastern Line unclipped themselves from their stations on top of the train, where they rode and directed the smooth magework wyrm to its destination. The head of the train was a stylized dragon, bright colors accenting the metal to give it the look of scales. They would be in the belly of the beast.

Tevin shuddered.

"Oh, get over it, you big baby." Despite Brouchard's not-too-subtle hints that she should go home, Val had stayed with Tevin.

"Trains explode sometimes, Val."

"Not in ages," Val said, a hand on her hat as someone jostled her. "They fixed that design flaw."

"I can't help not liking it," Tevin said. "It's unnatural."

Val frowned. "My mother explained it to me once. Something about the mages using the force of the earth and possibly magnets? I wasn't really paying attention at the time."

"Pretty girl?"

"Baroness Lafayette and her daughters."

"That explains it, then."

Val rested her hand on his wrist. "It's safe, Tev. The mages spend years learning their trade. If the whole muster doesn't pass the examinations, they don't get a license. Which means every single person in those blue jumpsuits is well seasoned and knowledgeable. We'll be there faster than you can say *cricket*."

Tevin nodded, but couldn't make himself believe her words.

The mages would stay at the station, and a fresh muster would take their place. Once they were clipped in, boarding began. Brouchard left them for the first-class cabin that was all cream leather and metal accents, every comfort considered. Tevin and his siblings originally had tickets for third class, but between Kate's savvy and Tevin's charm, they'd managed to get bumped up to second. Not as posh as first, but they had their own berth, and it was clean and quiet.

They took their seats, Amaury sitting across from him, his golden eyes fixed on Tevin.

"I'm not a mouse," Tevin said, leaning against the wood paneling of their berth.

"A mouse wouldn't get sick in our cabin," Kate said. "A mouse would be preferable at this point." She pointed a demanding finger at Tevin. "Be the mouse we all know you can be."

Val slid the door shut and locked it. "What's going on? Your father was as tight-lipped as a magistrate."

"Our illustrious mother got nicked." Amaury leaned forward, his elbows on his knees.

"That's all we got." Kate's face scrunched up in frustration. "Father's being very evasive. I don't like it."

For a brief moment, Tevin wished his sister was still the tiny, whirling redheaded dervish he used to be able to take onto his lap while looping an arm out to pull his quiet little brother to his side. That was the only time he'd known for sure that they were safe.

"I'll be home after this. No long-term or out-of-city jobs for a while."

Kate turned her gaze on Amaury, sharing something silent between them. "Tev, it's okay—"

"I gave them my savings." Amaury tucked his arms in, his hands clasped tight as he looked at his brother. "After the rug was gone."

Tevin tried to hide his frustration and knew he'd failed when Amaury scowled at him. "You didn't need to do that."

The corners of Amaury's lips tipped up in the faintest impression of a smile. "I forgot. Sacrifice is your job. Sorry to steal your thunder."

"It's not a sacrifice," Tevin said. Not when it was for them. It was a gift gladly given. "But you shouldn't have to—"

Kate growled at him. "You're exasperating. Why won't you let us help?" She slung her arm around Amaury. "We don't like you killing yourself for our sakes."

"I'm not killing myself." Tevin closed his eyes against the rolling of the train. He hated feeling at the mercy of his nausea—weak and helpless. They could run. Fake papers wouldn't cost much with Amaury making them, and they'd scrape by with their gifts, but what kind of life was that? Always looking over their shoulders for their parents, always hiding. If he saved up enough to get his own place, they'd have somewhere to live, but he had no guarantee they'd be able to move in with him. He was afraid then that his parents would need help, and he wouldn't have enough on top of his own living expenses. Tevin couldn't take the risk. He'd gone through the options so many times. There were no good answers.

"I'll be okay." Kate's voice was gentle but somehow also firm, simultaneously comforting her brothers and reprimanding them. "I know you're both worried, but it's not your job to rescue me."

"It most certainly is," Tevin said, cracking his lids to glare at her. Amaury didn't respond, keeping his eyes fixed on the scenery passing out the window.

Val grinned. "Did you think that was going to work?"

Kate shook her head and heaved out a breath. "It hasn't yet, but I keep trying."

"You're almost sixteen," Tevin reminded her, as if she would ever forget. "What if they decide to marry you off? Trade you to someone?" She'd have no legal right to argue and nowhere to go. "What if they ask Amaury to counterfeit something that finally gets him caught? Do you know what they do to forgers?"

"Prison, deportation, the breaking of fingers. So many delightful options." Amaury rolled his eyes. "I'm not going to get caught."

Amaury was smart—his razor-sharp intellect deliberate and thoughtful . . . most of the time. He could be rash when it came to the small handful of people he loved.

"You might not, but you're not always in charge, are you?" Tevin hated reminding either of them that they were powerless. He wanted to reach across the gap between him and Amaury, hug his brother close. Amaury wouldn't appreciate it, so he settled for wrapping his arms around his gut, tightening the hold he had on himself. No one had a good response to his question, and the car filled with the murmur of the train as it slid along the track.

"How did it go with Downing?" Kate asked, changing the subject.

Tevin closed his eyes and smiled, trying to ignore the rocking movement as the train accelerated away from the station. "Funny thing about Lydia Downing—she had her heart set on an impoverished third son. Good lineage, but no money to speak of. Her father was well against the match, but he'll see it much more favorably now." He peeked at Kate.

"So she paid you to play fiancé while her father paid you to go away?" Kate asked.

Tevin's smile grew. "Brouchard only knows about the second part. The first payment is ours." His stomach lurched, and he curled toward the wall, but it didn't dampen the tiny victory of sliding something past his parents. "I wish they were all like

65

this." He never felt bad about taking money from the parents, but sometimes he was haunted by the broken hearts he left behind. Not enough for him to stop pulling the con. Each ill-gotten copper added up, and he'd have swindled Queen Lucia herself if it meant keeping his own safe.

• • •

The train trip went about as Tevin expected—he threw up twice into a bucket while everyone else catnapped, and occasionally broke into a cold sweat. He arrived at the station stiff and sore, but grateful to be stepping onto solid ground that didn't move, lurch, or hurtle at unnatural speeds.

Veritess was a juncture city, sitting on the boundaries between three baronies. Juncture cities acted as common ground—a neutral territory where only the queen's laws and whims mattered. It was the kind of city where the sometimes far-flung fairyborn aristocracy owned houses so they could meet, do business, arrange marriages, and conduct all the other mysterious workings that the upper crust managed. It was the kind of place the DuMonts went to make quick money—a target-rich environment.

The train they caught had been an overnight making many stops and moving slowly through the countryside, so when they hit the cobblestone streets of Veritess, they were greeted by pre-dawn birdsong. The city around them was waking up—young shop workers were out sweeping the walkways out front, ready-ing themselves for the long day ahead. They walked quickly through the winding streets, stomachs grumbling at the smell of fresh bread wafting out of a bakeshop on the corner.

66

Brouchard didn't let them linger, herding them all directly for the local jail. Tevin's father, having used the facilities available to first-class passengers, was cleanly shaven and fresh as spring rain. He'd also likely had breakfast. Everyone else had a rather rumpled and disgruntled look about them, which seemed fitting for a trip to jail.

Veritess Jail was situated on the outskirts of town, and it took them a half hour of quick walking to get there. As penitentiary institutions went, Veritess's was of a nice sort. It was clean and well made, the stone a bright, unrelenting white. The outside even had fresh flowers, a riot of color and types that a constable was watering as they approached. Amaury sniffed derisively, and Tevin hid a smile. Veritess Jail was one of Amaury's least favorites—and over their years, the DuMonts had seen many. He thought it lacked the gravity of similar institutions.

Tevin waited for it, knowing what the next words would be.

"Glitter bars." Amaury growled the words.

"No self-respecting nick should glitter," Tevin, Kate, and Val chorused. The building used a local ore that, when treated, had an almost sparkling finish. In the bright light of morning, the place practically shone.

"We'll get her and go," Tevin said, slinging his arm around his brother, his voice low. "We'll be on the next train back to Grenveil. You'll see."

They went in the front doors and greeted the desk clerk. Despite the early hour, the clerk, an older man, was in a crisp uniform, his tight gray curls cropped close to his deep brown skin. He took one look at the group and snorted. "No need to say who you're here for." He poked his head out the door and whistled. A young boy ran up, half asleep on his feet at the early hour. Despite this, he took off at a run as soon as the guard finished speaking.

"Follow me." The guard stood and escorted them through a set of doors and into a hallway. They followed him past several cells, most of their denizens still snoring on the wooden slats attached to the wall. Fresh hay dampened their footfalls, and the atmosphere was quiet, with the exception of someone muttering in their sleep. At the end of the corridor, they stopped in front of the last cell. Florencia DuMont sat primly on her bench, her cell conspicuously empty of other prisoners.

"We learned quick to keep her by herself. She starts trouble," the guard said when he noticed Tevin taking in her single status.

The DuMont clan nodded. This was an accurate assessment of their mother. The guard took out his keys.

"It's about time." She stood, her chin high. "I couldn't stand another breakfast of runny eggs and questionable sausage." She eyed the guard. "It tasted like rat."

The guard gave her a tight smile. "It's not all tied up in a bow just yet. I've sent a runner. It's up to Lady Merit now."

Val frowned. "What? We don't need to pay a fine? Sign something? Why do we have to wait?"

The guard's eyebrows rose, and he looked at Florencia, then the family, and back to Tevin's mother. He laughed, a deep bass sound. "Of course you didn't tell them."

Tevin looked at his father. "What didn't you tell us?"

Brouchard's face was placid, though he tapped his foot, eager to be gone. "In order for your mother to be free, someone must take her place."

Somehow Tevin knew without asking who it would be. "You're trading me?"

Brouchard rolled his eyes. "We couldn't very well leave your mother here, now, could we?"

Florencia's gaze was hard. "The beast wouldn't make a deal until she took a good look at you." She scowled at Tevin's rumpled appearance, her gaze lingering on the tears and the two missing buttons. "You couldn't tidy yourself?" When Tevin went to argue, her scowl deepened. "You'd best hope she likes rumpled and scruffy. If she turns the deal down, I'll have to offer something else."

Tevin didn't have to ask what she meant. He had to stop himself from pushing his brother and sister behind him. "You can count on me."

"Such a good boy." Florencia patted Tevin's cheek through the bar. "Don't kick up a fuss. We'll handle everything."

He hated the small part of him that gobbled up her scant praise. He glanced at Val.

"Then we'll all wait for Lady Merit," Val gritted through her teeth.

The guard shrugged and opened the cell, letting Brouchard in to sit with his wife. When no one else followed, he sighed, locked the cell, and opened up the second one for everyone else to use.

The guard grimaced at them, turning the key in the lock with a decisive click. "Welcome to Veritess Jail. We hope you enjoy your stay."

Amaury shook his head. "Absolutely no gravity at all."

CHAPTER 5

IT'S PRETTY, BUT WHAT
DO I DO WITH IT?

The Cravans' city home was a confection of wrought iron and red brick, nestled in a piece of land on the corner of a street lined with large oaks. Their parcel was large enough for stables and a decorative garden, while the house had enough rooms to host not only Merit and her mother, but several guests and the small flotilla of staff such a household required. Merit always stayed the night after one of her gatherings, keeping a suite of rooms on the second floor for her own use. The morning sun was bright, the day promising to be warm, when Merit joined her mother for breakfast at a table set out on the garden terrace.

Lady Zarla, baroness of Cravan and Merit's mother, sat across from her at the exquisitely laid out table and slid the snowy linen napkin into her lap. Her rich ebony hair was swept up in a complicated knot, the whole thing kept in place by a thin silver netting interspersed with pearls. With her hair up, there was no missing the delicate tipping of her ears, or the way the deep brown of her eyes and hair set off the pearlescent sheen of her skin. Lady Zarla dressed for a day about town with the careful deliberation of a warrior choosing armor. Merit, conversely, had barely looked at the dress her maid had put out—a cotton day dress, cream-colored, with a lilac print.

"I wonder," her mother said, pouring coffee into both of their cups, "if you're ever going to stop being childish about this."

Merit added cream and sugar to her coffee, pretending ignorance. "Childish?" Her relationship with her mother, always a little strained, had worsened after her curse. In Lady Zarla's mind, Merit had failed by refusing to marry her betrothed. That refusal had led to her curse, and seeing Merit's beastly shape only reminded her of the failure. On her end, Merit felt that her mother should have listened to her complaints about the betrothal in the first place. Which meant these weekly breakfasts were a frequent—if quiet—battleground.

Lady Zarla sipped coffee from the delicate china in her hand and raised one elegant brow. If someone were to apply one word to her mother, it was *elegant*. Lady Zarla embodied everything one expected from the fairyborn—grace, beauty, wealth, style— and she was not to be trifled with.

"If you had an issue with me showing up to breakfast as a beast, then perhaps you shouldn't have let Godling Verity curse me." Merit gave her a tight-lipped smile. As an opening salvo, it lacked subtlety. Merit had found that if she swung in, conversationally ham-fisted, it would escalate the argument faster and save them both time. She couldn't avoid the fight, but she could at least make it more efficient by drawing first blood.

"One doesn't say no to a godling, daughter." Lady Zarla placed a bottle on the table, the brown glass making the contents look darker than they were. "Drink."

The beast wanted to growl. She wanted to knock the table

over, screeching until her mother had to cover her ears. The restraint it took to keep the beast in check made her movements slow and precise. She set her coffee down just so before taking the napkin from her lap and dabbing at each side of her fanged jaw. When the skin around her mother's eyes tightened, the first warning sign that her patience, such as it was, had almost evaporated, Merit caved. She unstoppered the bottle and tossed the tonic into the back of her throat.

Tincture of Caen's bloom tasted peppery, earthy, and unpleasantly biting, and its effects left her feeling like she had been pulled inside out through her own belly button. Merit's horns receded, her tail disappeared, and her fur melted away to reveal a fine spray of freckles across her strong nose. Her fangs became white teeth, and when all was said and done, she was once again a young woman of seventeen, somewhere between awfully plain and almost pretty. She had her father's stubborn chin, her mother's wavy brown hair and pointed ears, but the almost overwhelming anger at this moment was a thing all her own.

"Was that so difficult?" Lady Zarla asked.

Merit ignored the question. "I'm here, as promised. And changed, as demanded." She fished her father's old pocket watch out of her dress pocket, making note of the time. She set the dial, which would sing a warning to her when her time was up. "You have me in human form for four hours, though in reality you only have me for breakfast. Tick tock."

"Except I have more than breakfast now, don't I?"

Now it was Merit's turn to arch that single brow. "I'm not sure what you mean." They both smiled politely as a young maid deposited a tray of scones onto the table along with sweet cream and artfully arranged berries. Merit's stomach rumbled, and she helped herself to the offerings. She wasn't so stubborn as to turn down a good meal.

"I spoke to Ellery."

The words made Merit still, even though it wasn't a surprise. Last night Merit had given the healer permission to share pertinent health details with her mother—but for some reason her mother having that knowledge made her feel naked. Vulnerable. "Oh?"

Her mother filled her own plate. "Your birthday approaches."

Merit broke the still-warm scone in half. "That it does."

"You can hardly go gallivanting back to the country *now*. So I have you for more than this morning. I have you for six weeks." She would never smirk, considering the facial expression beneath her, but her satisfied smile flirted with smugness. "Have you given any thought to resolving your curse? You'll not find anyone with the right qualifications skulking about the manor house."

"I've thought of putting out an ad in the paper so they'll come to me," Merit said, silently marveling at how much easier it was to sip her coffee with human hands. "Prize heifer to the highest bidder. Fairyborn aristocracy only."

"Really, Merit." Lady Zarla stacked pounds of disapproval on only those two words. "This is hardly the time for sarcasm."

"I disagree," Merit said, sipping her coffee. "It's the perfect time for sarcasm."

"Six weeks, Merit." Lady Zarla speared a piece of strawberry with her fork, then placed the morsel daintily in her mouth. "That's not a lot of time."

After that, the curse became permanent. After that, she was a beast, mindless and snarling until her last breath. This hadn't bothered her before, not really. Her birthday had seemed so far off, the repercussions nebulous and far away. But then she'd started having her episodes. Stretches of time where the beast took over and her mind went away. She could cope with the physicality of the curse, but she refused to let her mind—her self—slip away.

When Merit didn't respond, a muscle in her mother's temple began to twitch. "Someday, Merit, I will die. You will take over my barony. There's no one else. No cousins or kin. It's time you stopped this childish nonsense and started accepting your responsibilities."

Merit dipped a piece of scone into the cream. "Have I shirked my duties? Learning how to govern our people? The land or the ledgers?"

Her mother ignored her. "Someday, sooner than you think, it will be your turn to rule." Lady Zarla set her cup down firmly, her voice dry. "I'd like to dandle a few babes on my knee before I go to the summer lands, daughter."

Merit choked on her scone.

"You will get married, my child. You will break your curse, and you will do your duty and create the next heir for the Cravan barony."

Merit couldn't help it—she pictured them. Fat-cheeked, brown-eyed babies with Jasper's nose and mouth, their mother's stubborn chin, and the diluted blood her mother had so despised. Oh, Merit had known for three years now that he was a fortune hunter. She wanted to forget. She'd been so foolish, and somehow part of her still loved him with an intensity that burned. Which made her feel even more the fool.

"You could have had that marriage, those babies." Merit stared at her scone, no longer hungry, the old pain rising up and howling. She crushed the remaining scone with her fingers. "You chose the beast."

"He was unsuitable." Her mother's face remained serene, but Merit knew those signs. Knew the pulse point of Lady Zarla's anger. Good. *We'll see whose anger is bigger, mine or yours.* Even though she hated herself, too, for still loving him. Hated herself for still wanting her mother to tell her that she was worth loving, instead of reminding her that the one boy who'd promised his heart had loved only her wealth. Not even all of it, either. A smart man would have held out for the marriage and taken it all. No, he'd been happy with a bag of coins, which made it all worse somehow.

"I loved him." Merit said the words unthinkingly as she stared at the remaining crumbs of her scone. A treat lovingly constructed that had taken a sweet second to destroy.

"He was a fortune hunter!" Lady Zarla paused, smoothing the napkin in her lap with shaking fingers, reining in her temper.

"I chose him all the same." Merit kept her own hands folded so her mother couldn't see how tightly pressed they were, how white her knuckles. "And what does it matter? I choose either someone after my coin or someone after my blood. What's the difference?"

"He never would have respected you, that's the difference. Or understood you. How could he? You need someone of your own class. Someone you can build a relationship with rooted in common bonds, respect, and good breeding." Lady Zarla's eyes flashed. "Your conjecture is wasted breath. He chose the money and ran. Let the past fade, Merit."

"How can I when the past has shaped my present?" She would not cry. Would not give in to that old, scarred pain, or let her mother win this piece of her. This battle was hers, even if she'd lost the war.

"You can decide how much it affects you," Lady Zarla said, her chin up. "You're a Cravan. We're the ones who do the shaping, not the common clay." Her lip curled. "For godling's sake, Merit, the choice was you or the money, and he made his decision."

Merit looked at her mother then. "And you made yours. I chose him, he chose coin, and you chose the beast. Everyone lost, and no one is happy." She stood and threw down her napkin.

"Merit, sit down!"

Merit walked away, striding through the foyer and toward the front step where her carriage waited. She only had to keep it together until her carriage. Her mother's voice followed her, not yelling, but carrying with authority. "You will wed, Merit. There isn't a lot of time. Do not remain cursed simply to spite me."

Merit paused, her eyes closing. She wanted to outstubborn her mother—oh, how she wanted to *win*. But she didn't want to be a beast forever, not when it took her mind. She might have Caen's bloom for now, but even that would stop working after her birthday. Merit dropped her chin. "Yes, Mother."

"You will start making the rounds." The voice came from close behind her, meaning her mother had followed her in.

"Attending dances, clubs, and other social events where acceptable suitors are available. I will find you someone worthy of our house. I'll make a list."

You mean you will find an entitled, pompous ass, but one of proper lineage. She kept those words to herself. "Of course. What am I if not your dutiful heir and daughter?" Merit didn't wait for a response, pushing open the front doors and stepping out into the sunshine.

She almost bumped right into the messenger.

The young lad looked at her skeptically. "This where the Beast of Cravan lives? Only, I got a message for her."

"I'm the beast," Merit said.

The boy was even more skeptical now. "You don't look like one."

"I'm only a beast in the afternoons. You have a message?"

"You're to come to the jail. Guard says someone's waiting for ya."

"Thank you," Merit said, handing him a copper. "If you go around to the back door, the cook will give you breakfast." The boy took off for the back before Merit even finished speaking. She wished her own problems could be as easily fixed.

• • •

Merit stepped through the front doors of Veritess Jail, hailed the guard, and identified herself.

The man stood up from his chair. "It's about the prisoner your people brought in. Florencia DuMont."

Merit rubbed her temples. With everything else going on, she'd forgotten about the DuMont woman. She hadn't decided what to do with her yet. "Ah, yes. The horrid woman who wanted to trade her child." Exactly what today needed. She squared her shoulders. "What does she want?"

"Her family is here. The whole gaggle of them is in the back cell," the man said.

"Gaggle?" Merit was beginning to wish she'd stayed and argued with her mother long enough to have a second cup of coffee. She was exhausted, and it wasn't even lunchtime yet.

The guard pulled out his keys. "It's best if I show you." He led her down to the last cell. Merit pulled up short. There was a man with Florencia in her cell who looked like he'd stepped out of a painting—the romantic kind with lush colors and fat cherubs cavorting in disheveled bedding. From the way he was holding Florencia's hand, Merit assumed it was her husband. They were talking softly to one another and pointedly ignoring the cell next to them. That cell held four younger people, three of whom were probably DuMonts. She wasn't sure about the freckled young woman in the trousers.

The four occupants, oddly enough, weren't the interesting part. Every other cell was clean but spare—wooden planks attached to the wall for sitting and sleeping, bucket for necessities, straw-covered floor. The young DuMonts' cell had a rug. Their planks had blankets and pillows. They had a lantern, a basket full of food, and a mostly empty bottle of wine. The four people in the cell were playing cards, sitting on the rug, and sipping from delicate glasses. By their empty plates, she could guess that they'd already eaten their fill.

"Where," Merit said, her tone deceptively calm, "is their bucket?"

The guard shuffled his feet. "They said it smelled. We've been letting them use the guards' lavatory."

Merit covered her mouth with one hand. Dropped it. "And the other goods? Where did those come from?"

"The guards, mostly." He paused, licking his lips. "They seemed like reasonable requests at the time. And it's not like they're *real* criminals. They're being traded *for* the criminal, or at least that one is." He pointed at the card player who had his back to her. "It seemed wrong to leave them in there without . . ." He looked at Merit, his eyes wide. "It's just, they're so charming, ma'am."

"We're only defenseless children," the young woman with the freckles drawled, throwing down an ace. Merit could just make out tipped ears from where she stood. "Well, Kate is, anyway."

"Defenseless?" the DuMont girl—apparently named Kate—asked.

"No, a child," Freckles corrected her. "As you haven't reached your majority yet."

Merit took the guard's keys, sending him back to his station without looking away from the game. She wondered briefly if she should simply leave them all in the cell and throw the keys in the garbage.

Kate frowned at the ace. She plucked it off the pile and handed it back to Freckles. "Not that one. Honestly, Val, if you can't play properly, don't bother."

Freckles placed it back into her hand, confused. "I thought I was playing properly?"

Kate shook her head and held out her palm. "Let me see your

hand." She took the cards from Freckles, who was apparently named Val. Kate quickly rearranged them, pulled out a two of clubs, and tossed that into the pile. "There. Trust me."

Val eyed her warily. "I trust you with my life, cousin, but I'm not sure I trust any of you with cards."

The taller, leaner young man sitting by Kate threw down a jack. "You're finally learning."

"Don't be condescending, Amaury," Kate said. "You should apologize."

"Why? She won't believe it."

"He's right," Val said. "I won't."

Merit decided to ignore all of this and focus on the pertinent details. "Which one of you is Tevin?"

The quiet one raised his hand without turning, keeping his back to her.

"May I speak to you, please?"

He stood and turned then, moving slowly to the bars, his cards hanging forgotten in his hand. Her first impression was that he was tall, with wide shoulders and eyes that were a startling shade of green. A few days of stubble covered a masculine jaw, seeming to highlight lips that looked so soft she almost reached out to touch them. She watched him move all the way to the bars until the tip of his hat touched the metal. Merit swallowed. It had to be a trick of the light. No one could be *that* handsome. She surreptitiously pinched herself, and yet Tevin DuMont remained completely, unbearably, almost ridiculously good-looking.

Tevin tilted his head, taking her in quickly. She had to fight to not straighten her dress or fuss with her little half boots.

80

Merit assumed he would, like most men her age, glance at and then dismiss her. Instead, he kept watching, like he was attempting to figure out a puzzle where the pieces didn't quite line up. "You don't look like a beast." His voice—the deep velvet of it—made her knees actually weak.

She felt something then—almost a push. A strange desire to please him. Merit didn't like that feeling. She'd spent too much of her time the last few years feeling pushed into things. It also reminded her unpleasantly of Jasper. She shook off the compulsion, like a dog casting off pond water. "You, however, are exactly as advertised."

A slow, smug grin spread across his face. "Am I, now?"

"Yes, when your mother was trying to sell you to me. Practically singing your praises." That wiped the grin off his face. She hadn't meant to be so petty, but she couldn't say she wasn't appeased by the results. Merit wanted him as off balance as she was. Still, it was something she would have been more likely to say as a beast. Not as herself.

He didn't look over at his parents, but Merit got the feeling he was focused on them all the same. "What did my mother do, exactly?"

"She went off the path in my family's estates and took a cutting of Caen's flower."

"That's the plant they use to make bloom, right?"

She hadn't seen Val walk up, only noticing her when she spoke. She'd been too focused on Tevin. "Yes. It's one of our main exports."

Tevin leaned his shoulder against the bar, his eyes unfocused. "That's bad, isn't it?"

"It's a difficult plant to grow. Very sensitive," Merit said, focusing on Val. It was easier to look at her. "And for the cursed who need it, it's priceless. It's not a cure, but it gives people four hours of relief from their curse."

"That's why you're—" Tevin waved at her.

"Yes, my mother insisted I take it earlier." Merit pulled her father's watch out of her pocket, glancing at the scratched face. "I have about three hours left."

"So my mother cut your plant, of which you have many. Now she's in jail?" Tevin asked. "Seems a bit much." Merit didn't think it was possible for him to move closer, but he managed, letting his voice grow soft and conspiratorial. His disarming smile had a practiced ease as he leaned down to look her in the eye. "What say we apologize and everyone can move on about their day?"

Merit couldn't tell if he was being deliberately obtuse or was simply that cocky. She tucked a strand of her brown hair back into her updo. "We welcomed her as a guest. She broke hospitality and stole from me. A cutting of bloom is worth a great deal, yes, but she also endangered the plant." She pursed her lips. "Well, it's more of a shrub, if you want to get technical. The cutting wasn't done carefully, and it's left the plant open to disease and parasitic infection. It's not only the theft—it's also the loss of priceless medicine for a lot of people."

Tevin glanced at the neighboring cell. "Mother never does anything in half measures." He focused back on Merit. "Where does that leave us?"

"Your mother offered *you* to cover the expenses and serve her time." She crossed her arms and tilted her head, looking at him again. "The only thing is, I'm not sure what use you'd be beyond decorative."

Val barked a laugh. "That's a first."

"Decorative?" Tevin ran his thumb along his lower lip as he weighed her words. Merit hated that she was automatically drawn to the motion. "Like a vase?"

Merit shook her head. "I don't wish to be disrespectful. I have a guard, a healer, and a full staff." She dropped her voice low. "I only considered the trade because I was tired of dealing with your mother and thought she deserved to sit and stew over the loss of her eldest son."

She didn't need to glance at Florencia to know she'd been wrong.

Tevin's full focus was on her now. His gaze had an almost physical weight to it. It made her want to squirm, but instead she stared back, her spine straight, her chin level.

The corners of his lips tipped up. "Surely the Beast of Cravan needs something." His voice promised her so many things, if only she'd be brave enough to ask.

"What makes you think that?"

"Everyone needs something," Tevin said. "Besides, I'm very good at reading people. Family skill, I'm afraid."

Merit really thought the deep velvet of his voice ought to be illegal. As she considered his words, the beginning of an idea occurred to her. She turned the idea around in her mind, looking at it for sharp edges. Tevin didn't rush her as she thought, which she appreciated. The more she considered it, the more she liked it.

"You're *very good at reading people*—what does that mean?"

She found she couldn't really look away from him. It was like the jail, the other people, all of it fell away.

"Most people," he said, his voice soft, "think their secrets are their own, and no one could possibly guess them. Everyone thinks their secrets are special, because they assume the rest of the world is upstanding and perfect. Only they aren't. Once you know how to read the signs?" He gave a small shrug, flipping his hands open like he was holding a novel. "Open book."

Merit felt a little thrill rush through her as she considered her idea some more. It was outlandish. Her mother certainly wouldn't approve, which was an added bonus, really. A flush of triumph swept through her. "You're right. I do need something. I need a husband."

Surprise slapped his face. "Pardon?"

"I need to get married." When he continued to stare at her in a blank, uncomprehending manner, Merit began to question his intelligence. "Because of my curse." She spoke slowly, enunciating each word carefully. When that didn't seem to help, she turned to Val. "Is he well? I was under the impression that he was quite bright, but perhaps his mother exaggerated?"

Val leaned closer, a small, mirthful light dancing in her eyes. "Give him a moment."

"You want to marry me?" Tevin said abruptly. "For a plant?" He spluttered the words, casting the last part at Val. "I'm worth a flower?"

"Hold out, Tev." Her grin was wicked. "You might be worth the whole shrub." She patted his shoulder. "If Kate negotiates, that is."

"Stuff it, Val." Tevin crossed his arms. "I'm not marrying you. No offense. There has to be something else."

"Full offense." Merit mimicked him, crossing her own arms. "I didn't ask you to marry me."

That seemed to cut his indignation off at the knees. "I beg your pardon, but that is what you *implied*."

"Then you inferred *wrong*." Only years of training kept Merit from rolling her eyes. Honestly. Why was it that so many men thought they were the answer to a question no one was asking? "My curse states that I need to marry by my birthday, which is six weeks away. Specifically, I need to marry someone who meets my mother's approval, which doesn't include you, or someone who loves me, which also doesn't include you *and* seems unlikely."

"Why?" Tevin said, looking her up and down again. Not leering, but assessing. "What's wrong with you?"

"I have a brain," Merit said dryly. "They don't like it."

"Yeah," Val drawled. "That'll do it."

Tevin's eyebrows shot up in surprise as he looked at her. "Since when have you thought brains were a negative? You like smart women."

"We're not talking about me," Val said. "I'm reasonable. We're talking about peacocks." She waved a hand at Merit. "Someone like her? Trust me, that's what she's dealing with."

Merit nodded approvingly. "Small brain and lots of plumage shaking. Very apt."

Tevin grimaced. "Right." He turned his attention back to Merit. "Still a little hazy on my part in this."

Merit tented her fingers around the ring of keys in her hands, attempting to find the best way to phrase it. "Your family is very comfortable here, which leads me to think this isn't your first time in a cell."

"Not even this week," Val offered, her grin cheeky.

Merit let that pass. "From your mother's account, you're charming, witty, a good dancer, and smart." She waited for Tevin to confirm or deny any of these assertions, but he simply took them as his due. "In the past, I chose . . . poorly. I let charm and a pretty face blind me. I don't wish to do so again. My options aren't without limit; nevertheless, I wish to make the best of them." She gestured to Tevin. "You're the very definition of everything I'm trying to avoid. I'm hoping you can recognize your own and help me avoid them."

Tevin ran his fingers down his jaw, his eyes unfocused. Merit could almost see his brain sorting through the information. Perhaps he was intelligent after all.

"To clarify—you can't avoid marriage, but you want to approach it on your terms and get the best bargain?"

She nodded.

"How did you choose poorly before?" Tevin asked. He must have seen her stiffen, because his gaze softened. "I mean no harm, honestly—but it's a question I must ask."

"I was betrothed to someone I didn't wish to marry, which left me very unhappy. When a boy closer to my age started courting me on the sly, it seemed like a sign of what was meant to be. He was enchanting and handsome. I lost my head. When I told my mother we'd marry, she gave him a counteroffer in coin behind my back."

"He took it." His words were more confirmation than any hint of a question.

"Didn't even say goodbye."

"You think he set you up?" Tevin asked. There was something carefully neutral in his gaze now that Merit didn't like. She would have expected outrage on her behalf, or perhaps not *outrage*—maybe at least mild indignation.

"Yes, I think he did."

"You were conned once, and you don't wish to be conned again. That's why you want me to accompany you on your husband hunt." He was amused now, which Merit didn't understand. It seemed like a sound idea to her.

"Yes. Like I said, you remind me of him." She waved a hand at him. "All of this. The handsome and charming thing. I don't want to be charmed. Marriage is until death, Mr. DuMont. I'd like to make it at least a few years before I start considering poisons and a shallow grave for my husband."

Amusement lit through him. "You're too practical for a shallow grave. If you murdered your husband, no one would ever find the body." He looked at Val and they busted up laughing.

It irritated Merit, that laughter. "You don't think it's a good idea?"

When he finally stopped, leaning on the bars and gasping for breath, he managed to shake his head. "On the contrary, I think it's brilliant. And you have no idea how qualified I am. How long did you say you have?"

"A hair under six weeks."

"And I'll stay with you until then? In exchange for my mother's freedom?"

Merit nodded.

Tevin stuck a hand through the bar, only to have Val grab him at the wrist. She clucked her tongue. "Six weeks is a very long time."

"It's a bargain when you consider what his mother owes me."

"Excuse us," Val said, not waiting for an answer before she yanked Tevin away to speak to him at the back of the cell. His siblings joined them. They all whispered harshly back and forth, Tevin doing most of the actual talking. After a few minutes, Tevin cut everyone off and returned to the front.

"Forgive me," Tevin said, his smile wide. She felt that weird push again, the one she didn't like, and once again she shook it off. Something must have registered on her face, because Tevin lifted his hands in a placating gesture. "If at all possible, Lady Merit, I'd like to discuss the terms of our contract alone."

She nodded, using the key to unlock the cell and let him out. "That seems like a solid notion." Once he was through, she relocked the cell and motioned him on. "After you."

CHAPTER 6

A DEAL IS STRUCK

Tevin followed Lady Merit through a door, down a hall, and into a snug room with two chairs separated by a table. A long, narrow window sat high on the wall, letting in light and air, but keeping any enterprising criminals out. She'd taken him to an interrogation room. Tevin wondered if she meant something by it, but determined from her demeanor that this was likely the closest space for them to have privacy. He took the chair that had manacles dangling from it, waiting to see if she would make use of them. Merit settled into the chair in front of him, her posture straight. From that posture alone, Tevin could have guessed her social class. Merit stared at him, her gaze direct, her hands folded.

"There are a few things we need to discuss." Tevin leaned forward, his elbows resting on the table in front of him. He took her measure for a long moment. Tevin hadn't been lying when he said he was an expert at reading people. In order for this to work, Merit was going to have to trust him. As someone who'd had her trust snapped in two, that wouldn't be easy for her. They needed a solid foundation to work from, and Tevin had an idea how to do it, but it was a gamble. If the gamble failed, he might end up cooling his heels in Veritess Jail until his hair turned gray.

"Before we go any further, I'm going to need to be completely honest with you, which is a bit of a novel concept for me." He tapped his finger on the scarred wooden table between them. "You're not going to like it, I promise you. All I ask is that you listen."

Merit stared at him, and Tevin got the feeling she was flipping through his own pages; he didn't care for it. Lies were weapons, but they were also shields, and he was used to having that armor. With no small amount of hesitation, he let them drop.

"The boy that ran off—what was his name?"

"Jasper Sullivan." Merit said the name with no inflection, treating it like any other word, but Tevin wasn't fooled.

"Jasper. Right. What he did, there are lots of names for it, but it's a kind of honey trap. Do you know what that is?"

Merit shook her head.

"It's a type of con. The grifter wants something—money, information, a horse, it doesn't matter. In your case, they wanted money. Jasper was the bait." He kept his eyes on hers. It would be so easy to look away, but he needed her to believe him. "They probably watched you for weeks. Talked to your friends, maybe. Talked to your servants, your butcher, your dressmaker—anyone who knew you. If they couldn't sneak the information, they'd bribe them. Jasper knew all about you before you even spoke a word. Everything from your favorite dessert, favorite song, even the color of your bedroom walls."

"You can't know that," Merit said.

"Yes, I can." Tevin watched as Merit swallowed hard, struggling to absorb this new information.

"How are you so certain?" She was still prim and proper looking, but Tevin was paying attention and caught the fine tremor in her voice. It was the only indication she gave that their discussion was upsetting her at all.

This was it. No going back after he told her this part. Still, he didn't rush it. "Because my family has pulled every kind of cheat and swindle you can think of. We might have even made up a few." He tapped his chest. "My specialty? The honey trap. I'm bait, Merit. Professional bait." Several emotions flickered across her face, so faint that anyone else would have probably missed them. Dismay. Pain. Anger. Her eyes welled, and she blinked, causing two tears to trail down her cheeks.

"I'm sorry," he said, his own throat suddenly tight. "But I needed to tell you before we went any further."

Her voice was completely steady when she spoke. "Tell me one reason why I shouldn't put you in that cell and toss the keys in the sewer."

"Because I *can* help you. With me at your side, Jasper won't happen again."

"You're exactly like him," Merit said, drying her cheeks with the back of her hand. "How can I trust you?"

"Because I don't think the Beast of Cravan should ever cry for the likes of a Jasper Sullivan." He leaned back in his chair. "And I will never be a Jasper to you."

"Of course not." Her voice was stiff as she scowled at him. "You are not, nor will you ever be, an option, Mr. DuMont."

He tapped his thumb on the table, all of his focus on her.

"Believe it or not, I understood that after you said 'full offense, I didn't ask you to marry me,' earlier. What I mean is, I won't lie to you, Merit. I might tell you things you don't want to hear. I may keep secrets that aren't mine to tell, but I will never lie. Not to you."

She growled, a very beastlike noise. "How do I know I'm not being foolish right now?"

Tevin wondered if she knew, just by asking that, that she'd already decided to trust him. "You were never foolish to begin with, Merit. I've seen some of the smartest and wisest fall for the honey trap. It's very hard to not reach for something that you want, and he made sure you'd want him." He gave her a hint of a smile.

Her eyes narrowed.

His smile bloomed fully, stretching wide across his face. "You already said I'm not an option. If I ask you to marry me, say no." He spread out his hands. "See? Nothing to lose."

She shook her head, and the weird, intense moment they'd been sharing broke. "I can't tell anymore if this plan is brilliant or demented." She huffed out a breath, causing a few of the tendrils around her face that had escaped her braid to float into the air. "It's not like I can get more cursed. Fine. The deal is back on. But that means no little fibs, white lies, or anything of that nature. If a dress is hideous on me, you say it. If I step on your toes while dancing, you tell me. I need to trust someone for this to work. Apparently, you're it."

Tevin couldn't help it—he laughed. "You just walked me out of a cell. My mother *stole* from you." He wasn't sure why he'd reminded her. He didn't exactly want to talk her out of it.

"My mother is going to have fits." She leveled her gaze at him. "As for your mother—her choices don't reflect on you. I don't believe that blood will tell. I will judge you on your actions from here forward, no others." She tilted her chin up, the watery light from the window making her look like an illuminated engraving in an old book. "So we're in agreement, then?"

Tevin leaned back in his chair. "I have conditions."

"Of course you do." Merit crossed her arms and leaned back in her chair, mimicking him. "What are they?"

"I'll need to be your shadow—live in your home, go with you when you're out." He held up a hand to stop her from speaking. "Wait until I'm through, please. We only have a short time to get you a good match, so I'll need you to listen to me. I don't expect you to mindlessly agree, but do take everything I say with consideration. Val comes with me. I need another set of hands, and I trust my cousin implicitly."

"And she'll offer to come out of the goodness of her heart?" Amusement tinted her tone.

Tevin nodded slowly. He had no doubts about Val. She'd think it was a lark.

Merit watched him as she considered this, her eyes unfocused. When they sharpened on him, he knew he'd won.

She stuck out her hand. "Deal."

His hand swallowed hers when they shook, but her grip was strong and steady. Jasper might have dented her confidence, but there was a lot of mettle in her. He grinned. "Great. Now let's go find your Prince Not-Charming."

CHAPTER 7

PRINCE NOT-CHARMING

His Highness Prince Eric Latimer of the kingdom of Huldre looked in the long silver mirror and liked what he saw, as he had every morning since the day he realized that the handsome devil staring back was him. His eyes saw no blemish, no wrinkle of fabric, nor any hair out of place. The bright light of midmorning favored the deep sapphire of his eyes and highlighted his dimple, giving him a roguish air. The stylized yoke on his new shirt accentuated his broad shoulders. His valet had braided the long blond hair back from his face, bringing out the exquisite cut of his cheekbones and showing off his delicately tipped ears. His skin sparkled in the light, like he was carved out of a beam of sunshine.

He spun, checking the hang of his duster, which draped over a tightly fitted—and massively bejeweled—vest. The coat swirled, revealing the cut of his trousers and his fine leather riding boots, which hugged his calves as he turned. When everything seemed in place, he added his bowler hat and assessed the whole look.

"What do you think of the new duster?" he asked no one in particular, as that would require him to remember the actual names of the staff, which was, of course, beneath him. A chorus of "very fine, sir," came back to him, with murmurs of appreciation. This was the expected—and really, the only—response. When he murmured that the vest might be a *bit* much, he was assured that it was exactly enough. Latimer stopped twisting and leaned closer to the mirror, licking his index finger and smoothing his shapely golden eyebrow. "And the tail?"

This was met with silence. Latimer looked behind him in the mirror at the faces of the staff. If Eric Latimer, prince and only heir of the kingdom of Huldre, had been a man who thought about others' feelings, he would have understood that he'd caused them palpitations because they weren't sure what response to give. Should they sing a chorus of praise to his fine and royal tail? Pretend they didn't know what he was talking about? Produce a manly, bejeweled (possibly fringed—he was really into fringe right now) ribbon to bedeck it? But Latimer wasn't the type of man to consider his own feelings deeply, let alone those of others. In fact he was actively discouraged from doing either. His right foot started tapping, his impatience driving the movement. "Well? Can you see it?" It may have been a royal tail, but it was still a *tail*, and he didn't always want it advertised.

Grateful for this cue, the handful of staff behind him quickly assured the prince that no, they couldn't see it at all before they began praising the luxurious fabric, delicate stitching, and vibrant hue of his new duster, which of course brought out the color of his eyes (like glittering jewels), the color of his hair (rich as spun gold, soft as new lamb), and framed his strong, masculine torso (the envy of the kingdom).

Appeased by their obsequious replies, he dismissed everyone

and sent them gratefully scurrying into the depths of the castle. He finally tore himself away from the mirror and made his way to the grand dining hall downstairs.

The Castle of Huldre was an aberration of time, jutting out of the hill like a calcified thumb bone amongst the forts and holdings of neighboring baronies that belonged to Queen Lucia's people. But when Latimer's great-great-great-grandfather had sailed over in a fleet and ruthlessly conquered these holdings and claimed this land, he had wanted a castle built like the ones in his homeland of Tirada. He'd wanted trappings of the old country, and so a castle had been built, and his family hadn't seen fit to do much beyond the occasional repair or update since. Latimer, like the rest of his family, was rather fond of the prodigious monstrosity. The single royal holding on what was otherwise Queen Lucia's lands. What it lacked in subtlety it made up for in pompous grandeur.

If anything encapsulated the magnificent estate that the Huldre family owned, it was the dining hall. The ceilings were vaulted, the tapestries intricate, and the table an ancient and hulking thing that had been carved within an inch of its life. A great stone fireplace took up one wall, the fire crackling with subdued merriment. The castle was a monument to times past, and if the hall was drafty and prone to cobwebs, no one mentioned it.

At the table sat the remainder of the Huldre family. If they had any family left in his ancestors' homelands of Tirada, he wasn't aware of them. His mother, Lady Angelique, had golden hair so pale that it was bordering on white. Today it was up in an intricate knot, revealing the delicate curve of her tipped ears. Sitting still, as she was now, a teacup in her hand, the faint morning sunshine through the stained-glass window bathing her, she looked like a creature woven of light and air. She was, quite simply, breathtaking.

At the other end, his father crowded his place setting, his broad shoulders carving space for the rest of his body. He fit their surroundings, more ancient warrior than modern king. Henrich would look more at home with a sword and shield than in the suit he was wearing now.

The table could, on any given day, seat sixty people. Latimer's mother sat at one end. His father at the other. Neither was willing to give up their position as head of the table, both choosing to either eat in silence or have the footman run messages back and forth between them, and both insisting that every morning Latimer choose where to sit. When he was mad at his father, he sat with his mother. If he wanted her attention, he sat with his father. If he felt petulant toward both, he sat in the middle, refusing to let the footman carry any messages between them and forcing his parents to shout.

When Latimer was younger, he used to find the whole thing upsetting, but that was before one particular day when he'd chosen his mother and happened to glance up to see the king's face. Henrich Latimer, king of Huldre, didn't look angry or even irritated. Instead he'd looked at his wife with a strange mix of pride and a heat Latimer didn't understand at the time. That was when he'd realized. His father, who hated losing to anyone, *liked it* when he was bested by Angelique. It was a game, and though Latimer was a piece in it, he wasn't an important part. That realization took some of the pressure off his choice.

Latimer dipped a bow to both. The king nodded, the sunlight filtering through the room making his circlet wink. His father had a ceremonial crown but preferred the circlet for daily life.

"The morning greets you well, Father?" Latimer did not sit, still waiting to choose his allegiance for the day. He didn't get to make many choices for himself, so he savored the few available to him.

"It does, my son, it does. A fine day for hunting, perhaps?" The king placed a meaty fist on the table. "People in the western fields have been complaining about wyrms. Scaring the livestock and all that." He drummed his fingers. "They only sent half of their tithe, so I'm tempted to leave them to it, but the weather is pleasant, and a wyrm would look fine over the mantel, don't you think?"

Latimer considered this. Hunting *was* entertaining. He had a fine new crossbow to break in as well.

Before he could accept, his mother patted the spot next to her with one hand. When he didn't join her immediately, she added, "Come, my son. Your mother needs you." His chest tightened, hope in his heart, despite years of layering indifference onto the infernal organ. His mother never *needed* him. No one really needed him. Sometimes he wondered if he was any different from the decorative vase in the hall, and while that idea once depressed him, now he took pride in it. If he was going to be an ornament, then he was going to be the *best* ornament.

Still, to be *needed*? Latimer couldn't pass up the sliver of a chance that it was true. He went to her, and her face glowed, her victory evident. Without looking back, Latimer took the seat she'd indicated.

For once, curiosity got the best of the king. Unable to stay on his side and be left out, the king reluctantly gave up his chair and took the one across from his son. The harried steward, who had been waiting in the doorway for the final seating arrangements to be made, clapped his hands to alert the serving staff. A small boy ran out and placed a linen napkin in each noble lap. A young woman followed him, silently filling cups with black coffee before another girl placed a pot of tea next to his mother. The girl poured a steaming cup before retreating, never making eye contact.

After that came plates of food—duck eggs with asparagus and mushrooms, kippers, toast, and raspberry jam. Thick slices of ham steamed on a platter surrounded by pickled quail eggs. Sticky buns with candied oranges, figs in honey, and delicate apple tarts. The king loaded up his plate until no porcelain was showing while Latimer held his mother's hand.

"What is it?"

The queen dismissed the staff, waiting until the door swung shut on the last of them. Then she turned to her son and stroked his cheek with one delicate hand. "You have grown into a fine man, my son. Strong, handsome, brave—a mother couldn't ask for more in a child."

Unease churned in Latimer's gut. His mother wanted something. From her lavish praise, she *really* wanted whatever it was, too. He hoped it was something he was willing or able to give, for he knew there would be no stopping her. While it was lovely to be needed, nothing was worse than not being able to provide the service in question. "Thank you, Mother."

"We've given you everything, asking for so little in return."

The unease doubled. "Milady?"

She took his larger hand in her long, delicate fingers. "I'm tired of watching this kingdom struggle. I'm tired of watching our coffers empty while Lucia paves her streets in gold."

Latimer didn't know much about streets, but gold ones sounded impractical. Gold was soft. It would flatten under horses' hooves and cart wheels, surely. "What is wrong with our coffers?"

"Nearly empty," Angelique said mournfully. "I had an idea to fix it—I didn't want you to worry." Her eyes filled up. *Oh no, tears.* Latimer glanced at his father, who was already leaning toward the queen, his face panicked. If the queen cried and Latimer didn't do anything to stop it, his father would be furious.

"I'm sure you did your best." Latimer awkwardly patted her hand.

"I did. Only the woman I hired *failed.*"

Henrich handed her his handkerchief, and she dabbed at her eyes. He glared at his son, his command clear. *Fix this.*

"How did she fail?"

But the queen ignored his question. "I was so upset. Such a simple task." She sniffed, and when she looked up, her eyes were bright. "Then I realized—I was thinking too small." She handed her plate to Latimer, taking out a small folded piece of paper from a hidden pocket in her gown. She gently placed it on the table in front of her. "Why does Queen Lucia's kingdom prosper?"

Latimer responded without thinking, this lesson being one that had been drilled into him at an early age. "It's larger than ours and rich with resources. Minerals, lumber—"

"And Caen's bloom," his mother cut in as she delicately pinched the edges of the paper, tugging it open. "Our kingdom spends a fortune importing it, and they have the temerity to dictate what we charge for it. Is that fair, I ask? No. And we can't do anything about it. Delicate thing won't grow here in *proper* soil. Good Huldre soil. But what if our botanists could produce a hardier strain?" She'd finished unfolding the paper, and it appeared to be a map.

He could see their lands butting up against Queen Lucia's on one side, the ocean on the other. A shaded area denoted the large sprawl of the Enchanted Forest that began in their kingdom and spilled into the other like ink. "Our people would rejoice—cheaper medicine," he said.

"We would rejoice in full coffers and throwing off the powerful hold Lucia has on us. We'd be a power in our own right. No more threats to swallow us up into her kingdom." She tapped a highlighted area. "This land right here. It's not far, and yet here the Caen's shrub thrives. What if we had access to this land, access to the flower? We've held our borders since we first came here. I think it's a fine time for us to grow a little."

"Are we going to invade?" It seemed unlikely to Latimer. Wars cost coin, and they were running low.

"In a manner of speaking." His mother was smiling now, the shine of tears completely gone from her eyes as if it had never even been. "This area belongs to Lady Zarla, the queen's cousin. She has a daughter. Her heir. Her *only* heir."

Latimer stared at the map, hoping it might tell him the rest of her plan, but all he saw was the thick lines of borders and the squiggles of rivers. "We're going to kidnap her?"

"You're going to marry her, my son. Marry her, and we'll have access to her lands, the flowers, *and* claim to a new piece of Queen Lucia's kingdom." She took his hand again. "Marry her, and I get what I want. I gave you life. Surely you can give me this."

Despite having a border in common, Latimer had never met Lady Zarla's daughter. He had no idea what she looked like. What kind of person she was. But he'd heard one thing. "Isn't she cursed?"

"Yes," his mother said, waving that away. "Quite terribly. Turned into some sort of hideous beast, I hear." The grip on his hand increased. "Which will make your job that much easier." She touched his face again. "To be a beast and courted by one such as you? How easy it will be. Smile. Charm her. Marry her. Then everything we want is ours."

Latimer pulled his hand back before his mother could feel his palms sweating. Certain things came with marriage, and he didn't want to do a single one of them with a beast. "There will be other suitors, surely? If she's rich and an heir? There's no guarantee she'll pick me."

"Make sure you're the only possible choice." Lady Angelique picked up her tea, taking a long sip. "Shouldn't be difficult. Look at you. Handsome. Rich. Good bloodlines. A literal prince among lordlings."

"Perhaps I'm not her type," Latimer hedged. "Or her heart is already engaged."

Angelique's eyes narrowed, and Latimer felt a chill run down his spine. "You will make sure that she chooses wisely, then." She set down her cup.

The king harrumphed. "He still has to court a beast. I don't envy him that."

Latimer paled. How bad would it be? Did she have scales? Slitted eyes, like a goat? "Even if we wed, the lands would remain hers until we passed them on to an heir, assuming we have children. What until then? And what if she denies me access to her funds?" He may not know the beast, but he couldn't imagine anyone raised as an heir would cavalierly toss any part of their birthright away. "Unless something happened to her, we'd be beholden to her charity."

"You let me worry about all of that. Concern yourself with courting her, winning her, and bringing her home. Mother will take care of the rest."

What did that mean? Did he even want to know? "As you wish," Latimer said, finally filling his own plate and putting everything else out of his mind. His mother would handle it. It was best to let her have her way.

CHAPTER 8

WHAT WE NEED IS A MONTAGE

Merit had the guards release Tevin's family. His parents decided to take the reluctant DuMont siblings with them. Merit got the impression that the only reason Tevin had been allowed to hug his brother and sister goodbye was that he did it before Merit unlocked his parents' cell. Once she did, they swanned out, taking Kate firmly in their grasp while Amaury followed quietly behind.

Merit thought she heard them toss a "we'll be in touch!" casually over their shoulders, but she couldn't be sure if it was meant to be reassurance or a threat.

Tevin watched them go, a lost look on his face, which he quickly covered with a blank mask. He held the door open for Merit and Val before following them up to the front desk so Val could collect her things.

Val accepted her belongings—a leather belt and side irons—back from the guard. Merit waited for the guard to bring something for Tevin, but nothing else appeared.

"Where are your things?"

Tevin scoffed. "Like I'd bring anything of value with me into a jail. Prisoners' things have a tendency to evaporate into the ether."

"Hey!" Val said, her ears pink. "Why didn't you say anything to me?"

"Losing a pistol or two would have been a fantastic learning tool, wouldn't it?" Tevin asked mildly. "As an elder, it's my duty to enlighten the youth."

Val punched him in the arm. "You're full of it. I know for a fact you didn't bring anything with you."

Tevin jammed his hands into his pockets, his step light. "The lesson stands." Then he laughed as Val took another swing at him.

Merit wondered, briefly, if she'd made the wrong decision. She'd traded a prisoner for unknown quantities that seemed quite used to trouble. It occurred to her that maybe that was what she needed. A little trouble could sometimes do a lot of good, couldn't it? Either way, it was too late now. All she could do was make the best of it.

Merit had borrowed one of her mother's carriages to come over to the jail, and now she wished she hadn't. It was fancier than she liked—the carriage a glossy cream and airy as spun sugar. Gilding caught the light even when it wasn't moving, drawing the eye. It practically shouted, *Look at me,* and she didn't care for drawing stares. The metal constructs pulling it were shaped like hieracosphinxes, their hawk heads so lifelike Merit wanted to touch the feathers that blended into the lion bodies that made up the rest of the animals. The blue spark of mage light shone out of the construct's eyes as she stepped close and tapped the lead hieracosphinx, whispering her location to it.

Then they all clambered in, Val bouncing on the leather seats. "Fancy."

"You're the only fairyborn we have," Tevin said. "Try to be dignified."

Val shoved him over. "My family's barony is rural. We don't have much use for fancy carriages. But I do know hog-tyin', and if you don't hobble your lip, I'll be demonstrating it right quick."

"What do you look like when the bloom wears off?" Tevin crossed his legs and made himself comfortable in the plush leather. Merit caught the sharp look in his eyes. He might pretend to be idly curious, but Merit thought he missed very little.

"More horns, I bet," Val said, stretching her arms out over the back of the seat, clearly enjoying herself.

"Furrier." Tevin grinned, getting in on the game. "I heard she has wings and haunts the night."

"You're both very funny," Merit said primly. "Have you considered becoming street jesters?"

Val leaned over and carefully grabbed Tevin's hand. Merit didn't think he'd even realized he'd been chewing on the tip of his thumb. A nervous gesture that obviously embarrassed him as he glanced to see if Merit had noticed. She pretended she hadn't, fussing instead with the shade that blocked the window. It was stuck and wouldn't come down. She didn't want people trying to peek in at her. She'd have enough of that soon with all the balls and social parading.

"Yes to the fur and the horns, no to the wings." She yanked

too hard, and the shade snapped off. "Blast." She huffed out a breath. "Wings would have been interesting."

Val pulled down the other shade with a deft tug while Tevin took Merit's seat and edged her over and away from the open window so no one could see her. They really were good at reading what people needed. She felt better about her decision.

Merit felt the warmth of Tevin along her side, tempting her to lean into him. What would it be like, to have someone to hold her up? To comfort her? To have siblings who pretended they were fine but hugged you so hard you knew they were desperately sad at the idea of you leaving? Or a cousin who loved you so much they didn't think twice about throwing their chips in with yours and jumping into a beast's carriage?

• • •

Tevin had felt shabby sitting in the jail. Amaury might have used his sewing kit on the train to mend Tevin's shirt—he'd been too sick to do it himself—but he was still missing two buttons, and hadn't shaved or showered. Gently cushioned in Merit's elegant hack, he'd moved beyond "shabby" and somewhere into "seedy and disreputable." He ran a hand over his jaw and wondered how he was going to set himself to rights when he only had the clothes on his back.

Val pressed her face against the side of the hack to get a better view out the window. "I think we're here."

Seconds later the hack slowed, proving her right. Val opened the door, revealing the Cravans' city home, a beautiful brownstone in a nice neighborhood. Too big for two people, but Tevin didn't think that Merit and her mother were ever only two

107

people. There would be a cook, maids, a butler, a secretary, and who knew how many others. The aristocratic fairyborn always lived with an entourage.

What he hadn't expected was to see Amaury leaning indolently against the bricks beside Merit's door.

Merit stopped next to him, placing her fingers on the back of his wrist. "How did he beat us here?"

Tevin swore.

Merit ignored his cursing as she breezed into her home, leaving Tevin, Val, and Amaury to follow her lead. Normally, someone like Merit would hand off gloves and perhaps a hat to the butler. Tevin realized that she wasn't wearing gloves and had no hat, though a butler had, indeed, opened the door. Merit requested refreshments and was walking into a cheery yellow parlor when she was accosted by a young Hanian woman who moved like a fencer.

"You dashed off without me."

Merit blinked. "Oh, Kaiya. I'm sorry. This morning I was just so—" She cut herself off, seeming to remember that they weren't alone. "Kaiya, this is Tevin DuMont and his younger brother, Amaury. The young woman with the hat is their cousin Val. Two of them will be staying with us. Amaury was about to explain what he was doing here."

Val took off her hat, bowing to Kaiya with a flourish. Then she straightened, hitting Kaiya with a smile that was pure flirt. If Kaiya noticed it, Tevin couldn't tell. She assessed them all with an equally critical eye as Tevin and Amaury greeted her while Val frowned and handed her hat off to the butler.

Tevin swallowed a laugh, and it came out like a strangled

cough. Val was obviously used to getting more of a response from her flirty grin. Irritated, Val snatched his hat off his head, tossing it into the waiting butler's hand. Val lingered until everyone else had started following Merit into the parlor before throwing Tevin a rude gesture with her hand.

The parlor was decorated to within an inch of its life, and Tevin knew it was probably Merit's least favorite room. He wondered, then, why she chose it.

After they settled in, the butler came in with a tea service, coffee, and sandwiches, followed by a slender dark-haired man about Tevin's age. Though he still had his bowler on, he wore no jacket, just his shirtsleeves, trousers, and a gray waistcoat. He took off his hat and hung it on a hook behind a door. "Milady, I—" He paused, adjusting his wire-rim spectacles and looking about the room. "I was unaware we had guests."

Merit waved a hand at him. "I'll explain later." She rattled off their names again, this time to the newcomer, whom she introduced as her healer, Dev Ellery Detante. Tevin caught the honorific, even if Merit didn't stress it, and he wondered if she was testing him to see if he knew what it meant. He immediately discarded the idea. Merit wasn't one to play games like that, especially if the outcome could prove hurtful to her friend, and Ellery was obviously a family friend. Tevin glanced at Val and Amaury to make sure they caught it. Dev was the honorific sprigganborns used instead of Miss, Mr., or Mrs., because their culture didn't have a strict gender binary. Just in case Val and Amaury had missed it, Tevin stepped forward, offering his hand to the healer. "Pleased to make your acquaintance, Dev Detante."

Ellery shook his hand, their expression guarded. "Pleasure's mine, probably."

Merit collapsed into a chair. "Tevin and Val will be staying here for the foreseeable future. Amaury, I assume you are as well?" She rested her head against the chairback. "I suppose it's only sporting that I warn you both that all three of them are criminals."

"Allegedly," Val said, though Tevin kept his mouth shut. Amaury only acknowledged that he would, indeed, be staying, by nodding his head.

"Allegedly," Merit repeated. "Though I did bring them directly from a jail cell."

"Pleased to meet you." Val stuck out a hand to shake Ellery's. "And I have no current arrest record."

Tevin coughed into his hand.

"Except for the occasional tavern brawl," Val conceded.

"I have the honor of being Merit's healer," Ellery said, shaking her hand before placing themselves between Merit and the DuMonts. By the obstinate set of their jaw, Tevin decided that Ellery didn't care for them much. Tevin batted his eyelashes at the healer. Ellery cared for that even less.

"Is my mother at home?" Merit asked, smoothing her skirt.

"No, milady. She's on a social call." Ellery fetched Merit a cup of tea and pressed it into her hands.

Tevin was tempted to let the scene play out. You learned a lot more by being quiet and letting people forget they had an audience than by barging in, but his nerves were strained by the day, he was tired and dirty, and they had a timeline.

"Speaking of your mother, we'll need her list of prospective

suitors as well as a list of the social occasions you'll be attending."
Tevin wasn't that hungry, but he grabbed a sandwich anyway.
You never knew when you'd be fed again. "You're going to need
to let your mother know that we're staying here, Merit."

Ellery's expression was scathing. "You should not address her
so familiarly."

Merit sighed. "Ellery, there is no need to be protective." She
looked at her watch. "In thirty minutes, I will revert to my
curse. If they do something wrong, I'll simply bite them."

Ellery looked like they wanted to argue, but Kaiya spoke
instead. "Merit, I'm dying to know why I'm not throwing the
criminals back onto the street. I hate to be nosy, but as your
guard, it is *actually my job*."

"You love being nosy," Merit said. Kaiya shrugged.

"I'm here to help Merit pick a husband," Tevin said.

"I'm here to help," Val added.

Everyone looked at Amaury. His grin was a feral thing. "And
I'm a spy."

"I don't think spies are supposed to tell you that they're
spies," Merit said.

Tevin dropped his head into his hands. Had he really thought
his parents weren't going to put their hands in, or would pass up
an opportunity like this? He was going to spend weeks among
the pigeons—it wasn't enough for him to trade himself for his
mother's freedom. He'd be expected to come home with coin in
hand, or at least some leads for them to follow. Always schem-
ing, that was his parents' motto. They should engrave it above
their mantel and be done with it.

"He's telling us so we can choose what information to pass

on. They let us go too easily. I should have guessed." He rubbed a hand over his face. "I'd put you on the next train home, but you'd just come back. If you're here, who's taking care of Kate?"

"Kate is taking care of Kate." Amaury brushed at something on his sleeve. "Novel idea, but we're seeing how it goes."

Tevin wanted to argue but knew it to be a futile endeavor. Even if Amaury desired to go, Florencia and Brouchard wanted him here. He'd simply be sent back. "Fine."

"Merit, based on this conversation alone, you can't possibly let these people stay. Kaiya, back me up on this, please?" The healer sent a beseeching look to Kaiya.

Kaiya grinned. "Oh, no. They should definitely stay."

"Thank you," Merit said.

The look Kaiya gave Tevin made him squirm. "I like to know *exactly* where my enemies are."

Ellery glowered at her.

Tevin carefully set his empty plate aside and stood. He was taller than Ellery and broader. Though the healer was in good shape, judging by the muscle tone he could see, Tevin wasn't worried. He knew how to size up an opponent, and he could take Ellery easily. Not that it would help him any. If he beat up Merit's friend and healer, she would be unhappy. If she was unhappy, she wouldn't listen to him. He needed to defuse this. Tevin crossed his arms, his stance not aggressive, but sure and steady. "Merit can give you more details, but we're here by her request and invested in her happiness. We're on the same side." The more he talked, the more Ellery softened. Most people didn't notice, but Merit's healer seemed alarmed by the change.

Ellery looked almost panicked when they glanced at Merit.

"I want to listen to him and trust him, but I don't. I want to toss him out on his pretty face. What's happening?" They rubbed their hands over their arms. "I don't like it."

Tevin felt sorry for Ellery. It was bad enough to be manipulated, but worse to know it was happening and not be able to do anything about it. It was a feeling Tevin knew well from being around his parents. "What you're feeling is my fairy gift. All of my siblings have gifts. Mine is charm." He gestured to Ellery's arms. "The more I talk, the more my magic will try to mold your will so that you're disposed to like me."

"Well, cut it out," Ellery said, their body stiffening.

"I can't." Tevin crossed his arms, trying to ignore his wrinkled shirt and the fact that he desperately needed a bath and a shave. Ellery would have been less suspicious if Tevin didn't look so disreputable. He *was* disreputable, but he didn't usually look it. "I'm sorry, but I can't control it."

Ellery jerked a finger toward Merit. "Is that why she agreed to bring you here? Your charm?" They didn't wait for Tevin to answer but strode toward the bellpull. "Don't worry, milady, I'll take care of this riffraff."

When the healer went to reach for the pull, their hand met Amaury's chest. Tevin's brother shook his head and pointed Ellery back to the sitting area.

"And let him charm us more?" Ellery scoffed. "I think not."

Amaury continued to block Ellery, waiting for Tevin, who was staring at Merit and thinking back through the morning. "Actually, Merit's immune to my charm."

Ellery glowered at him again. "Convenient, don't you think? How could we know that's true?"

Val, ignoring the tense undercurrents of the conversation, was selecting a pie from the tray and sneaking glances at Kaiya. "She's been arguing with him. Wouldn't do that if she'd been charmed."

Tevin leaned his hip against Merit's chair, his smile meant only for her. "Merit, you should fire your healer."

"Absolutely not," Merit said, frowning up at him. "Are you mad?"

"I'm awfully cold," Tevin said, dropping down into a crouch, his face inches from hers. The faintest hint of peach tinting her cheeks was the only indication that she was affected by how close he'd come. "May I have your dress?"

Ellery choked in outrage, but Merit only sipped her tea. "Now you're being cheeky."

"Why'd you pick this parlor?"

She blinked at the abrupt change in topic. "My tincture will wear off soon. The beast has claws, and I despise this parlor. This way I don't have to worry about the furniture."

"But you're not worried about your dress? It's a pretty little thing." His words were soft, intimate, but they carried through the quiet room. "Don't you think it would look good on me?"

"I have no doubt that it would," Merit said dryly. "But I'm attached to it."

Tevin laughed, delighted at her response. "Ellery, if my charm worked, you'd be fired, and I'd have a new dress." He grinned, still crouched close to Merit and enjoying how pink her cheeks had gone. "Some people simply don't want to be charmed."

"He can't charm me, either," Val said. "Or Amaury."

Everyone looked at Kaiya. She gazed back steadily. "Don't

114

worry about me. He can be as charming as he wants. Wouldn't stop a blade, now, would it?"

"I still don't believe you, any of you," Ellery said, indignant.

"Ellery, do sit down," Tevin said, suddenly realizing how long he'd been staring at Merit. He straightened abruptly, waving his hand at the tray of food. "And have something to eat. Your fussing is upsetting Merit."

Ellery walked across the room and sat by the tea service, taking a plate before they blinked and looked at Tevin. "Oh."

Tevin sat back down. "I cannot make Merit do anything she doesn't want to do. I'm here to help her *not* be charmed by any of the suitors her mother has picked."

Kaiya waved a hand at Amaury and Val. "What about them?"

"They'll be endlessly useful," Tevin said. "I promise."

Ellery's mouth opened, and Merit huffed. "That's enough, Ellery. They're staying until I decide they aren't." She frowned over her tea. "So all your siblings have fairy gifts? It's unusual to have so much wealth in one family, especially when you have no fairy blood. Are your parents gifted, too?"

Amaury grunted in the negative but didn't elaborate.

Tevin helped himself to a piece of shortbread. "Our parents have lied, cheated, and stolen to make sure we all have gifts that are helpful to them, but they themselves are not gifted."

"Why not?" Merit asked.

"If you'd spent time with Florencia or Brouchard DuMont, you wouldn't ask that question." Val's face twisted into mild disgust. "They would never give anyone that much power over them, even for a second. Fairy gifts can cut both ways, and they wouldn't endanger themselves."

Tevin looked up through his lashes to catch Merit's reaction. He didn't want pity and was relieved that he didn't see it. She looked thoughtful, her lips pursed, but nothing more, like she was waiting for more information to come in before she decided something. Tevin finished his shortbread.

Merit tapped her finger on the side of her cup. "When will my mother be home?"

Ellery took out their watch. "Two hours, I imagine."

"She left some papers for you on your desk," Kaiya said, shifting forward on the settee. "Including the list of approved suitors." She smiled so wide her eyes crinkled. "I'm sure you just can't wait to see it."

Merit nodded. "Kaiya, can you fetch the maid for me? Have her find rooms for the DuMonts and get them situated." She set down her tea. "I've got some things to do before my mother gets here. I need to decide how to handle her."

Tevin exchanged a look with Val. Amaury, still leaning against the wall by the bellpull, dipped his head to hide a grin.

"Don't worry about your mother," Tevin said, standing. "Bring her to us when she gets here. We'll take care of everything."

Merit looked like she wanted to argue, but Val stopped her.

"Let us earn our keep," Val said. "You won't regret it." Val grabbed another small pie before snagging Tevin's arm. "Come on. I've got an idea."

• • •

Tevin almost felt bad for Lady Zarla. Oh, she was rich and titled, with the fortunate existence that came with that. She seemed

116

intelligent, and nice enough as these things went, which was a bit of a surprise. She could likely hold her own in most situations, but against the DuMonts? She was to be pitied, really.

Lady Zarla came back from her social engagements and strode into her sitting room only to find it in complete and utter disarray. The room teemed with activity—Val's idea set in motion. It was a large room, but even so, there was very little space left to move around. Amaury was flipping through fabric samples, occasionally stopping to show one to the tailor's assistant. Val examined boots that had been brought in by a local cobbler while simultaneously trying on hats from the milliner. Tevin, freshly bathed and clean shaven, stood on a stool in his underthings, sipping coffee as the tailor took measurements. There were boxes upon boxes of goods and several very harried assistants running around. To be honest, the room looked like the entire fashion district had thrown up in it.

There was also, inexplicably, a harpist.

Lady Zarla's expression remained serene, every inch in control from the soles of her finely made walking boots to the jeweled clips in her ebony updo. Out of the corner of his eye, Tevin saw one of her gloved hands briefly fist against the ruby fabric of her walking dress. Without batting an eye, she sent one of the servants off to fetch Merit. She didn't speak to Tevin or anyone else in the room, only glared as she stripped the gloves from her hands. Tevin ignored her and continued to sip his coffee and move when the tailor asked him to.

Merit strode into the room after that, and everything stilled. One of the assistants gasped, his face bloodless. The harpist fainted over her harp, causing the instrument to make a mangled sound. Tevin ground his teeth as the tailor stuck him with a pin.

Gone was the Merit of before. What strode into the room was the Beast of Cravan. Curved horns sprouted from her skull, curling around her ears, much like a ram. The horns themselves were black, almost delicate, rising out of rich brown fur. She had a snout, reminding Tevin of either a dog or a bat. He cocked his head. More bat than dog, he decided.

Her hands and feet were clawed, and though her hands were still vaguely human shaped, her feet were closer to paws. She moved differently, too—sinuously, like a predator. When she crossed to her mother, he caught the faintest hint of a tail. Orange eyes blinked at the room, and though they looked different, Tevin could still see the intelligence and resolve he was already associating with Merit. Changed on the outside into something bestial, she still wore the same cotton dress with the tiny purple flowers from this morning. He relaxed. He looked down at the tailor. "That's not where your needle is supposed to go." His words were loud in the quiet room, breaking the spell. The room lurched back into motion. The tailor apologized and went back to pinning.

"You were right," Tevin said. "Horns."

Val snorted and pulled a boot onto her foot. "Furry, too. We were both right."

"Could someone please revive the harpist?" Tevin said, pitching his voice louder. "The lack of music is killing the mood." A second passed, and music once again filtered into the room, though softer and a little wobbly. Tevin caught Merit's gaze and smiled over his coffee cup.

"Did you empty all of High Street?" Merit asked, taking one of the coffee cups her own butler offered.

"Only the best shops." Val eyed Merit. "Do you need anything? They're a little overloaded with the three of us, but I'm sure they'd figure something out for you."

"She makes a point." Tevin's brow furrowed as he examined the room. "We should have checked if you had adequate gowns for the upcoming social whirl."

"I'm fine," Merit said. "Merely confused. Especially about the harpist."

"We couldn't find a fiddler on short notice," Amaury said.

"We thought music would make things go faster." Tevin handed his coffee off to an assistant and held his arms out so they could fit him with a ready-made suit. They'd have to alter it for him, but it would be faster than making it from scratch. "We didn't exactly plan to stay in Veritess." Tevin slipped into a shirt, his deft fingers making quick work of the buttons. "And we only had the clothes on our backs. They're decent clothes, but they won't do for what we have in mind."

"What we have in mind?" Lady Zarla finally found her voice and choked out the question.

"I'm going to be your honored guest." Tevin moved as directed while the tailor pinned the shirt. "And Merit is heir to the House of Cravan. So I can't be *me*, and I can't pretend to be one of you, either. Which leaves a very specific strata of society."

"Industrialist," Val said. "A head of a mage concern, here to discuss business with your barony. It would make sense for Merit to be showing him about the place. If he's rich and handsome—"

"And I can pretend to be rich," Tevin said, checking the suit in the mirror behind the tailor. Since he'd had a chance to bathe earlier, his hair had returned to its usual golden brown. He'd brushed it back, revealing high cheekbones and a firm jaw. The deep purple of his new vest made the rich green of his eyes bright in the mirror. He nodded at the tailor.

"Then if he's seen attempting to ingratiate himself and court Merit?" Val yanked off the boot she'd been trying on.

"Human, but with money and power," Amaury said, setting the fabric samples down. He looked at Merit. "I'm going to need coin."

"They'll bill us." Merit looked around the room again. "A lot, probably."

Tevin had to hand it to Merit: She didn't even wince at the thought. Full, high-end wardrobes for three people were going to cost some serious change. Not to mention the harpist. He glanced over at Lady Zarla, whose face was a rather strangled-looking red.

Amaury shook his head. "Not for this." He waved away the frenzy of workers in the sitting room. "Supplies. Identities."

"Pardon?" Merit asked.

"What is going on?" Lady Zarla snarled. "Someone has five seconds to tell me before I call for the constables."

Val came over to Lady Zarla and smiled, placing a light gray bowler onto her head. "That is splendid on you, Baroness Cravan. It brings out your eyes. May we call you Zarla?"

"No, you may *not*." Lady Zarla looked like she was going to grab Val by the belt and toss her out the window.

Val laced her arm through Lady Zarla's, steering her out of the teeming mess of things and closer to where Tevin stood.

Tevin exchanged the purple vest for a silver one from the tailor and put it on. "Lady Zarla, please forgive my cousin. She fell off her horse recently and hasn't been right since."

Val surreptitiously scratched under her eye with her extended middle finger. Tevin ignored her and turned a bright smile on Merit's mother, one his own mother referred to as his "matron stunner." She'd made him practice it in front of a mirror until he achieved the perfect balance between slightly wicked and boyishly innocent. He took Lady Zarla's free hand, bowing over it as best he could without upsetting the tailor. "I have to say, Val is correct. That hat looks dashing on you." Before his eyes, Lady Zarla softened, her cheeks becoming rosy.

She touched the hat. "You think so?"

"I do." Tevin nodded.

Val patted her arm. "Lady Zarla, we're here to help your darling child—the apple of your eye—bag and tag a suitable suitor."

"Val," Tevin remonstrated.

Val didn't look the least bit chastened. "To do so, Tevin has to be with her. What better way to do that than by waltzing at her side? Fetching her punch? Escorting her to museums and whatnot?" Val didn't wait for her to answer but plowed on. "The thing about young bucks is they always want what someone else has." She waved a hand at Merit. "They see your daughter on Tevin's arm? A handsome—and in their minds totally inferior—suitor about to snatch her away? Suddenly, they're looking at her with new eyes."

Lady Zarla's brows winged up as she faced her daughter. "Merit, darling, who are these people?"

"Oh, they're criminals, Mother," Merit said casually as she

reached out to adjust Tevin's vest. "You're going to need to take this in at least an inch." The tailor's hand shook, but he nodded and moved a few of the pins.

"Criminals?" Lady Zarla blinked.

"Criminally good at our jobs," Amaury crooned, taking over from Val. "Think of us as marriage consultants."

"Consultants?" Lady Zarla crossed her arms, her brow creasing. A flash of hurt in her eyes, there and then gone, like emotional lightning.

"I think we might have broken my mother," Merit whispered, her face tilted up to Tevin's, her eyes twinkling.

"I'm sure she'll recover," Tevin said softly.

"Now, Lady Zarla," Val said, stepping in front of Merit's mother and pressing a hand to her shoulder to turn her attention away from her daughter. "We can't just go to a ball and announce to all and sundry that Tevin's wealthy and chasing after your daughter. It's simply not done. He must act the part, sure, and he can do that. Should the need arise, he might even have to prove *who* he is. Now, how are we going to do that?"

Lady Zarla opened her mouth, but Amaury barreled in before she could speak. "Without getting into specifics, I'm going to create identities for us that are tight enough to carry water. But I can't make them out of thin air." They would all need identification papers. Of course, what Amaury was talking about was *technically* illegal. Normally, they wouldn't have told her anything, just appeared with new identities intact. But they didn't have time, which made Tevin decide to bring Lady Zarla in on some of it and hope his charm was enough.

Tevin slipped his arms into the jacket. "He'll need paints,

paper, wax, and so on and so forth. I'm sure you'd find the details boring, and besides, plausible deniability is a lovely thing, isn't it?" He beamed at Merit's mother.

She stared at him, then at Amaury, and finally landed on Val. "And what about you?"

Val went back to the boots she'd been trying on. "I'm here to add a hint of respectability to the enterprise. Besides, if he gets into a scrape, he can't hit the broadside of a barn."

Lady Zarla turned a pained face to her daughter. Merit grinned, revealing sharp fangs. The tailor swayed on his feet.

Lady Zarla gave up. "I don't care what you do as long as she gets married before her birthday. If anyone needs me, I'll be in my study drinking a very large brandy." She pointed at the gray bowler. "Add this to the tab." Then she strode out of the room.

Tevin watched the door swing shut behind her. "That went well."

"It did." Merit's voice was gleeful. "The charm certainly comes in handy."

"Yes," Val said, admiring her new boots. "And I have to say, the harpist has made the shopping almost fly by."

Amaury grunted. "Fiddles would have been better."

CHAPTER 9

PRIZE HEIFER SEEKING SAME

Another problem with being a beast, Merit reflected, had to do with seating. The cushioned chair at the delicate writing desk in her room didn't have an outlet for her tail, so she had to sit in a sort of perched manner, like an awkward bird. She kept fidgeting. Every time she fidgeted, the chair squeaked.

"How's that letter coming?" Ellery asked. They were keeping her company in her private sitting room while she wrote a letter to the staff in the country. She'd only planned on being here for a few days. Now she didn't know how long she'd be staying, and needed to make sure things ran smoothly without her. Ellery relaxed on the love seat, sketching in a notebook. It should have been a perfect time to catch up on a few things before she had to meet with Tevin to go over the list of suitors. Her sitting room was light and airy, the windows thrown open for a pleasant breeze. She could hear the drowsy sounds of the city through the windows, and Ellery was an excellent companion, never feeling the need to chatter aimlessly.

"It's going well." She fidgeted. The chair squeaked.

Ellery made a thoughtful little hum that somehow managed to convey skepticism.

Squeak. "It's just my tail."

As a healer, Ellery was used to controlling their expressions, maintaining a calm and confident exterior. So they didn't so much as smile when they said, "That's quite a whopper."

"A whopper?"

"A whale of a tale, as my gran would have said."

"I don't know what you mean." Merit returned to her letter. Dash it all, what had she been going to write?

"Are you absolutely sure it's your tail and not, say, the image of Master Tevin in his undergarments?"

Merit dropped her pen, splattering ink. "Blast." The letter was ruined. "Of course it's my tail."

"Only, you use that desk all the time, and it's never been more than a minor annoyance."

The problem with friends, Merit thought, was that they could not only see your little self-delusions, but felt comfortable calling you out on them. Also, you couldn't toss them out the window, because you loved them and they were right. Even if they were annoying.

Merit paused, her pen hovering over the paper. The upside of friends was that it was easy to go on the offensive in the hopes that they would retreat. "Have you apologized to them yet?"

"The criminals?" Ellery glanced up from their notebook. "No, I have not."

"You were rude, you know." Merit set aside the ruined letter to use for scrap and pulled out a fresh sheet. "It was very unlike you."

Ellery paused over their sketch, tapping the pencil against the paper. "I suppose I owe them an apology." Their eyes met

125

hers. "I'm not saying I don't have concerns. I'm your friend. Of course I'm concerned when you surround yourself with criminals. I've been attempting to remind myself that you're an intelligent, levelheaded person and that you know what you're doing. Except where your mother is involved. It's like a chemical reaction. You're a stable variable on your own, but put you together?" Ellery flicked the fingers of one hand out, mimicking an explosion.

Merit couldn't argue. They did tend to bring out the worst in each other.

Ellery returned to sketching. "That being said, I should try to keep an open mind. Tevin can't control his gift any more than I can control my reaction to it."

"Is it bad?"

"Not bad, but annoying. It's like ants crawling all over your skin." Ellery was fairyborn like Merit, but descended from an entirely different fey creature, a spriggan. One of their peculiarities was being sensitive to magic directed at them. Godlings weren't fond of spriggans. They were immune to their brand of magic, which meant godlings had no control or influence over them. Which made Ellery the perfect healer for Merit and others like her. Godlings couldn't retaliate against a spriggan.

"It shouldn't even work, you know. His magic," Ellery grumbled as they sketched. "Not on me. It's godling magic."

"Maybe you want to be charmed?"

Ellery grunted, indicating that while they didn't agree, they didn't have a very good counterargument, either.

Merit jotted off her letter quickly, rolled it up, and tied it with a red ribbon. "It needs to go express." And she couldn't send it, because the beast couldn't whistle.

"I don't see why you don't just mirror your staff." Ellery stood, taking it from her hands. They leaned out the window and whistled.

"They do better with a list, and I like writing," Merit said, neatly capping her pen.

After a second, a raven settled onto the ledge. He looked like any other black raven, except for a small band on his leg, which held the Cravan crest. Ellery placed the letter on the sill. "No dawdling, hear?"

The raven pecked Ellery's hand and snatched the letter with its claws before taking flight into the bright blue sky. Ellery shook out their hand. "What was that for?"

Merit snorted. "His way of saying, 'You're not my boss.'"

"Your ravens have a bad attitude," Ellery said, crossing their arms right as the door opened.

"We actively encourage it." Kaiya closed the door softly behind her. "That way they accurately represent Merit."

"How angry is she?" Merit fiddled anxiously with her pen.

Kaiya waffled her hand back and forth.

Merit had to admit that she'd loved witnessing Tevin and his family handle her mother so neatly. She'd made the right choice. Hadn't she? "Am I being foolish?"

Ellery and Kaiya exchanged a look, but it was her guard who spoke. "I can't see the future, Merit." She shrugged a shoulder. "Which I'm grateful for. So while we can't answer that question for you, I can tell you that no matter what, we're both here if anything goes wrong."

"Thank you," Merit said, feeling a little better.

Kaiya handed her a folded piece of paper. "From your mother."

"Thanks, Kaiya." Merit took a steadying breath, filling her lungs with air, missing her country home as her beastly snout filtered the scents of the city. "Tevin?"

"In the library." Kaiya tipped her head. "Would you like me to go with you?"

Merit shook her head.

"Just don't forget to frisk him when he leaves, milady." Ellery left the window, resuming their spot on the love seat. "Lots of valuables in there." They picked up their pencil and notebook, flipping it back open, only to pause when Merit's chair squeaked. "I take it back. It's not the valuables I'm worried about. It's you."

"I'm pretty sure I can manage one afternoon in a library with Tevin DuMont without losing my heart." Merit stood up, shaking her hem out.

Ellery's shoulders shook as they laughed. "Heart? I was more concerned about your knickers."

Merit gave her friend a playful shove as she walked past. "Ellery, you're a dear friend and I love you, but there is not a man on this soil who would try to seduce the knickers off a beast."

"Don't sell yourself short, milady. You never can tell what someone likes," Ellery called from the love seat.

"Hush, you," Merit said before she shut the door firmly on Ellery's laughter. Kaiya had followed her as she left, and they went downstairs, walking quickly to the library.

Kaiya paused outside the room. "You sure you don't want me with you?"

Merit squeezed Kaiya's arm. "If he so much as steps wrong, I'll roar."

Kaiya nodded before disappearing down the hall, leaving Merit staring at the library door. She took a deep breath and entered, the wood cool on her paws until she stepped onto the thick rug. The library was twice the size of the sitting room, with built-in cherrywood shelves taking up every wall. Two delicate golden chandeliers cast warm light down onto the thick rugs on the floor. At one end of the room was a long table with six chairs grouped around it, their seat cushions embroidered with delicate branches and brightly colored birds. At the other end, a large fireplace was surrounded by a love seat and two overstuffed chairs. Long windows cut into one wall between the shelves, the heavy drapes framing them held back by thick golden cords. Merit loved natural light, but it wasn't always good for the books. It was a warm, inviting room that smelled like beeswax, leather, and old paper.

Tevin stood with his back to the door, his hands loosely clasped. He was wearing one of the new suits, though he'd left the jacket draped across one of the chairs. As Merit watched, he reached out and selected a red leather volume off a bookshelf, examined the cover, and slid it back.

"That's wise," Merit said.

"Not your favorite poet, then?" Tevin asked without turning.

"He only discusses women in their relationship to men or to himself, so no, not my favorite."

129

Tevin took the volume back out, flipping through the pages before settling on one in the middle. "'Her heaving bosom draws my unwanted eye, lily white, thrusting—'" Tevin slammed the book shut. "Well, that's rubbish. Why do you still have it?"

"Sometimes I need a coaster." Merit made to sit at the table, pausing as Tevin gracefully came over and pulled her chair out for her. "That's unnecessary."

"More like awkward. My sister always complains about the chair banging her knees. It is, however, the sort of asinine thing you need to get used to if you're venturing out into the courting scene. Courting is strange. Courting at your particular level of society is a farce." He took the seat across from her, pulling out a worn leather notebook and a pencil.

Merit watched him as he flipped to a clean page, and wondered again at her choices. She had to admit he was better-looking than Jasper had been, but he seemed less . . . slick. Did that mean he was being honest with her, or was Tevin a more talented con man?

Tevin caught her watching and stilled. Merit wasn't sure what he saw, but he put everything down, closing his notebook. He leaned back in his chair. "Out with it, then."

"What?" Her question was a squeak. She hadn't been doing anything wrong by staring at him, but felt caught out nonetheless. Which irritated her and made her want to growl. This was a drawback of the beast. Her emotions were closer to the surface, harder to control. It was also the upside of the beast, which made sense to Merit only when she looked at it from an angle.

"Merit, for this to work, to work *well*, we need to be on the same side." He grimaced. "Which I recognize isn't going to be easy. Your trust has been violated." He stood, coming over to her side of the table. Tevin grabbed the chair next to her, pulling it out so he could face her. "May I see your wrist?"

She placed it on the table.

He took it, fingers slipping through fur to find the skin fluttering over her pulse. "This would be easier without your fur coat." He smiled faintly and caught her eyes again. "What I need to do is help you get your confidence back, so you can trust your gut. Take back what Jasper took away. First lesson. How do you know someone is lying to you?"

Merit frowned, thinking. "They fidget? Sweat?" She gestured to the wrist he had trapped. "Their heart beats harder?"

Tevin didn't answer but kept his gaze steady on hers. "Tell me three things and make one of them a lie."

"What kind of things?"

"Anything." He waved his free hand in the air. "Any small detail or big truth. It doesn't matter."

"I had an orange with my breakfast," she said. "I'm gifted at sketching. I love living in the country."

"The first two were lies." Tevin huffed a laugh. "You cheated."

"You said make one of them a lie, not that I couldn't make two of them." Merit tugged against his hold.

"Agree to disagree." Tevin let go of her wrist, grabbing her hand, carefully avoiding her claws as he uncurled her first two fingers and placed them on his own pulse. "I can't dance. I hate horses. I've never been arrested."

Merit frowned at his wrist. "I didn't feel a change."

"That's because lying doesn't bother me. Your pulse kicked

131

up because it bothers you." Tevin leaned back in his chair, pulling his wrist free from her hand. "People fidget even when they're telling the truth. Some talk too much." He straightened, crossing his legs so that one of his feet was dangling. "It's easiest to read someone you know well—because you know how they normally sound or move. For everyone else, there are other things you can check." He jiggled his foot, pointing at it. "Look at anchor points—feet, butt, whatever connects to a surface. Look at these the second someone answers you—that's when someone is going to give themselves away."

He stopped bouncing his foot. "People will groom themselves—check their watch, fix their hair, straighten their skirts, touch their face." He rested his elbows on his knees. "Listen to their response, how they're saying it. They might get overly aggressive, or talk a lot without actually answering the question. If they do two or more of the behaviors mentioned— that's important, too. If they scratch their nose but don't do anything else, it's just an itch."

"The behaviors have to be clustered?" Merit clarified.

He nodded. "We'll work on it. I'll point out examples. That's what you'll be getting with me at your side, Merit. An education." He tapped his thumb against the table. "I can accompany you anywhere. I know every dance, custom, and social grace. Take me to any dinner party, ball, or picnic, and I will seamlessly blend in. I can recite the lineage of any fairyborn aristocrat with accuracy to at least four generations. If you like someone, I have the contacts that will let you know what their vices are, their history, their bank accounts down to the half copper. I'm charming and funny, and I can help you *shine*." He crossed his arms over his chest. "This time, you'll be the bait. Not the trick."

"You're not fairyborn. How are you going to blend?"

"Trust me, Merit. I may not look like one of you, but I can guarantee that no one will care."

Merit considered what he'd said. She might have decided in the jail to trust him, but it wasn't really the sort of thing one could easily decide to do. She wasn't sure she *wanted* to trust him. It made her feel wobbly. "If our roles were reversed, what would you do? Would you trust so easily?"

"I would not." He went quiet for a while, then rubbed a hand over his face, clearly having decided something. "When you met my mother, did you trust her?"

"No."

Tevin tapped his forehead. "When we meet people, we're bombarded by information. The way they speak, their tone, the way their body moves; all of it is collected by the animal part of our brain. We read what they aren't saying without realizing we're taking it in, and when people ask, we say we had a 'gut reaction.' " He rested his elbows on the top of the table. "Only, it's not our gut at all, but our mind." His focus narrowed, his eyes glinting emerald green in the light. "Your curse—what does that do to your senses? Better? Same?"

"Better," Merit said. "My hearing and sense of smell are improved. My sight is the same, except I can see better in the dark."

"That's helpful."

"What does this have to do with me trusting myself, exactly?"

133

"I'm charming." He eased back into his chair. "That's not always a positive thing. I'm charming because of my gift, and because I've been trained to be. It's something I've actively worked on." He grinned, and Merit's stomach fluttered. "I'm also stunningly handsome."

She grunted. "And cocky."

"Yes," he said. The grin faltered. "Merit, I have to be cocky. I'm not saying I secretly think I'm a hideous troll." He waved a hand in front of his face. "This is a commodity, and in my business, you have to know what your strengths are. When I say I have to be cocky, I mean it—people are more likely to believe what you're selling if you act like you believe in it, too." He leaned his head against his fist. "What I meant is, my charm, my charisma, it can be overwhelming. Only it doesn't influence you the way it does other people. Because of your history, it makes you trust me less. We'll work to get you to the point that you trust your gut again, okay? Is that enough to work with me for now?"

Merit nodded. "I think so."

He gestured to his notebook. "Would you mind if I took notes?"

"Not at all."

He moved back to the other side of the table and opened his notebook, flipping to an empty page. "According to Kaiya, you have your mother's list, along with the social engagements she'd like you to attend." He looked at her. "We can discuss the pluses and minuses of the events, but the decision about whether to attend will always remain yours. Okay?"

"We'll also have to decide which ones I want to be *me* at."

He paused, his pencil over the page. "How do you mean?"

Merit filled him in on her episodes and how Ellery had warned about overdoing it on her doses of tincture.

His brows dipped in concern. "Should you be taking it at all, then? Is it safe?"

"As long as I don't take it too frequently."

Tevin's expression didn't ease—if anything, his brows dipped lower—but he continued on. "I also need you to think about anything in particular you do or don't want in a partner, and what you have to offer."

"I hate this." Merit slumped in her chair. "It's very difficult not to feel like a prize heifer up for auction."

Tevin's green eyes met hers. "That goes both ways, you know. You're buying as much as they are."

Merit perked up a little. "I just wish it felt less mercenary."

"It feels mercenary because it is." Those jewel-green eyes of his assessed her. "You were hoping for love?"

Merit could tell by the careful way he said it that he thought she was naive to hope for such things. "No, of course not." Wanting and hoping weren't the same thing, so she wasn't really lying. She wanted love, but she didn't dare hope for it.

He went back to his journal. "It would be nice, though, wouldn't it?" The words were soft, almost like he was speaking to himself.

"Yes, it would."

He held out a hand. "Your mother's list."

Merit handed over the list, careful not to tear the paper with her claws.

"Have you looked at it?"

Merit shook her head. "I received it right before I came here."

135

"Well, let's take a gander." He plucked the list out of her claws and studied it. Frowned. Reread it. Frowned harder. Finally he looked up at Merit. "Did you tick your mother off recently? A lot?"

"Always." Merit tilted her head, her horns catching the light. She waved a hand at herself. "I give you exhibit A."

"Right, yes, cursed. Wait, your mother cursed you?"

"I don't really want to talk about it."

"You're going to have to talk about it a little." He shook the list at her. "Because you clearly have some unresolved issues."

She leaned closer, trying to peer at the paper. "How can you get all that from a list of names?"

Tevin lifted the paper. "Marshall and Tanner Muldavi, the heir and spare, respectively, of the Muldavi barony. I believe Val once referred to them as 'depraved layabouts,' and it didn't sound like a compliment when she said it. Val respects a bit of depravity, but it sounds like they take it too far."

"Next, please."

"A Mr. Wainsborough."

Merit frowned. "I don't know him."

"That's probably because he's twenty years older than you and, since he doesn't have two coppers to rub together, probably doesn't run in your circles. He lost all his lands to gambling debts. Solid bloodline, though."

"You're right. This is a terrible list," Merit groaned. "His wealth isn't an issue. We have plenty, but I don't want anyone twice my age. Cross him off."

"Maybe she made the first ones intentionally horrible, so you'd give the others a chance?"

Merit rested her head against the table, the wood cool against her fur. "It's possible. Please tell me the next one has some redeeming qualities."

"Suitor number four is Cedric Fedorova. He's not bad. Well-mannered, if memory serves."

"Cedric?" Merit tipped her face up. "He thinks of himself as an old-fashioned knight. Lots of chivalry. I will get miladyed to death. He will probably try to serenade me."

"Is he any good?"

"By all accounts, his music could be used to scare cattle." Merit gently thumped her head against the table. "But compared with the others, he's a possibility. Leave his name."

Tevin read the next name. "Frederick Dowerglen, second son of the House of Dowerglen." He tapped the pencil against the table. "His family's okay. They're well-off. I seem to remember Val saying he's especially enthusiastic about riding and hunting."

"Oh no," Merit said. "Not Freddie."

"Why not Freddie? He's your age, which is good."

"He decorates his residence with antlers, skins, and stuffed prizes," Merit said. "And when he isn't hunting, he's drinking."

Tevin tapped his pencil against Merit's horns. "I wouldn't go off with him unescorted, then. Just in case."

Merit fixed him with a glower.

"I'm simply looking out for you," he said, his expression all that was innocence. "You don't want to be stuffed and mounted, do you?"

"I'm going to stuff and mount you in a minute."

"No need to be filthy, Merit." He used his pencil to make a note on the paper. "We'll leave him as a maybe."

Merit wanted to claw the furniture in despair. "Don't even tell me anything bad about the next one. No, tell me. Otherwise I'll just make up something really terrible like he eats babies or hates puppies."

Tevin contemplated the name, trying to pull up everything he remembered about the family. "Actually, I don't think I have anything bad to say about Padraig Emer. All I can remember is that he's shy and that his family's barony is small. A little shabby, but respectable."

Merit leaned against the desk. "That's my best option so far? The man you can't remember anything specifically terrible about?"

"You told me not to sugarcoat things." He made another note. "I'll have Val put some feelers out, see what she can learn about him."

Tevin moved his pencil down the list quickly. "I'm not even going to read you the next three. Trust me on this. Which leaves us with our final prospect, Eric Latimer, crown prince of Huldre." Tevin tossed the paper onto the desk.

Merit grabbed the list. "Let me see that. She must really be desperate."

"Why?" Tevin sorted through what little information he had on the Huldre line. "By all accounts they're well-off and fine-looking. Maybe a bit high in the instep."

"Our marrying would be complicated." Merit stared at Eric Latimer's name on the paper in her mother's beautiful swoopy handwriting. It didn't make any sense. Why would her mother list him as a possibility? "As far as I know, he's the only heir, like I am, and not to a barony, but a sovereign land."

Tevin canted his head to the side, frowning. "I see. So who would govern what? Would you have to rule them both together?"

Merit splayed her hands out. "We'd have to come to some sort of agreement before we wed. But my mother wants an heir. If Latimer and I only had one child, that would complicate succession. One child would inherit both the barony and the kingdom. With two children, I suppose, we could split it, which might cause some headaches."

"What would happen if you don't have children?" Tevin asked.

"If I die without an heir, then technically the barony would go to my husband," Merit said, her face troubled.

"Worrying if that's to a husband of even status—other baronies might grumble at someone suddenly doubling their land. But a prince from a sovereign nation? Can't see Queen Lucia loving that. She'd lose that barony, another bite of land taken by the Huldres." He tipped his chair back from the table. "We have to be missing something, or choosing him makes no sense. Tell me about your curse, please. You don't have to go over the whole story, only the actual curse part."

Merit rested the weight of her chin on her fist. "It's the usual story, I think. I fell in love with a boy. First love and all that—I was very young."

"How young?"

"Almost fifteen."

"As opposed to the crone you are now," he murmured.

She was tempted to push her boot against his chair and knock him flat onto his back. "As I was saying, he was kind, handsome, and sweet."

"He sounds boring." Tevin pushed too far back and had to catch the table with his hand so he didn't tip over. "What happened?"

"We decided to marry. I wanted to elope, but he wanted to do things right."

"If you'd eloped, there would have been no chance at a payoff," Tevin said, his voice flat. "He insisted you tell your mother?"

"She was livid."

Tevin's expression was sympathetic. "Too young? Too soon?"

"Too common."

"Ah." Tevin managed to get a wealth of meaning packed into that one syllable.

She cleared her throat, which suddenly felt thick. "What did matter was that my mother had already arranged a betrothal for me."

He shook his head ruefully. "I've seen this song and dance so many times, I know the tune and steps by heart."

"My mother and I fought. I've never seen her so angry. I don't think I've ever *been* so angry." She sighed, straightening up and squaring her shoulders. "I locked myself in my room. Refused to go to the betrothal party she'd planned for me and the man she wanted me to marry. That's when I found out she'd offered Jasper money. I'm not sure how much. It didn't matter. I never saw him again." Merit's words were sad but steady, an old, scarred-over pain. "She told me I was being beastly. That he didn't love me, only wanted my money. The fairy godling she'd invited to bless the union overheard and agreed." She waved at herself. "This was the result. I either need to marry for love alone or accept someone of my mother's choosing."

Tevin reached out and squeezed her hand, careful to not touch her claws.

"I was so sure he'd come back. I told her I wouldn't marry anyone but him, despite everything."

"Merit, I'm sorry."

She didn't answer. What was there to say?

"No one should do that to their children."

Merit examined him for a minute. He seemed genuinely upset on her behalf. It was nice to have someone listen. "They shouldn't trade them off to cover their own debts, either."

He turned his head away, looking suddenly uncomfortable. "It's not the same thing."

"Isn't it? Our parents have traded our futures to suit their needs. I bet your mother didn't ask what you wanted, either." She tilted her head. "And you didn't even argue or get angry. No, you *negotiated*."

Tevin didn't answer, his lips pressed into a flat line.

"We're not so different," Merit whispered.

Tevin laughed. "We're not even remotely similar." He took back the list. "Moving on. The first event your mother has listed is tomorrow morning. A party by the lake. That sounds perfect."

"Peachy," Merit said. "A beast in a summer dress."

"Don't give up yet. There are weeks left for that." Tevin tucked away the paperwork. "Rest up. Tomorrow will be the lake party, and then dinner and dancing at home so I can see what we're working with."

"That sounds ominous."

He winked.

"Winking is creepy."

He winked again, only slower.

CHAPTER 10

A WASTE OF GOOD TOAST

The next morning found Tevin and Val eating breakfast across the table from Ellery. Tevin sat quietly at one end of the table, enjoying coffee and thick slices of toast with marmalade. Val was currently working her way through an impressive amount of bacon, while Ellery sipped tea and read the paper, ignoring everyone. Which was impressive, really, considering both what was going on at the other end of the table, and the fact that the table wasn't that long.

Merit's mother, her coffee forgotten, had shoved her chair to the side as she stood, leaning over the table, while her daughter unconsciously mirrored her stance. Merit had just thrown her toast at Lady Zarla's head, either because she was angry or because she wasn't a big breakfast person. She'd missed, sadly, and it was now sliding down the wall, leaving a bright orange smear on the charming silk wallpaper. The argument had started with Merit telling her mother that they'd already crossed several suitors off the list, and it had now sidestepped into a new segment involving when she was going to take her tincture.

"You cannot honestly think to show up like *that* at the party and be taken seriously by any of the gentlemen there."

Tevin assumed by "that," Lady Zarla meant Merit's beastly countenance.

"I can and will!"

Tevin could see Merit's tail lash back and forth as she attempted—unsuccessfully—to rein in her temper. It hadn't taken him long to realize that you could read a lot of her mood by watching her tail. She was like a cat in that way. Right now her tail was telling everyone to back away before she scratched them to ribbons.

Tevin took a gulp of coffee, riffling through the ways this fight could go and deciding how he wanted to steer it. Lady Zarla was right—Merit needed to be herself at the party. She needed to flirt, and he suspected she was bad at it under normal circumstances, but as a beast? He pictured her fanged mouth tipped into a coquettish grin and shuddered. No, that wouldn't work. But did it need to work today? He couldn't side with Lady Zarla, either, or Merit would immediately respond like the cornered animal she obviously was.

The toast finished sliding down the wall, surrendering to its fate on the floor with a sad little *plop*. The problem, he decided, was that they'd each been hurt acutely by the other, and yet they still loved each other desperately. Either they didn't know how to express it properly or they had chosen to do so in the worst possible way. He couldn't tell which. No two people loved the same way, each heart speaking a different dialect of a similar language. What they needed was an interpreter who could quickly and delicately help them sort it out. Tevin felt he wasn't the best choice, but he appeared to be the *only* choice. Mother and daughter were equally strong-willed, which meant he had to find a solution where both could compromise without feeling like they'd surrendered.

Tevin reached out with one hand and carefully shoved Ellery's paper down. "How frequently can she take her tincture?" He kept the question quiet for them alone.

"I'm not sure," Ellery replied softly. "She doesn't have a disease that responds in a scientific manner. It's magic. Godling magic is as stubborn and petulant as they are—it doesn't like to be circumvented forever. The magic will have its pound of flesh, one way or another."

"Meaning?"

"The curse might come back stronger, she might have another episode—I don't know." Ellery's eyebrows pinched together in thought. "Think of the magic like a river. You can dam it, but there will be leaks and you can't always tell where they will be. Understand?"

"I think so."

"We'll have to keep an eye on Merit and see." The healer snapped the paper back in place, deciding the conversation was finished.

"One more thing," Tevin said, pulling the paper back down.

"Yes?" Ellery looked similar to how they had the day before— same manner of dress, short sable hair, and wire-rimmed spectacles. Identical irritation with Tevin and his gift.

"Is my magic still bothering you? I'm sorry if it is."

Ellery gave up and folded the paper. "You can't help it. Spriggans are sensitive to godling magic."

145

Tevin groaned inwardly. No wonder Ellery disliked him. "Is there anything I can do to help?"

"Yes." Ellery finished their tea, took the paper, and stood. "I suggest you concentrate on the problem at hand." They tucked the paper under their arm and left the room without hurry, not even looking over at Merit and Lady Zarla as they argued. Apparently fighting matches were as much of the household breakfast ritual as Tevin's coffee and toast.

He got up from his chair, taking his second as-yet-untouched piece of toast, and slid it onto Merit's plate. "The marmalade is a little heavy on the left side, so if you choose to throw it and waste perfectly good toast, adjust your aim accordingly."

Merit blinked at him, her mouth snapping closed. He guided her back into her chair with one hand while snatching up the silver coffeepot with the other and refilling Lady Zarla's cup. As Merit sat, so did her mother.

"Sugar?"

"Thank you, no," Lady Zarla said.

He set the pot down with a decisive *thunk*. "Lady Zarla, there are good reasons for Merit to go as herself today." He had to raise his voice for the next bit to be heard over Merit's growl. "But Merit also makes good points. Might I make a suggestion?"

"No," they both said. Well, at least he'd managed to get them to agree on something.

"Today Merit can wear a veil and take a parasol. It won't hide what she is, but it will soften it and give her an excuse to lean on my arm." Lady Zarla was already relaxing into his charm, but it wasn't her he had to convince. It was Merit. "Today can be a fact-finding mission. We'll talk to anyone there on the list and make revisions if necessary. We'll gain focus."

Merit's shoulders relaxed, but her gaze remained sharp. "That doesn't sound too terrible."

"And that will leave you free to take your tincture for the ball and dinner tomorrow night," Tevin said. "I'm sure Lady Zarla would agree that is the more important of the two events."

"Fine," Lady Zarla said, picking up her coffee and taking a sip. "But I want you on your best behavior today, Merit. You may look like a beast, but you will not act like one."

Tevin's eyes met Val's, and he could tell they were sharing the same thought—*famous last words.*

• • •

Just because her mother had conceded on the tincture didn't mean Merit got off completely free. Lady Zarla desperately wanted to minimize the visual impact of the curse, so she'd instructed Merit's maid very carefully about how she needed to dress. They'd selected a vivid blue hat with a cluster of silk flowers and a heavy veil along the rim. The dress was a rich cream color, and it covered her from neck to wrists to ankles. Boots concealed what the hem of her dress did not. Merit drew the line at gloves. Even if she managed to get them over her misshapen hands, her claws would shred them. The party was scheduled early in the day so people could attend and still keep their evening engagements. By the time Merit climbed out of the hack, sweat was already pooling along her lower back. There was no breeze to be found, and the sun was beating

147

down upon the lake like a relentless golden hammer. Beautiful, yes, but comfortable? No.

Merit felt less like a beast and more like a fetid swamp troll. It didn't help that Tevin looked crisp and cool in a lightweight suit that matched her dress. His vest was a verdant green the same color as his eyes. He looked comfortable and handsome, and Merit considered pushing him into the lake.

"I don't recommend it," Tevin said, offering her his arm. "You'll only ruin the suit."

"Is mind reading one of your fairy gifts?" Merit grumbled as she hefted her parasol. Lady Zarla climbed out of the carriage behind them, impeccably turned out in a lilac summer dress. She immediately flitted off to speak to friends, without a backward glance at Merit. She'd already lectured her daughter in the carriage, and there were no final orders to give. Val sauntered out last, dressed in a similar manner to Tevin, except she'd ditched her jacket in the hack and was wearing a new version of her ubiquitous telescope hat.

"I don't have any other gifts," Tevin said. "You mumbled your threat out loud." He kept his face pleasant, but his voice was tinged with worry. "Are you going to be okay? It's a real melter. I don't want you swooning into the clam dip."

Merit snapped her parasol open with a deft flick. "I never swoon."

He grinned at her, and her stomach twisted. "I bet I can make you swoon."

"I bet I can push you into the lake," Merit said.

A delighted laugh tore out of him, making more than one

woman turn. Merit held up her chin. "Are we going to stand here all day?"

Tevin rested a hand on hers, guiding her to the gathering. Merit couldn't see much through the thick veil; she could make out silhouettes, but she mostly relied on the murmur of Tevin's voice for the details. Linen-covered tables had been set out under the trees, taking advantage of what small shade they cast. Plates of sandwiches, appetizers, cakes, and fruit covered most of the surface. One table held a punch bowl full of what appeared to be lemonade. Brightly colored blankets stretched out here and there on the grass for people to sit and eat. Music flowed from a white gazebo, the roof keeping the sun off the string quartet housed inside. People milled about, talking and enjoying the beautiful sunny day.

As they grew closer, Val peeled off and disappeared into a crowd of young fairyborn who had clustered near the punch bowl.

"What is Val doing?" Merit whispered.

"I showed her the list earlier. She's going to information-gather for us. That way you can concentrate on talking to your prospects."

"No one here knows Val," Merit pointed out, then suddenly wasn't sure. "Do they? I mean, how will she get them to talk to her?"

"She might know some, but even if she doesn't, Val is one of them. That goes a long way." Tevin pretended to nod and smile at someone he recognized. "Do you see anyone from the list?"

Merit tried, but the veil made it too difficult to distinguish faces from this far. "No, but if Freddie's here, he'll be by the punch table, waiting for an opportunity to upend his flask into it. And Cedric will be monopolizing some poor pretty girl." She was fairly certain both would be here today. "I'm not sure about anyone else."

"We'll have to make the rounds and see, then. Let's start with the punch bowl."

"Where is Amaury?" Merit asked, suddenly realizing she hadn't seen the younger DuMont since yesterday.

"I find with my brother it's best not to ask. He'll surface when he wants to."

Tevin guided her through the crowd, eventually getting them close to the drinks, despite Merit stopping to greet a few acquaintances along the way.

They didn't have to look long before Freddie found them. He tipped the edge of his boater hat at Merit before doing a quick once-over of Tevin and then dismissing him. Though he was dressed much like Tevin, he had a thin, aristocratic look to him and had either swiped a lady's lacy parasol or brought his own. He spun it in his long fingers, giving Merit a rakish smile. If there was a word for Freddie, it was *languid*. He seemed to think if he waited long enough, whatever he wished would be brought to him.

Merit wondered how they had managed to have such similar upbringings yet end up so very different. When she pictured him hunting, he was always stretched out in a sedan chair, rifle in hand while someone led the quarry forward on a gilded leash.

"Lovely to see you, Merit, as always." He tipped back the last of his drink, shoving the glass at Tevin. "Be a good fellow and refill this for me?" When Tevin stared at the glass but didn't take it, Freddie gave a sly smile. "You were going to fetch one for the lady, were you not? It's so beastly hot." He winked. "Apologies, Merit."

"Of course," Merit said absently. Why did every young man think winking was cute? She made no move to indicate what she was thinking, yet somehow Tevin knew.

"It's not creepy when I do it."

She didn't argue. It was true.

"I'd be delighted to refill your drink." Tevin snatched the glass gracefully away from Freddie. "Be right back."

Tevin eased his way into the crowd, leaving her with her would-be suitor.

Freddie offered his arm. "Let's walk down by the lake, shall we?"

Merit followed, careful to keep her parasol from bumping his. "I see my mother has talked to you."

Freddie turned them to follow the edge of the lake before they strolled onto the short wooden pier that people used to launch small dinghies and canoes. "Of course. Not that I'm surprised. We'll make a lovely match. I can send someone around with the contracts when you're ready."

Merit stopped, halting their progression and letting go of his arm. "Contracts?"

Freddie's free hand flicked at the air. "Naturally. Why wait until your birthday, I say? Let's get this hemmed up." He grasped the edge of her veil and fluttered it. "Get you out of this business."

Merit stifled a sigh. How very like Freddie to assume that

he wouldn't have to work for his bride. "I haven't decided yet. You're on a list—a short list, of course." She was careful to add the last bit. Despite their power and privilege, Merit had learned that the egos of the men in her class tended to be as fragile as soap bubbles.

Tevin reappeared, shoving Freddie's glass into his hands but keeping Merit's. "Give me the parasol, so you don't have to juggle."

Freddie's brow scrunched in irritation. "This is a private conversation."

"Is it?" Tevin traded his glass for Merit's parasol with a smile.

"Merit, who is this forward creature?" Freddie huffed.

"Freddie, may I introduce you to Tevin? He's a guest and business contact of my mother's. I'm showing him around." Merit moved her veil so she could sip the tepid lemonade. It was far too sour, but she didn't care. The delicate glass curved at the lip, making it easy to pour into her mouth.

"Business, eh?" Freddie was already losing interest, though he did look closer at Tevin. "Not on the list, then."

The grin Tevin gave him would have looked at home on a shark. "Not yet."

"Not likely." Freddie's smirk was a stamp of aristocratic smugness.

Overly hot and already irritated, Merit didn't have the patience to deal with their posturing. She had turned to go down the pier when someone hailed her.

"Merit!" Cedric Fedorova waved one hand at her, the other taken up with a thin silver chain that led to a large peacock. Cedric's suit was a deep charcoal, his waistcoat an iridescent blue to match the strutting bird. Multiple watch chains led into a single pocket, catching the light, along with the golden rings he wore on several fingers. His hat held a few of the peacock's tail feathers, which he doffed over her hand. "So lovely to see you, my angel."

One thing Merit liked about Cedric was that though he was ridiculous, he was always trying new things. He often tried too hard, but at least he tried. She thought that if he could just figure out who he was as a person, he would be a joy to be around. As it was, she was trying not to giggle as he bowed deeply while the peacock made a sort of *wha* sound, like it was asking a question but was already alarmed about the answer.

"Cedric, it's lovely to see you. I should warn you, though, that birds don't seem to like me in my cursed state. The beast upsets them."

Cedric righted himself, placing the hat back on his head. "Nonsense, milady. He needs a moment, is all, then he will see past the façade to the elegant beauty beneath." His voice, much like the young man himself, had a theatrical quality to it. There was a sweetness to Cedric, an almost wholesome demeanor that showed when he smiled. He wasn't tall—only an inch above Merit herself—and appeared gently rounded when compared with Freddie's whippet-like leanness. Merit tried, for a moment, to picture herself with either of them. A union with Freddie would be appealing for its very separateness. She couldn't see him taking much interest in her daily life. He also seemed likely to cede most decision making to her, letting her run her barony as she saw fit. Cedric, however, would make a kind and attentive companion. He would also run up an impressive clothing bill, and most likely outshine her at any formal event. Cedric was a man who truly loved clothes.

The peacock honked, startling her. She leapt back, knocking into Tevin and losing control over her cup.

"Cedric," Freddie drawled. "Nice bird. Are we roasting him later, or is he decorative?"

Cedric began to respond, his tone argumentative, but Merit didn't pay attention to what he said. She was too busy trying to get away from the peacock, which had gone on the offensive.

Tevin grabbed her arms. "Wait a second, your skirt—"

But he didn't get to finish the statement. The peacock hissed and lunged at her, causing Merit to dart back. Tevin, hampered by Merit's skirts, hadn't moved back fast enough. Each of them tripped over the other, falling in a tangle of limbs into the cool waters of the lake.

The water was murky, their fall stirring up the thick layer of silt on the bottom. Merit was tempted to stay under. It was peaceful here. But a hand reached down, grabbed her arm, and pulled her up.

Tevin stood next to her, the water lapping at his waist. He pushed the sopping hair off his forehead before shaking the fabric of his suit, which clung to the lines of his body. Merit spluttered next to him, throwing up her veil. She roared at the peacock, startling the bird into flight before it was yanked back by its silver tether. Merit shook then, trying to get the excess water out of her fur. When she stopped, the first thing she noticed was how quiet it had become. The music had stopped, and everyone—*every single person*—was staring at the beast. She wanted to shrivel up and crawl back into the lake water.

Tevin threw back his head and laughed.

"Have you lost your mind?" she hissed.

Tevin bent down, rescuing her bedraggled parasol from the water and giving it a shake. "Go with it." His words were quiet and for her ear alone. Then he tipped back, parasol and all, and fell into the water.

She followed suit, collapsing back into the lake and swimming next to him. If she had to be a spectacle, she could at least control what kind of spectacle she'd be.

CHAPTER 11

DANCE, MONKEY, DANCE

Tevin stepped into the formal dining room, taking a moment to appreciate the room under the warm and steady glow of the mage light cast from the chandeliers. The walls were painted a cream color, setting off several large oil paintings and an ornate mirror. The pristine white of the tablecloth was interrupted only by the china settings, a simple but elegant silver design. Even though the dinner would just be him, Amaury, Val, Merit, Kaiya, and Ellery, it was set up to be every bit like one of the formal dinners they would encounter.

Merit was already seated, so Tevin bowed over her hand and took the seat across from her. Val, Tevin noticed, took the seat across from Kaiya, smiling at her. Kaiya smiled back before turning to speak to Ellery. Amaury coughed a laugh, quickly smothering it. Val scowled before elbowing Amaury in retaliation.

"You look lovely tonight," Tevin said, unfolding his own napkin. After their impromptu swim, they'd both had several hours to dry, rest, and dress for dinner. Merit had taken care with her appearance, wearing a fine gown. Someone had put a delicate diamond tiara on her head. The effect was ludicrous.

"You're lying through your teeth," Merit said, placing her napkin on her lap.

"I am."

She paused with the water glass halfway to her lips.

Tevin waited for the staff to fill his glass. "What gave me away?"

Merit put her water down. "Tevin, I'm wearing a tiara between my *horns*. This dress had to be designed to make room for my tail. Of course I don't look lovely. I'm cursed, not stupid."

"Fair enough, but you won't always be in beast form. You need to watch the faces of your suitors when they say flattering nonsense to decide if they mean it or not."

"As if these events weren't exhausting enough," Merit mumbled.

Once everyone was seated, the first course was served. Tevin dipped his spoon into the soup and carefully tasted it.

Merit watched him with amusement. "Does it meet with your approval?"

He reached for a roll, a warm brown bread, and broke it in half. "I'm keeping all opinions to myself until after the meal, thank you." He had to ask Val twice to pass the butter dish. Kaiya was finally talking to her, and Val was ignoring everyone *but* her and almost dropped the butter dish into his lap. He caught it at the last minute, putting it on the table before grabbing his knife and buttering his roll. "When we're out next, will you be dining in this form or your other one?"

"My mother will want me to take my tincture, which of course makes me want to do the opposite." Merit glared at her soup. "Which would you suggest?"

Tevin bit into his roll, the slightly sweet bread contrasting beautifully with the salt and fat of the butter. The baker, at least, knew what they were doing. "Which way are you more comfortable?"

Merit carefully angled the spoon, attempting to get it into her mouth without spilling. It wasn't easy. She had the teeth of a predator, but she was trying to eat like a human. Next time he'd have to think of a gentle way to recommend that she skip the soup course.

"*Changing* is uncomfortable." She attempted another spoonful.

"And?"

Soup dribbled down Merit's chin, and she dabbed at it with her napkin. "You've heard Ellery's speech. I can't take it all the time."

"We'll have to decide by event, weigh the risks." Tevin sipped his wine, watching her struggle to eat. "Your curse must make everything so difficult."

"It's a curse, Tevin. That's kind of the point." Merit tried to sip her own wine, which had been served in a metal goblet. After this afternoon, she didn't trust herself with glass. Even so, she had to be careful drinking with a face not made for traditional dining ware. "Frogs and snakes fall from my friend Wilhelmina's lips when she speaks. Some of them are poisonous. Her sister, Diadora—the fairy godling liked *her*, so she gifted her with flowers and gems when she talks."

Tevin put down his glass. "That . . . I was going to say that doesn't sound bad, but I take it back. That sounds uncomfortable."

"She's allergic to pollen, so she sneezes all the time. She's chipped several teeth on precious stones and has almost given up on marriage entirely."

"That sounds awful, but it doesn't negate your own struggles. You can't trust your suitors, either, and you gave the harpist the vapors. I nearly screamed and embarrassed myself when you first walked in as a beast." The staff whisked the soup away and moved on to the next course, some sort of lightly breaded fish. They ate quietly for a few minutes, both apparently lost in thought.

"You didn't seem to be in danger of screaming." She pushed a piece of fish with her fork. "In fact, my curse doesn't seem to bother your family at all."

Tevin took a good look at her. It wasn't like she wasn't terrifying in appearance, and yet he didn't feel scared. Snarling jaws and horns aside, it was Merit who looked out at him, even now. He paused, dangling his fork over his plate. "I once courted a girl who had this tiny lapdog called Muggins. Well. I assume it was a dog. It had long, frizzy fur, bulging eyes, and an overbite, but it was *vaguely* dog shaped. Completely hideous. The girl doted on it, so every minute I spent with her, I spent with the dog. She used to dress it to match her."

"The dog had its own wardrobe?"

He nodded. "The maid had to dress the dog's hair as well as the girl's. Total nightmare."

"Muggins drove you away, in the end?" Mirth lit her orange eyes.

Tevin shook his head slowly. "The dog grew on me. It was her I couldn't stand." He went back to his food. "Besides, at that

159

point, my parents had their money, so I was ushered on to the next debutante."

Merit stiffened, bristling at the reminder that Tevin was so much like the boy who had hurt her. She set the thought aside, returning to the original discussion. "Am I Muggins in this scenario, or the girl?"

"Oh, you're a Muggins. You haven't changed, but as one spends more time around you, you're less . . . overwhelming."

"Thank you, I think."

"You're welcome." Tevin signaled the steward for another glass of wine. He felt a stab of annoyance at Lady Zarla and the fairy godling who'd cursed Merit. She would end up in, at best, a tepid and loveless union. She deserved better.

The next dish was seared bison and roasted vegetables. The meat was lightly seasoned, letting the natural flavors come through. Merit had a hard time with the vegetables. She was forced to use a large spoon to scoop them up and shovel them in.

"Efficient," he said, watching her chew. "But lacking a certain elegance."

"If I didn't do *something*," Merit said, taking another spoonful of vegetables, "I'd starve. Would you rather the beast look foolish or eat the guests?"

Tevin fought a smile. "Is the guest in the situation Freddie? Because I wouldn't mind if you chewed on him a little." Merit snorted and shoved the spoon into her jaws. It was becoming increasingly clear to him why she preferred the country and avoided society. A chunk of carrot fell from her spoon, causing Merit to growl, the spoon bending in her fist.

Frustrated, she dropped the spoon and reached to pick up

another when Tevin stopped her. He snatched it from her place setting and tossed it over his shoulder. Then he undid his cuff links, slipped them into his pocket, and carefully rolled up his sleeves. Without a word, he picked up some bison with his fingers and popped it into his mouth. He raised his eyebrows at Merit as he chewed. Hesitantly, she picked up a piece of meat from her plate, stacked some of the vegetables on it, and carefully placed the food on her tongue.

Tevin smiled and went back to his entree. "We won't be able to do this when we go out, but you need to eat, Merit. Take a break and finish your meal, then we can move on to the nightmare that is formal dance."

Merit skipped the silverware, attacking her food with her claws. "I used to love dancing."

Tevin nodded. "Have you danced since the curse?"

Merit shook her head. "Not a formal dance. Snuck off to the nearest town for a barn dance or two. Never as the beast."

Tevin gave her a sympathetic smile and waved one of the staff over. "Have another glass of wine. You're going to need it."

• • •

Even before the curse, Merit had never been a tall, willowy beauty like her mother. She'd been light on her feet, however, and truly enjoyed dancing, so she'd practiced until she glided through each step. What hadn't come naturally came from hours of work. It had been years since she'd danced formally— they had a few informal dances at Cravan House for friends and family, though that usually involved a country reel and jigs and nothing at all where anyone had to look stately. She also usually took her tincture before the dance. Attempting to waltz in beast form was going to make her feel like her bumbling twelve-year-old self, tripping over her own feet.

Tevin cued the musicians, watching as Ellery took Merit into their arms. Val and Amaury were on the floor as well, since Merit didn't particularly feel like being the center of attention for this, even if Tevin was watching only her. Kaiya sat at the piano, ready to play when Tevin signaled. He adjusted Ellery's hold, stepping back to look at them again, one hand cupping his chin, thumb pressed into his lower lip. Merit had started to have a lot of indecent thoughts about that lower lip. Earlier at dinner, when he'd rolled up his sleeves, putting her at ease so she could feed herself, a genuine smile on his face? Beasts don't swoon, but blast it all if she hadn't wanted to.

Ellery squeezed her waist. "Relax, Merit. I'm not a pin-cushion."

Merit apologized and relinquished her death hold on Ellery.

Tevin waved a hand and stepped back, watching Ellery and Merit as they moved to the music. They took one turn around the room before Merit glanced at Tevin to gauge how they were doing.

He'd dropped his face into his hands.

"That can't be good," Ellery murmured.

Tevin didn't halt the music, but he strode across the floor, avoiding Val and Amaury as they glided by, and stopped at their side. "You said you could waltz." He directed this to Ellery.

"I can," her friend said defensively. "I took lessons."

Tevin rubbed his forehead. "Demand a refund."

Ellery cocked their head. "Surely I'm not that terrible."

"You are at leading. Have Amaury pair with you in the next set. He's patient and an excellent dancer." He waved Ellery away, taking their spot. He pulled Merit close, his hand hot on her hip. "Lift your frame. You're slouching." She placed a hand on his shoulder, the other in his grip. He slid his free hand from her hip to her shoulder blade. Ellery had held her the same way, but it felt completely different. She sucked in a breath, which was a mistake. Tevin smelled like a heady mix of spiced soap and his own underlying scent, and she wanted to lean in and *sniff him* like the beast she was, and for a split second she couldn't remember why that could be considered off-putting.

"Remember, it's all about the upper frame. Lift, separate, and trust that I'll take you where we need to go. Okay?" He waited as Kaiya paused and restarted the tune she'd been playing. "Let's try again." He looked down at her, and his expression gentled. "Relax, Merit." He leaned in closer. "Believe it or not, this is supposed to be fun."

"Right." She could do this. "Fun. I remember fun." She straightened her spine and followed his lead as he twirled them along the floor. She watched Amaury and Val spin past, trying to ignore the warm grip of Tevin's hand on her back. When she looked up again, Tevin had a funny expression on his face.

"What?" she asked.

"You don't want to dance with me."

She didn't. Tevin, though not a beast, was scary in his own right. Not scary, but dangerous. Which she absolutely couldn't tell him. "I want to dance with you."

He laughed then, his body shaking. "No you don't. You look like you're taking your medicine." The song ended, and he waited for Kaiya to pick another tune. Amaury bowed before stepping into Ellery's hold, his lips moving as he instructed the healer through the steps. Val sauntered over to the piano, offering to turn the pages of the music for Kaiya. When she agreed, Val slid next to her on the piano bench. Kaiya smiled in thanks, and Val lit up so bright, Tevin was concerned she'd combust.

"You're a hot commodity at every ball you attend?" Merit asked once Kaiya had picked a tune and started playing.

"Yes." He pulled her back into position, twirling her around to the music. "For me, it's part of the job. I'm like one of those little monkeys you see dancing at the circus."

She snorted. "Tevin, put a jaunty little hat on me, and I *am* that dancing monkey."

He grinned at her. "What can I do to help you relax?"

"It would be easier if you weren't"—she waved a hand at him—"you know."

"I can wear a bag over my head, if that helps."

"No, I don't think it will." She would still be able to feel his hands, hear his voice. That voice alone was trouble. "Tell me something. Anything that will make you less perfect."

He barked a laugh. "I'm far from perfect. You may look like a beast, but I *am* one." He twirled her, and it felt like she was floating along the dance floor. "Besides, as your assistant, don't you want me to be perfect?"

"Perfect for everyone else, but not for me, okay?" Merit settled into his embrace as he thought. She really had missed this, and Tevin was an excellent dance partner.

"When I first met Val, she punched me in the face."

Whatever she'd been expecting, that wasn't it. "Excuse me?"

164

"She thought I was trying to steal her girl. Insults were exchanged. We'd just met, and Val didn't think much of me yet."

"What did you do?"

Tevin's eyes took on a far-off look, his attention more on the memory than her. "I showed her how to throw a better punch. Val is great with pistols, but she neglects her up-close work. We ended up outside the saloon, jackets off, having an impromptu boxing match."

"What happened to the girl?"

Tevin's eyes came back to hers, but they'd warmed, and that barrier he kept between himself and the rest of the world was down. "While Val and I were rolling in the dirt, she found someone more civilized to spend her time with."

"Smart girl."

"I thought so."

• • •

As the evening wore on, Merit lost track of how long they'd danced. She was tired, her patience frayed, and she was having issues with her tail. She'd stepped on Tevin's toes enough times to worry that he'd have a permanent limp. Ellery had made excuses twenty minutes ago to go soak in a bath. Val badgered Amaury into taking over at the piano so that she could dance with Kaiya.

"I'm done," Merit said. "Amaury, stop, please." The music immediately halted as Amaury removed his fingers from the piano keys.

Tevin shook his head. "You're still having balance issues. We don't have much time to prepare, Merit. You're going to have to push yourself." He whirled her around the floor. How was he not tired?

"I'm well aware of the situation, *Tevin*." Her tail snapped back and forth, causing her to tip too far to one side and trip on his feet again. He didn't say anything, but his expression clearly implied, *See what I mean?*

"I wouldn't have tripped if I wasn't so tired."

"Fairly certain it was more about the tail." His voice wasn't condescending, but it was *placating*, and she hated it.

She growled.

"One more round, Merit," Tevin coaxed, but he didn't wait for an answer.

She roared in his face. Not a bellow, not a yell, but a roar worthy of the beast she was. Merit's mother had raised her to believe that you should never raise your voice. Powerful ladies shouldn't need to, but she wasn't a lady right now, was she? She was a beast, and she was going to *act like it*. The claws on her feet dug into the floor as she bellowed again, her tail lashing now. "I said I was done!"

The ballroom was silent. Val and Amaury stared. Kaiya, blast her, had a look of worry on her face. Merit *never* yelled unless her mother was involved.

Tevin dropped his arms from around her and calmly took out a handkerchief, wiping the spittle off his face and vest. It had been a solid roar. She waited for him to yell back. To make his own growl. But he seemed to be made of nothing but patience. He simply crossed his arms and watched her, like a parent waiting for a child to stop their tantrum. Despite the fact that she was, essentially, doing just that, she didn't care for the condescension. She roared again, the sound coming up from her toes and echoing through the angry chamber of her body. She went on for so long she was panting at the end of it, her vision sparkling from lack of oxygen.

Tevin tucked away his handkerchief. "As milady wishes." He bowed. Then he walked away, and Merit was left with the feeling that neither of them were happy with how the evening had ended.

CHAPTER 12

A BALL GONE HORRIBLY WRONG

He shouldn't have pushed her during practice. It had been an amateur mistake. The number one thing he was supposed to be good at? *Reading the room.* Merit had obviously been tired. What was he thinking? He'd taken control away from her, knowing full well that it was a bad idea. The beast didn't like to be bossed around, and neither did Merit. She got enough of that from her mother. He wished he'd been able to apologize earlier, but Merit had avoided him all morning.

"Your bow tie is crooked," Val admonished, stepping close and adjusting it for him.

He slapped her hands away. "You'll only make it worse. I'll have Amaury do it."

"You can tie a bow tie sleeping upside down in a dark room," Val said. "You missed your calling as a vampire with formal wear. What's wrong?"

"Nothing." His tone promised pursuing the subject would lead to a horrible death. "Amaury!"

Amaury sauntered into Merit's main foyer, dressed flawlessly in a white waistcoat, black swallowtail jacket, trousers, and black bow tie. He was tucking a red carnation into his button hole. Tevin noticed with consternation that his bow tie was perfect.

"For shame, older brother."

"I don't know what's wrong with me." Tevin glowered at Amaury.

He had the cheek to almost smile, or as close as Amaury usually came to it. "I do."

"What does that mean?" Val asked, biting into an apple she'd filched from somewhere. To no one's surprise, Val was dressed identically to Amaury. She even had her red hair slicked back with oil.

"You look very dapper," Tevin said. "Amaury, help me with my tie."

"Thank you," Val said. "I'm trying to impress Kaiya." She raised a single brow. "Think it will work? Nothing seems to be catching her attention so far."

"You mean she's not instantly swooning into your arms? How dare she." Tevin stole her apple and took a bite. "We've only been here a few days, Val. Kaiya probably has standards—"

"Standards?" Amaury's expression turned stony. "You're doomed, Val."

"That's not what I meant, so stop messing with Val." Tevin tossed the apple back to his cousin. "Kaiya knows her own worth, meaning Val is going to have to put some effort in."

Val snatched the apple out of the air. "She's worth it. Now spill, Amaury. I want the skinny on Tevin."

Amaury looked smug as he loosened Tevin's bow tie, smoothing it before he began to retie it.

"I take it back," Tevin bit out. "You don't look dapper. You look like a hayseed from a provincial backwater."

"I *am* a hayseed from a provincial backwater. Tern is a rural barony. Now, stop avoiding the discussion."

Tevin's suit was too tight. His very skin felt too tight. It had to be the tie. He glared at Amaury. "You're choking me."

"Hogwash." Amaury let go of his tie with a flourish. "The suit is perfect. You owe Merit an apology."

"Hogwash? You sound like Val." Still, it was a veritable speech from his brother. He'd screwed up. "I know. I should have listened to her." He ran a hand over his face. "Why didn't I?" He'd asked the last question to himself, but Amaury answered it anyway.

"You were having fun." Amaury's lip twitched again. "Every time she growled or hissed, you *smiled*." His gaze grew speculative.

"I don't like that look," Tevin said. "That look leads to trouble. Stop it."

Kaiya walked in with a man at her side and introduced him to the group as her uncle Glendon, the ambassador from Hane. Tevin greeted him, seeing the faint resemblance to Kaiya in his face. Glendon was tall and broad-shouldered, his easy smile bright against the tan of his skin, his dark hair brushed back.

Glendon grinned. "So you're the lot that has Lady Zarla in an uproar." The grin became a sly one. "I approve. The Cravans need to be shaken up a bit."

Kaiya touched his shoulder, her eyes twinkling. "You look very handsome tonight, Uncle. I'm sure Lady Zarla will agree with me."

"Thank you," Glendon said, shooting his cuffs. "I try."

Tevin glanced over and realized that Val was frozen with the apple halfway to her mouth. A faint flush marked her cheekbones as she openly stared at Kaiya in her evening finery. He nudged Val with his foot, reanimating her. Val blushed harder and looked away, biting into her apple.

Kaiya was pretty on a normal day, but she'd gone out of her way tonight. Her sleeveless dress was black, simple in design but expertly cut, the fabric flowing along the lean lines of her body. The skirt reached the floor, and when she moved, Tevin could see a flash of skin through the slits that reached almost to her thigh. She'd braided a silver ribbon into her black hair, the contrast catching the eye. It was simple, sophisticated, and causing a slow flush to crawl up Val's cheeks.

"You're going to choke on that apple if you're not careful," Tevin whispered. Val elbowed him.

"I've not forgotten my duty," Glendon said. "I'll save several dances for Lady Zarla. As a favor to you, of course."

Kaiya snorted. "You would dance with her anyway. You like—"

Glendon mock-scowled at her. "That's enough, I think."

"I would appreciate it. Thank you for coming," Tevin said. Merit and her mother had gone separately, and were supposed to meet them there. He thought it would be better if people witnessed him seeking Merit out in the crowd and then doting on her. Not that he'd had much of a choice. Merit had all but insisted in the note she'd sent him. A *note*. She was so mad she wouldn't even track him down in her own house.

"I'm happy to escort you," Glendon said, smoothing the

front of his jacket. "If only to make sure no one contests your invitations." He straightened, looking every inch the fairyborn gentleman, absolutely at ease in his finery. He examined the group. "I'll say this, I highly doubt anyone will question your story. You lot look like a bunch of moneyed upstarts. It's going to be difficult getting some of the starchier aristocrats to accept you, though."

Val patted his shoulder. "You've never seen the DuMonts work a ballroom. Trust me, Glendon. They'll have them eating out of their hands."

• • •

Tevin sipped his champagne, the bubbles hitting the back of his throat. He was tempted to drink a whole vat of it and erase this entire evening from his mind. Somehow they'd beat Merit to the ball. A few of the dowagers had surprisingly quick hands, and as a result, he was gaining a large bruise on his back end. He was starving, bored, and worried about Merit.

"You're scowling again," Val said under her breath. "You might not want to kick up your heels with these lovely ladies, but I do, and you're scaring them off. I want Kaiya to see what she's missing. Or if that fails, to distract myself for a little bit."

"You're welcome to them, cousin. Just don't forget to gather information as you cavort about the place." He'd danced with several young women, and they'd spent the entire time blushing and twittering. He hadn't realized how annoying that was until tonight, and he couldn't help comparing it with the night before. Amaury was right. He *had* been having fun. Oh, not when Merit got upset, but dancing with her as she snapped and scowled had been refreshing. Obviously there was something wrong with him.

"That's a little uncharitable of you, Tev. You're a handsome fella, with fairy-boosted charm. These sheltered chits don't stand a chance. And need I remind you that I'm a seasoned cavorter? I can manage some high-spirited capering and dig for dirt at the same time."

"You're right. I'm sorry. I'm in a mood." Tevin scanned the room for the fiftieth time. Glendon was currently chatting with a horsey-looking gentleman of indeterminate age. He'd lost Amaury about ten seconds after walking through the doors. He'd danced with Kaiya when they first arrived, but hadn't seen her since. Only Val stood by him.

"Stop staring at the entrance. She'll get here when she gets here." Val tipped her head at a pretty young woman swathed in a puffy confection of white lace. Tevin thought the dress made her look like an uncooked meringue. He *was* being an ass. The Meringue blushed at Val and flicked open her fan.

"Blast. I forget what that particular flick means." Someone walked in front of Val, and she stood on her toes to get a better look.

"Get down, you're not a prairie dog." He grabbed her shoulder and gently pushed her back onto her heels. "It means she's amenable to meeting you on the terrace for some 'air.'"

Val's side-eye was heavy on the skepticism. "She said that with her fan? Are you yanking my chain?"

Tevin shook his head and swapped his empty glass with a fresh one from a tray floating past on the hand of a liveried servant. "I would never."

Despite Val's lineage, or Tevin's lack of one, they'd spent about the same amount of time in ballrooms over the last few years. Fan language, a subtle way for young people to pass messages, had developed as a way to get around chaperones. The DuMont siblings had memorized it quickly for obvious reasons, but Val hadn't really needed to. Tevin might tease her about her country ways, but that didn't change the fact that Val still had fairy blood in her veins and a barony in her family. A connection to her was desirable. A connection to Tevin was not.

Val still eyed him. "How do you remember all of this?"

"It's my job. Now, if you'd care to join her, I would recommend heading to the terrace. Be nice about her horrific dress."

"What's wrong with it?"

"Everything."

"You're grouchy," Val says. "Go waltz with someone. Cheer yourself up."

Val took a meandering route to the terrace, stopping to greet a few people, then heading out the open patio doors.

Tevin figured his cousin was right and he needed to circulate and see what he could learn. He managed two country reels before he found a partner who could stop giggling long enough to speak a whole sentence to him.

"I'm not looking to marry," the young woman said, her gray eyes meeting his. Her round face and pointed chin were framed by a short black bob with bangs, giving her a puckish air. Tevin's seasoned eye knew that her beaded silver dress meant money. He'd been wondering why she'd been holding the wallpaper up and not dancing, but if she started every conversation this bluntly, that was probably his answer.

"I think we're supposed to at least pretend to consider it," Tevin said, twirling her about. She danced gracefully. So far everything was falling into the positive column, so either she hated the concept of matrimony, or . . . "Ah, besieged by fortune hunters, are we?"

She grinned. "I'm considering building a moat and filling it with them."

Tevin chuckled. "Milady, I will help you dig it, but I will not help to fill it."

"You don't want my money?" she said, one sable brow winging up.

"I have plenty," he lied. "After some point, it's unfair, isn't it? We must leave some for the others."

"Oh, I like you." She smiled up at him. "Wilhelmina. My friends call me Willa."

"Tevin," he said. "I don't have any friends."

She laughed. "I find that hard to believe."

"Is it only the fortune hunters that have soured you on marriage, or is it something else?"

Willa looked over his shoulder, her face thoughtful. "My sister was granted a fairy gift—every time she speaks, precious jewels or beautiful flowers fall from her lips. The fairy thought this a grand idea. Only now she's constantly pursued by men who wish to benefit from that gift. My sister is beautiful and kind—it's hard for her to tell them to go away or to believe that they don't have better motives."

Her story seemed familiar, and Tevin realized he'd heard it from Merit. This must be her friend. "It seems we have someone in common. I'm currently a guest at Lady Merit's house." He stuck with the official story. If Merit wanted to tell Willa the details of their partnership, she was welcome to, but it wasn't his secret to share.

She brightened. "Really? Well, if you're looking for friends, she's a good one to have. Merit's really been there for me and my sister."

"It sounds like it hasn't been easy," Tevin said, keeping their steps light, even if the conversation wasn't. "For any of you."

"Diadora chipped a tooth on a ruby once, and she's allergic to flowers. The only way she can enjoy an evening such as this is by taking a tincture of bloom." She shook her head. "If a husband marries her for her gift, he'll encourage her to talk until she's broken her teeth and her nose is raw from sneezing." She dipped her head. "People are monsters."

"I can see how watching suitors pursue her would put one off." Tevin twirled her around a couple who were out of step. "What about you? Are you gifted, too?"

Willa grinned. "Cursed. I had the cheek to imply that Diadora's gift was less than welcome."

"So no gems and flowers for you?"

"I get toads and snakes. That's the other reason I'm not marrying."

"Because you think your chosen partner would find it revolting?"

"I can't take bloom all the time, Tevin, and I talk in my sleep."

Tevin laughed. "You and I have the opposite problem."

"What, people don't run away when you speak?"

Tevin kept his face very serious. "I'm absolutely enchanting, and I mean that literally. The last two debutantes I danced with are smitten. They can't help it. I start talking, and they start swooning."

She clucked her tongue in mock sympathy. "Poor man."

The song came to an end, and she curtseyed as he sketched a bow. "Care to walk with me, Willa?" He held up a hand before she could respond. "I still don't want to marry you, but you provide a pleasing buffer between gigglers."

She took his arm. "I would be delighted to be your moat." She led him over to the edge of the crowd, ignoring the people trying to catch Tevin's eye. "Why am I not giggling and fainting?"

Tevin glanced over the ballroom, looking for Merit's brown hair. "Some people don't want to be charmed."

Willa thought about this for a moment. "It's a relief, isn't it? To simply . . . be for a minute. No snakes. No gigglers."

"It is, actually." He stopped then, in both word and deed. Merit was descending a set of steps into the ballroom. He actually caught sight of Lady Zarla first, as she was taller and difficult to miss in a silver gown that caught the light when she moved, sending off a sparkle. Merit's dress was more subdued. The fabric had been dyed a deep blue with a silver filigree covering it—he was too far away to see if the silver was embroidery or not. Her hair was up, a few brown curls draped artfully around her face. She looked lovely and also like she absolutely didn't want to be at the ball, not that she let any of it show on her face. Tevin could just tell.

"Ah," Willa said, her tone knowing. "Now we get to the real reason you don't want to fill my moat."

"It sounds much worse when you say it that way."

"Are you pursuing Merit, or is this a forbidden longing?" She paused. "Unless you're aiming for her mother?"

"I'm pursuing forbidden longing," Tevin said, hoping she'd be satisfied with the murky answer. "Now take back what you said about Lady Zarla. She's *terrifying*."

"Her mother is a bit of a tyrant, yes." Willa grabbed his arm, dragging him away from where they'd been standing. He followed without complaint because she was taking him toward Merit. "Merit and I belong to the same curse support group. Let's just say she's had a time of it."

"I can imagine." Well, he could try. He had a feeling that Merit's daily life had been very different from his—they were opposites in many ways. But as she stepped down into the crush of people in the ballroom, she managed to look very alone. That, Tevin understood.

Willa halted their progress. "You're going to be nice to her, right?"

He'd been deep in his own ruminations, and it took him a moment to surface; he'd missed her question. "Pardon?"

Willa turned so he had to look at her. She was a tiny thing, so Tevin had to look down.

"I consider Merit a friend," Willa said frankly. "If I find out you've added to her misery, I will break into your room in the middle of the night and read you a story."

"As threats go, that one is weird."

"It will be a long story, and I won't be using any tincture. Have you ever woken up in a bed of snakes?"

178

"I can honestly say that I haven't."

She poked him in the chest. "Best keep it that way. It takes getting used to." She turned back around and continued on her path to Merit.

• • •

By the time they'd reached her, Merit was talking to a tall blond man. A tall, blond, handsome man who was making her smile. Tevin sized him up, a purely academic assessment, and had to admit that if he'd actually been after Merit, he would be worried.

The man was smiling down at her, so Tevin could see that his teeth were white and even. His long hair was braided back, exposing a masculine jaw. Tevin glanced at his clothing. You could tell a lot by how someone dressed. Because the ball was formal, the man's suit was similar to Tevin's, with the cut, the stitching, and the material all of the finest quality. Some men padded their suits to give a more muscled appearance, but Tevin could tell that his athletic build was the real deal. Everything about the man was picture-perfect, except for the leonine tail. Would he bond with Merit over it? Were they swapping charming tail stories right now? Was that why he was smiling at Merit and she was actually smiling back? A *real* smile. Which was what Tevin wanted, wasn't it? He suddenly wished he hadn't had quite so much champagne. He was feeling a little dizzy and not at all like himself. That had to be the reason he was feeling a stab of jealousy over Merit's interaction with the stranger. He had to stomp on that feeling. Hard.

Willa gave a low whistle. "I think you've got competition."

Tevin mentally ran through aristocratic lineages. Of course, the man could be cursed, but he didn't think so. "Latimer of Huldre."

"The fairy prince?" Willa asked, her eyes wide. "How do you know?"

"Our queen has wings because that's what her line manifests, but his kind have tails."

Willa sighed. "He looks like a golden dream, doesn't he? Can't say I trust the pretty ones, no offense. Why do they call him by his last name, do you know?"

"None taken." Tevin didn't know much about the Huldre barony. "He's a prince. Can't have everyone doing something so common as referring to him by his actual name. I bet even his parents call him Latimer. It's Eric, I think. His first name."

"That's kind of sad," Willa murmured. They were cutting their way through the crowd and getting closer. "Do I have to worry about my moat? I don't think I'd like to be a fairy princess. So many rules."

"I think you're safe," Tevin said. "They wouldn't sully the bloodlines with mere mortals such as us."

"I've learned that a lot can be overlooked when a boatload of coin is involved," Willa said. "And it's well known that my father has a boatload."

He tilted his head closer. "You could reconsider your moat. I'm sure you'd get used to the tail. You'd get a crown, and everyone would have to do what you say."

"You don't make it sound like people bowing and scraping to your will is much fun, so I'll pass."

"Handsome fairy princes don't grow on trees, Willa." Tevin stared down his nose at her, affecting a haughty expression.

She glared at him. "Bed of snakes, Tevin. Bed. Of. Snakes." She herded him the rest of the way to Merit.

Lady Zarla's reception of them was icy, naturally. Oh, she was polite to Willa, and she wasn't openly rude to Tevin, but he had the impression she was mentally flaying him, layer by layer. Tevin, being a DuMont to the bone, couldn't help but poke the dragon. He took Lady Zarla's gloved hand and bowed over it. "Lady Zarla, you are an absolute vision. It's obvious where your daughter gets her beauty." *And her claws.*

He could easily imagine the flames in Lady Zarla's eyes, but her face and tone were serene as she softened to his magic. "My, don't you have a silver tongue." She waved an elegant gloved hand toward Huldre. "May I present to you the exalted Latimer of Huldre, heir to the kingdom of Huldre?"

Latimer glanced at Tevin. "Charmed, I'm sure." Then he went right back to his conversation with Merit.

Tevin smiled, reached out, and grasped Merit's glove. "My apologies, of course, but I'm afraid Merit has promised me a waltz." He pulled her to him. "The music is already starting."

"I can't hear it," Merit said.

"It's faint. Opening strains." He urged Willa forward. "Huldre, have you met Wilhelmina? Capital girl. Interesting ideas about moats. Loves to waltz." Willa glared at him, and he mouthed an apology. She rolled her eyes and shooed him off.

"Tevin," Merit whispered. "That was rude."

"Was it?" Tevin kept his face averted. He had the odd feeling that if Merit looked into his eyes right now, she'd see past the pleasant face he was wearing, past the social mask, and into the confusion that plagued him. How was he going to explain stealing her away when he should have left her to talk to Latimer? "My apologies, then."

"You're not sorry in the least." Merit sounded cross, but hadn't let go of his hand.

"Nonsense. I'll send him a note and some very manly flowers on the morrow." His words were flippant, but she'd believe what he said more than what he actually thought, which was, *I didn't like the way you smiled at him.* And perhaps he was imagining it, but had there been something oddly predatory in the way Latimer had looked at her? He couldn't be sure, because he didn't know whether his dislike was a jealous response or an accurate one. Everything was all tangled, and he couldn't sort it now. He decided to blame that on a head full of champagne.

There was also something about the way Merit had looked standing next to her mother. She'd appeared . . . meek. It felt wrong to him on a deep level. Merit was a lot of things—argumentative, intelligent, strong-willed. She should *never* look meek.

By the time they were close to the dance floor, the band actually was playing the first few notes of a waltz.

Merit made an irritated noise. "A waltz. Of course. Does anything not go your way?"

Tevin pulled her close instinctively. "Considering you pulled me out of a jail cell quite recently, I think I can say things go against my wishes all the time."

Merit's eyebrows lowered. "But your setbacks are fleeting.

You may have been incarcerated, but today you're flitting about a grand ballroom, in the finest threads and without a worry."

"Ah," Tevin said softly. "That's where you're wrong. There's always worry. When circumstances change so frequently and are so disparate, you know how quickly you can lose everything. It's exhausting."

"We shouldn't be talking about any of this here." Merit glanced up at him through her lashes. "Even quietly."

"Just so," Tevin said. "What was your impression of Latimer?"

"I barely met him."

"Merit Cravan, I haven't known you long, but I know you've already gathered some data, processed it, and judged him accordingly. If I'm wrong, I'll eat my boutonniere."

Merit shook her head. "He was very tall and very blond."

"That's it?" Tevin dipped his head to catch her eye. "I don't believe you."

"Fine. He's handsome, and he was very attentive after my mother introduced us. I would say that it seemed he was interested in me, but as someone has blabbed that I'm looking for marriage, it could have been an act. If so, it was a good one." She frowned. "I still don't understand why he's on the list. Why would my mother pick him if it meant he could take me away?"

"We'll figure it out." Tevin lost the conversation for a moment as they danced, Merit's face turned up to his. Trust. She was looking at him like he had all the answers. He'd never felt more like a fraud in his life, and he was suddenly overcome with the fear that he would let Merit down. He cleared his throat before forcing a levity into his tone that he didn't feel. "Later

I want a full report—every little irritating detail. Make some up if you want. For now, you need to act like you're enjoying this dance." When she frowned up at him, he smiled back at her. "I'm supposed to be your mother's guest, right? And you're supposed to sparkle. Try to look like you're having a good time."

"But I'm not. I hate everything, and I want to get out of this dress."

"That can be arranged." He winked at her.

"Stop it," she growled. "So creepy."

Tevin acted affronted. "I happen to know that I have a very sexy wink. Sensual, even."

"I don't know how you can say things like 'sensual' with a straight face." Merit continued to scowl at him. It shouldn't have made him feel lighter inside, but it did.

He sighed. "Fine, pretend you're at home reading and don't have to deal with a single human soul."

Now she sighed, and it was simultaneously wistful and ir-ritated. "How is it you've only known me a short time, but al-ready know exactly what to say to me? It's annoying."

Tevin pulled her close. "If you manage to look absolutely smitten with me for the rest of the dance, I'll reward you with a trip out to the terrace for some fresh air and a moment of not smiling at anything."

She beamed up at him and batted her eyes.

"That's my girl."

• • •

The cool air was a welcome respite after the stifling ballroom. The terrace itself was long and surrounded by a railing, except

184

for two spots left open to accommodate stairs. From the stairs came several brick paths that led out into an elaborate garden. The staff had lit torches along the path so that revelers could take a walk, get some air, or find a semiprivate corner. Tevin thought it very likely that Val was currently in such a corner with the Meringue and envied his cousin a little. Not for the girl, but for his cousin's freedom to gad about in the first place.

"Oh no." Merit's whisper held genuine dread. She pulled Tevin down the stairs.

"What?"

"My mother is talking to Freddie and clearly looking for me." She yanked him along by his arm.

"Isn't that why we're here?" Tevin asked, rocking back on his heels to slow her. "To talk to the suitors your mother approves of?" It was a good reminder for both of them, though he hated bringing it up.

"I just talked to him."

"Yesterday."

"That doesn't mean I want to do it again today," Merit said, yanking harder.

"I think the fact that you can't handle talking to him two days in a row doesn't speak well for his chances." He followed Merit down the stairs, but instead of entering the garden, she cut away from the paths, lifting her skirts an inch or two to keep them from touching the grass.

They made their way to the side of the house, where Merit found a narrow and unassuming wooden door, likely a quick way for the servants to reach the back lawns. Merit opened it without issue and stepped inside, Tevin close behind. Tevin gently shut the door behind him, plunging them into darkness. They navigated their way up by feel, his hand on her shoulder so he wouldn't lose her. Merit's dancing slippers made little sound, and Tevin tried to keep his steps light—they didn't want to create a ruckus and draw attention to themselves. At the top of the stairs, Merit hesitated, pressing her ear to the door. Hearing nothing, she cracked the door and peeked out. After a moment, she led Tevin into the hall.

"Which way do you think will take us back to the ball-room?" Merit asked, pushing one of the curls out of her face. The faint strains of the orchestra floated through the air, but Tevin wasn't quite sure which direction the sound came from.

Tevin rocked back on his heels. "Who says we need to go back right away?" He grabbed Merit's hand. "You needed a break, right? Let's take one. It'll be fun."

"I think you confuse fun with trouble." But she took his hand anyway and led him farther away from the music.

He followed Merit up another set of stairs, down a hallway—where they ducked behind some curtains to miss running into a maid—and finally to another door.

Merit slowly and quietly opened the door, peeked in, and then pulled Tevin in by his lapels. As soon as they were inside, she shut the door behind them.

They stared at each other, eyes wide, before they both burst out laughing.

Tevin felt his body relax—they'd made it this far undetected. He nearly jumped out of his tux when someone leaned in close to him and said, "Boo."

• • •

"Amaury, I'm going to punch your teeth in." Tevin shoved his brother away from the door, but Amaury only smirked.

Merit had a hand over her heart and was blinking rapidly. "I think my soul temporarily left my body, and I became a ghost. What are you doing here?"

Amaury flopped back into the desk chair, picking up a bottle of champagne and drinking from it. "I do this at every ball I go to. Don't you?"

"No," Merit said, sitting on the desk. "I actually dance and talk to people." She examined Amaury's calm and contented sprawl. "Obviously I've been doing it wrong." She grabbed the bottle and took a sip, grimacing. "Ugh, it's warm."

Amaury snatched the bottle back. "If you're going to complain, then you don't get any."

Tevin rubbed the spot between his eyes that seemed to be growing a headache. "You were both supposed to be gathering information." Val was too, but she was likely still gathering information from the Meringue. Useful information, no doubt, but not to Tevin.

"I know my orders, thank you." Amaury set the bottle on the other side of the desk, away from Merit.

"Your orders are stealing champagne and, what, looking through drawers?" Merit asked.

He glanced at Tevin, a silent question in his gaze. *How much do you want me to tell her?*

Tevin sighed. His promise to Merit didn't cover his brother, exactly, but it felt wrong to keep this from her. Besides, maybe

187

they both needed a reminder of what kind of people Tevin came from. "Go ahead."

"I scan correspondence, ledgers, bank drafts, grocer bills, whatever's handy." Amaury shrugged.

"Of course you do. That makes perfect sense," Merit said. "Except, I'm sorry, but it doesn't at all. Why do you do this?"

Tevin moved to stand by the door so he could keep an ear out for company. "Because that's where secrets are hidden. You can keep a fake finance ledger and burn all your letters, but you'd be surprised what can be gleaned from a grocery bill."

Merit blinked. "Like what?"

"It can be a good way to hide embarrassing expenses," Tevin said. "Say you're spending serious coin on a mistress. Don't want to put *that* on your ledger, so you inflate something else to explain the expense away. Bolts of cloth you didn't buy, pork chops that didn't cost quite that much, a charitable donation."

"I see," Merit said. "Except for the part where Amaury does this at every ball."

"Mimicry." Amaury waved his hand at a pile of papers he'd left on the desk.

"Amaury's gift," Tevin supplied when she still looked confused. "If he sees something, he can re-create it exactly. Signatures, invitations, anything."

Amaury put his shiny shoes up onto the desk. "I see it once, it's in my head forever." He put his hands behind his head. "Useful and terrible."

"Useful how?" Merit asked. "I get the signature thing—forgery. But why would it matter if you knew what groceries the baron ordered?"

Amaury tilted his head, his eyes shining in the lamplight. "I like her. She's precious."

"Don't be condescending, Amaury," Tevin said, leaning against the door.

He blinked, sitting back up properly in the chair. "I meant it." Amaury opened a drawer and pulled out a cloth notebook, flipping it open to the bookmarked page. He showed it to Merit. "What do you see?"

She scanned the list quickly. "I see that Baron Everslee is spending way too much on hothouse fruits instead of eating what's in season." She flipped to the page before. "And no one should eat that much cabbage."

Amaury nodded. "The hothouse fruits are new. They've also nearly trebled their purchase of gingerroot." He looked knowingly at Tevin.

"What does that mean?" Merit asked, clearly irritated that she had missed something.

Tevin gave a low whistle. "Naughty girl." When Merit glowered at him, he held up a hand. "Not you. Lady Everslee. She's having another man's child."

Merit snatched the notebook back from Amaury. "You can't possibly get that from a list of groceries."

Tevin placed his ear to the door, listening. When he heard nothing, he straightened. "Ginger for morning sickness. Hothouse fruits—something they didn't splurge on before—for cravings. Typically both happen during the first trimester and then taper off. Not definitive, for sure. Every woman handles pregnancy differently." He put his ear back to the door—he thought he heard giggling.

"So she's possibly pregnant," Merit said. "That's a big leap to 'someone else's child.'"

"Context," Amaury said, spreading his hands out. "Tonight's ball is to celebrate Baron Everslee's return to Veritess. He's been jaunting about the rural estates of his own barony for the past six months. His wife has been here." Amaury moved his hands to his chest and brushed them down through the air. "Empire waist."

"Any male staff laid off recently or received an unaccountable promotion?" Tevin asked absently, his attention mostly on the sounds through the door.

"Stable lad," Amaury said. "Now personal footman to her ladyship."

Merit frowned thoughtfully. "Lady Everslee is a fashion plate. Empire waists aren't in this year, but they do cover a multitude of sins, and her footman is very handsome." Merit handed him back the notebook, pointing a finger at him after he took it. "What are you going to do with this information?"

Amaury hesitated, glancing at Tevin. "Nothing."

"We can't go back to our parents empty-handed." Tevin rubbed a hand over his chest, trying to ease the sudden tightness there. "While we're with you, we're supposed to keep our eyes and ears open. Either we come back with information they can use or coin in hand."

"You mean blackmail," Merit said with a frown.

"Why do people always say that word like it's a bad thing?" Amaury asked, giving the champagne bottle a little twist on the desk.

"Because it *is* a bad thing, Amaury." She scowled at both of them. "You're not going to tell them about the Everslees, are you?"

"No," Tevin said firmly.

Amaury's eyebrow rose. *We'll have to give them something, brother.*

"Not this." Tevin stared at Amaury until he nodded.

"I'm not sure I believe you," Merit said, crossing her arms.

Amaury shrugged. "That's your choice." Then he tilted his head, looking at Merit funny. "When'd you last take your tincture?"

Merit's eyes went wide and she looked at her watch, which she'd pinned to the inside of her sleeve. "Oh no. Is it bad?"

"Your eyes are orange."

She began digging through her pockets frantically. "Mother made me take my dose, and then we were ages getting here—said she wanted to stop off at a friend's, but it was actually a thinly veiled attempt to make me meet one of the suitors I'd crossed off the list already." The digging got more frantic. "I can't find it. I can't find my second dose!" She looked at Tevin, eyes wide. "It must have fallen out somewhere."

Amaury grabbed the champagne bottle and took a healthy swig. "So instead of the belle of the ball, you're going to be the beast of it."

Merit's face twisted in panic.

"You don't understand," Tevin said, his heart squeezing painfully at that look on her face. "Merit isn't always herself when she changes."

Merit was breathing fast now, her eyes wide. "I could hurt people. I could—"

Tevin strode over to her and grabbed her arms, hushing her. "What can we do?"

"Find Ellery! If anyone would have a spare dose, it would be Ellery." Tevin could feel her trembling. "Oh, find them, Tevin. Hurry!"

CHAPTER 13

OBJECTIVELY HANDSOME AND
SUBJECTIVELY BEASTLY

Tevin ran down the stairs and through several hallways until he heard other people, then was forced to slow. He couldn't draw attention to himself, not if he wanted to keep this contained. More people had arrived since they'd been gone, and the crowd was thick, so Tevin stayed on the steps, searching.

He couldn't see Ellery, but his eyes caught on a familiar redhead. Val, her bow tie slightly askew and her hair looking like she'd finger-combed it back into place, caught sight of him and wove her way through the crowd to stand by his side. Tevin spent a few precious seconds finding out that Val had no idea where the healer was before he saw Willa a few yards away chatting with a group of women. Tevin maneuvered through the throng of guests until he was close enough to touch her elbow. He smiled at the women. "Excuse us for a moment." Then he drew a confused Willa away a few steps.

"Merit has a problem, and we need to find Ellery. We need them now, and we need absolute discretion. Any chance you've seen them? Or have a dose of tincture on you?"

Willa shook her head. "I didn't bring any. Ellery was playing cards in one of the little side rooms fifteen minutes ago." She stood on her toes. "That door there to the left of the terrace." Her dark eyes were solemn. "Anything I can do to help?"

"That's help enough, thank you," Tevin said over his shoulder as he cut through the crowd, Val at his heels.

"What's going on?" Val whispered.

"Later," Tevin said. It took him several minutes to get to the card room. Val waited outside as Tevin slipped through a mostly closed door, coughing when he breathed in the air thick with smoke. Two of the gray-haired women playing had cigars in their mouths and were so focused on the cards in their hands that they didn't look up when Tevin entered. Ellery sat between two young men, who, based on the level of flop sweat on their brows and the loosened state of their ties, were getting absolutely fleeced by the older women.

Ellery glanced up, saw Tevin, and frowned. Tevin mouthed Merit's name, letting a little of his panic show. The healer put down their cards. "I'm sorry to say, I have to fold." They waved off the chorus of complaints and stood. "I'm sure my seat won't even have a chance to get cold."

"This better be an emergency," Ellery said after they'd closed the door behind Tevin. "I was going to win that hand."

In a few sentences, Tevin filled both of them in as quietly as he could. Ellery's smile vanished, and they were suddenly all business. "We need to stop by the cloakroom for my bag."

The trio detoured and got Ellery's bag, walking swiftly until they made it up the stairs and out of sight. Then they ran.

The library door was locked when they reached it, so Tevin

rapped his knuckles against the wood. "Amaury?" There was no answer.

"We'll have to find a member of the staff," Ellery said, frustrated. "We don't have time for this."

Tevin was already kneeling on the floor, Val automatically turning around to play lookout. He peered at the keyhole while he slipped a hand into his jacket pocket and removed his lock-picking kit. The lock took a simple skeleton key, so it wouldn't be difficult. He pulled two small hooked metal wrenches out of his kit.

"Why am I not surprised," Ellery said dryly.

"You want to debate the ethics of what I'm doing, or do you want me to open the door quickly?" Tevin asked, slipping the first metal tool into the keyhole and using it to push the lever up.

"I will take option two," Ellery said absently as they popped open their bag. "Because I put Merit's health above this slight ethical dilemma." They pulled out a thin case. "Speaking of which, I'd like to measure your face." Ellery opened the case, withdrawing a vial. "For science. Not now, of course."

"If you help Merit, I'll let you measure anything you want." Tevin put in the second metal piece and used it to move the deadbolt a fraction of an inch, until he could feel it holding the lever up. He took the first wrench out. "Why do you want to measure my face?"

"My help is not contingent on your answer. I'm a healer." Ellery tsked. "That means something to me. As for your face, I think your features might be perfectly symmetrical. People find that pleasing. I'm curious to discover how much of your power comes from your fairy gift, and how much comes from being objectively handsome."

"Why objectively handsome?" Val asked, her gaze never leaving the hall. "Isn't that usually a *subj*ective thing? Based on preference and such?"

Ellery closed the snap on their bag. "Yes, but in this case, it's less about subjective tastes and more about things that your people generally look for in a male specimen. Like a chair everyone wants to sit in."

"You hear that, Tev? You're a popular chair," Val said. Tevin didn't look, but he could hear the grin in her voice.

"I feel objectified and insulted." Tevin used the second hooked wrench to capture the deadbolt and finish pulling it in. "But I'm used to it." He stood up, putting his tools away, and opened the door. The library wasn't much different from when they'd left. But now the desk was turned over, the champagne leaving a small puddle on the rug. Amaury had climbed up one of the tall bookshelves until he was dangling off. The beast crouched below him, snarling. She swiped at his leg with her clawed hand, causing Amaury to yank up his upper half barely out of reach. He mostly made it, though the beast had taken one of his shoes.

"If I'd known we were going to play this game," Amaury wheezed, "I would have drunk less."

Val shut the doors and locked them behind her.

"It's going to be difficult to get the tonic in her now." Concern pinched Ellery's face. "She's completely changed, which means there will be no reasoning with her."

Tevin quickly assessed the room. They could right it if they acted quickly, but even if they got Merit back to her normal self, her dress was ruined. Long tears sliced through the fabric, revealing fur. There was no way she could return to the ball.

"Val," Tevin said, taking off his jacket. He'd need to move freely. "I need you to go down and find Glendon. Tell him Merit's unwell and that we'll need to take his carriage home. We can send it back for him. He needs to inform Lady Zarla but give us a good head start." He didn't want her mother interfering. "Once you do that, find Kaiya. She can get the carriage pulled up to the house and ready." He removed his cuff links and dropped them in his pocket before rolling up his sleeves. The beast turned, revealing more tears in the fabric. If he could see that much fur now, she would be practically naked when she reverted. "Ellery, she just needs to drink the tincture, right? Nothing else?"

"Yes," they said, handing the vial to him. "After this kind of episode, she'll likely be woozy and tired." Ellery grabbed Tevin's wrist. "Are you sure, Tevin? This is quite dangerous. Once she's in this state, Kaiya and I usually try to keep her contained and quiet until she calms down. Merit would never forgive herself if she hurt anyone."

"I'm sure. Go with Val. While she's handling the carriage, I need you to find a cloak of some kind—I don't care if you have to steal it, but it needs to be something that covers her from head to toe. Understand?"

They both said they did as they ran off, leaving him with the beast. He locked the door behind them before moving slowly toward the creature as she paced, eyes on Amaury.

"Not to add to the problem," Amaury said, his voice

surprisingly calm, "but she has both my shoes now. I like my feet, Tevin. I've grown attached to them."

"I'll try to keep you in one piece," Tevin assured him, before letting out a sharp whistle. The beast whipped around to look at him. She was moving on all fours, her tail lashing behind her. Teeth flashed as she snarled; a thin line of drool hit the carpet.

Tevin kept his hands up, the tincture held in place by one thumb. "Hello, beautiful." The beast blinked slowly at him. Amaury stayed where he was, but Tevin could see the strain from holding himself up on the shelves' narrow ledges. Still, his brother appeared calm and, because he was smart, didn't say a word. Tevin had the beast's attention now, and it was best if no one reminded her that there was another target in the room.

"I didn't move fast enough, did I?" Tevin took another step. "You trusted me, and it took too long, and here we are. I think from now on, maybe one of us should carry a backup vial, too?" She sat back on her haunches, watching him. The beast appeared curious, not like she was going to pounce, which was a small relief. "Well, now," he said, his smile wide. "Merit might not want to be charmed, but you do, don't you?"

Behind her, Amaury carefully and silently climbed down. When his feet hit the rug, Tevin tossed him the tincture. Amaury caught it one-handed and tiptoed closer to the beast. Tevin kept talking, and once he got close enough, he kneeled down, leaving them eye-to-eye. The beast grew momentarily uncertain. "It's okay. It's just me. I won't hurt you, you know that, right?" The beast leaned forward and tentatively sniffed his hands. Tevin kept talking and getting the beast used to his hands, stroking the fur around her face. Touching the velvet of her ears. After a minute he was scratching under her monstrous chin—her neck was extended out with feline grace, her eyes closed.

Once her snout was vertical, Amaury carefully uncorked the tincture and leaned close. He mouthed, "Three, two, one."

At one, Tevin grabbed her snout and held it up while Amaury moved in, blocking her from backing up, and poured the tincture down one of her nostrils. She whined, scooting back and knocking Amaury down. Then she shook her head and sneezed, covering Tevin in a fine spray of what he hoped was spittle and not tincture. With a final hiccup, she collapsed back onto her hindquarters. Hair receded, horns curled in, and claws disappeared like they had never been there. In the span of a few breaths, Merit sat before him. Her dress in shreds while she hiccupped, her eyes wet like she might cry. Tevin didn't think, but pulled her into his lap and held her while Amaury fetched Tevin's jacket. Once that was draped around her, he settled her into a chair, and Amaury and Tevin quickly did their best to set the room to rights. They'd barely finished tidying the desk when the others returned, and they swiftly and quietly snuck Merit out of the house and into the waiting carriage.

CHAPTER 14

SHE'S ALWAYS PREPARED—
LIKE AN EVIL BOY SCOUT

The next morning, in a rented suite with a view that over-looked the river, Latimer of Huldre was talking to his mother in the portable magic mirror that had been included in his luggage. Lady Angelique was anxious for an update and wasn't too pleased with her only son.

"You barely spoke to her?"

"I've been in town less than a day." Latimer chose his words carefully. His mother was in a mood, and he didn't wish to set her off. "The ball was heavily attended. Her mother was keen to introduce us, but she was almost instantly whisked away by another man."

Angelique tapped her paintbrush against her lips. She was fond of watercolors and had been trying to capture the gardens when he'd called, making the servants take the mirror out to her. They'd set up another easel to hold it so she could talk and paint in relative privacy. "The mother was keen—that's a positive. Did you stay and charm her?"

Latimer attempted to appear relaxed as he perched on the plush love seat in his rented rooms. His mother wasn't going to like his report, but he had to act like he had it all under control. She could sense weakness like it was blood in the water. "Of course. I wanted to make a good impression."

"Surely you could have danced with Merit later? Or dined with her?"

Latimer shook his head. "She disappeared early. Rumor has it she was unwell. Still, the night wasn't a total wash. I danced with her mother and learned a lot that will help as I go forward."

She scrutinized her painting. "And got information about the man, I hope?"

Latimer stretched, wishing he was still in bed. The dance had gone late, and he was too tired for verbal fencing with his mother. He made mistakes when he was tired. "Yes. His name is Tevin. A business associate of Lady Zarla's."

"Is he a threat?" She dipped her brush into the water next to her, swishing it around to clean it, looking like she was little invested in the conversation. Latimer knew this for a ruse, thinking carefully before he responded. How should he play this? What did she want to hear? If Latimer wrote down the facts on paper, Tevin didn't look like much of a risk. But Latimer had seen how comfortable they'd seemed with each other. They looked *cozy* together. Tevin was also the person Merit had been with when she disappeared out onto the terrace. Part of him knew that Tevin was a very real threat, whether logic agreed or not. People weren't always logical about these things.

"He's handsome, but the mother doesn't care for him, and he's of common stock." Latimer said this easily, pushing down his worry. "And while her mother does approve of me, there's competition. Other fairyborn heirs." Latimer had made note of

201

every name Lady Zarla had mentioned. She'd made it clear that her daughter had other options. It was a delicately made threat, and he appreciated her skill.

"Are they as handsome as you?" the queen asked, dipping her brush and gently applying it to the paper.

No," he said quickly, then admitted, "Tevin is, though."

"Human," she said dismissively. "The other names she mentioned, are any of them as distinguished as we are? None of them have our title. Never underestimate what people will do to gain a higher rank."

"I understand," Latimer said. "But I think it would be a mistake to discount any of them."

His mother swept her brush across her paper, leaving a dark purple stain. "Of course." She leaned back and smiled at her work. "Don't worry, dear heart. I'm leaving nothing to chance. The best defense is a ruthless and preemptive offense." For the first time since he called, she looked away from her painting and smiled into the mirror. "I sent some helpful things in your trunk. You just be your handsome and charming self. I'll handle the rest."

Latimer had already found the case of vials, potions, and coins for bribes, though he hadn't looked at it thoroughly. He'd been hoping he wouldn't need to look at it at all.

"Thank you, Mother."

"Think nothing of it."

CHAPTER 15

BLOOM WORN

The day after the ball left Merit feeling like someone had stripped away some invisible buffer between her and the world. Every nerve felt exposed—lights were too bright, sounds too loud, and her mother too much. Lady Zarla had cornered Merit in her room as she was applying brush and tooth powder to the beast's fangs, sleepy-eyed Ellery and alert Kaiya hovering behind her. Merit leaned against the door frame of the bathroom and continued to brush her teeth, knowing both things would annoy her mother.

"I want an explanation," Lady Zarla said, her hands held in front of her, her shoulders squared. She might be in Merit's sitting room, but she was clearly the mistress of the house. "Changing at a ball. What if someone had seen? What happened to your second dose of tincture? And why didn't I hear a single word about it until after you'd disappeared? My own daughter, and I'm the last to know."

Merit held up her toothbrush. "Can I at least finish brushing my teeth before I submit to your interrogation?"

Lady Zarla harrumphed and flounced her way to Merit's

settee. "Deserting halfway through—you barely spoke to Latimer, completely ignored Freddie, and you only danced once and it was with Tevin. Hardly a good showing on your part. I thought you were going to make a real effort."

"I am making an effort. I'm fine, by the way."

"Don't get smart with me, young lady. I didn't ask because I've already spoken to Ellery this morning—not that they would tell much. Still, you will submit to a checkup before you go anywhere." She leveled a scowl at Ellery. "I assume that this time I will get a full report. That shouldn't be a problem, should it?"

Merit flicked her eyes to Ellery, catching the weary smile on their face before they set their leather bag down and turned back to face Lady Zarla. Ellery didn't even get a chance to open their mouth.

"If you say 'patient confidentiality' to me one more time, I will scream," Lady Zarla ground out between her teeth.

Merit's rescue came from Kaiya. "I gave you my report, Lady Zarla. Leaving early was necessary for Merit's health and well-being, which I believe you have put in my care when you're not around. Unless things have changed?"

Lady Zarla's nod of acquiescence somehow managed to be both graceful and irritated.

"Then trust me to tell you if that changes," Kaiya said.

"Fine." Lady Zarla turned her attention back to Merit, who chose that moment to step into the bathroom and gargle her water in an unladylike fashion before spitting it into the sink. "Merit, please."

Merit wrapped her robe tight around her and took one of the chairs across from her mother. Kaiya stayed standing by the door, and Ellery sat on the window seat. Ellery would give Merit a checkup, but would wait until her mother was gone.

"To make up for last night, I've accepted an invitation on your behalf to a grand dinner being thrown at Cedric Fedorova's home. You will also be meeting Latimer of Huldre this morning."

"Mother—"

Lady Zarla waved her off. "Don't argue. You owe me for last night. The only person you spoke to for any length was that dreadful DuMont boy."

"Fine." Merit pulled her feet up into the chair, covering them with her robe. "Why Latimer, Mother? I understand the logic of everyone else, but the prince?" She watched her mother very carefully as she responded.

Lady Zarla fussed with her dress, her foot jiggling. "He's got impeccable lineage." She adjusted her bracelet.

She'd *lied*. Merit was sure of it. Oh, the lineage was important, but that wasn't the reason Lady Zarla had chosen him. Merit could let it go. Why did it matter? Except it felt like, once again, her mother was making choices for her life without discussing them with Merit. She needed to draw a line, and this was as good as any. "And?"

Lady Zarla frowned at her. "Do I need another reason?"

"Yes." Merit watched her very carefully. "In this case, I think you do."

Her mother fidgeted for a moment before she gave up and straightened. "If you must know, he was added as a favor to the queen. Huldre is a thorn in her side—the only parcel of land in Pieridae that isn't under her rule."

"And marrying me would fix that how?"

"The queen is looking at this long term. Your children could inherit both the barony and his kingdom. She's seeing it as a peaceful way to join the lands."

Merit drummed her claws along her thigh as she considered. It had the stamp of the queen on it—she thought years and steps ahead of anyone else. "What do you get out of this concession?"

"The queen agreed that, should our effort to break the curse fail, I could adopt an heir of my choosing. Someone to shepherd our lands and people after we're gone."

Merit threw her hands up in the air. "And why didn't you discuss this with me?"

"Why should I?" Lady Zarla asked, affronted. "My barony, my decision."

"It's mine, too! I—never mind." Her mother would never understand. It wasn't that she disagreed, but that she'd had no say in something that would affect her.

"Merit—"

Merit turned her head so she could gaze out the window. If she looked at her mother right now, she would cry, and she couldn't bear it. "Ellery needs to examine me, and then I need to get ready for the day."

Merit could hear the rustling of fabric as Lady Zarla stood. Then she waited, because she knew her mother would want the last word.

"I won't contest anyone on that list, Merit. But I don't have to tell you that the queen's choice should be given special attention."

Merit didn't respond, counting the seconds until she heard the door shut quietly behind her mother's retreating form.

• • •

"Now that the dragon has left the cave, how are you feeling?" Ellery asked, pulling up a chair in front of Merit.

"Do you want me to leave?" Kaiya used one hand to vault over the back of the settee and land on the cushions where Lady Zarla had sat. She sprawled indolently, one boot hanging over the side, the other on the floor. Kaiya had returned to her usual ensemble of black everything—from shirt to boots.

Merit managed a small smile. "You clearly expect to stay. No, I don't mind. Please do. You need to know." Her mother probably did, too, but Merit wouldn't tell her.

Ellery rolled back Merit's sleeves, then picked up a wrist and took her pulse.

Merit considered how to answer Ellery's earlier question. "Remember that time we snuck out to one of the local barn dances, and I drank something called white lightning, and I—"

"Aired the paunch all over my shoes?" Kaiya asked.

Merit winced. "Yes, that."

Ellery let go of her wrist before tipping Merit's chin up to get a better view of her eyes. "Then you must feel right awful. Because I remember the White Lightning Incident, as I refer to it in my diary." The healer quickly and methodically went through the rest of the exam as they spoke. "Well, you're dehydrated, I can tell you that. Lots of water today." Ellery dug through their bag and pulled out a small packet. "I would recommend a day of quiet and rest, but you're not going to get it. So when the inevitable headache blooms, here's some willow bark tea to take the edge off."

Merit took the tea, knowing she'd need it. "I should get ready before Latimer gets here." She stood, retying her robe. "What about tincture?"

Ellery considered their answer as they put away the rest of their things. "I'll tell your mother that you shouldn't have any today but leave the final decision up to you. Be careful, Merit."

"I know," she sighed, looking at Kaiya. "Want to be a third wheel today?"

"It would be my fondest wish, Merit," Kaiya said, a faint smile on her lips.

• • •

Merit ultimately decided that she'd be best served as a beast for her date with Latimer. She was tired, and even after the tea she felt lousy, which wouldn't be as apparent in her beast form. Besides, Latimer was incredibly, awfully handsome, and she didn't wish to remind him that she, well, wasn't. If she went as the beast, her looks were out of the equation.

She donned a light cotton day dress patterned with lemons, the material covering her from neck to ankles. Her walking boots were buttery-soft leather, embroidered with ladybugs and whimsical greenery. She chose a straw hat with a lighter veil—her face would be obscured, but she'd be able to see. Merit didn't want to rely on Latimer to lead her around. Last, she grabbed a parasol, found Kaiya, and was ready for the prince by the time he arrived. She tried, very hard, not to wonder where Tevin was.

Latimer didn't say a word about her cursed state as he held out a hand to help her into the waiting hack before offering a

208

hand to Kaiya. Once they were in, he paid the fare and joined them inside. He was much more casually dressed today—his hair pulled back into a low ponytail, his shirt the style seen more in the rural western baronies.

"That's . . . a lot of fringe," Kaiya said, looking at Merit.

Latimer held his arms out so they could get the full effect. "It's great, isn't it? I know people in the city prefer to take their fashion from Tirada or the Ivani Islands, but there's something so rugged about the western rustic look." He shook his arms. "I really like fringe right now."

Merit wheezed a laugh, glad that the veil obscured her face. Kaiya handed her a handkerchief with a completely straight face. "Allergies."

They chatted on the drive, Latimer being surprisingly easy to talk to as long as you kept the topic light. He could converse effortlessly about fashion, for example, and horses, but couldn't offer up much in the way of his thoughts on the use of mage tech. When the hack came to a halt, Merit was surprised to find they were in front of Godling Arestia's city home. The godling hadn't lived in her residence for years, but had opened up the grand estate for tours.

Latimer took Merit's arm in his own, while Kaiya wandered behind them. "I took a gamble that you hadn't been here before. So many of us don't take advantage of our local history."

"You're right," Merit said, deciding not to mention that the reason she hadn't gone was that she wasn't overly fond of anything godling related after her curse. Still, it was an amazing place. Palatial and intricately landscaped gardens took up the front of the house, and the back had a grove of fruit trees. The home itself was seven stories, with cupolas and a peaked tower, the top studded with so many chimneys it looked like the roof had broken out into hives. All told, it was a stunning creation of wood and mortar, and yet Merit took an instant dislike to it. She was reminded of the way some plants give off a sweet scent to lure in unwary insects, only to trap and digest them.

Latimer took an almost childlike delight in reading the markers that had been set up to tell visitors about the history of the house. Despite her lack of enthusiasm for the place, she enjoyed it with him. He went out of his way to charm and draw her into conversation.

"There are one hundred and sixty rooms, forty-seven fire-places, and six kitchens," Latimer whispered as they walked down one of the hallways. The hallway itself was lavishly papered, interrupted by paintings of dogs. Sixteen paintings so far. Merit had been counting.

"What I don't understand is why you would have two separate ballrooms." Merit ran her fingers through the strings of beads hanging off a lampshade as they walked past. "In case you wanted to throw two dances at once?"

"Maybe she threw big parties," Latimer said, "and put the really great people in one ballroom, and the so-so people in the other."

Kaiya leaned close and examined a painting of a litter of spotted dogs, nestled in a basket. "I think one of the ballrooms was for dogs."

Merit snickered, imagining dogs in fancy dress, bowing and waltzing and drinking punch straight from the bowl. "Oh, I'd love to see that."

"According to the plaque down the hall, she hates dogs." Latimer tipped his head up to read yet another plaque. "I think it's all the hair."

Merit paused midstride. "But there are so many dog portraits. Why do that if you don't like dogs?"

Latimer shrugged. "Maybe she only likes the idea of dogs."

And that, Merit thought, *is godling mentality in a nutshell. They like the idea of things, but can't stomach the reality.*

Though she enjoyed Latimer's company, she found the whole house to be depressing. It was a gigantic home that no one lived in, filled with paintings of dogs that were loved by other people. By the time Latimer dropped her off at home, her feet and heart were sore, and she was ready for another dose of willow bark tea.

CHAPTER 16

THE SPINNAKER

Though it was midmorning and the sun hung bright and cheery in the sky, in this area of town, the tall, close buildings kept anyone on the street from noticing it. They also blocked the breeze, causing the stench coming out of some of the alleyways to linger. The cobblestones were worn, but spotted with rubbish and broken bits of things, making Tevin wish he could buy shoes for some of the children running around. Through innovation and magecraft, humans were spreading into the nicer neighborhoods now open to their new wealth. The reverse wasn't quite the same. The poorer sections were overwhelmingly human.

Amaury doffed his bowler—worn only under protest—at a passing group of gentlemen. From their clothes and demeanor, it was obvious that they were young fairyborn lords, slumming it with humans and looking for adventure. Though it wasn't early for Tevin, it was still early for them, making him think they were heading home after a night of carousing. There certainly was no good reason for such a group to be down among the pigeons, as it were. Even Val's lip curled in disgust at their attitude. Then she shoved her hat further down, covering the tips of her ears. Val didn't want to be associated with them, even if they were as far from her as apples from wagon wheels.

The gentlemen glanced at Amaury, sniffed, and turned away, a genteel response so bred into them that it looked choreographed. Which meant they didn't notice when Amaury palmed two of their money purses, handing them to Tevin, who tossed them to a pair of street urchins. The boy and girl didn't question their luck, and instead disappeared down a nearby alley.

"Tell me again why we're here?" Tevin handed over a couple of coppers to a flower girl, tucking a fresh pansy boutonniere into his buttonhole before handing a similar one to his brother and another to Val.

"We needed to chat, and I didn't care to do it in a house full of people we don't know." Amaury stopped to purchase an iced bun.

"And I need ammunition," Val said. "There's a shop down this way."

"You could have picked somewhere nicer," Tevin said.

"I feel quite comfortable here." Amaury licked icing off his thumb. "Besides, we have Val, and Val has her pistols."

"Really, Amaury? You just ate."

Amaury held up a finger, stepped back to the baker's stall, and bought two more buns. He shoved one into Tevin's hand. "And yet I'm able to buy a bun for no reason except that it's delicious and I want it." He held the other bun up and waited. "You can't hoard every single copper, Tevin. Sometimes you have to enjoy what you've got."

Val snatched it from him. "Bless the dancing fairy lords and their tiny shoes," she groaned as she took a bite. "That's good."

213

"Val," Tevin chided. He reached over and wiped her mouth with his handkerchief.

"Leave off." Val batted his hands away. "I've got some gossip from the dance." She took another bite. "I found out why we haven't seen Padraig yet."

It took Tevin a second to remember who Padraig was—he had been on Merit's short list of possibilities, but they hadn't heard a thing about him coming to Veritess.

"I was right, thinking he needed coin," Val said, her mouth full of bun. "But it turns out he solved the problem hisself, so you can cross him off your little list."

"How did he solve the problem?" Tevin said. "And for fairy's sake, can you not talk and chew at the same time? I don't need to see your bun. I have my own."

Val swallowed and then stuck out her tongue. "He solved it by marrying a wealthy cattle rancher. Local fella, fairyborn, I think, but not aristocratic. Pots of cash. They eloped."

"Well, congratulations to them," Amaury said, "but boo for us. I was hoping he'd show up and be decent. I like Merit. Can't say I fancy the idea of her marrying any of the twits we've met so far."

Tevin grimaced. Amaury's assessment was, unfortunately, accurate. "We'll figure something out for her."

"I think you should marry her," Val said. "You'll treat her nice, and then you'll have pots of money and Amaury and Kate can stay with you and you won't have to go."

For a brief second, Tevin allowed himself to picture it, then ruthlessly quashed the idea. "She would be stuck cursed, for one. Since my job is to help her avoid men just like me, I don't think Merit would find me acceptable marriage material. That's two." He'd barely managed to convince her that he was a step up from Jasper. From where Tevin currently stood, the top of Merit's list was entire leagues away.

"Three," Amaury said, slinging his arm around Val. "Would you really want to inflict her with Florencia and Brouchard as in-laws?"

"I guess not," Val said sullenly.

Tevin swung his arm around her shoulder as well, sandwiching her between him and his brother. "We'll think of something, Val. I promise."

There was a loud squawk behind them as several men's voices blended together in mutual outrage. Val didn't glance back, but she grinned. "It would seem a few esteemed gentlemen have misplaced their purses. Tut-tut. Such carelessness."

"I doubt they'll connect us," Amaury said, "but let's put some distance between us anyway."

• • •

A few blocks and several turns later, Val found an ammunition shop and ducked in. Tevin and Amaury waited outside, having little interest in pistols. He'd closed his eyes, face tilted up to catch some sun, when Amaury cleared his throat.

"Yes?" Tevin asked without opening his eyes.

"About the Everslees . . ."

Tevin opened his eyes. Amaury had a distinctly uncomfortable look on his face. Not quite shame—Tevin wasn't sure the DuMonts possessed the ability to feel shame—but he wasn't *happy*. "Spit it out, Amaury."

"I mirrored the house to check in." He held up his hands, stopping Tevin from yelling. "I kept the Everslees to myself. You promised Merit." Amaury's gaze roved over the street, taking in everything on a constant swivel as he cracked his knuckles. "I told them about a few of the people we've met, that's all. Didn't want them getting antsy and showing up."

Tevin straightened, tipping his hat at a few ladies passing by. "Everyone we've met?"

Amaury puffed out a breath. "No one we liked. I'm not stupid, and I'm not cruel, no matter what you think."

"Amaury—"

He tilted his hat down and dropped his chin to his chest as he leaned against the wall next to Tevin. "Forget it."

He bumped his shoulder against Amaury's. "I'm sorry."

Minutes ticked by before Amaury finally spoke again. "I don't want them here, Tevin. I like Merit and her friends."

"I do too." It was like his parents were a slow-acting poison. If they stayed somewhere long enough, someone would get hurt. They ruined good things. It was what they did best. "I'll do what I can to help Merit. You do whatever's needed to keep Florencia and Brouchard appeased. I trust you. I'm sorry if I made it seem otherwise."

Amaury nodded, and though he didn't smile, he did tip his hat back up, relaxing against the warm bricks of the wall.

• • •

When they returned from their errands, it took Tevin only a few minutes to find Merit. She was back in her favorite room, the library, sitting in front of a fire, despite the heat of the day. A red leather-bound book sat open in her lap, forgotten. Her tail rested on the floor, the end twitching in a slow beat. If Tevin were to paint a portrait of her as she was, right in this moment, he would have titled it *Pensive*. He thought about everything Merit had gone through since he'd met her, added that to the things he guessed at, and he could see how she would feel that way.

Tevin ignored the other chair and sat on the floor, his legs crossed, arms on his knees. He rested his head against the side of the chair and closed his eyes. It was too hot for a fire, but that didn't stop it from being comforting.

"You've got to be sweating in all that fur," he murmured after a moment.

She tilted her head to the side, considering. "I am, but I hadn't noticed until now. You look miserable."

"Oh, good, we can be a matched set."

There was a slight tickle as she reached out, running her claws gently through his hair. He didn't move, afraid she'd stop. She paused a moment, waited for him to complain, and when he didn't, she ran her claws through his hair again. He leaned into the touch. It was like the fire. He didn't need it, but oh, how he *wanted* it.

"Want to talk about it?" he asked.

"Not really," she said.

That surprised a laugh out of him. "I won't make you." He kept his eyes closed, thinking it was somehow easier to apologize when you didn't have to look at the person. "I never did say I was sorry for the other night. The dancing lessons. I should have listened. I'm sorry, Merit."

"Thank you," she said simply. She scraped her claws a little deeper, scratching along his scalp. After a minute, Tevin realized he was almost completely collapsed against the chair, languid like a cat.

"Okay, now that you've mentioned it, I can't stop thinking about how hot it is," Merit said.

"Want to get out of here?"

"And go where, exactly?"

Tevin shrugged himself back into a sitting position. "Somewhere fun."

The beast frowned down at him. "I'm supposed to get ice cream with Freddie."

He stood and held out a hand. "Do you want to get ice cream with Freddie?"

"Not even a little." She took his hand. "And he's nice enough. It wouldn't be awful or anything. It's definitely what I'm supposed to be doing."

"You just don't want to go," Tevin said, pulling her up and catching the book with his free hand. "Send him a note, take your tincture, and meet me back here in ten minutes." He set the book on the chair and nudged her to the door.

They didn't manage to get out completely free—Kaiya somehow caught wind and was coming with them no matter what, which meant Val had to go as well. Tevin didn't bother arguing, shoving them all into the hack he'd waved down. It wasn't in the best shape, the metal horses visibly rusted in spots, but it would do. He put a coin into the box and whispered the directions to the metal as he did, trying not to think about the coin this trip would cost. He didn't want to think about money tonight, or debts, or his parents. No, tonight was his version of Amaury's sticky bun. He was going to do it because he wanted to and he could.

Merit spent the ride trying to guess where they were going. Val spent the ride staring at Kaiya and trying to pretend she wasn't. Kaiya, for her part, stared at Tevin in a way that looked both gleeful and slightly threatening.

When the hack stopped, they all clambered out, the dust puffing up from the ground as they landed. Noise assaulted them, and Merit's eyes lit up as she clapped her hands. "The carnival!"

Waites Family Traveling Carnival was set up on two acres of land, in what was normally a vacant lot in the city, closer to the neighborhood Tevin had been in with his brother this morning than to where Merit lived. Even from the gate, the carnival was a feast of the senses. Brightly painted signs and lights advertised rides and spectacles, while barkers competed for attention. *Hot dogs! Candy apples! Visit the house of mirrors! Only one ticket!* All of it blended with the noise of the crowd, and the underlying scents of animals, people, and food. Packs of children—both fairyborn and human—were chased by parents, older siblings, and nannies, darting through the other adults like minnows.

On his suggestion, Merit had worn an older summer dress, short-sleeved blue gingham. Her hair was in a simple braid, and she looked at home among the crowd, which was mostly working-class Veritess. People who'd traded in their overalls for jeans and cotton shirts or day dresses. A little girl in a sailor suit, holding on to the belt loop of an older boy's trousers. Young women in sensible blouses and skirts, their eyes bright at the joy to come. A tall Ivanian woman, her hair wrapped up in a bright scarf, her arm linked with someone who looked like her mother as they lined up to get tickets. It was nothing at all like the balls and fancy parties he'd been attending with Merit, and he felt a flicker of doubt. He glanced at her, relieved to see her smiling and pointing out the sights to Kaiya.

Merit's eyes were immediately drawn to the tallest ride, the Spinnaker. People stepped into large gilded birdcages before strapping themselves into the metal swing suspended in the middle. A group of mages would then power the machine, making the cages spin as they hurtled up, suspended almost horizontally along a metal pole, for one hundred and fifty feet into the air before coming back down. Tevin felt the blood drain from his face simply looking at it. This was an incredibly foolish idea.

Merit was practically dancing, her leather half boots kicking up dust. "That one! I want to do the Spinnaker first!"

Tevin elbowed Val before she could say anything. "Of course. Let's get our tickets." He paid their entrance fee, getting them tickets for the rides. Though he refused to let anyone else pay since it had been his idea, he didn't stop Val from surreptitiously sliding him a few coins.

Merit grabbed Tevin's hand and beelined for the Spinnaker, passing several smaller, tamer rides. He didn't bother trying to talk her into those. He couldn't. Not when she was beaming ear to ear, pink-cheeked with excitement.

The line was short, and before Tevin knew it, he was buckling himself into the cage next to Merit, his back to Kaiya and

Val. He wrapped one arm around the metal pole supporting their seat. He closed his eyes, focusing on Merit's excited chatter instead of the cold fear slithering through him.

"Tevin, are you okay?" Merit whispered.

He'd promised not to lie to her. "Mildly terrified."

"What?"

But at that moment, the mage dropped the lever and the cage spun outward into Tevin's own private misery. He clenched his jaw. It was only a moment. How long could the ride be, anyway? Still, when Merit's hand slipped into his, he held on like he'd drown without it. Time seemed to slow into an eternity. The world spun at a hideous rate, his stomach trying to climb out through his nostrils, but the only thing that mattered was the small hand in his.

After the ride was a different matter. Tevin got off first, making a beeline for the trash can sitting behind the fencing around the ride, where he was immediately and disgustingly sick. He felt a hand on his back, rubbing circles.

"Is he going to be okay?" Merit asked.

"Yeah," Val said. "He'll be fine. I'm not surprised—he gets sick on trains."

"I probably shouldn't have slipped the mage an extra coin to send us through twice," Kaiya said.

Tevin stared into the garbage can and tried not to breathe in. There was a cacophony of smells waiting to assault him when he did. "You don't have to stay. I'm fine."

"I don't mind waiting," Merit said. "We can get something to drink."

"Well, if you don't mind, Tev, we passed some games on the way. I thought Kaiya might like to try her hand at ring toss," Val said, sounding hopeful.

"I would destroy ring toss," Kaiya said.

He waved a hand at them, keeping his head over the garbage can. "Go."

Val gave him a quick pat on the shoulder before blazing a trail to the nearest game.

Once Tevin could walk without feeling queasy, Merit found a vendor who had glass soda bottles sitting in ice, along with puffy cakes rolled in cinnamon and sugar. She bought two sodas and a basket of the cakes, and they walked to a spot where they could watch a woman wearing a large snake around her neck juggle fire.

"Why didn't you tell me you get motion sickness?" Merit asked.

Tevin stole one of the fried cakes and popped it into his mouth, breathing around it quickly when he realized it was too hot. What he said was, "You really wanted to go," but it came out closer to "Oo eely anted ta ga."

"Yes, but you didn't have to go *with* us. You could have waited," Merit pointed out.

"I didn't want to," Tevin said. And that was the crux of it. Merit doing something that lit her up inside meant he wanted to be part of it. He couldn't do that as a bystander. He didn't want to just watch her have fun; he wanted to be in it.

"I don't think I'll ever understand boys," Merit said, shaking her head.

"That's probably because you're too reasonable. You've got to

222

let that go first thing." Tevin grabbed another cake, blowing on it carefully this time. "Do you think that snake is real?"

"Yes," Merit said. "I do." She sipped her soda, the condensation sliding down the bottle. "How do you think someone becomes a fire juggler?"

"I have no idea," Tevin said. "Why, do you want to change careers?"

"No." Merit smiled. "Not that I have an option to. But don't you ever see someone doing a job, something that you maybe didn't even know *was* a job until that moment, and then wonder how they got there?"

"Merit, I often can't even figure out how I got to where I am, let alone worry about someone else." They finished off the cakes and found a place to drop off their basket and bottles. Merit linked her arm through his so she didn't get jostled away from him in the crowd as they explored rest of the carnival. Tevin tried to win a prize by throwing a ball and knocking over milk bottles (he lost), and Merit proved to be very adept at a game involving darts, where she won a small stuffed badger with wings.

"Have you ever seen a fladger?" she asked as she handed off the stuffed toy to a sticky-faced little boy with a gap-toothed grin. He immediately used it to chase his little sister.

"I don't think they're real," Tevin said. "I've never seen one."

"I have—they live in the forest by our country home."

Tevin frowned down at her. "You're making that up."

"Hand to heart. They get into our gardens. Drive our gardeners batty. They call them the 'nuisance from above.'"

"Now I know you're making it up." He followed her into one

of the tents, this one advertising wonders of the world. They watched a contortionist for a few minutes, followed by a brother and sister duo who were deadlifting humongous weights and demonstrating other feats of strength. After a few minutes of that, they exited into an adjoining tent that housed a cage. The cage was metal, maybe ten by ten, and had a layer of old straw at the bottom. Inside was the biggest cat Tevin had ever seen.

"A marar!" Merit gasped in dismay. Reflexively, she reached for the bars, stopping herself from getting too close. "He looks absolutely miserable."

Tevin had never seen a marar but thought Merit might be right. The large cat was sprawled and a little listless. His dark fur didn't look very clean, and Tevin had to lean close before he realized that the cat wasn't solid black. There was a faint rosette pattern covering his entire body, except for the flat black of his broad nose. A thin, jagged scar cut along his nose and down to his cheek. A ruff of gray fur barely hid the collar around his neck.

"What are we going to do?" Merit looked up at him, her brows pinched. "We can't leave him here."

Tevin couldn't see how there was much they could do, but he couldn't say that. Not when she was looking at him like that. "We could come back at night and bust him out, but then we'd have to figure out how to get a large carnivorous cat out of the city."

She frowned at him. "Or I could just buy him? Our first option doesn't have to be illegal, you know."

"Buying him seems wrong," Tevin said.

Merit shrugged, but she had a determined look on her face.

"Perhaps. But I can get him out of here and onto a train, then released back into the Enchanted Forest where he belongs." Her grin turned slightly evil. "And then I'll see what I can do to keep them from using the money to buy another. There has to be some law I can pass." She leaned close to the cage. "Hang in there, my friend. You'll see freedom soon."

Reluctantly, they left the marar behind for now, exiting back into the sun. "You don't have to do any of that, you know," Tevin said, guiding her back toward some more rides.

Merit took his arm. "It would be a sad world if we only did what we had to do. Besides, what's the point of having power and money if I don't use it for good?"

Tevin knew there was probably an argument against her logic, but he couldn't think of it. They stopped when another ride caught their attention. As they watched, pairs of riders climbed into large wooden swans. Once the couple were seated, a mage activated it, and the swan became amazingly lifelike, stretching out graceful wings and arching its neck as the couple floated down a river into an archway covered in vines.

"Should we try another ride?" Tevin asked, nodding at the line that led to the swans.

"You want to go on this one?" Merit said, dubious. "Won't you get sick?"

Tevin pulled her forward. "It looks safe enough." He stopped to hand over their tickets and helped Merit climb into the swan before he followed her into the seat.

"How do you think it works," Merit whispered, "with only one mage?"

"Like hacks, I suppose. The mage group makes them and

225

then sets up a simple activation system." The mage tapped their swan, and it swam forward, the motion gentle. The magic made the wood under Tevin's fingers feel like warm feathers. They ducked, laughing, as the swan went through the vines.

The realization of what kind of ride they were on came swiftly and simultaneously to both of them. Probably when they caught a glimpse of the couple ahead locked together like they had decided to become one being.

"Oh," Merit said, her cheeks heating. "I should have guessed." She eyed the décor. The scenery was whimsically fashioned, full of flowers and weeping willows, the soft glow of mage light making the riders feel both alone and overwhelmingly aware of the romance.

"They're not paying any attention to the décor," Tevin said.

"They're missing everything," Merit agreed. "Like that tree over there. That is some tree."

"Yup," Tevin said. "With branches, even."

They both sat very quietly then, trying *desperately* to look at the décor.

"Hey, more vines. Oh, now we're in some sort of grotto," Merit whispered. "How wonderful."

The light in the grotto was soft, giving one the feeling of being on a pond at dusk a few moments from nightfall. To Tevin's absolute horror, there was also music—the sweet, smooth strains of a violin playing a romantic tune. Soft rain fell, and Tevin brushed flower petals off of his sleeve. "Whoever made this ride is a monster."

Merit reached up and very carefully pulled a rose petal out of his hair. "The absolute worst." She started giggling then, her hand over her mouth to stifle the sound. Her eyes lit up; her cheeks flushed. Tevin couldn't help but join her, and they giggled until they were gasping, her face in his shoulder.

By the time she looked up, they were in another part of the ride, about to go under a sweetheart bridge. The violin music swelled, the scent of flowers strong from the earlier shower of petals.

Merit's brown eyes met his.

If he leaned forward, just a few inches, they would be doing what every other person on this ride was doing. Which he absolutely, 100 percent, *should not do.* He was supposed to be helping her find a husband, which had nothing to do with kissing.

What would it hurt, though? One kiss. He could steal *one* kiss, a little voice inside him coaxed. That voice was like a slap. *Steal.* Because it would have to be stolen, wouldn't it? She wouldn't give one away, not to him. Not to someone so much like the boy who'd hurt her.

Her face was still tilted up at him, laughter leaving her rosy cheeked. He needed something to break the moment, and clearly the ride was not going to be any help *whatsoever.*

"I think I should remind you," Tevin said, his voice the barest of whispers, "that I threw up earlier. A lot."

This announcement made Merit collapse into another fit of giggles, laughing until her eyes were filled with tears.

They went under the bridge and then the ride was over.

They found Val and Kaiya after that, Kaiya's arms full of a giant stuffed cat. The fur was black, with faintly purple rosettes, the eyes a vivid emerald green.

"Look, Merit!" Kaiya said. "I won!"

"What, Val, empty-handed?" Tevin asked.

Val glowered at him, clearly grouchy that she hadn't been able to win the big cat for Kaiya. When she noticed that Merit's hands were empty, she clucked her tongue. "What, *you* didn't win Merit anything?"

"Of course not," Tevin said. "*She* was supposed to win something for *me*. And she did. Then what did she do? She gave it away." He glared down at her. "You, miss, owe me a fladger."

Merit's watch chimed, and she took it out of her pocket, glancing at the time. "We should go. My tincture is going to wear off soon."

Kaiya bought them all candy apples as they left, which they ate in the hack on the way home. Once Kaiya poked her head in and said the coast was clear, they snuck through the back door into Cravan House, everyone tired, sticky, and happy.

When they reached the stairs where they'd go their separate ways, Merit stood up on her toes and kissed Tevin's cheek. "Thanks for today."

"Anytime," Tevin whispered, watching her as she lifted up her skirts and took the stairs two at a time, racing to her rooms before she became a beast once more. He stood there for several long minutes afterward, listening to the ticking of the clock down the hall. The hour chimed, and Tevin wished he was a man very different from himself. The kind who could take Merit out without sneaking her through the back door. The kind who could have a day like today as a gift, instead of something he had to steal.

CHAPTER 17

A CURSE, MILADY

Merit stared at the gown her mother had picked out for her. Tiny pearl buttons ran up the back. She'd need help fastening them. With a sigh, Merit took her tincture, hating the feel of being pulled inside out, before she pulled the dress over her head. She'd cut it as close as she could—barely enough time for a simple hairstyle and to get dressed. She'd been able to skip her dose this morning when she went to meet with Freddie to make up for missing ice cream yesterday. He'd taken her for a ride in a rowboat on the lake, got tired halfway through, and made Merit paddle back. Which had actually been fun. She liked rowing, and he was amusing as he pretended to be dying from exertion.

Freddie hadn't cared that she came as a beast on their outing, which was great. She didn't want so many doses of tincture so close together. As it was, she felt worn thin and tired. The beast was pacing inside her, she could feel it, and one good slice of claws would break down her barriers.

Which might explain why she snarled at the door when someone knocked.

"Is that a 'come in' snarl or a 'go away' snarl?" Tevin's voice was muffled by the door. She couldn't even see him, but part of her started to relax. Tevin would help her fix this, her dress, her mood, all of it. Somehow she knew he would, and that also irritated her, because she should have been able to fix it herself.

"It's both," she said, the snap still in her voice.

"Okay," Tevin said, slipping through the door. "Then I'll come in, but I'll be careful about it."

She pulled her hair to the side. "At least make yourself useful."

Tevin came up behind her, gamely lining up buttons. "These are terrible. Either my fingers are too big or the buttons are too small."

Merit huffed a laugh. "Both, probably."

"Did you go back for your marar today?" Tevin asked.

Merit shook her head. "I couldn't go myself, so Ellery went. I paid an exorbitant sum, but the marar will be loaded onto the train in the morning, bound for my estate. I had to mirror my groundskeeper. He'll be in charge of letting it go. I'm going to have to pay the man a bonus."

"Aren't you worried about the creature coming back onto your lands?"

Merit shrugged, making him miss a buttonhole. "I don't think so. The forest is large, and it's where they belong. It's not like he's a tame house cat, Tevin."

He continued to button, cursing softly under his breath. "How did your outing this morning go?"

"Pleasant. Freddie was very entertaining. Why, have you dug up terrible things?" Merit asked, looking at him in the mirror.

He fumbled one of the buttons. "No." None of them had uncovered anything newsworthy about any of Merit's possible suitors, much to his irritation. His gut insisted that Latimer was off, that there was something there, but he couldn't help but wonder if that was jealousy rearing its snaggle-toothed head.

"You promised not to hold anything back." Merit's lips firmed, her gaze sharp.

"I don't like Latimer." How many buttons did a blasted dress need, anyway?

"Why?"

Her scrutiny made him want to fidget. "I don't know, okay? Val, Amaury, we've found nothing so far." That didn't change the fact that he wanted to strike Latimer's name from her list. Tevin scowled at the buttons. He couldn't look at her.

"That's all? You just don't like him?" She tried to turn, and he had to nudge her shoulder so she'd stay in place.

"You're going to pop the buttons."

"So I wear a different dress." Exasperation filled every word. "Latimer has been nothing but polite and attentive so far. He's also the queen's choice. I ask you, truthfully, has he said a single thing—done a single thing—that you can point at as evidence of a poor character?"

Why had he promised her he wouldn't *lie*? He always lied. Lying was as easy as breathing. So why had he not only promised, but why was it so blasted important for him to not break the promise? Whatever it was, he couldn't. He could keep information from her, but when she asked him directly like that, he felt the unbearable urge to vomit up the facts into her lap.

No," Tevin ground out, concentrating fiercely on her ridiculous buttons. "But you also promised to listen to my suggestions." Another button. Why was he sweating? He stared blindly at his fingers.

"I *am* listening. I'm simply not doing what you want." Her hand holding back her hair tightened. "So far he's been nothing like Jasper. That's what you're supposed to be protecting me from."

It was just the verbal wallop Tevin needed—a reminder that he was here because of everything he had in common with Jasper. Jealousy was a sneak thief, taking all his good sense.

"Tevin—"

He finished the last button and straightened, blinking rapidly and looking away. "It's silly to put tiny buttons that you can't reach on your gown. What happens if you need to get out of it quickly because your tincture wears off?"

"I've told Mother, but she doesn't listen." Merit's words were tentative, as if she wasn't sure she should let the subject drop.

Tevin ran a finger down the line of buttons. "Your mother can run an entire barony, but she can't take two seconds to think about your buttons."

Merit tried to smile and mostly succeeded. "That's what you're for, I guess."

It hung heavily in the air between them as they both tried not to think about the fact that Tevin was only around until her birthday.

"I have to finish getting ready," Merit said. "I promised Mother I'd dote on Cedric and Latimer."

"Right," Tevin said, turning to leave. "I'll see you in the carriage."

• • •

Tonight's entertainment featured a formal dinner at the home of Cedric Fedorova, next in line for the Fedorova barony. He lived in a palatial home on the outskirts of town, far enough away that despite the speed of Lady Cravan's carriages, it still took them half an hour to get there. The immense back garden was walled in, boasting several rows of fruit trees, a fountain, an assortment of tulips, lilacs, and other flowers, and several bushes planted to draw butterflies. The Fedorovas had decided to host the dinner outside, festooning the trees with brightly colored lanterns. At least fifty other people—mostly fairyborn with a smattering of humans—wandered around the gardens in their finery.

Long tables had been brought outdoors and covered with silver tablecloths before being burdened with candles, plates, silverware, flower arrangements, and, for some reason that Tevin couldn't decipher, pineapples.

"Why pineapples?" Val asked, leaning close, her eyes on Kaiya as she escorted Lady Zarla over to talk to Glendon.

"I'm more concerned about the birds," Tevin whispered back. He probably should have guessed after the whole leashed-peacock lake debacle that Cedric had an inordinate fascination with birds. What he'd failed to consider was just how far an idle fairyborn gentleman could take it. There were several peacocks, yes. But also pheasants, a chivalrous parrot, an irritated swan, and doves in cages.

"I have questions," Amaury said. "Also concerns."

A distinctly avian voice cackled from the tree above them. "Be you friend or knave, good sir?"

"Did the parrot just call me good sir?" Tevin asked.

"At least it didn't call you fair maiden," Val replied.

Merit leaned close to Tevin's ear. "Yes. Prepare to be good-sirred and miladyed to death, if not by Cedric, then by his parrot."

They greeted Cedric, who was of course overjoyed to see Merit and her guests—he was probably less overjoyed to see her guests but was kind enough to pretend that wasn't the case.

"I want to hate him," Amaury said. "Because—" He waved at everything around them. "But it would be like kicking a baby duck."

"He's too nice," Tevin said. There was a certain softness to Cedric that Tevin both envied and disliked. He was annoyed by the very idea that anyone had been allowed to grow up to be that gentle. He also felt an overwhelming urge to shelter the baby duck that was Cedric for the same reason.

Merit hissed out a breath.

"What is it?" Tevin asked. "Did you see the peacock from the park? Is it back for revenge?"

"They invited a godling." Merit's voice was shaky, though she appeared calm. Tevin followed her gaze to a thin, hawkish-looking gentleman who was currently nudging away one of the peacocks with his foot. His lip was curled up in distaste, the wings at his back starting to hum as they flickered. They were folded away, but Tevin thought that if he extended his wings, they'd look like a dragonfly's.

A short, plump woman in a gold evening gown laid a placating hand on the godling's shoulder. "My apologies, Godling Price." She held the other one up, hailing her son. "Cedric! Please come help with the peacocks."

Cedric, who had been in deep discussion with a few other guests, went to help immediately, but instead of shooing the birds away from the godling, he allowed them to stay where they were and started to tell the godling interesting facts about them. As he was talking, one of the peacocks fanned out his tail, causing a gentleman to leap back, knocking into one of the tables. The table shook, and Tevin was worried for a second that one of the candles would topple, setting the linens ablaze. From the far end of the party, one of the peahens shrieked, the sound not unlike someone being murdered horribly. Everyone startled at the sound and at the following crash when someone dropped their glass. One of the servants ran over, trying to clean up before someone stepped on it. Cedric didn't seem to notice any of it.

The godling's ears reddened like he was about to explode all over the babbling Cedric just as one of the birds in the tree pooped, the white smear of it blossoming on the lapel of Price's suit.

"Oh dear," Cedric said good-naturedly. "Apologies, of course." He snapped his fingers, and one of the staff ran up, face pale and fingers shaking as they offered to take the godling's jacket and clean it.

"Do you want to leave?" Tevin asked. "We can get you out of here."

"No," Merit said, giving him a brave smile. "It's fine. I can manage one night."

Shortly after that, dinner began, and Tevin scanned the neatly drawn placards until he found his name, unsurprised that he was at a different table from Merit.

The frustration over his argument earlier with Merit had left Tevin with a piercing sort of headache, and trying to make his way through the delicate razor wire that passed for conversation among Merit's circle wasn't helping. Tevin's real problem was that Eric Latimer, heir to the kingdom of Huldre and absolute pompous ass, sat across from Merit and very far from him. How was he supposed to keep investigating the man if he was across the room?

Cedric probably had no choice but to place his competition close—Latimer's title was too high for him to be stuck on the outskirts like Tevin. Which meant that while Cedric sat at the head of the table, Merit sat next to him on one side and the godling on the other. Cedric had to divide his attention between Merit and the godling so he didn't give offense, and Latimer was using that to his advantage, monopolizing her time.

Lady Zarla was doubtless overjoyed. Latimer was the best catch out of all of them, and Tevin had to grudgingly admit that he seemed genuinely interested in his discussion with Merit. He was hanging on her every word, almost to the point of neglecting conversation with the people around him.

This was what they wanted, and yet Tevin had been imagining a variety of scenarios that involved him shoving various

236

things into Latimer's face. He'd started with rolls, quickly escalated to cutlery, and was currently envisioning himself picking up a chair and bringing it down on Latimer's immaculate golden locks. Next dinner party, he was sneaking in and moving the placards around until the seating suited him better. He'd put Latimer in the privy.

He kept reminding himself why they were here—to get Merit married off to someone like Latimer. She'd get married, he'd be free, and then he'd return home to keep an eye on his parents and take care of his siblings. That's what he needed to do—focus on the future.

He sipped his water, trying to keep his hands busy. The wine was tempting, but he didn't need it as much as he needed a clear head. It wouldn't help the headache that was quickly morphing from piercing to pounding, either.

"Copper for your thoughts?"

Tevin turned to blink at the voice. The chair to his left had been empty for the first course, and he hadn't bothered to look at the placard. He was pleasantly surprised to see Willa placing her napkin in her lap as she sat.

"Pardon?"

She darted her eyes to the head table and dropped her voice. "You're giving someone over there hot eyes—the nonsexy kind." Willa took a bite of her salad. "What *is* this?" She grimaced. "Fennel. I hate fennel."

"Ah, a kindred spirit."

Willa stared at his empty plate. "You ate it anyway?"

"No, I traded plates with Val when she wasn't looking." Tevin kept his voice low so only Willa would hear it. "I assume

237

she'll do the same to Amaury. Who knows where the fennel will end up."

"Brilliant. So, who are you trying to murder with your eyes?" She was very good at speaking so that her voice didn't carry.

"Latimer. I'd like to cover him in honey and leave him for the rats."

Willa paused in shoving the salad around on her plate to look at him. "Do rats like honey?"

"I'm not sure. We can experiment. If they don't go for honey, we can cover him in something else. Jam, maybe. I'm a patient man. I can see it through until we get a favorable result."

Willa stifled a snicker and put her fork down, giving up on her salad. "My poor sister."

"Which one's your sister?" Tevin glanced around the tables, but there were several young women he didn't know, so he couldn't guess.

Willa nudged him. "She's down at the end closer to Cedric. She's sandwiched between Freddie and Lady Zarla."

Tevin glanced down the table. It was difficult to see everyone. The middle of the table was a dividing line of flower arrangements, candelabras, and decorative pineapples. Tevin counted four interspersed among the other decorations. "Do you know what's going on with the pineapples?"

"They're imported." Willa poked at one of the arrangements in front of her with her fork. "I think he's trying to make a statement, and that statement is 'I have money.'" A peahen landed on the table, causing one of the servants to dart forward and shoo it away. Everyone pretended not to notice.

Next to one of the pineapples at Cedric's table was a young

woman with tight brown curls, a dimpled smile, and warm brown skin. He looked back at Willa. "That's your sister? But she looks so nice. Very anti-moat."

"Diadora *is* nice." Willa grinned at him. "She supports my moat because she loves me, but she's trying to convince me not to fill it with bears."

"Bears would be pretty great," Tevin said, "but then they'd have to put up with the suitors. Would you do that to bears?"

She laughed. "Yes, we must think of the bears."

"Well, your sister is lovely, and I support her anti-bear agenda."

"Poor Merit," Willa said, pushing away her plate. "I think Cedric has decided to pull out all the stops."

Cedric appeared to be composing a song on the spot in honor of Merit, serenading her from his seat. Tevin couldn't hear the actual words over the din of conversation, but based on the look Godling Price was giving him, Merit's assessment of Cedric's troubadour skills was accurate.

Willa reached for her water, pausing with the glass close to her lips. "Oh, Cedric, no. Someone needs to stop him." She indicated the hawkish man. "That's Godling Price. He looks really irritated, and he's not exactly the forgiving sort."

"Are any of them?" Tevin looked closer at the man while pretending to smile at the staff as they came through, took the salad away, and brought the next course. Cautious after the fennel, Tevin poked it warily with his fork.

"It's pheasant confit with an oyster stuffing," Willa whispered. "I asked."

Val leaned over. "Is anyone else surprised they're serving

239

pheasant? I feel weird eating it while all the decorative pheasants look on."

"It does seem like a taunt," Tevin said, taking a bite. "You're right, Willa—Godling Price doesn't look happy with Cedric."

Tevin ate a few more bites, giving Willa a break to eat. She seemed fine, but he wondered if, like Merit, she had a difficult time sharing space with godlings. When he next spoke, he changed the subject, spending the rest of the dinner chatting with her and stealing glances at Merit to make sure she was okay.

After dinner, the guests were all ushered inside so they could play cards, have an after-dinner drink, or head into the ballroom to listen to music and dance.

Tevin ended up in the ballroom, stuck in a conversation with Glendon and Freddie—the latter telling them a long story involving a case of wine, a drunken wild pig, and a pair of pinstripe trousers—as he tried to catch Val's attention. She took one look at Freddie, who was gesticulating wildly with his hands and spilling his drink in the process, and shook her head.

Tevin gave her puppy dog eyes. She silently but dramatically groaned before excusing herself from the group she'd been talking to and came over.

"Tevin," she said, grabbing his arm and interrupting Freddie. "There you are." She threw an apologetic look Freddie's way. "I'm so sorry to interrupt, but I'm afraid I must steal Tevin here." Glendon sent her a pleading glance. "And of course, the ambassador."

Freddie looked crestfallen. "But I haven't got to the best bit yet."

"You know who would *love* to hear about this?" Val pointed to Latimer, who was deep in a conversation with Merit and her mother. "The prince. Loves a good pig story, he does. Can't get enough."

Freddie brightened. "Thanks." He patted her shoulder and left.

"I am deeply in your debt," Glendon said, sipping his drink. "Do you think we even need to leave now, or is he sufficiently distracted?"

"Let's step out, just in case." Val ushered them into the hall. "I figure we can stay out a minute and then go back in."

There was a noise down the hall, and Tevin turned to see a servant helping Godling Price back into his jacket. Even from here, Tevin could see that there was a mark on the lapel.

Glendon cursed into his drink. "I better go find Cedric's parents. They'll need some serious diplomacy to get Godling Price back into a good humor. If you'll excuse me?" He left quickly, and Tevin and Val decided to sneak back into the ballroom.

"Where's Amaury?" Val asked.

"Probably reading grocery lists somewhere," Tevin murmured. People were mingling and laughing, though the center of the ballroom was clearing to make room for dancers as the musicians tuned their instruments.

Merit, her smile fixed as she nodded at something Cedric was telling her, practically snatched his arm as he walked by. "Tevin! There you are." She stepped closer to him. "I'm so sorry, Cedric—but I promised Tevin the next dance." He waved her off good-naturedly before wandering away to find his own dance partner.

241

Tevin followed Merit gratefully onto the floor. "Do you actually want to dance, or was that a clever ruse?"

Her eyes twinkled at him. "Can't it be both?" The first tinkling notes of a slow ballad came from the piano, and Merit let Tevin pull her into his arms. "Tonight has certainly been interesting—you should have heard Cedric's song. At least Latimer was good company." Her brow arched, making the last bit a question. One he wished he had a rebuttal for. But all he had was a throbbing head and a heavy heart.

Tevin spun her across the floor easily. He didn't want to think about how well they moved together. He didn't want to think at all, really. "I bet he even ate his fennel."

She tipped her head. "What does *that* mean?"

"Never mind. I'm pleased for you." He thought for sure she would argue, but instead her shoulders softened, and she settled more firmly into his arms. They flowed together like water, like creatures of a same piece. For a few precious moments, they didn't do anything but simply exist in the music. No matter what else happened, Tevin felt he'd remember this dance until he was buried deep in the earth and his flesh went to the worms.

When the music stopped, they paused, their eyes locked. Tevin's throat felt thick, his skin hot and somehow cold at the same time. Merit's brown eyes were wide, her lips slightly parted.

"Merit—"

That was as far as he got before there was a large *clang* at the end of the room, followed by the crash of champagne flutes hitting the floor and shattering. Amidst the mess, Cedric, heir to the Fedorova barony and questionable troubadour, flailed on the floor. Feathers flew, and even from where Tevin stood, he could see a fine spray of blood as the glass sliced into a large set of wings. Cedric bellowed and his body bowed. Someone screamed, and Tevin looked up in time to see an older man— the spitting image of Cedric in thirty years—faint dead away, only to be caught by Cedric's mother before he hit the floor. She looked torn between holding her husband up and going to her son.

Merit left Tevin's arms and ran over. He went after her, trying to stop her before she stepped out onto the broken glass.

"Merit!" Tevin grabbed her shoulder.

"He's changing," Merit said. "It hurts, and he's fighting it—he doesn't realize there's broken glass everywhere. He'll cut himself to ribbons."

Tevin didn't argue but pulled off his jacket. He tossed it to Merit and bent, scooping up Cedric. Val had snagged his feet, and they lifted, dragging him out of the glass. They didn't make it far—Cedric was a writhing mass of heavy limbs—before they had to lower him down again. Merit quickly spread Tevin's jacket under him. He watched blood splatter the cloth as Cedric's spine bowed back. Tevin and Val held him down as Cedric bucked, his eyes rolling back, his skin bubbling like he was made of melted wax.

"I remember this part." Merit stood, her eyes haunted, grabbing Tevin by the shoulders and dragging him back and away from Cedric's flailing body. "He's almost done." She tucked her face into Tevin's chest, though she kept an eye on Cedric. She was trembling, so Tevin put an arm around her and pulled her close. Val stood next to him, her face stoic.

There was a shriek and an awful bubbling sound, and then silence.

Cedric was gone. In his place sprawled an unconscious ostrich, his tux in tatters and blood seeping from half a dozen small cuts.

"Poor Cedric," Merit whispered.

Tevin squeezed her and let go, sparing himself the feeling of her pulling away first. "He'll be okay. We'll make sure." How they would help Cedric, he had no idea, but he didn't want it to be an empty promise.

"What happened?" Val asked.

"He's been cursed," Merit said, her voice breathy. She was pale, the pulse at her throat fluttering like a trapped butterfly.

Tevin didn't like the look of her. "We should go." She didn't argue, letting him lead her away. Servants scrambled to clean up the mess, while someone shouted for a healer. Tevin was almost out of the room when they walked past Godling Price. He stood by the door, calmly listening as Cedric's mother pointed at her son and pleaded, "With all due respect, you cannot leave him like that! He's our son—"

The godling cut her off, his face cold. "Think of it as a temporary gift. He likes birds so much? Now he'll get to be one for the next three months."

Lady Fedorova seemed torn between wanting to argue on her son's behalf and not wanting to anger the godling further. "Three months?"

Merit shivered again, and Tevin ushered her out and away from Cedric's distraught mother and Godling Price.

CHAPTER 18

THE REAL GIFT IS REGRET

Latimer calmly put on his jacket and took his leave, declining the offer of a carriage or a horse from the stables. He needed to walk right now—he could grab a hack later. It was too far to go on foot this late in the evening. The night air was sticky and warm, clogging his nostrils as he put one foot in front of the other. He didn't dare open his mouth, even to breathe. Every step took him farther away from the ballroom, the blood, and Cedric's screams.

And with each step, his hands shook a little more.

He managed to keep himself together, his spine straight, the picture-ideal fairy lord, until he was several blocks away and back into the city proper. Then he turned into an alley where he threw up everything he'd consumed at the dinner, which had been precious little to begin with.

He became aware of himself in degrees—the bite of brick on his palms where he held himself up. The cold sweat on his brow. The stink of the alley in the warm air—rotting garbage and who knew what else. The faint wash of mage light filtered in from the streetlamps, competing with the cold light of the moon and stars. He wanted the night to swallow him up.

Latimer had spent several years very carefully avoiding

self-reflection and deep thought. It was easier and better for everyone if he just did as he was told. He didn't concern himself too much with the outcome of his actions, because that wasn't his job, was it? He had staff to clean up his messes. Only tonight, he couldn't avoid it. Oh, he had no compunctions about planning to do something about Tevin. He didn't like him, and sensed on a certain level that the man could take care of himself.

But Cedric? What he had done to Cedric was like tossing a piglet into a lion pit. All because, what? Merit had been kind to him at dinner. While he wasn't as much of a threat as Tevin, he was still a threat. And the opportunity had practically fallen into his lap—catching Godling Price outside, muttering about his jacket and Cedric while he took a boot to one of the roaming peacocks. It had been laughably easy to pay off Godling Price. He'd been halfway to cursing Cedric already. He hadn't had enough coins with him, but they'd managed to come to a deal. He'd never seen a curse so cavalierly violent and cruel as the one he watched tonight.

If the featherbrained chit likes birds so much, I'll make him one.

All because Latimer couldn't take any chances. His mother had been clear: There was no room for mistakes. Merit had to be his, and he had little time and fewer resources. He needed to be creative with what he had, because the idea of going home empty-handed and facing the disappointment of his mother made him want to be sick all over the cobblestones again.

• • •

Merit didn't remember getting into the hack. On some level, she knew that Tevin held her carefully, comforting her with gentle noises, but none of it sank in. Not even the sound of the wheels on the cobblestones registered.

In Merit's mind, she was back in time, reliving one of the worst nights of her life. She'd insisted that her mother cancel the betrothal ball, only Lady Zarla hadn't *listened*. Her mother never listened.

Watching Cedric had been like being cursed all over again. The feeling of her bones shattering, rearranging themselves into the new and complex pattern of the beast. Waking with the thin hope that her mother had been wrong, that Jasper would come back for her. That he *loved* her. Days slipped into weeks, and the hope thinned, until it became a dried-out husk disintegrating in the next big breeze. She'd broken. Like Cedric had broken. Would it feel that way when her curse became permanent? Was tonight a portent of her future?

She threw back her head and screamed, but the sound that came out was never meant for a human throat. The sound was all beast.

• • •

Tevin had never been so grateful to be in a hack. If they'd been in a regular carriage, the beast's roar would have startled the horses. He'd tried to hold on to Merit as she changed, but it had proven impossible. The beast didn't want to be held. The beast wanted *freedom*, and it took freedom easily, the door of the hack shredding under her claws like so much paper. Then Tevin was alone in the hack, though he didn't stay there.

He jumped out of the moving vehicle, rolling into the fall as he hit the stones only to come back up onto his toes. His back would be a mess of bruises in the morning, but it couldn't be helped. The beast was loose in Veritess. Tevin had stared into the creature's eyes and hadn't seen an ounce of reason or intelligence. Merit had completely disappeared.

And now she was running the streets alone. If she hurt anyone, Tevin knew that she wouldn't be able to forgive herself. He tore after her, arms and legs pumping; the skittering of his heart echoed in his footfalls as he practically flew down alleyways and side streets.

Tevin wasn't sure how long he'd been running. It had to have been some time—they were almost to the river. He could smell the water in the air as he gulped down greedy lungfuls.

Despite pushing himself, he kept losing her—she was faster than he was, for certain—and he had to pause and check cross streets when he did, looking for any clue of her passing. Sometimes he would hear her, or see fresh scratches clawing through the mud between the cobblestones. The fact was that he was falling more behind with every delay, and he wouldn't be able to run forever.

If the beast hadn't stopped to eat, he probably would have lost her in the tangled streets of lower Veritess. Instead he found her, mouth full of feathers and blood, her foot caught in the torn wire of a chicken coop. Tevin slowed then, pausing to bend in half and suck in air. "You led me for a merry chase, didn't you, sweetheart?"

The beast snarled and continued to chew on what was left of the chicken.

"Naughty thing," he said, inching closer. "Those aren't yours to eat, are they? No, they were supposed to be someone else's dinner." He eyed the coop carefully. The beast had practically torn off a whole side of it, and whatever chickens she hadn't eaten had escaped. Not only would the family have to pay for materials to rebuild the coop, but they'd also lost a source of food and income. From the look of the neighborhood, they couldn't afford to lose either.

A window opened, and the beast ignored it except for tightening her hold on her meal. A young boy, probably the age of ten, peeked out. "That your dog, mister?"

"No," Tevin said. "She's her own master."

The boy snorted. "Well, I'm thinkin' she's yours and you don't want to be payin' for her mess." The boy leaned out farther, trying to see better. "She's a big 'un. You can pay for her kibble, you can pay for our coop."

"Right enough," Tevin said. The problem was, he didn't have a coin on him. "She's not mine, though. Belongs to the baroness of Cravan."

The boy whistled. "What kind of dog is it?"

"A big one, like you said," Tevin said. "And not in the best of moods. Do you have a rope?"

The boy nodded but didn't move. *Smart lad.* "You get me some rope for tonight, and tomorrow you stop by Cravan House. She'll pay for the whole mess, promise." The boy gave Tevin's finery a good inspection before making a sharp nod of agreement. Even dirty and torn, his clothing still looked respectable, or the boy would have laughed him out of the alley. Relieved, Tevin rattled off the address of Merit's home and waited for the rope.

In reality, he didn't think the rope would hold the beast. No, he had to hope that his charm would do that. But it was a long walk back to Merit's house, and it would go better if people thought he was walking a large, ugly dog. Sticking to the shadows wouldn't be enough. He'd have to be charming. The boy tossed down a length of thin, grimy rope and closed the window, leaving Tevin alone with the beast. He slid the rope into a slipknot, leaving a loop big enough to put over the beast's head.

Tevin stepped closer to the coop, dreading the walk home. If he needed to charm the beast and the people around them, he would need his voice to carry. Which either meant shouting all the way home . . . or singing.

He wasn't a very good singer.

Not that it mattered to anyone else but him. For now, he kept his words soft and constant, moving closer and closer to the beast, hoping he could manage to get her home while a coop full of chickens was still the worst of her damage.

CHAPTER 19

CHICKEN FEATHERS GET EVERYWHERE

Merit woke up in her own bed, warm and safe. She wanted to burrow down deep into the mattress and never leave. Sunlight filtered in through the curtains, birds chirped, and someone was snoring softly. She was tired and didn't want to move, but she couldn't ignore that last part. She blinked her eyes against the sunlight and took in the room. She was in her bed, nestled up against Tevin, who was still wearing what was left of his suit from last night. His jacket, tie, and shoes were gone. His shirt and pants were torn, dirt caked in more than one spot. He only had one sock. His eyes were closed, the thick fringe of his lashes resting against his cheek. *Beauty at rest.* She should wake him. She should get up. Instead she curled back against his side and closed her eyes.

"You decided not to get up, then?" Tevin mumbled, not bothering to open his eyes. His voice was rough, barely pitched above a whisper.

"If I get out of this bed, nothing good will happen," Merit said.

"What makes you say that?"

"The compiled evidence of every day before now," Merit grumbled.

Tevin rasped a laugh. "Well, if you don't get up, nothing good will happen either."

"What's wrong with your voice?"

"I had to serenade half the city last night on my way home," Tevin said. "It was a long walk."

Fear shot through her, and she tensed, but Tevin held her against him. The feeling surprised her so much she stopped struggling. Very few people felt comfortable touching her when she was a beast. Merit missed freely given hugs, and the gentle connection that touch could bring. "What did I do?"

"Nothing terrible," Tevin said. "Rest easy on that. You destroyed a chicken coop, the door of a hack, and ate an ill-gotten dinner. No one was hurt, and you can pay for the damages. It's okay."

Someone knocked at the door. "Merit?" It was only Ellery, which relieved her. It was too early to take on her mother.

"Yes, Ellery?"

"You have a visitor. I told your mother that you needed rest and an exam after last night, but she wouldn't send him away."

"Give me a moment," Merit said, levering herself up and out of the bed.

"It's going to take more than a moment," Tevin murmured.

"What do you mean?" Merit stood, her legs wobbly.

Tevin pointed at the mirror. Merit peeked and instantly understood what he meant. Her dress was shredded. She was caked in dirt and, worse, feathers sticking out of her fur. She needed a bath and a change of clothes. "You let us crawl into my bed like this?"

"Merit, if you think I had any energy to do more than that, you're delusional." Tevin rubbed his eyes, and Merit could see the shadows of exhaustion under them. "And I didn't exactly want to summon one of the maids."

She was grateful that he hadn't, but now they had a problem. "Ellery, how long can you stall?"

"If I skip the exam until later, twenty, maybe thirty minutes." Ellery hesitated. "You okay?"

"Yes," Merit said. "Thank you."

"Tell Ellery to come back when they're done," Tevin whispered.

"Ellery—can you run back here as soon as you let them know?"

"Of course," Ellery said. "Consider it done."

"Why do we need Ellery?" Merit asked, pulling Tevin out of the bed.

"Because you need help, and I'm not exactly a lady's maid. I'm not sure how great Ellery is at it either, but at least no one will think twice about your healer being in here with you."

Tevin moved past her and into her private bath. He turned on the spigots and let water fill the tub.

"I don't have time for a bath."

"Merit, you're covered in who knows what, and neither of us are exactly springtime fresh."

"My fur will take too long to dry," Merit said.

Tevin tapped his fingers along the copper edge of the tub. He stood up, sifting through the different-colored glass bottles

253

that sat on a ledge next to the tub. After a second, he picked up the purple bottle, took out the stopper, and sniffed. "Lily. Strong fragrance. That's what we need." He poured a little in the water and then turned off the spigot. "Step into the tub— you're going to need to wash your hands and feet the most. Use a wet washcloth to wipe down your fur. It won't be perfect, but it will do for now."

Tevin started pulling feathers out of her fur.

Merit stood in front of him, not moving. "Are you going to leave?"

"As soon as I get these feathers out," Tevin said. "Look, I understand you don't want to strip down, but we don't exactly have time left for modesty. At least get down to your chemise. I think that's mostly intact. I'll have Ellery take over as soon as they get here."

She stripped out of her dress and tossed it into the hamper. Maybe someone could use the material for rags. Tevin helped her into the tub. She dipped her washcloth and started wiping as he continued to pluck feathers, stopping only when Ellery arrived.

Ellery didn't bat an eye at the scene, stepping up to help Tevin remove the feathers as quickly as possible. "Can't say I've ever helped pluck a patient before."

"Can't say I've ever wanted to be plucked," Merit grumbled.

Ellery laughed.

As soon as all of the feathers were gone, she was left to finish her quick wash alone. Merit moved swiftly, getting the worst of it off. She would take a proper bath later. Once she was done and dried as best she could, she wrapped herself in a robe and cleaned her teeth before stepping out into her room. Tevin was gone, leaving only Ellery to help her. Ellery handed her a fresh chemise. The one from the night before followed her dress into the hamper, and then they brought her a light blue belted day dress, the hem decorated in small embroidered flowers.

Merit heard the door open and shut a second before Kaiya peeked in. "Tevin said you might need some help."

"Yes," Merit said. "Can you brush while Ellery handles the dress?"

Kaiya nodded, grabbing a brush and jumping to swipe at the fur around her face and head.

Ellery did up the buttons and turned her in front of the mirror. They both stared at their reflections for a moment.

"You'll do, I think," Ellery said.

"Do you want a veil?" Kaiya asked.

Merit shook her head. "If they're going to show up unannounced, they can deal with the full beast treatment."

"Quite right," Ellery said. "In my country, it's considered acceptable to launch people who show up unannounced from a trebuchet. We all keep them by our doors as a reminder."

"In Hane, we keep crossed swords in our entryways for the same reason," Kaiya said. "Keeps people polite."

"I think you're both making that up." But Merit couldn't tell just by looking at them. They were both remarkably skilled at keeping a straight face. Something caught her eye and she started snickering.

"What?" Ellery asked, checking Merit's appearance.

"You have a feather in your hair," Merit said, before reaching up to pluck it out.

• • •

Her mother met her in the hall outside the library. "There you are." She examined Merit quickly, clearly not liking what she saw. "I'm glad I waited for you. Merit, you can't go in like this." She pressed a vial of tincture into Merit's hands.

"Mother—"

Lady Zarla shook her head. "No, Merit. No arguments. I've given you a lot of leeway. You disappeared from one ball, ducked out of dinner last night, and didn't come home until who knows when, and you've let those people practically infest this house." She crossed her arms. "I'm trying to be patient with you, but I must put my foot down *now*."

Merit knew better than to argue with her mother when she got that look on her face, so she didn't bother. Why waste her breath? She wouldn't listen. Merit carefully unstoppered the bottle. After all, she'd had one of her episodes last night. It should be safe for now, shouldn't it? She'd never had one so soon, anyway. But then the curse was changing in ways she didn't understand . . .

She drank the tincture, closing her eyes until the awful feeling of shifting from the beast passed.

When she opened her eyes, her mother was looking at her critically. Lady Zarla turned her around, adjusting the dress, which hung on her awkwardly after the transition. After that, she tightened the belt around the waist and took off her own shawl and draped it over Merit's shoulders. Her mother turned her back around, examining her work. She licked her thumb and wiped at Merit's cheek. "You've got dirt—"

"Mother, I'm not five."

Lady Zarla smoothed Merit's hair. "I wish you were five. You were so sweet at that age. And quiet." She paused, holding Merit's face. "I do all of this for you, you know."

"I know you think you do," Merit said, gently removing her mother's hands from her face. "I have to go, Mother. My guest is waiting."

Lady Zarla looked like she wanted to say something, but changed her mind, shooing Merit into the library.

Merit shut the door gently, turning to see Latimer waiting for her. His back was to her so he could look out the window. The light flooded in and gilded him, making him look like a dream come to life.

She smiled. "Latimer."

He turned, presenting her a fluid bow. "Lady Merit, you look lovely. I'm sorry to drop by so unexpectedly."

Merit tried not to picture him flying through the air in Ellery's trebuchet and was mostly successful. "My apologies for making you wait."

"Now that we've both apologized, can we sit?" Latimer waited for her to settle herself on the love seat before taking the seat next to her.

"I don't want to intrude on your time too much. You probably have a busy morning planned, and we're still practically strangers." He caught his lower lip in his teeth, looking charmingly unsure of himself. "When you left last night—you looked upset. I wanted to see if you were all right."

"Oh." Merit couldn't help but feel touched. He'd stopped by just to check on her. "That's sweet, thank you."

"We don't know each other well yet, but I do hope you realize you can talk to me if you want." He laughed self-deprecatingly. "I won't claim to be good at this sort of thing. I'm not the kind of man people confide in." He took her hand in his. "But I'd like to try. For you."

His hand was warm and comforting in hers. She realized she was comparing it with holding Tevin's hand and stomped down hard on that line of thought. Latimer deserved her full attention. "Last night, it brought up some things. About my curse. When I was first cursed, that is."

He gave her hand a reassuring squeeze. He really was gorgeous, sitting there on her couch. Every inch the golden prince. Only, it was like looking at a painting. She could recognize that he was handsome in an abstract kind of way; it just didn't mean anything to her. Why didn't she care more that he was handsome?

"I can't imagine what you've gone through," Latimer said. "But you're feeling better today?"

"Much." She realized that while she might not care that Latimer was handsome, she was genuinely enjoying his company now. They could be friends, at least. That was something. Lots of people based relationships on friendship, didn't they? She didn't like the very real possibility that she would have to live in his kingdom and bid her beloved country home goodbye, but she liked the idea of him more than she did Freddie or Cedric. Though those two had the advantage of being local. Of course, Cedric was temporarily an ostrich.

"I couldn't help but notice that you left with that DuMont fellow. You seem to be spending a lot of time together."

Merit stilled. She didn't like what he was implying, even if there was truth to it. He didn't lay claim to her or her time—not yet. "He's our guest."

He nodded. "I don't wish to speak ill of a guest, of course, but I will speak bluntly. You would do yourself a disservice if you married him." His gaze was steady on hers. "It's just the way things are, Merit. I've heard he's rich, and I know he's decent-looking, but he can't ever offer you the things I can."

Decent-looking? Latimer must really think Tevin is competition if he can't even admit that he's gorgeous.

"What can you offer me that Tevin can't?" Merit asked the question knowing the answer, of course, but it wasn't the information that mattered. It was how he presented it. You could learn a lot about a person by how they said things. What words they used, the tone, and how they held themselves. Tevin had taught her that.

Latimer laughed and leaned an arm over the back of the settee. He reached up and touched a lock of her hair that had come loose from her braid. After examining it for a moment and letting it run through his fingers, he tucked it behind the curve of her ear. "My bloodline may not be local fae, but it is a royal one. Someday I will be king. You would continue in your current lifestyle with someone who would *understand* you— with someone who has been raised the same way and can anticipate your needs because of that." His tone was gentle, like he truly regretted that he had to tell her such things. "He will never know what it's like to be one of us, Merit." He brushed his thumb across the back of her hand. "I'm not offering love. We don't know each other well enough for that. But

259

I think we get on well. I respect you. We could have a solid partnership."

"Why now?" Merit wasn't shocked by his practical approach. Her own parents had married for such a reason. "I have my curse to drive me, but what's making you consider marriage?"

"I'm an only child. My parents worry. They don't want me to put my duties off, such as they are." His smile was apologetic. "It's my understanding that you need to marry soon, correct?"

"I have to be married by my birthday, or the curse is permanent."

Latimer regarded her with sympathy, and part of her bristled at the possibility that it might be pity, but another part . . . a rather large portion, to be honest, welcomed it. He was right—it was nice to have someone understand, and Latimer understood having to marry for duty. She wondered what it would be like to be married to him. Until now she'd mostly considered him in terms of his title, but what of Latimer himself? She thought back to their day at the godling's house and felt a trickle of hope. They'd had fun, been easy in each other's company. Marriage to him held a hint of possibility.

"I hope I'm under consideration." He stopped her before she could respond. "You don't have to tell me, and I don't expect any decisions today of course, but I wanted you to know that I'm serious in my attentions."

She nodded. Her mother would be over the moon.

He released her hand so he could dip into an inner jacket pocket and pull out a small wooden box, tied neatly with gold ribbon. "I also brought you something." He handed the box to her with a flourish.

"A gift?" She took it somewhat reluctantly. "Latimer, you don't have to—"

"I know." He bit his lip, and Merit couldn't tell if he was doing it unconsciously or trying to draw her attention to the perfect curve of his mouth. Something told her it was intentional. "I would love to claim to be completely altruistic, but the truth is that I'm willing to bribe my way into your affections."

She laughed, as she was meant to, and opened the box. The inside was lined with silk and held a delicate silver chain with a small, ornately carved locket. Merit carefully took it out, releasing the catch so the locket folded open. Inside was a small painting of his face. It was well done, capturing him exactly. She wasn't sure what to say. The locket was lovely, but he'd still given her a picture of himself as a gift. "Thank you."

"There's a trick to it." He took the locket from her hands and showed her another spot on its side. "It's a pressure switch. Press it." He pushed down, and the portrait of his perfect face popped forward, revealing the delicate surface of a magic mirror.

She clapped her hands together in genuine glee. "That's ingenious. And so generous!"

He undid the clasp, holding it out for her, a wicked look on his face. "I'm not going to pretend otherwise—it *is* a very generous gift. Thoughtful and helpful. Not only do you get to look at me, but you can call me whenever you wish."

"And you're hoping this will put you ahead of the competition." She gathered up her hair and held it away from her neck.

"Of course." He leaned to put the chain around her throat. "I aim to win. I think we would make a good match, Merit. We both come from long and distinguished lines. Everything I've seen of you does you credit." He connected the chain, letting his fingers trail down it to straighten the locket. "But I also know what it's like to be different. To have people look at you and treat you as other. I'm not a baron. My fairy line comes from Tirada. Even in my own lands, I'm different." His voice was gentle and lulling, but there was power in it. Not the power of fairy magic, but the very human power of charisma.

His fingers lingered on the chain. "It suits you." Latimer's smile was as soft as his voice and held that same power. Merit felt herself drawn in, wondering what he thought of her. Remove her bloodlines and wealth, put her in a country dance, and she wouldn't turn any heads. But the way Latimer looked at her made her feel as if she were that kind of girl, someone lovely, enchanting. *Special.* He leaned in, his fingers brushing the edge of her jaw. When she didn't draw away, he dipped his head, his lips meeting hers.

Before her curse, Merit had kissed a few boys. Her early kisses were fairly terrible, but after much discussion with her friends, she'd decided that was normal. There was a learning curve to kissing. A learning curve that involved an awful lot of drool and unpleasantness. When you thought about it too much, tongues were weird.

Two kisses stood out from the pack. The first was from Jasper—she didn't think he'd been particularly skilled, but she'd adored him and forgiven a lot. The second had actually been post-curse. Merit had taken a dose of Caen's bloom and joined Ellery and Kaiya at a local barn dance. She'd danced for two hours, ending the night in a dark corner with a tempting boy with fine eyes. The kiss had been sweet, but nothing had ultimately come of it. Still, it was a pleasant memory. For a second she wondered what kissing Tevin felt like, then felt guilty.

Latimer's kiss was nice. His lips were warm and firm, his touch gentle. He obviously had some skill, even if it didn't set her world on fire. The kiss was pleasant. She could work with pleasant. Latimer pulled back, pausing to take her hand and press it to his mouth.

"With that, I will leave you." He released her hand and stood. Once he was at her door, he paused, giving her a formal bow. "I do hope you'll continue to think of me favorably and consider what I've said."

Merit couldn't suppress a small smile. "How could I not?"

Another bow, and then he slipped out her door.

Merit touched her lips and tried not to think about riding under the sweetheart bridge and the kiss that didn't happen. She failed miserably.

CHAPTER 20

A CHARMING MASQUERADE

That night, Freddie took Merit to see a play. His family had their own box in the balcony, the seats made of plush red velvet. Merit liked the theater, but she was tired of going out. Weary of smiling, nodding, and making small talk. Freddie didn't try to kiss her or even hold her hand, but he hinted—broadly—that his parents were hoping to hear from her mother about wedding contracts. She excused herself at intermission, claiming a headache, and he didn't question her. He kindly put her into his own carriage with instructions to take her home, then continued with his evening out. She was absurdly grateful for his inattention.

Merit's mother was in the entryway when she got home, dressed elegantly in a rich burgundy gown and adjusting her earrings as she waited for the carriage to be brought around. "You're home early. Something wrong? Shall I send for Ellery?" She lifted Merit's chin. "Perhaps I should stay home tonight. You look peaky."

"I'm just tired," Merit said, pushing her mother's hand away.

She felt a pang of sadness, wishing that she had the kind of mother who would help unburden her, instead of adding to the weight on her shoulders. A mother who *listened*. "Nothing to worry yourself over."

Lady Zarla pursed her lips. "Of course I'm worried. I'm your mother." Her eyes narrowed. "Was it something Freddie did? I'll mirror his parents."

"No," Merit said, a little too sharply. "Freddie was fine. I really am tired. I'm not used to this."

Lady Zarla nodded, accepting the answer. She picked up her beaded clutch from the table, only to set it back down again. Instead she stepped close to Merit, grabbing her shoulders. The faint jasmine of her perfume teased Merit's nostrils, bringing with it the memory of so many nights of her mother kissing her goodbye before leaving for the next ball or dinner party. She rubbed Merit's shoulders briskly. "No, I'm not going to leave it at that. Not used to what, exactly?"

Merit hesitated. Her instinct was to say something glib, end the conversation, and get them both on their way. But could she really complain that her mother didn't listen if Merit didn't at least try to talk to her? When had she stopped giving her a chance? Her betrothal ball? That didn't sit right with Merit. She couldn't control her mother, and it was likely she would disappoint Merit again. But that didn't mean Merit wanted to cut herself down to manageable pieces, not anymore. Not even for her mother. She would give her the truth, and if she didn't like it, so be it.

Merit lifted her chin. "I like my nights in the city—I enjoy the theater, some dancing, seeing my friends. But I also like being home. I miss playing games with Ellery and Kaiya, or sitting by the fire with a book. I just miss home."

Her mother picked up her evening wrap from the small table by the door. She draped it around her shoulders as she stared at the door, her eyes unseeing. "I hadn't really thought—" She shook her head. "We're so similar, sometimes, that I forget that we are also quite different."

"You think we're *similar*?" Merit was sure she hadn't heard the words right.

"Oh, yes," her mother said, the corners of her mouth twitching. "We both overanalyze everything, and we can be more stubborn than mules when we want something." Her smile faded. "I love Veritess. Always something to do. I forget that you need more quiet." She reached out and traced her fingers along Merit's hairline, tucking away a few stray tendrils. "Why don't we throw a house party out in the country? Invite Freddie, Cedric, and Latimer?"

"You—you would let me do that?" Merit was afraid to so much as breathe in case it ruined this fragile peace between them.

Lady Zarla's lips curved in a gentle arc. "Of course. It's a brilliant idea, actually. I can't believe I didn't think of it before. You'll get to really compare them, side by side, no distractions. I'll send out invitations tomorrow morning, and we'll be out in the country before you can blink."

"Thank you, Mother."

Lady Zarla straightened her wrap. "You're welcome, darling." She took a step to the door and then stopped, turning her head back to Merit. "I don't suppose we could leave your new friends here?"

Merit shook her head.

Lady Zarla sighed and left, mumbling about their home being overrun by peasants.

They didn't quite leave in a blink. Her mother was not a light packer, and things needed to be organized, invitations sent. They lost a full day to that but were on the train the next morning. Besides the suitors, Lady Zarla had invited Glendon and a few of her friends, and let Merit invite Willa and Diadora. Merit thought Lady Zarla was secretly hoping that one of the sisters would take a shine to Tevin and keep him out of the way. Merit didn't disabuse her of this notion, mostly because she wanted to see her friends.

The Cravan country house was a shining thing—white brick that occasionally sparkled in the light, and a gabled roof outlined in intricate silver woodwork in a curving pattern, with two tall towers jutting off to the sides. A large stable joined the house through a covered walkway. The grounds were immaculate, the colors of the flora pleasing—Tevin saw purple foxglove, pink and red rhododendrons, white lilacs, and some vibrantly orangey-red flowers that he couldn't identify. Though the colors were bright and striking, the planting had been done simply, to avoid taking attention from a fountain in the center of the grounds. The fountain was white marble and tiered— wyrms ringed the bottom, forming the base. The center was a column of water and hippocampi, swimming upward. At the top, the water crested and a phoenix, its wings spreading for flight, emerged from the waves.

Val let out a low whistle when they arrived. "That's something, isn't it?"

"Pick up your jaw, Val, or they're going to think we're hayseeds."

"I'm proud of who I am," Val said. "And see no reason to pretend otherwise."

Even though she likely wanted to put Tevin, Val, and Amaury out in the stables, Lady Zarla wouldn't have been able to explain why she put her guests in such accommodations, and had grudgingly agreed to give them a set of rooms in the east wing of the house. Exactly opposite Merit's rooms.

On the first night, Lady Zarla had planned a masquerade ball to welcome everyone to her home. The Cravans were thoughtful enough to provide masks for those who didn't have them just lying about at home. Considering the kind of lifestyle most of the fairyborn aristocracy led, it was quite possible that many of them had entire trunks full of costumes in their closets gathering dust.

Tevin got ready for the masquerade while being stared at by the unfortunate glass eyes of a large stuffed marar. The fur was a rich black, covered in darker rosettes. It looked like the kind of creature who could move soundlessly through the night. He was surprised to find it in the house, because he didn't think Merit would care for it, but had decided it was a family heirloom.

"I swear it follows me as I move," Tevin told Amaury as he checked his suit in the mirror. Black tie, naturally. The fact that they might be tired from their travels didn't seem to occur to Lady Zarla.

"Yes, and it's judging you." Amaury set a box down. "I asked the maid, and she said it's a local forest creature."

"A marar," Tevin said. "Merit and I saw one at the carnival."

"The carnival you went to without me, I might add." Amaury opened the box, pushing aside layers of tissue paper. "They're apparently named after the sound they make sometimes."

"Sometimes?"

"If you're lucky, you hear the sound. If you're not lucky, you hear nothing and you're dinner." Amaury finished sorting through the layers of paper and pulled something out.

"Is that my mask?"

"Yes, Merit apparently picked out ours especially." Amaury blinked at it and barked a laugh. Tevin couldn't honestly remember the last time he'd heard Amaury laugh, so he stopped what he was doing and looked at the mask.

"I'm beginning to really like your lady," Amaury said, his eyes gleaming.

"She's not my lady." Tevin picked up the mask. It covered most of his face, leaving only his bottom lip and chin free. Curved horns curled up over the top, the beastly face a twisted and angry grimace. It was a thing of fine craftsmanship, if not actually beautiful. "She made me a beast."

"She picked all our masks. I have no idea when she had the time. Naturally, I'm a fox."

Tevin sighed. "I suppose I should be grateful she didn't make me a snake."

"You'd make a poor snake." Amaury made for the door. "Also, I'd check on Val if I were you. She's usually dressed before me, but I haven't seen hide nor hair of her yet." He shut the door softly behind him, not waiting for Tevin's response.

Tevin stared at his mask for a moment, trying to decipher what Merit meant by it. Finally he gave up and went to look for his friend.

• • •

Tevin tapped a knuckle on Val's door, but didn't wait for her to answer before he walked in. He wished he had once he caught sight of Val. The jaunty tune he'd been whistling died abruptly. Val stood in front of a mirror, her hands on her hips as she stared at her reflection. She was wearing a sunshine-yellow dress with lace detailing around the hem, sleeves, and bodice. Her hair poufed oddly, like a small dog that had been struck by lightning. Repeatedly. Strips of pink stretched across each cheekbone as well as her lips, and someone had attempted to darken her eyelashes and eyebrows. The overall effect was one of perpetual surprise.

"What happened to you?"

Val scowled at him, and her hand went self-consciously to her skirt. "What?"

"You're wearing a gown."

"It's a ball."

"Yes, which is why I expected a suit, like you've worn to every other ball I've ever attended with you. You hate gowns."

"I don't. There are some good things about them."

"Let me rephrase: you hate gowns *on you*. Last time your mother wanted you to wear one, she had to bribe you with new tack for your oaf of a horse."

"People can change," Val said defensively. She twirled, eyeing the dress in the mirror. "Does it look that terrible?"

Tevin sighed and examined his friend carefully. It wasn't that the dress was terrible. Or at least wouldn't be terrible on someone three inches taller, ten pounds heavier, and with drastically different coloring than Val. But the combination of the dress, the hair, and the rather heavy-handed approach to lip paint and eyelash tint gave the overall appearance of terrible. Okay, if he was being honest, the dress was also ghastly. But he wasn't sure he could be honest with Val. He considered lying to her, since his usually confident friend had clearly lost all of her good sense.

He took her gently by the shoulders. "I think you should burn it and then sprinkle the ashes in a river. Maybe separate rivers." So much for lying to her.

Val collapsed onto her bed. "I don't know what I'm doing."

He squinted. "What, exactly, did you do to your hair?"

"I tried to curl it." She reached up and patted the top of her head. There was an audible crunch.

Tevin crouched down so that he was on eye level with his friend. "This? It isn't you, Val. What's going on?"

"Kaiya."

Tevin tipped her face up to his. "Kaiya snuck in here and did this to you? Was this revenge, Val? Did you do something to her? Something unforgivable?"

Val sniffed, blinking rapidly, a sure sign that she was trying not to cry. Val cried when she was frustrated. Tevin had been so wrapped up in his own mess that he hadn't been paying enough attention to Val's mess.

"I can't get her to *see* me, Tev. I've never had that problem before."

"Yes, well, when you're an adorably dashing yet rough-and-tumble fairyborn, debutantes do seem to fall in your lap."

"Right?" Val sniffed. "So why hasn't she?"

Tevin crossed his arms and leaned onto her knees. "Because Kaiya isn't a debutante. She's not a blushing barmaid swooning over your title. Not that there is anything wrong with any of those things, but Kaiya is a trained warrior. Her uncle is an ambassador. If you want to impress her, you're going to have to actually work for it. This isn't the way to do it."

"Are you sure?" Val ran her hands along the fabric. "I figured maybe she was more into this sort of thing?"

Tevin shook his head. "Val, you're wearing a hideous dress that you hate and makeup, which you also hate. It makes your skin itch. Trust me, this isn't a good gambit."

Val played with her cuff. "Kaiya's . . . She's—" Val let out a breath. "She's amazing, Tevin. Have you ever seen her practice her knife work?"

"I haven't, no."

"The way she moves," Val gushed. "I think I'd stand still and let her gut me, just to keep watching. She makes me want to be conquered."

"I think she's cracked your brain," Tevin said. "I'll get Ellery."

"I watched her training yesterday, and she's just as fast with her hatchets and crossbows—"

"Yes, nothing is sexier than a woman who could easily hack you into pieces."

"Right?" All the air went out of her then, her shoulders

272

slumping. Val was almost completely deflated by the time she flopped back on the bed. "She's the *best*."

"And this is bad because?"

"It's not. It's amazing."

"Your words say this is a good thing, but the rest of you is disagreeing," Tevin said.

"It means there's no way she'll be interested in me. I'm not even the floor beneath her boot. I'm the dirt under the floor beneath her boot. I aspire to be the floor." Val sighed.

"It will work out, Val. Have a little faith in your own ability."

"I've changed my mind. I'm not going tonight. I'm never leaving this room again."

"Val, you are the best person I know, despite . . . whatever is happening here," he said, waving at the dress. "I will help you, I promise. But please, as your friend, I'm begging you to wash your face and undo whatever horrible thing you've done to your hair."

Val didn't cry, but her eyes were bright. He grabbed her chin and tweaked it. "You've finally found someone as impressive as you. We just need to show her that. Come on." He stood, holding out a hand for Val and pulling her to her feet. In doing so, he caught a whiff of something *strongly* floral. "On second thought, perhaps a quick bath is in order? I'll stay here and rummage through your wardrobe. And Val? Leave the dress. I'm going to give it a proper funeral." He handed her a robe.

Val came back bathed and scrubbed and looking much more like her usual self. Tevin handed her a set of fitted cream trousers and a matching shirt. Over that, he layered a formfitting emerald waistcoat. The design around the edges was a mix of acorns, clovers, and other flora. Tevin had shined Val's dress shoes to a warm finish. He helped her into her formal dinner jacket—a matching cream—and tied her bow tie set in the same shade.

Val went to touch the waistcoat, and Tevin smacked her hand away. "Careful, it's silk."

"Where did you get this? It fits perfectly."

"Because it was made for you. I commissioned it for you when we had the tailor at Merit's. You simply never looked." He turned Val toward the mirror. "There. This is you. The color is good for your eyes and your hair. The cut flatters, but also moves easily, so you can showcase your form and grace."

Val looked at him in the mirror. "Do I need to use the lash tint? Or the perfume—"

Tevin squeezed her shoulders. "No. You don't need any of those things, and from what I've seen of Kaiya, she doesn't strike me as one impressed by such, anyway. You want to sway her? Be upfront—no game playing. Stop hiding your interest. Be *you*. That's what she'll find impressive. You are extremely competent. Don't underestimate how sexy that is." He handed her the mask Merit had picked out for her, the feathered likeness of a falcon. "If none of that works, she doesn't deserve you."

"Thanks, Tevin."

"You're welcome. Now let's go downstairs and never speak of that dress again."

• • •

The ballroom was lit by several chandeliers, the mage light a warm and steady glow. Tables were scattered around the sides, letting the dancers sit and eat when they chose to do so. Every-

274

thing appeared enchanting or possibly enchanted, depending on how you looked at it. Through a clever use of paper cutouts over mage lamps, shadows of branches and leaves, or sometimes whole trees, stood out against the walls. Small tables were set here and there along the edges, their tablecloths dark and sparkling, making the fabric seem like snatches of night sky. Single candles graced the tables next to bouquets of twigs and fresh flowers. The effect gave the dance floor the aura of a clearing or midnight glade where creatures frolicked.

Tevin saw all this from the doorway, as Val had stopped dead when she entered. Kaiya stood off to the side, speaking to several other fairyborn, including Glendon, Lady Zarla, and Latimer. Kaiya had veered away from her usual look, choosing a more Pieridaen-style gown of pure silver. The light material flowed around her like water, with no hint of lace or flouncing. She'd also left her hair down, a wall of jet falling straight and fine to the middle of her back.

Val actually sighed, and Tevin imagined that he could almost see tiny hearts floating above her head. Then she started to edge backward. "This was a mistake."

Tevin, being the kind and supportive friend that he was, gave Val a good, hard shove against her back so that she had no choice but to start walking toward the table. Sometimes love needed a gentle nudge, and sometimes it needed a boot to the behind.

It didn't take long for Tevin to find Merit. She was dancing with Cedric, who was still getting used to being an ostrich. He didn't have a mask, but he was wearing a bowler hat and a bow tie, and that was good enough, really. Merit was wearing the face of the beast, but as a mask, which rose several inches above her forehead and ended over the curve of her lips, leaving that fraction of her face free.

Without the guise of the beast, Merit appeared smaller, even with the full skirts of her dress. The tight bodice was a deep purple and had elaborate silver embroidery that caught the light, building and growing as the design followed the pouf of her skirts. Small white flowers were braided into her hair, which had been pinned to the crown of her head. She spun and smiled, and in that moment, Tevin wanted to give her anything that would make her happy. Which meant marriage, the sooner the better, so she didn't have to worry about her tincture. Didn't have to worry about losing herself to the beast.

"You think he knows he's out of the running?" Amaury asked, surprising him. He hadn't heard his brother approach.

"No," Tevin said. "I don't."

"It's down to Freddie and the prince now," Amaury said. "Poor Merit."

Though most of those not in dresses were in formal tuxes, Latimer had adjusted his to match his mask. His gold suit paired with a lion mask that covered his face. His hair was down, and it was difficult to tell where the mane of the mask ended and his own hair began. The suit did everything it could to accentuate Latimer's regal bearing and robust stature. Tevin also caught sight of the sisters, Wilhelmina and Diadora, dressed as a raven and an owl respectively.

"Did you see the necklace he gave Merit?" Val said, returning with two glasses of champagne.

"Yes." It had been a smart gift, too. Tevin hated it. "He's a paragon."

"I don't like him. He's smug," Amaury said, rolling his shoulders.

"They're all smug." Tevin downed his champagne. "If you've got something better, I'm listening."

Amaury crossed his arms, tapping his fingers along his biceps. "He smiles too much. How's that?"

"Amaury, that's hardly incriminating," Val said with a grin. "Besides, you don't like anyone."

Amaury clucked his tongue. "Hyperbole. I like at least four people. Possibly five." He used his finger to point and count. "Val, Kaiya. Ellery is growing on me, and Glendon." He held up his hand with a flourish. "See? Four whole people."

"I'm not on that list?" Tevin asked.

Amaury's eyes were sharp behind the fox mask. "Tevin, you're my brother. I love you more than air, but keep it to yourself. I have a reputation."

Tevin snorted. "Of course."

Amaury carefully touched his shoulder. "You're my *brother*. We're monsters, but we don't eat our own." His head tilted to the side. "We may not always like what we've become, but I would slaughter every single person in this ballroom if they hurt you or Kate."

Val squeaked indignantly.

"Or Val," Amaury amended. "Because if I don't add her, she'll use me for target practice."

"What about Lady Zarla?" Val asked.

He held his hand out, waffling it back and forth. "This close to shipping her off to Tirada."

"Thank you," Tevin said. "For everything."

"Oh, I'm not doing it for you. Merit happens to be one of the people I'm fond of, which brings the total number to five. Aren't I the belle of the ball? Five whole people." He slapped Tevin on the back. "Now, go dance and keep an eye on the King of the Savannah over there, and I'll do what I do best, shall I?"

Val squinted at Amaury. "What are you going to do?"

"What I always do at a ball. Go through other people's things." With that, Amaury disappeared into the shadows, leaving Tevin confused and a little overwhelmed, but feeling better than he had all evening.

After a few minutes, Tevin caught sight of Kaiya, now wearing a marar mask, dancing with Glendon. Merit was still dancing with Cedric. As he watched, the song ended, and Merit curtseyed to the ostrich, who handed her off to a fairy lord in a rabbit mask. Tevin couldn't place him.

"It's Freddie." Val used one hand to adjust one of the falcon's feathers away from her mouth. "I saw him at the drinks table a moment ago."

Merit smiled at the man in the rabbit mask as he reached for her hand. Tevin took a glass of champagne from Val and watched the dance. Even from here, Tevin could tell that Freddie was doing his best to charm Merit. He managed to make her laugh a few times, and she spent most of the dance smiling. Once the dance was finished, Latimer stepped up, handing his drink to Freddie and whisking Merit away. Freddie seemed surprised to have his prize stolen so quickly and efficiently. In the end he shrugged and drank Latimer's champagne.

Tevin didn't even get close to Merit for the first hour. Instead he had to watch both Freddie and Latimer dance with her again, along with a handful of other people, all while feverishly reminding himself that this was a good thing. Besides their friends from Veritess, the baroness had invited local acquaintances as well, and either they were all very friendly or Lady Zarla was specifically sending people to him to keep him occupied and away from Merit. He finally had to excuse himself on the pretense that he needed to visit the privy, before ducking behind Glendon and circling around the ballroom so he could grab Merit's wrist and sneak her out onto the veranda and into the shadows of the garden.

"Tevin, slow down." Merit yanked her arm back, not hard enough to break his grip, but enough to make him stop. "Why are you dragging me out into the gardens?"

"It was the only way to get a moment with you," Tevin said.

She tilted her head, her mask sliding slightly to the side. "What's wrong?"

"Nothing's wrong, I just—" Tevin was suddenly irritated by the fact that he couldn't see her face. He reached behind her and undid the ribbons. "I hate talking to people when I can't see them."

She spun her finger in a circle, telling him he needed to turn around. "Is that because they're harder to read?" She untied the ribbons of his mask, and he grabbed it, setting both masks on a bench.

"Yes."

"And you need to read me?"

No, he simply wanted to see her, but he couldn't say that. Instead he cupped her face and held it up to the moonlight. Faint bruises purpled the skin beneath her eyes, which looked feverishly bright. "Merit, how much tincture have you had today?"

"Two doses," Merit admitted. "With a third in my pocket."

"Merit—"

She jerked her chin out of his hands. "My mother did a lot to bring this together. For me, Tevin. She made an effort because I wanted to go home. I don't want to disappoint her."

"So you'll put yourself in danger?"

"Did you bring me out here so you could lecture me?" Merit crossed her arms over her chest. "If so, you can skip it. It was my choice to double up on the tincture. She didn't ask."

"Then why—"

"My time is running out." She fingered the silver locket around her neck absently. "And seeing Cedric the other night." She clasped the locket in her fist. "I ate a live chicken, Tevin. Do you know what it's like, waking up and not remembering something like *that*?"

"It scared you."

Her eyes were wide when they met his. "I can't stay a beast forever, Tevin. I just can't."

He nodded, the lump in his throat hard to swallow around.

"I need to choose, while I still have time." She placed a hand on his chest. "And I can't do that out here with you."

"I know," he said, telling himself to step away. To take her arm and lead her back into the ballroom. It was the smart thing to do. The *right* thing. Instead he pulled her into his arms, cursing himself even as he did. She wrapped her arms around his waist and set her head on his chest. "I'll take you back in. I promise. One song. Can we have one song?"

She nodded against his chest, and they swayed to the music that floated out into the night air around them. They didn't waltz. The dance had no name as far as Tevin knew. He didn't want anything fancy. Dancing was an excuse to hold her close, to breathe her in. To feel the heat of her against him, her small hands fisted into the cloth at the small of his back. Neither of them admitting, even to themselves, that they wanted something they couldn't have.

When the song ended, Tevin stepped back and helped her put her mask on, but stayed in the garden when she returned to the ballroom. After a moment, he would go in. He wasn't sure he could watch. But he had to stay, in case she needed him.

He sat down on the steps, setting his mask beside him, and buried his face in his hands.

Val sat down next to him, handing him a glass of punch. "Thought you might need this."

"You are my best friend," Tevin said, raising the cup to his lips.

"I know," she said. "What are you going to do?"

"I'm going to finish this punch."

"After that?"

"We'll do what we're here to do. Get Merit married." He needed to remember why he was here—what his goal was—and to refocus on that. "Then go back to where we belong."

"I'm not completely sure where that is," Val said. "The magical place where we belong."

"Me, either."

Val leaned against him, resting her head on his shoulder. "I wish we could stay."

"Me too." Tevin put his arm around her and wondered why he could never seem to stop reaching for the things he couldn't have.

CHAPTER 21

SHE'S VERY PRACTICAL

Merit slept fitfully. The dance had gone on for hours, and she'd taken another dose of bloom. It had been a bad idea, but for once, Merit had fun at a social event. She'd had so many dance partners, and having someone as handsome as Latimer hanging on her every word . . . She just couldn't go back to the beast. She knew none of them really wanted *her*, but it had felt so nice to be desired that for a short time, she chose not to care.

When she'd woken up this morning, she'd been on the floor. At some point during the night, she'd ripped off the sheets and coverlet, torn down the draperies, and made a nest in the corner of the room. The nest had been lined with feathers that must have come from her down pillows. She didn't remember doing any of it.

After several minutes of fighting off a clawing sense of panic, her throat loosened and she was able to draw calming breaths. Early-morning sun hit her windows with a gilding of wan gray light. The maid would come soon to draw the draperies and bring Merit a cup of tea, because for some reason last night she'd promised Freddie to get up early and go for a

283

ride. She wouldn't be able to set the room fully to rights. The pillows wouldn't restuff themselves, and she didn't have the tools to mend the window hangings. She extended her hands, grimacing at her claws. Even if she had a needle and thread, she couldn't hold the wretched things. A sense of hopelessness washed over her. What good was her title, her bloodline, any of it, if she couldn't do something a child could do?

Merit didn't have time to wallow. She carefully folded the drapes, accidentally clawing a new hole in the process. There was nothing she could do about the pillows. As she tried to scoop up some of the feathers, she found claw marks on the floor. Embarrassment snaked through her. These weren't the rooms of a fairyborn heir. These were the rooms of an animal. Her eyes stung as she squared her shoulders. This was the best she could do. Messy and damaged, but at least the nest was gone, making it look less like a creature's den.

She wrapped herself in a dressing gown and rang for the maid to fetch Ellery.

• • •

Ellery arrived looking immaculate and neat, like they'd been up for hours.

"I hate how well rested you look," Merit grumbled.

"Upside of not dancing the night away," Ellery said. "Instead I haunted your billiard room for a few hours." They considered the room and Merit, taking it all in but not saying anything. "Made a few coins, and then retired early like the sensible spriggan that I am. How are you feeling?"

"Lousy," Merit grumbled.

Ellery nodded as if this was to be expected. The healer dug around in their bag and pulled out a paper envelope. There was a knock on the door, the maid arriving with the tea at last. Ellery took the heavy tray, which included toast, tea, coffee, a pitcher of water, and a glass, from the maid before shooing her away. Ellery set the tray down on a small table in front of Merit before handing her the packet of powder. "Take all of this. I suggest following it up with a large glass of water. It will taste wretched, but you'll feel better."

"What is it?" Merit said, tipping the envelope into her mouth. Ellery was right. It tasted like licking a dirty metal bowl.

"Spriggan hangover cure." They handed Merit her tea before taking a seat by the small table. "You could cancel, you know. Stay in bed."

"I could do that," Merit said. "Or I could take another dose of tincture and go ride a horse like a normal person."

Ellery poured a dollop of cream into their coffee, stirring the liquid slowly. "That's a lot of tincture in a short time." They set their spoon carefully onto the saucer, so it didn't rattle. "You're playing with fire, Merit. You keep pushing, and the curse will push back."

"Are you telling me no?"

Ellery took a sip of coffee, their eyebrows raised. "Would that stop you?"

"No." Merit selected a piece of toast carefully with her claws.

"Then I will tell you to be careful and hope that you call for me when you need it."

• • •

Despite Ellery's misgivings, Merit had taken the dose of bloom and had another in her pocket just in case. The air had a cold snap to it, the sun hiding behind cloud cover that Merit was sure would burn off. The stable yard bustled with riders, horses, and stable lads getting everything ready.

The ride that was supposed to be her and Freddie had escalated into a group event. Latimer, Freddie, Tevin, Val, Willa, and Kaiya were there, along with Glendon, who was hoping that his presence would civilize the expedition.

Kaiya adjusted her stirrups. "So much for a quiet ride."

"It will be fine, I'm sure," Merit said, fixing one of the pins in her hair.

"I'm just coming along to keep you all alive," Kaiya said, swinging into her saddle. "And to keep any of your exalted guests from riding into the Enchanted Forest."

"The Enchanted Forest?" Merit frowned. "Why would any of them do that?"

Kaiya looked over at Freddie climbing into his saddle. His foot kept missing the stirrup, and Merit wondered if he was still drunk from last night.

Kaiya settled into her saddle and grabbed the reins. "You know how during the rutting season rams slam their heads into each other and you think, *Wow, that's really stupid, why would any creature voluntarily batter its brain*?"

"Yes?"

"You have a riding party full of rams, Merit." Kaiya glanced over at her. "You look very pretty today. Blue is a good color on you."

Merit wore a deep blue velvet riding suit. She didn't wear trousers very often—difficult with a tail—but she hated riding in a skirt. She wasn't comfortable sidesaddle or bareback, and the saddle had a curve to it that pinched if she didn't sit just right. It was a relief to ride comfortably as herself.

The rest of their party was equally turned out. Latimer looked very dashing on his white charger, Prince. Tevin was off to the side holding the reins of his bay and talking to Val. Freddie swayed like he was going to fall off his horse, but he would do so stylishly.

Glendon brought his horse forward, a tall black thoroughbred. The Hanian ambassador looked like he was born in the saddle, much like his niece. "I'm glad I'm coming with you. Between the lot of us, I'm sure we can keep the bloodshed to a minimum."

She looked out over the stable yard. Everyone seemed ready now. People were now mounted, their tack jangling as the horses moved in anticipation. Merit nudged her heels into her horse's side, urging her forward. The mare danced to the right, sensing Merit's excitement. She couldn't wait to get out onto the trail.

• • •

They left the house behind, cutting through the fields and down to the river. Lady Zarla had sent one of the grooms ahead with a picnic basket so they could enjoy lunch on the riverbank. After an hour, the cloud cover was already burning off, the sun starting to patch through. They'd been mostly riding slowly, half of their party feeling a trifle delicate from the night before. Merit rode with Willa and Freddie on one side and Latimer on the other. Kaiya and Glendon rode ahead of them, while Tevin and Val brought up the rear. They lagged behind far enough that Merit couldn't hear them talking.

"Fine day for it." Freddie grinned as he surveyed the countryside. "Nothing quite like being in nature. Good for the spirit!" He sipped from his flask. When Merit raised an eyebrow, he held up a hand in supplication. "It's tea, I promise."

Freddie straightened in his saddle, putting the flask away. Now that he was out riding, he perked up, looking more alive than he had earlier. Though he didn't seem much taken with nature walks, Freddie was clearly happy on horseback.

"We could do this all the time, you know," Freddie said, sweeping his arm out. "After the wedding."

Next to Merit, Latimer twitched.

"The wedding?" Willa said, her eyebrows raised in question.

Freddie shrugged. "She could do worse, right?"

"That's quite a proposal, Freddie," Willa said with a laugh.

He squinted at her. "Merit doesn't need me getting down on one knee and all that rubbish." He sniffed. "Always seemed the practical sort."

"All the dancing lords, Freddie," Willa said, her words coming out on a groan. "Here I thought romance was dead, but you're currently beating the corpse just to make sure."

"What?" Freddie asked, genuinely surprised.

"It's all right," Merit said with a forced laugh. Romance, after all, was for a certain kind of people. Charming, gorgeous creatures who called love to themselves like an errant falcon. Even before she was a beast, that wasn't her.

"Is it?" Latimer murmured, soft enough so that only she could hear.

"I didn't think Merit would want that kind of frippery," Freddie argued, exasperated. "Flowers, chocolates, and all that rot. She's sensible."

Be still my beating heart, Merit thought. *I'm sensible.*

Willa groaned again. "You're killing me, Freddie. Talk about damning with faint praise."

"I was being complimentary." Freddie continued to be perplexed. His face brought to mind a puppy being scolded for piddling on the new rug.

Willa leaned over her saddle, her bob swinging with the movement of the horse. "She's not a hunting dog. Have a little charm." She jerked a thumb back over her shoulder. "You think the fellow in the back is calling her sensible? Bet he's been writing her sonnets. All you can manage is a dirty limerick." She jerked her chin at Latimer. "I bet even golden boy has pulled a little game out of his sleeve."

Freddie was surprised now, glancing back at Tevin and then to Willa. "DuMont? But he's *human.* Surely she'd pick me over *him.* I may not be first in line for the barony, but at least I'm in line."

Willa laughed. "Of course, my lord, wouldn't want to forget that. After all, no lady's head would *ever* be turned by a handsome, smooth-talking lad with pockets full of money. No, she'll definitely think of pedigree first."

289

Freddie spluttered. "She wouldn't pick him." Then he looked at Merit, suddenly unsure. "Would you?"

"Oh, did you remember that I was here? Shall I take part in the conversation you've been having about me?" Merit's tone was breezy, meant to only partially take the sting from her words. "How lovely to be able to discuss my own proposal."

"Don't be like that," Freddie said, his voice cajoling.

"Fine. Of course I'll consider your quasiproposal, Freddie. I am, after all, *sensible*." She stretched the word out, her eyes half-lidded.

"That's a compliment!" Freddie's cheeks reddened when Willa snickered.

"It *is* a compliment," Merit conceded. "And one I appreciate, but it's not what one usually leads with in a proposal, and it makes the lady think you're not mentioning her other charms because they are lacking." Her tone was gentle now. Freddie hadn't meant any harm, so she was hoping he'd listen and not make the same mistake in the future. "I like being sensible, but that doesn't mean I'm not vain enough to want to hear *some* frippery."

When Freddie looked confused, Latimer sighed. "It's like this, Freddie." He turned to Merit. "That's a fine outfit, Merit. The color brings out your eyes."

"Why, thank you, Latimer," Merit said, playing along. "It's new."

Freddie still looked confused. "But Merit knows I don't think of her like that. We're pals."

Willa looked skyward, either begging for patience or for lightning to strike her down. "Yes, Freddie, we know. Doesn't mean she doesn't want to hear nice things anyway."

"I just don't see the point," Freddie grumbled.

Willa turned in her saddle. "Hey! DuMont! Ride up, will you?" She turned back around. "Watch. Bet you he can have her blushing in under a minute." When Freddie started to splutter a rebuttal and Latimer looked irritated, Willa just shook her head. "Just watch and try to learn something."

Tevin pulled his horse up to them, his expression calm, though Merit caught a wary glint in his eyes. "Yes?"

Willa leaned back in her saddle and waved a hand at Merit. "Latimer here was complimenting Merit on her choice of outfit. Brings out her eyes, don't you think?"

Freddie stared hard at Merit's eyes, jumping in before Tevin could respond. "They're a normal shade of brown. Nothing spectacular. Pedestrian, really. They're just eyes. No offense, Merit."

She shrugged.

Tevin tilted his head, looking at her as if he'd never really thought about her eyes before. "I see. Yes, rather pedestrian."

Merit couldn't help it. Her heart sank, and she had to tighten her jaw to not lash out.

"Of course, there can be beauty in ordinary things," Tevin said slowly. "Her eyes might bring to mind the richness of soil after a good rain, when the world feels new and filled with promise. Or they could remind you of the sweetness of choco-late, and that moment of undeniable decadence when it first hits your tongue." Tevin tilted his head the other way. "It's pos-sible you could say that the shade and sharp intelligence in her eyes invokes the majestic eagle as it spreads its wings, owning everything in its shadow."

The entire group was quiet now, hanging on Tevin's every word. Merit's throat tightened, and she could feel her skin flushing, but she couldn't look away from Tevin. *He's playing a part. He has to say these over-the-top things to get the others to admire me.* Her heart wouldn't listen to logic. No, her heart couldn't even hear her whispers over its own shouts for more.

"Yes, you might say any of that and more," Tevin said, finally looking away from Merit. "Or you could say pedestrian. I rather think it depends on who's doing the viewing and the speaking." He tipped his bowler hat. "Gentlemen. Ladies." Then he turned his horse and went back to riding next to Val.

Willa looked at Merit and cackled, smacking the side of her leg. "Now, that is how you do it, Freddie."

"But he didn't even really say anything. He just said 'might' and 'possibly.'" Freddie looked between Tevin and Merit before throwing up his hands in surrender. "I will never understand women. I give up."

Willa looked skyward again. "You're useless, Freddie."

Freddie sighed. "My proposal stands, Merit."

"I'll take it under consideration." Merit smiled at him to show that there were no hard feelings. Outwardly, she looked carefree, but inside, her mind spun about. Had Tevin made up those things to flatter, to charm, or did he actually mean them? Was this his way of nudging her suitors along—and her—to get her married sooner, or was it something more? And did it matter? After all, marrying Latimer or Freddie was meant to break her curse. Anything else was a gamble, and she wasn't sure she could toss any more dice with her future.

CHAPTER 22

DANGER PICNIC

They got to the river just before noon. Their pace had been lazy on the way, no one feeling in a particular rush to get there until the end, when everyone started to get hungry. The trail had curved along the side of a hill, spitting them out into a naturally flat area next to the water. The grass was rich with clover, coaxing several fat and fuzzy bees to swagger drunkenly through the warm air. Light sparkled off the river, a deep, inviting blue.

Merit laughed at something Willa said, her eyes lighting up.

Tevin hadn't been jesting earlier. He liked Merit's eyes. They were warm and rich in color, but it was her sharp intelligence that drew him in. Only a fool would disregard them as Freddie had done. And yet there was a very real possibility that fool was going to get to look into them every day for the rest of his life. Unless she chose Latimer, and that appeared more likely with each second.

Tevin slid off his horse, handing the reins to a waiting groom. Two quilts had been spread on the ground, each with a basket just waiting to be unpacked. Tevin took off his jacket, giving in to the heat of the day. Merit slid her arm into his, pulling him close.

"You're right, competition helps. Latimer has been by my side since you said the eye thing, and I'm feeling very doted upon. I find I like it."

"You deserve a little doting."

She grinned at him before letting go and running over to join Willa on one of the blankets. Tevin watched her go.

"Be careful, Tevin," Val said, her voice soft. "You're *playing* suitor, remember?" She adjusted her hat, as if she were waiting for him to argue. "I don't want you to get hurt."

Tevin smiled and grabbed the edge of Val's hat, yanking down the flat rim. "Ah, you love me."

"I've changed my mind," Val said. "I hope she strings you up like a deer."

• • •

After lunch, Tevin stretched out in the grass with Val, enjoying the sun. Soon they would saddle up and head back to the house, but right now everyone was taking advantage of the fine weather. There was a shout from down by the river, and Tevin looked up to see Latimer running along the bank, chasing after something thrashing in the water. Tevin cursed when he realized Freddie had fallen in. The river, while looking gentle and idyllic, moved at a deceptive pace, and either Freddie was panicked and not thinking or couldn't swim well. Latimer was taking a few precious seconds to remove his boots, which was smart, but Freddie was getting farther away.

"There's no way Latimer will catch him." Val levered herself up next to him, scrambling to her feet.

"Get your horse." Tevin yanked off his own boots, glad he wore ones suited for riding that slid off easily.

Val bolted to where the horses were tethered, shouting at the groom to untie her mount. She practically vaulted into the saddle before swinging the equine around with practiced ease. Tevin may tease her a lot about being country, but Val's family herded cattle. She could ride better than anyone he knew. She leaned low over the horse's neck, hooves pounding as they aimed right for Tevin. When she got close, she didn't slow but leaned down, catching his arm along the elbow, helping him swing up. It was a move they'd practiced before, but Tevin was still surprised when he landed heavily in the saddle behind his cousin.

They aimed for a spot downriver from Freddie, careening through the grassy hillside toward the water. When they got close enough, Val pulled back on the reins, causing the horse to skid to a stop. Tevin slid off, ran to the edge of the river, and dove in.

The chill of the water bit at his skin as Tevin kicked up from the river bottom. He broke the surface, paddling around until he could see Freddie hurtling toward him. Freddie screamed for help, sucking in a mouthful of water for his trouble. Tevin knifed through the water toward him, grabbing the neck of his jacket and dragging him close. Freddie, still panicked, was flapping his arms around, hitting Tevin so hard in the face he almost lost his grip.

"Cut that out," Tevin said, spluttering out his own mouthful of water. "You'll drown us both." The fight went out of him—

unfortunately, all of it went. The fairyborn became a limp weight as Tevin tried to drag him closer to shore. It was tough going, fighting the current of the water and the pull of Freddie in his arms.

Tevin heard a sharp whistle and looked up, seeing Val. A groom had brought her a length of rope while Tevin had been swimming. She knotted a loop at the end, swung it, and tossed it out over the river. It fell short, the current taking it away before Tevin could get close enough. Val pulled it back and tried again and again, moving her horse farther down the river with each toss. By the fifth attempt, Tevin was able to grab the rope. Val nudged her horse, and the beast leapt forward to help drag Tevin and Freddie out of the water. A few seconds later, they were pulled ashore. Tevin flopped exhausted onto his back, doing his best impression of a landed fish.

Glendon grasped Freddie, pulling him farther onto the grass before turning him over and smacking his back. Freddie vomited up several mouthfuls of water, then lay shivering in the grass as Glendon took off his own jacket and covered Freddie with it.

Val walked her horse over, leaning so she could see Tevin. "You okay?"

"Perfect." Tevin closed his eyes.

• • •

The ride home was a lot less fun than the ride out. Freddie rode behind Glendon, stuck to his back like a limpet and wrapped in one of the picnic quilts. Tevin was able to ride, but Val had to stay close to him for the last mile. Exhaustion seeped in, making him sway in the saddle, his eyes drooping closed. He couldn't stop shivering, despite the heat of the day.

Kaiya had galloped ahead, making sure Ellery was ready with supplies to greet them with when they arrived. Tevin was unceremoniously pushed by Val to his room and immediately cosseted into a hot bath. He didn't see Ellery until after they had taken care of Freddie, since he was by far the worst off.

By then Tevin was bundled up in a robe and blankets by the fire, drinking hot tea, but somehow still shivering. Someone knocked at the door.

"Enter." Tevin had to say it twice, his voice little more than a croak.

Ellery came in, bustling over to check his temperature, listen to his lungs, and make a general nuisance of themself. "Hear you're a bit of a hero."

Tevin pulled the blankets tighter around himself. "No. Probably would have drowned without Val."

"Oh, if you don't think your cousin isn't milking this for everything she's got, you're sorely mistaken. When I left, the staff was filling her with tea and cookies while she told them the story for the third time."

"Great, she'll be all sugared up. They'll regret that."

The healer grunted, putting all of their things back into the bag. "Well, I think you'll be fine. I suggest you finish your tea and go to bed."

"I want to argue," Tevin said, "but I don't think I have the energy."

"Good," Ellery said, holding out a hand. "Then I'll tuck you in and rest assured that for once a patient is doing exactly what I asked of them. How novel."

• • •

Merit, in all her beastly glory, was in a parlor with Cedric, telling him everything that had happened while waiting for Ellery to finish with Tevin. "How are you feeling?" Merit asked. She would say he smiled at her, but an ostrich couldn't smile. Still, it felt like he did.

"Better now with such delicate beauty to look upon. Thank you for inviting me, Merit. My parents were so distressed, and if I'd stayed home, they would have fussed over me. How are you?" The effect of his fine words was spoiled a little by the rasping hiss of his voice caused by his ostrich body. "The shock of this morning must be overwhelming. Poor Freddie." He bobbed his head. "And your friend, of course. You don't need to sit with me, good lady. You should be resting. Feminine nerves can't take so much strain."

"My nerves are fine, Cedric." Though she was used to his ways by now, she spoke firmly. Cedric had once compared her eyes to limpet pools. It was supposed to be "limpid pools," but she never corrected him, because frankly she liked the imagery of her eyes as aquatic snails. Cedric meant well; he just wasn't very attentive to the world around him.

The problem was that it never occurred to Cedric to actually tailor what he was saying to the person he was talking to. Merit was not a delicate beauty. More than once, her mother had referred to her as "sturdy," which she always kind of liked. Her shoulders could take weight. Her body could work. She wasn't fragile, and she wouldn't break, whatever Cedric thought of her nerves. But her eyes were neither limpid *or* limpet pools. Vague flattery was almost as bad as specific insults.

The brisk clip of footfalls on hardwood announced Ellery's arrival. "Cedric, would you excuse us?" Ellery's gaze cut to Merit. "Maybe see if someone will bring in a plate of cookies?"

Cedric's head bobbed. "I can see. I can't carry them, but—" Cedric's neck inflated, and he gave off this strange, muffled *rrrmm* noise.

"It's okay, Cedric." Merit patted his shoulder again, trying to comfort him. "Someone will do it for you."

After he left, Ellery took Merit's hand, careful of her claws. "They'll be fine as long as both of them rest. There's a small chance Freddie could get a fever or an infection in his lungs, but I'll keep a close eye on him." Ellery squeezed her hand. "How are you feeling?"

"I'm fine."

"I saw the nest this morning, Merit. You didn't get me or Kaiya to lock your door." Ellery's gaze was steady and sympathetic, but their words were no-nonsense. "These spells will become more frequent and last longer. The sooner you can get married and break the curse, the better." Ellery gave her hand another squeeze before letting go. "I'm so sorry, Merit, but your time is up."

"I'm going to have to choose." Merit took in a steadying breath.

Ellery took off their glasses, using a handkerchief to buff the lenses. "If there were anything I could do, I would do it. May Godling Verity's wings fall off and her legs go gouty."

As Merit let the devastating but not unexpected news go through her, she realized that a part of her had still hoped that somehow, someone would magically show up and just . . . love her. But no one was coming, and Merit would have to make the best of things. "Thanks, Ellery."

"Do you want me to go see about that plate of cookies?" Ellery asked gently.

"Yes, please."

Ellery hugged her before leaving, giving Merit what comfort they could. As soon as the door clicked shut, Merit put her head in her arms and wept.

• • •

After Merit ate an entire tray of cookies—and convinced Ellery that she might as well take her tincture because what did it matter now?—she went in search of Latimer. She found him in the stables, checking on his horse. Merit watched him for a moment as he brushed the animal, looking more casual than she'd ever seen him. His jacket was draped over the stall door, and his shirtsleeves were rolled up. He looked the picture of contentment as he currycombed Prince's coat with long strokes.

"He's a beautiful horse." Merit brushed her fingers along the velvet of his nose, letting the horse lip her fingers as he searched for a treat.

Latimer looked up at her, pausing in his motions. "Lady Merit. How are your friends? Are they well?"

She told him what Ellery had said, trying to ignore her own worry about their recovery.

"I see," Latimer said, his face serious. "I hope they mend quickly, then." Prince, unhappy with the loss of attention, nudged Latimer in the chest with his nose. Latimer chuckled, gently shoving the horse's head back in place before he resumed combing. "Sorry, he's a demanding one."

"You seem very fond of him."

Latimer put the comb away and scratched at Prince's ears. "I am. People come and go, but Prince is always there for me."

Merit considered that a moment, thinking how the comment was both unbearably sweet and kind of sad at the same time.

He pulled an apple out of his pocket as well as a pocketknife and sliced off a piece for the horse, holding it up for Prince to gently lip out of his hand. "Have you thought about my proposal at all?"

"I have." Merit stepped forward, holding out her hand. "May I feed him?"

Her grinned, looking boyishly sweet as he sliced off a piece for her. Merit fed it to Prince, enjoying the nuzzle of the horse's mouth on the flat of her palm. This was a new side to Latimer, one she'd never seen before, and one she rather liked. It made her feel better about her choice.

"Did Freddie say what happened today? How he ended up in the water?" Latimer asked, slicing another piece of apple for her.

"I don't know," Merit admitted, feeding Prince the slice of fruit. "I haven't had a chance to talk to him or Tevin yet. Only Ellery."

Latimer's brow furrowed. "It just seems odd." He fed the rest of the apple to Prince before wiping his blade clean and folding it away. "Freddie doesn't seem that careless."

"He could have slipped," Merit said. "He was hungover. Unless he lied and his flask wasn't full of tea at all, in which case he could have still been drunk."

"You should ask your friend Tevin. I'm fairly sure I saw him with the flask at one point." He opened his mouth to say something, but stopped, shaking his head.

Merit leaned in, putting a hand on his chest. "What is it?"

Still, Latimer hesitated. "He's your friend, and I don't wish to speak ill of him."

"Please." Merit licked her lips, realizing suddenly how close she stood to Latimer, the scent of horse and hay thick but pleasant. She didn't move away. "I need to know."

Latimer covered her hand with his, holding it on his chest. "You don't think he did anything, do you? To the flask? To get Freddie out of the way and keep you for himself?"

"Of course not." The denial was off her lips in an instant.

"Your title, to a man like him, would be quite a draw."

Merit didn't want to consider it. Tevin wouldn't do that, surely. But then, wasn't that what Tevin did? Charmed and conned people? What did she really know about him? She had no *proof* beyond her own gut that he'd been honest with her. He could have easily been playing along with her game, sabotaging it as he went. Doubt wormed through her, and she hated it.

"It doesn't matter," she said, gazing up at Latimer. "Not really."

"You've decided, then?" He pressed her hand gently, the other finding its way to her waist.

She hesitated. Once she accepted, that was it. She enjoyed several things about Latimer, but . . . there could be no arguments, really, because at the end of the day, she had to marry, and she had to marry a man of her mother's choosing, and he was it. She let out a breath. "I'm sorry, the whole thing just makes me nervous. I thought I was prepared, but it's still overwhelming."

Latimer pulled the hand off his chest and kissed her knuckles before threading his fingers through hers. "Yes, it is, but I have no doubt that we can handle the terrors of marriage together."

Merit managed a small laugh. Yes, Latimer could be pompous and a bit of a showoff, but he could be funny, too. The way he treated Prince showed that he could also be kind.

He brushed a lock of her hair behind her ear. "That's better." With a sheepish grin, he cleared his throat and pulled her a little closer. "I suppose I should do this right. Merit Cravan, heir to the barony of Cravan, will you do me the honor of being my bride?"

Merit didn't think—if she thought too much, she knew she wouldn't be able to go through with it. "Yes, Eric Latimer, heir to the kingdom of Huldre, I will do you such an honor."

His cheeks curved as he smiled, his eyes alight. He was so happy that Merit couldn't help feeling a little happy, too. It was over and done with—she had chosen a husband, and now only the details were left to sort out. She pulled his happiness to her, wrapping it around her like a blanket. Latimer's smile dimmed a fraction, his hand moving to cradle her face. The one on her hip pulled her closer as Latimer dipped his head and stole a kiss. She kissed him back because she knew she should, and when he finally broke it and leaned back, she wondered if he was as disappointed with it as she was.

CHAPTER 23

NO ONE GETS ANY CAKE

Merit wanted to let the betrothal roll over her like an out of control carriage—the damage done before she even knew it was happening. What Merit needed to do was tell Tevin and her mother, further sealing her fate. Latimer, thankfully, promised not to make any announcements until after she'd told them. Wanting to get the hardest part over first, she decided to start with Tevin. She had to wait. He didn't come to dinner, and there was no answer when she knocked on his door, so she assumed he was asleep. Freddie was, too. Ellery said it was understandable, considering what they'd both gone through.

She visited Freddie first thing in the morning. He was in a fine mood, propped up on pillows and eating breakfast from a wooden tray. His nearly empty plate showed that his appetite was unaffected, and Merit said so.

"I slept over twelve hours and woke up famished." He scooped a piece of egg onto his fork. "Nearly drowning does that to a fellow, I suppose. No fever so far. Your healer said if I rest today and my lungs sound good, I can get up for a little while this afternoon."

"That's wonderful," Merit said, opening up another window to let fresh air into the room before taking a seat. "Freddie, do you know what happened yesterday? How you ended up in the river?"

"No," Freddie said, using the last of his toast to mop up the eggs. "I remember getting dizzy. Then I was in the water." He shrugged. "Serves me right for going for a ride the morning after a party." He dabbed at his mouth with a napkin. "I owe your friends a thank-you. Not sure I would have made it out without them." He set his napkin on the tray. "Perhaps I'll send them a ham. Everyone likes ham."

Everyone did not like ham, but Merit kept that to herself. It was the gesture that mattered, and Freddie would probably forget anyway.

Freddie flopped back into his pillows. "You decided about this whole marriage business yet?"

Merit hesitated. She had wanted to tell Tevin first, but then she supposed Freddie deserved to know, too. "Yes. I accepted Latimer. Though I suppose I should call him Eric now. I'm sorry, Freddie. Are you mad?"

Freddie shrugged. "I'm disappointed. Figured we'd have an easy go of it." He took her hand and kissed it. "But no, I'm not mad. We're friends, Merit. Just make sure you invite me to the wedding. I do enjoy a good party."

• • •

Merit stayed a little while longer, keeping Freddie company before forcing herself to go find Tevin. He wasn't in his room. She found him sitting in the gardens with Amaury and Diadora, and since she didn't exactly want an audience for this, she tried to think of a good excuse to take him away. It ended up not being necessary. Amaury saw her walking up and told Tevin, shooing his brother away, so in the end Merit just had to lead him to a quiet space to talk.

Merit ushered him into one of the drawing rooms. Everything was already set up for afternoon tea. Cups and saucers of delicate porcelain were placed at each setting, along with trays of pastries, delicate cakes, sandwiches, and savory pies.

Tevin reached out and stole a chocolate-covered strawberry.

"Those are for later," she said automatically.

"I won't tell if you won't." He took a bite of the strawberry, his green eyes lit up with mischief. Merit felt a blush spread over her cheeks. He looked—well, he looked unbearably handsome. This wouldn't do.

"Latimer asked me to marry him. I said yes."

The light in his eyes died.

"He's my best option. My mother will be thrilled, my queen will be pleased. Everyone wins."

Tevin set the half-eaten strawberry on the table, the red berry staining the white tablecloth. He stared at it, the muscle ticking in his jaw.

"I'm succumbing to my curse, Tevin. I don't have time to be picky anymore." She was babbling. Merit threw her hands up. "Will you say something?"

"Are you happy?"

"Say something else." Because she wasn't sure how to answer that.

"What do you want me to say, Merit?" When he looked up,

his face was a complete mask. "Should I say sorry? Sorry we didn't find someone more worthy of you?"

"Worthy of me? Latimer is a handsome prince from a wealthy family."

"You don't need coin, and you already told me you don't need handsome. You don't give a damn about being a princess." He slammed his fist down on the table, making the little trays jump. "Blast it, Merit." His voice dropped low as he rubbed the spot over his heart with his palm. "You're funny and brave, and you tell me when I need to get stuffed." He stepped closer to her. "You have discerning taste in poetry and can rip open a chicken coop faster than anyone." He dropped his hand, a fist at his side.

Merit realized they were standing so close she could feel the warmth of his body.

"Amaury's right, you're wasted on him." His brow furrowed, his eyes pleading. "Give me a little more time, Merit. We'll think of something."

When she didn't respond, he let out a soft curse, cutting the distance between them and putting his mouth on hers.

Earlier, when Latimer had taken the liberty in the stables, she'd done her best to enjoy it. She hadn't succeeded. With Tevin, she was trying *not* to enjoy it and failing miserably. This wasn't a kiss; it was combustion. It wasn't pretty or sweet, the soft pressing of lips or gentle brushes. This kiss was a hungry thing. Tevin's kiss wanted, and Merit realized she wanted back. Her hands dug into his hair, while Tevin spun her back against the wall. Merit leaned into him until their bodies were pressed together in one firm line. She had no idea how long they stayed

like that. A second. Forever. An increment of time simultaneously too long and too short.

When Tevin pulled back, they were both breathing raggedly
and his cheeks were flushed. She looked up at him, every inch
of her feeling scorched. Tevin cradled her face in his hands and
gave her one more kiss, gently, like he couldn't help himself.
His eyes were wide, the pupils blown, and for a second Merit
thought he looked like someone who had been shaken right
down to his core.

Merit touched her lips, her fingers trembling. There was
no denying the fact that it didn't matter who she married or
who kissed her in the future. She'd compare every single one of
them with Tevin DuMont.

And it made her angry. "How *dare you*."

"How dare *you*," Tevin said, his voice rough. "It's not like I
was alone in that kiss."

"That's not fair." Her whole body was trembling now, with
hurt or anger, she couldn't quite tell.

Tevin smiled at her. "That's the difference right there, between you and me. You expect life to be a balanced game. I
grew up knowing life plays with loaded dice and all the good
cards up its sleeve."

She poked his chest with a single finger. "I can't control how
I was born. You don't get to judge me—"

"Oh, yes, that wouldn't be *fair*, would it?"

It was the smug look on his face that did it. She was exhausted, scared about her curse, confused, and she'd just had
the wits kissed out of her by the worst possible person. Merit
tipped completely over the edge. So instead of controlling

herself, she took a page from the beast's book. "You know what's not fair? Making a stupid choice when you're fifteen and getting cursed for it." She shoved him back away from her with one hand. "To be hurt and abandoned, and feel foolish because *everyone knows*." He opened his mouth, but she didn't let him talk. Her voice was getting louder now, an unstoppable thing. The howl of the wounded beast in human form. "To have your own mother bring the curse down because you're fighting at a dinner party and some awful fairy godling thinks it's a *good idea*." She gave him another shove, just because it felt good. The scene fractured for a second, and she paused to dash the tears out of her eyes with the back of her hand.

Tevin crossed his arms, his brow furrowed. "Worked out pretty good for you at the end, didn't it? You're happy now, right?"

"Happy? I have claws and a prehensile tail!" She was shouting now, her finger still jabbing into his chest. "I ate a *chicken. Raw.* I tore the coop up with my bare hands. I destroy perfectly good bedding sets."

"So you had a bad run. So what? You think you're alone in that?" Tevin moved back into her space. "My mother traded me, Merit. I have to keep my clothes pristine because next week our luck might be down and I'll have to sell them. I have to use my gift again and again to manipulate people, whether I want to or not, because I'm afraid of what will happen if I tell my parents no," he shouted back, then paused, temporarily at a loss for words, clearly surprised he'd shared so much. "And your prehensile tail is really useful! I've seen you carry stuff with it."

"That doesn't mean I want it!" She curled her fist, afraid

that the next poke would be a harder shove. "I can't go into the city without a veil. I can't wear gloves, and if I'm not careful, I crush my teacups." She stepped back, turning away from him. She couldn't look at him. "Do you know what it feels like to have your heart shatter into a thousand pieces and still wish you could see him one more time? No farewells. No chance to ask if it was all lies. Did he even care about me a fraction? Did I enter into his emotional equation at all?" She rubbed her eyes, furious at herself for crying, or for saying as much as she had.

He followed her. "Well, I'm really sorry!" For a second he softened, his hand reaching out before he yanked it back. "Merit, the best lies, they have truth in them. But if he didn't mean a single word, that's not on you. That's on him. You were desperate for any way out—if your mother had just listened." He grabbed the back of his neck, letting out a whoosh of air. "Who curses their own children, Merit?"

She threw her hands up. "Oh, like your parents wouldn't do the same thing if it would make them a quick coin? Like your gift is so great? You like me because I *argue with you*. So don't you dare judge my mother. That's my job. She was desperate—"

Tevin laughed. "Oh, I know all about desperate."

Ellery peeked into the room. "I just wanted to see if everything is okay—"

Their heads snapped to the side to glare at the healer.

"Never mind." Ellery closed the door with a decisive click.

Merit whirled around to face him. "I can't believe you kissed me!" She felt hot now, her anger boiling away the logic she'd been trying to protect herself with. All she wanted to do was rage, and since she didn't want to hurt Tevin, she grabbed the

311

nearest teacup and hurled it against the wall behind him. He dipped to the side, and the porcelain shattered in a way that Merit found really satisfying.

"I just told you I was engaged," Merit yelled. "*To be married. We've been together days and days, and *you pick now?*" She threw another cup. It felt good, so she threw the saucer, too. "You knew how important this was to me! I'm *this* close to ending this curse, getting a chance to be me again, getting a chance to mend things with my mother. What if Latimer saw? What if he calls off the engagement?" She reached for another cup, but it was too far away. Tevin leaned over the table and nudged it closer.

"Thank you."

"You're welcome."

She threw the cup. "I lost two engagements in a single day when I was fifteen, and what small relationship I'd had with my mother disintegrated to shreds."

"Merit, you can't blame me for that." Tevin shoved his hands into his pockets. "I didn't even know you then."

"But you knew about it, and now you're making it worse! You were supposed to be the one person on my side! The one here for me." Merit had reached the platter of tiny cakes and seized one, hurling it at Tevin. He didn't even bother to dodge, so the frosting and cake splattered against his chest. "Well, I'm tired of blaming my mother, tired of being so broken! I'm cursed because of *myself. I* made foolish choices. *I* didn't listen." She threw several cakes in a row, causing tiny explosions of sponge and frosting all over his torso. It was strangely satisfying.

"Merit—"

"No," she yelled, throwing another tiny cake. "We have to put away what we want and do what we *must*. That's what growing up means, Tevin." Her voice cracked. "Responsibility. I picked a man my mother chose." She sucked in a breath. "I didn't have any other options."

Tevin paled, his jaw so tight she could see the delineation of the muscles. Silence spread out as they stared at each other.

Merit turned, only to find the cake stand empty. She closed her eyes. She would not cry again. "We have to be responsible." She picked up the tiered cake holder and threw it. It crashed against the wall, crumpling into a heap. She threw the plates next, followed by the Danishes. It was only Tevin's warning that stopped her from reaching for the teapot.

Merit blinked, coming back to herself. The drawing room was an absolute disaster. Broken teacups and smashed desserts were everywhere. Merit stretched out her very human-looking hands. Where was the division? She might not have looked it, but she was cursed, even now. The beast was who she was.

Tevin reached for her. "Merit—"

She pushed his hand away. "No." The word came out resolute but soft, her throat sore from yelling. "It's over. Go. Get out!" When he didn't move, she brushed past him. "Go home, Tevin DuMont. Pack up your family and leave. I do not want you anywhere near me."

And with that, she turned, hiking up her skirts and moving swiftly around shards of porcelain and globs of cake. She opened the door with shaking hands and stepped through, not bothering to look back.

CHAPTER 24

SORRY, YOUR MIRROR IS
OUT OF ORDER

Tevin wasn't in the best mood. In fact, he felt like someone had scooped out his insides and filled in the space with jagged pieces of glass. It hurt to even move. Amaury and Val had gone to get train tickets—he didn't want to know exactly where Amaury had scraped up the money from. He didn't care. If a comet fell out of the sky at this moment, hurtling directly at him, he wouldn't even look up. He'd volunteered to mirror his parents to explain that they were coming home, because why not? There was a certain misery point that was like absolute zero—you were already at your lowest, so why not just pile more on? It wasn't like he could feel any worse.

The closest train station was a few miles from Cravan House, in a local town called Fladger's Drift. They hadn't bothered to even get their trunks, just packed what they could carry and walked. Amaury and Val had tried to talk to him, but he refused. What was there to discuss? Merit wanted him gone, end of story. Eventually, they'd given up and dashed to get their own things, as if afraid he would walk away without them. No way was Tevin waiting around to ask anyone for the use of a hack or to sort out travel details. Merit had been the only reason any of the fairyborn had been tolerating them, and with her welcome removed, Tevin knew from experience that the quicker they fled, the better. Besides, the idea of sitting through any sort of engagement celebration made him want to throw up.

Tevin ducked into a tavern, the Dog & Sparrow, looking for a local pay mirror. A town like this, most people wouldn't have the coin for their own. The tavern's pay mirror was in a dingy back room that doubled as a storage closet. The walls were thick, blocking out the noise from the people making merry. He tapped the mirror, putting in the code the barkeep had given him when he handed over his copper.

After a few minutes, Brouchard's face filled the screen. "Tevin, my boy. Aren't you a sight."

Tevin automatically took apart the greeting, scanning it for hidden meanings and criticisms. His parents never just said something. There was always a layer. This greeting meant to remind Tevin who was in charge, for though "my boy" could be an endearment, it also connoted ownership. Brouchard had also left out any sort of positive descriptors in the second part, meaning that the sight wasn't a good one.

He was definitely looking worse for wear after his fight with Merit. For a second, he contemplated telling his father that he'd almost drowned in a river yesterday but decided against it. What would be the point? Parental concern? Comfort? He'd get eaten by a pack of escaped circus bears before getting those things. Tevin responded the only way he could—by ignoring what his father had said. "We're coming home."

Brouchard sat back in his chair, legs crossed, his chin resting on his index finger, the rest of his fingers fanned out against his cheek. It was a calculated look, relaxed but also slightly dismissive. As a child, Tevin would have rushed to fill the silence, to do anything to get his father to shift from that expression to one of even the mildest approval. Last week he might have done it. Now he simply waited his father out.

"That's it? You're coming home?" Brouchard heaved a sigh. Tevin could almost feel the disappointment through the mirror. "Empty-handed, I bet. At least I can trust your brother to bring us some leads we can work with."

For a fleeting second, Tevin imagined siccing Willa and Diadora on Brouchard. They would eat him alive. "Is it safe to go to the house in Grenveil yet? Amaury mentioned something about anxious creditors."

"Oh, we found enough coin to tide them over." Brouchard extended an arm along the back of the settee, his fingers idly tracing the woodwork. "We used the money you had hidden in your trunk."

Tevin wasn't surprised, but he still felt a stab of disappointment. Just once, he wanted to be wrong about his parents. "You stole my money?"

Brouchard tsked. "*Stole* is a nasty word, Tevin. We needed to consolidate. For the good of the family. For the good of you, it turns out, since you're coming home hat in hand."

Tevin didn't know what to say. How do you even respond to such a thing? Did he expect him to say, *Thanks for having the foresight to steal from me so that I can go home and be besieged for your debts?* He probably did.

"Anyway, see you soon. Kisses from your mother, and so on." Brouchard nodded and signed off, leaving Tevin in the claustrophobic closet with a blank mirror. He stood there a moment, letting it all bubble up until he overflowed. Tevin slammed his fist into the enchanted mage glass, fracturing the mirror and slicing open his knuckles in the process. Then he dropped his head into his hands, giving himself ten seconds to roll around in the pain. That was all he got, and then he'd have to pull himself together.

Someone banged on the door, rattling the knob, which Tevin had locked. "Hey! You done in there?" The voice was slurred, the man too far in his cups to mirror anyone. "I need to holler at my girl! Tell her I love her." The man pounded his fist on the door again. Tevin calmly pulled out his handkerchief, folded it into a long strip, and wrapped it around his knuckles. He unlocked the door, letting the drunk man topple in.

"You'll have to wait, I'm afraid," Tevin said, waving at the fractured, blood-smeared magic mirror. "Doesn't seem to be working."

"How am I supposed to tell her how I feel?" The man swayed on his feet.

Tevin steadied him. "In the morning, clean yourself up. Go to her house with flowers and tell her everything in your heart. Don't mirror her while you're too drunk to stand. No one wants that." Tevin clapped him on the shoulder and went back into the tavern's main room, leaving the man staring in owl-eyed confusion at the dead mirror.

He jammed his hand into his pocket so no one would see the

317

bandage. When he walked out into the main part of the tavern, he was surprised to find Glendon at a table, talking to one of the last people Tevin wanted to see, Lady Zarla.

Glendon raised a hand in greeting, beckoning him to join them, making Tevin think they hadn't heard the news from the house. Why not join them? He had the time. Today was already a layer cake of awful, so why not put a cherry on top?

He dropped into the chair. "If you keep me here, you're going to have to pay the barkeep for a broken magic mirror."

"Are you okay?" Glendon asked, genuine concern in his voice.

Tevin waved him off. "I'm fine." He liked Glendon. It was too bad he was never going to see him again.

Lady Zarla went to speak, but Glendon, gauging from Tevin's mood that things were obviously not fine, tried to stop her. "Whatever you need to say, it can wait, Zarla."

Lady Zarla scowled at him. "I'll say my piece, Glendon."

He sighed. "For once, Zarla, don't do anything you're going to regret." She glared at him until he left, heading for the barkeep to discuss the mirror. "Good luck, Tevin."

"Thanks, Glendon. You're all right." He turned back around to face Merit's mother, jabbing a thumb over his shoulder. "That's a solid fellow, milady."

Lady Zarla ignored him and dropped a small purse onto the table. It jangled when it dropped, leaving Tevin no doubt what was inside.

"I know you have a deal with my daughter, but I'd like you to vanish. Leave. I've spoken to Latimer, and while he's made his intentions clear, he also has some concern about Merit's time

318

with you. I don't want you to ruin this for her. Not when she's this close to having the future she deserves."

He reached over and took the bag, pulling the strings until it opened. Gold glinted up at him. A small fortune in monarchs. He wouldn't have to go home empty-handed. Wouldn't have to worry about bills or food or his parents for at least a month or two. All he had to do was *take the bag*. There was a sweet irony to Lady Zarla bribing him to do what he was already doing.

Tevin couldn't help it—he laughed. He was getting exactly what he'd wished for and couldn't take a single coin because Merit would find out and it would hurt her. He laughed so hard his sides ached. The longer it went on, the more irritated Lady Zarla got, which made him laugh even more. Finally he slowed down, wiping tears from his eyes. "Oh, I needed that. Thank you, milady." He stood. "It was a pleasure to meet you, but I really must be going."

Lady Zarla frowned. "Aren't you going to take the money?"

"You can keep it for the ferryman in the underworld," Tevin said, tipping his hat. "Milady." And then he left, not even bothering to look back.

Tevin started walking to the train station, the throb in his hand echoing the steady beat of his heart.

• • •

They were back on the train, a first-class compartment all to themselves. There had been other people in it, but Tevin had asked them all politely to leave, and of course they had. He pressed himself into the soft leather seats, his body rigid, his hands white-knuckled on the armrests. All around him were

319

the hum of the train and the murmur of Amaury's and Val's voices as they played cards. Each mile the train whipped past took them farther away from Merit and made Tevin more miserable.

"I'm so sorry," Tevin gritted through his teeth. "I screwed up."

"You did fine." Amaury rearranged the cards in his hand.

"He's right," Val said, organizing her own cards. "Even though I'm thoroughly heartbroken over the result. I barely got to know Kaiya, and I didn't even say goodbye. We ran out like our tail feathers were on fire, and I missed a golden opportunity to ride stoically out into the sunset, thus impressing my lady love."

"Distance makes the heart grow fonder?"

"That is the biggest load of horse puckey you've ever shoveled, Tevin DuMont." Val threw down her cards in disgust. "Distance doesn't do a blasted thing except make it easier to forget all about me. Distance is the enemy. In a week it will be, 'Val who?'"

"You're not that easy to forget, Val, trust me," Tevin said while Amaury said, "Val who?" at the same time. Val smacked him in the arm.

"I really am sorry I got us chucked out. I didn't exactly want to leave, either."

"I wonder if she'll go with Merit when she marries," Val said, staring down at her boots. "How am I going to court her from another country?"

Tevin dropped his head into his hands, wincing when his makeshift bandage pulled tight.

Val threw an arm around his neck and squeezed him to her hard.

"Your love is aggressive and painful," Tevin said, but he didn't push her away.

"I liked Merit." Amaury carefully folded his hand before picking up Val's cards off the floor and stacking them neatly together. "Didn't like the Smug Prince. Even the ostrich would have been better."

"It's done." Tevin paused, swallowing hard as the train took a turn. He would not throw up. "Soon her curse will be broken, and she'll be married and happy." He pushed his palms against his eyelids. "I can't believe I turned down Lady Zarla's money. Amaury, you must hate me."

Amaury snorted. "I would have thrown it onto the floor, causing a bar fight, then snuck out and left her to deal with the repair costs."

Tevin dropped his hands. "Why didn't I think of that?"

"Because I'm the brains." Amaury tapped the side of his head. He gathered up the deck of cards from the small table attached to the window and handed it to Val. The green of the countryside whipped past behind him, making Tevin's gorge rise. Someone in another car was smoking a cigar, and the smell wasn't helping his nausea.

Val flicked her eyes at Amaury as she shuffled. "Lucky Merit, or should I say Princess Merit? Married happily to the handsome Latimer of Huldre. Walks on the beach. Holding hands. Lots of kissing. The most kissing. I wonder how many children they'll have?"

Tevin wrapped his arms around himself, like he could hold the queasiness in. "Please stop."

Val put down her cards. "No, my second-dearest cousin, I will not. You're losing, and from all accounts, DuMonts *do not lose*. You may cheat, but you still win. You're sullying the family name."

"Second-dearest?"

"I'm currently the dearest because I didn't get us kicked out of posh living, plus Kate's not here," Amaury said as he hailed a passing food cart, purchasing a thermos of coffee and several small tarts.

"And he's going to give me one of those tarts," Val added.

Amaury handed her the lemon one. "And I'm going to give her one of my tarts."

"What will you do when we get home?" Val bit into the flaky crust. Amaury shoved a raspberry tart into his mouth whole. Tevin wasn't sure if he wasn't getting one because he was in trouble or because he would likely cast up his accounts all over the nice train floor.

"I don't know."

Val crossed her arms, her face pinched up in annoyance. "Are we not even going to discuss the fact that you care for her? That you're not even attempting to fight for your girl?"

This time the heavy feeling in his stomach wasn't due to the train. "She doesn't want me to fight for her, Val. She doesn't want anything to do with me." He would *not* throw up. "Merit has her happily-ever-after, and I'm not it. She's got her fiancé, who will break her curse and give her little fairy-blood babies with tails. She made her choice, and I will respect it. I can live with her hating me as long as she's happy."

Val threw her hands in the air and flopped back in her seat. "City boys. You're all useless."

"I'm not arguing." Amaury settled into his seat, curling into it with feline grace and attitude.

"Too right." Val's tone bit at him. "Because if I had a second chance with the woman I love, I can't say I wouldn't be doing everything in my power to win her."

"And what, doom her to being a beast? How could I win her, Val? I'm not the one she needs. Latimer will break her curse."

"You could break the curse if you were in love with her, right?" Val asked. "Wasn't that one of the things?" When Amaury nodded, Val grinned. "See? No problem. You catch a train, tell her you love her, she swoons into your arms, the end."

"Merit doesn't swoon," Tevin said. "And she certainly doesn't love me. She chose Latimer. End of story."

Val snorted. "I'm not sure I agree with that, Tev. You don't throw a table full of crockery at someone if you don't love them."

"I don't think that's an actual indicator of affection," Amaury said, his eyes heavy-lidded and drowsy.

Tevin gave up arguing with them. "Fine, I'm not selfless at all, I'm just a big coward."

"It's funny how similar those things can be," Val said.

CHAPTER 25

ENTER THE IN-LAWS

Lady Zarla took the news of Merit's engagement with a combination of excited joy and focused pragmatism. It felt good to make her mother happy, to finally please her, but it felt even better to see her mother approach the wedding planning. Merit had seen her mother's to-do list and thought that this would be less of a joining of families and more of a ruthless negotiation. This was why Merit was traveling alone to Huldre. Lady Zarla would arrive a few days later with a small battalion of solicitors with which to lay siege to the king and queen of Huldre. Some people showed love with kind words. Merit's mother showed hers with lawyers.

That didn't mean Merit was going to get everything she wanted. She made her first concession before they even boarded the train. Merit would be traveling to Huldre with Latimer, and she would be doing it alone. If she brought Kaiya, Latimer said, it implied that Merit needed a guard from his family. It showed bad faith. After all, he had arrived without a guard, hadn't he? Merit didn't like it, but she didn't want his family to think she was weak, either. His family also had their own healers, so bringing Ellery would be an insult to them and his parents. Her mother hesitated but agreed. Merit understood the reasoning all around, even agreed with some of it, but it still allowed a sliver of unease to lodge into her heart.

A day after they announced their engagement, Latimer bundled Merit up in her shawl and they boarded the first-class car of the train. Lady Zarla had insisted on paying for their travel, getting them their own private car so Merit wouldn't have to worry about people looking at her. The thoughtful gesture warmed Merit, and she finally felt hopeful that the fracture between her and her mother could be mended. She was relieved that she wouldn't have to take any more bloom today, or even tomorrow. She had overdone it, and the last thing she wanted was to meet Latimer's parents and go into a mindless, ravening episode where she chewed up their favorite couch like a family dog.

Merit had always loved the smooth glide and gentle swish of the train as it ate away at the miles. She sat by the window, watching the countryside go by. Latimer sat next to her, reading the newspaper he'd bought at the station.

"I used to bring needlework on the train," Merit said. "In case I didn't want to read. I like making dolls for the children at our country house."

Latimer looked up over his paper. "Wouldn't it be easier to buy them a doll?"

"Perhaps," Merit said. "But I liked doing it myself. That way I could make it special for each child. Maybe it won't be as professional as a fancy one from a city shop, but the child would still play with her, love her, and know that someone cares about them enough to make them a doll."

Latimer stared at Merit in surprise.

"Didn't anyone ever make you anything?" Merit asked.

Latimer shook his head and went back to his paper. "Seems like a waste of time to me, but if it makes you happy, you can make whatever you want after your curse is broken."

The train was a slower one, frequently stopping to let people on or off, or switching out the mages who made the train move. The buttery-soft leather of the seats stayed warm and inviting, and Latimer would get anything they needed from the staff so Merit didn't have to interact with them. When they crossed the border into the kingdom, a conductor went around checking everyone's papers, making sure everything was in order for them to enter another country. The conductor skipped their car—there were some definite upsides to Latimer's nobility. Merit napped in her reclined seat, a soft blanket covering her. The beast in her slept as well, curled up and quiet for now.

The train chugged around hilly lands and cut through fields, coming closer to Huldre's holdings. Latimer wrapped her up and they exited the train, and Merit saw his homelands for the first time. They were pretty enough, but for some reason a wave of homesickness swamped her. What if they decided to live here? Not that there seemed to be anything wrong with it, but it wasn't home.

After they disembarked and their luggage had been dropped off, Latimer hired a hack to take her and their belongings up to the barony seat. He rode his own horse, Prince, leaving the entire hack for Merit to enjoy. The carriage was plain but well made, the creatures pulling it fashioned into the sturdy outline of horses. Latimer had chosen it because it was open on the top. The weather was fine, and he wanted her to be able to see his lands as they traveled. She stayed wrapped in her shawl, nestled far enough back in the fabric that her face would be difficult to see from the road.

Latimer made sure to point out the sights on the way to his house—his favorite hunting spot, the cottages that his people lived in, which were in various states of repair. Some of them were quite run-down. Merit looked at Latimer to see if he noticed. It wasn't his job to take care of such things now, but when he inherited, it would be. Latimer was smiling and merry. If he saw anything that caused him concern, he didn't show it.

The land itself was fairly pretty. Old, gnarled oaks and thick pines competed for the craggy soil. They passed several vineyards, long rows of grapevines clinging to wooden slats. His people didn't look particularly well clothed or fed. Much of the fencing needed replacing. When she started pointing these things out to Latimer, he made vague comments about his father's plans. Merit couldn't tell if Latimer just didn't know what his father had in mind or didn't really care. It wasn't unusual. Freddie or Cedric would have been the same way, but Merit wasn't marrying them.

She kept her shawl up as they traveled. Though none of the locals came up to say hello, she still didn't want to frighten them. Merit grew more and more nervous with each step. Meeting Latimer's parents would make everything feel real, and she wasn't sure she was ready for that. With each passing mile, the roiling knot of unease in her stomach grew.

The hack rounded a bend, and suddenly visible up on the ridge were the Huldre family holdings.

"What do you think?" Latimer asked.

Merit had never seen anything like it outside history books. The structure looked like the angry child of an ancient castle and a frontier outpost.

"It's very forbidding," Merit said. "Powerful-looking. Like an old castle." This response seemed to please Latimer. It was clear he was very proud of his home. They made the long trek up, the creatures pulling the hacks picking their way through the rocky trail as Latimer's horse easily ambled up. Once at the top, they were let in through a towering gate. Inside, the road was paved in cobblestones all the way up to the marble steps leading into the castle. A tasteful fountain stood off to the left, the stables off to the right.

"You can't see from here," Latimer said with a smile, "but on the other side of the castle there's an orchard and a lake. I'll give you a tour later."

"That sounds wonderful." And it did, but nerves were getting the better of her, so Merit had to force cheer into her voice. "I'd love to see your home."

Latimer turned away, his gaze lingering on the fountain. "It's your home now, too."

Once they were close to the steps, the hack rolled to a stop, and Merit climbed out. Latimer handed off his reins to a waiting groom. Then he offered her his arm and escorted her up the steps. At the top they were greeted by a large, imposing man that Merit assumed was Latimer's father. Merit could see Latimer in him when it came to height, coloring, and the shape of his forehead, but Latimer mostly took after his mother. She stood next to her husband, a wide smile lighting up her exquisite face. Her pale hair was swept up into a complicated mass of braids that complemented the simple silver gown she was wearing.

The king held his arms out as he beamed at Latimer. "My son! Welcome home." He hugged Latimer, kissing each cheek. Then his eyes zeroed in on Merit. She suddenly felt shabby and small by comparison. Beastly.

"Can this be my new daughter?" His mother stepped forward, taking Merit's clawed hands in her own. Though her smile was warm and welcoming, her hands were cold.

"We're not married yet, Mother," Latimer said, stealing one of Merit's hands back from her, causing her to drop the other to keep it from getting awkward. *Too late,* Merit thought. She already felt awkward. "Lady Merit, may I present my father and mother, Henrich and Angelique, the king and queen of Huldre?"

Merit curtseyed. "It's lovely to meet you."

"Of course," Lady Angelique said, and put her arm around Merit, drawing her into the house and away from Latimer. The queen led her into an entryway, their steps echoing on the marble floor. Two grand staircases swept up to the second floor, drawing the eye to a large crystal chandelier. Merit was surprised to see that it was lit by mage light, not candles. Latimer's parents struck her as old-fashioned, so it was a pleasant surprise to see they weren't.

Lady Angelique squeezed Merit to her in a one-armed hug, the pressure quick and unsatisfying, before she let go, leaving

Merit the impression of too much perfume and little else. "This is your home now, and we are your family. I'm so pleased you're here."

Merit smiled, trying to show that she was pleased, too, when really she felt more and more like she'd made a mistake.

CHAPTER 26

RISE OF THE BEAST

Merit shouldn't have had a lot of time to question her choices over the next few days before her mother arrived, but she somehow found it. While standing still for the dress fitting, during dinner with Latimer's family and local fairy nobility, even when she dreamed, Merit struggled to stay positive. She tried to picture her future, Latimer by her side, a happy marriage for them both.

It didn't work.

The dreams were the worst. Her mind stitched together pain past and present, an endless quilt of nightmares. Her nights passed with images of the beast, deep in the forest, calling out with an eerie howl. It would be here, soon, and then it would stay. The beast paced inside her, rage powering every rolling step, every rolling growl.

Though the beast haunted her dreams, Tevin haunted her waking hours. She missed him, even though she was mad at him, and confused, and so very lost over the whole thing. The ghost of their kiss followed her everywhere. What did he mean by it? Could someone kiss like that on a whim, a tactic to . . . what? Marry him instead of Latimer? She couldn't *marry* Tevin.

She'd remain a beast, and no matter how mixed up she was, she knew he didn't want that for her. He couldn't possibly love her, could he? Love had to be a gift freely given, something unknowable to someone who only calculated the cost of things. What did *she* mean by the kiss? She wasn't sure, but she knew that the dreams where Tevin walked by her side into the days ahead left her aching. Only the idea of reaching out, of discovering he really was just like Jasper, froze her in place.

Her spinning thoughts exhausted her, leaving her short-tempered, though she tried to hide it.

Despite all the wedding preparations, Latimer took time to keep her company. He walked with her through the orchards or down by the lake, talking for hours. Latimer was a good listener, though he shared few of his own stories. Oh, he talked. He told her things, but nothing that one wouldn't share with a new acquaintance on a train. He didn't tell her anything that really mattered. Merit hoped he would open up as they grew to know each other better.

Today they were walking along the lake. It was one of his favorite places, and Merit could easily see why. The glassy blue water reflected snowcapped mountains, trees, and sky, the sight almost taking her breath away. After an hour holding still for her dress fitting, she was happy to be outside, and as herself—she'd taken a dose of tincture before the dressmaker arrived.

"You should see it in the early spring." Latimer was dressed casually, his hair pulled back in a low ponytail. "There's a little purple flower called lover's tears that pops up, completely covering the lakeside. Makes the place look magical."

"Lover's tears? What a name for a flower."

"It's a pretty flower, but also quite poisonous." Latimer reached up, fingertips touching the green leaves of a tree they walked under. "We'll walk here in the spring, and I'll show you."

"I'd like that." She smiled at him, enjoying the sunshine off the water. Grateful to be lakeside in an eyelet dress instead of as the beast, covered and veiled.

"Are you excited to break your curse?" Latimer asked. "Less than a week left. Assuming negotiations between our parents go well." As heirs, their wedding could never be a simple meeting of two hearts. It was more akin to a business deal, both sides making demands and concessions until an agreement was reached.

"I admit I'm looking forward to it," Merit said, stopping to pick up a flat stone. She tried to skip it across the water, but it didn't go far. "The man I was originally betrothed to when I was cursed died a year later, did you know? Fell off a horse. If I'd gone along with the betrothal, I would never have gotten married. My fight with Mother, the curse, it was all for naught. I lost everything and gained nothing." Merit gave up trying to skip and instead threw her rock as far as she could. It curved up in a graceful arc before splashing into the lake.

"I'm sorry, Merit." Latimer pulled her close. She wished—oh, how she wished—she felt anything more than friendly affection for him. She knew her smile was a little watery.

Latimer rubbed his hands along her arms, soothing. "You miss your friends, don't you? Kaiya? Your healer friend? The other one, the one with the snakes?" When she didn't answer, Latimer frowned. "Is it DuMont?"

To her complete mortification, Merit started crying. A stranger at Latimer's castle, she had no one to turn to, and though she felt bad that her fiancé of all people had to hear it, she was relieved, too. After all the time they'd spent this week, she'd begun to trust Latimer. She genuinely liked him and considered him a friend. They would soon be married, after all—she needed to get used to leaning on him.

Once she was all cried out, Latimer kissed her forehead and leaned back, his hands cupping her face. "It's okay, Merit. It's common to have doubts before a wedding, and DuMont has you all twisted around, just like that Jasper person you told me about." He wiped away an errant tear with his thumb before letting her go. He glanced toward the water, rubbing a hand over the back of his neck. "What if I track him down, find his mirror location so you can talk to him?"

Surprise shot through her. "You would do that for me? You're not angry?"

Latimer gave her a close-lipped smile. "Consider it a wedding gift—I want no doubts in your mind when you walk down the aisle." He took her hand, resuming their walk. "And no, I'm not angry. DuMont is a consummate liar, but you consider him to be a friend. Sometimes in absence, we forget people's bad qualities and only remember the good. Perhaps you need a reminder of who Tevin DuMont really is—and I'll let him do that. I have no doubts that in comparison, I'll come out on top again."

She laughed, threading her arm through his. "So confident."

"I prefer to see it as knowing my own worth," he said, smiling. It quickly faded. "But, Merit, do me a favor? Don't mention the call to Mother? I don't wish her to . . ." He turned his gaze out over the lake. "I don't want her to worry."

Merit assured him she would not, feeling better than she had in days. Was it because she'd talked to Latimer about what was going on or because she was excited to talk to Tevin?

• • •

Merit spent the evening in the library. It didn't seem to be a very popular room—during her stay she'd never seen anyone else in it. Merit couldn't trust herself with the delicate pages of the old books, not with her claws, but she could sit in front of the fireplace and let the calm of the room fill her. She must have dozed, because she didn't hear Lady Angelique come in until a small tray was set in front of her. On the tray rested a teapot and cup made of rose-patterned china. The thick scent of chocolate filled the air.

"Forgive my presumption, but I thought you could use this. Chocolate can be medicinal, don't you think?"

Merit straightened, making sure her claws didn't catch the fabric. "You think I need medicine?"

Lady Angelique poured the chocolate into the cup, her hands moving with delicate grace. Merit couldn't help but compare them with her own. "I may be a queen, but I'm also a mother. You seem anxious, and having once been a young bride myself, I thought you might need a little help. And since your own mother isn't here yet, I was hoping you'd let me temporarily take her place."

"Oh," Merit said, taking the cup. "You've all been so kind." And they had been, but in an oddly detached way. To Merit it felt like their words said, "Welcome," but there was no *feeling* behind it. They smiled. They hugged, even. But it was like hugging a doll that couldn't really hug you back.

Lady Angelique straightened, her posture perfect as she perched. "It's normal to have doubts, my dear. When I first met Henrich, I was so worried. I feared we didn't have anything in common, but as I got to know him, I discovered a like mind. A partner." She gestured for Merit to sip.

Merit took a deep drink, happy for the warmth and comfort. It made her remember a far-off time when it had been easier to talk to her own mother, when she was a little girl and her needs had been simple.

Lady Angelique smiled. "Doubts are normal, dear." She flicked graceful fingers at Merit's cup. "Drink, drink. You'll feel *so* much better when you're done."

Merit finished the chocolate, catching a strange, bitter taste at the end. Almost . . . peppery. "You might want to talk to your cook. I'm not sure what's in here—" Merit froze, her clawed hand going to her gut.

"Oh, dear." Lady Angelique set down her own cup. She leaned in, her eyes suddenly sharp and cold, making Merit think of the snakes Willa often had to deal with. Snakes weren't mean or evil, but their perspective was so alien that she couldn't quite understand it besides agreeing that sunning on a hot rock was quite nice, thank you. "You don't look well, child. I'll have to send for a healer." She stood, heading to the bellpull that would summon the servants, her movements unhurried.

Merit doubled over, gasping.

Lady Angelique tugged on the bellpull twice before returning to her seat. She watched Merit, her eyes bright.

Merit tried to give the cup back to Lady Angelique, but her hand was shaking. She needed to get out of there—to find Latimer. He would help her, she was sure of it. The cup rattled in its saucer until Merit dropped both onto the floor, watching the beautiful rose-patterned china shatter against the hardwood.

"Pity," Lady Angelique said with a frown. "That was my mother's. Still, one must accept one's losses with grace."

Merit couldn't respond. Her heart pounded, and heat poured through her veins. Pain flared as her spine bowed, her clawed hands becoming gnarled.

Lady Angelique's face lifted as the door opened behind Merit. "Ah, there you are. We're in need of a healer. Quickly, now."

The servant must have left, because Lady Angelique returned her focus to Merit. "Unfortunately, Mrs. Humphries is out in the south orchards today, gathering a lichen that she needs."

Merit snarled.

"Now, now," Lady Angelique said, grabbing hold of Merit's jaw. "Don't fret. She'll get here eventually."

Merit tried to stand, but her muscles wouldn't obey. She collapsed against the floor, her vision fading. In the distance she heard the beast howl, and her heart howled back.

CHAPTER 27

A GIFT THAT KEEPS ON GIVING

Eric Latimer of Huldre stared at his bride-to-be and felt something in him wither. The beast that was Merit had been thrown into one of the cells in the dungeon. She'd destroyed the wooden bench, clawing it into so much timber. Yesterday he'd walked with her by the lake and planned their future, and now she was meticulously shredding a blanket with her teeth.

"Mother, I can't believe you did this."

"What?" His mother raised her brows, coming to a stop in front of the cage. Latimer stood there, scowling at the beast. "I think it's rather clever."

"She's in a cell. My bride is in a cell. We can't get married this way." He gestured toward Merit and the metal bars surrounding her.

"Of course not! I've had a *lovely* cage commissioned. It should be here the morning of the ceremony. You should see it—absolutely beautiful. I particularly like the filigree pieces." Queen Angelique stared at the beast. She bit her thumb, smiling as she did. "Ingenious, really."

"What did you give her?"

"An overdose of bloom." She frowned at him. "You're concerned things won't go smoothly? Darling, I've planned it all down to the last detail. You know me. Lists for days."

Latimer turned to his mother and wondered if he was truly seeing her for the first time. She stood next to the cage in a gauzy blue gown, a gold circlet holding back her hair, revealing her tipped ears. Her cheeks were flushed, her eyes bright. "I'm concerned that my mother attempted to poison my bride." He ran a hand over his face.

"Attempt to poison her! The very idea." She crossed her arms, one of her slippered feet tapping against the stone floor. "Not until after the wedding. What good would it do *now*?"

Latimer froze. He had to have heard her wrong. "Pardon?"

She shook her head. "If she dies before the wedding, we won't see a single copper." She tipped her head at the cage. "All of this would be for naught."

Latimer's blood froze in his veins. "You're going to *murder* my bride?"

"So melodramatic." Lady Angelique's brow furrowed. "What did you think was going to happen?"

He put his hands on his hips, afraid that if he didn't, he might do something he'd regret. The beast watched him from the cage, wary. "I don't know—a clever trick with the wedding laws, or maybe purchase another godling curse." Something terrible, like he had done with Cedric and Freddie, but not permanent.

She used her toe to push a shred of blanket between the bars and back into Merit's cage. "We couldn't leave her married to you. You're a prince, darling. Tiradian stock. When you marry, it will be to someone fit for you." She clapped her hands together, pressing them to her lips. "And with her coin, her lands, you'll have your pick of proper brides." She heaved a happy sigh. "I do love it when a plan comes together."

A chill ran its slippery fingers up his spine. "Mother, there must be another way."

"No," she said, dropping her hand sharply. "There is no room for doubts. Half of this wedding has been on credit. What do you think will happen if you don't go through with it? Creditors will start taking things. Our clothes. Our art and furniture. Your horse. Everyone will *know*."

Latimer's hand fisted, but his face stayed serene. "So we get married, and then what? What if she tells everyone about this?" He tipped his chin toward the beast and her cage.

"What will she tell them? She's mindless now, darling. Once her curse is broken, I hardly think she'll be able to remember who gave her the tincture. If she has doubts, our staff will remember me summoning the healer. Me, trying to help her. Alas, it was too late."

Her eyes glittered as they looked at the beast. "You just make it through the ceremony." She patted his cheek. "We'll give her a perfect wedding trip. When you come back, without your bride, we'll mourn young love and tragic accidents. After a proper mourning period, you move on." She smoothed her dress. "I look terrible in black. Still, we must bear up under adversity."

"Mother," he said so softly, it was barely sound. The beast raised her snout. "She's my friend." He regretted the words instantly. He *knew* better.

She glared at him. "Don't be weak." She grabbed his chin, yanking his face down to hers. For a long moment, she stared at him, her eyes cold. Then she brightened and released his chin. "Besides, you don't need friends. You have family."

Latimer's shoulders slumped. "And when the guests ask why my bride is in a cage?"

She dismissed the idea with a flick of her wrist. "We'll tell a pretty story beforehand, make it seem like intentional theater. They'll eat it up. Honestly, my boy, you must trust your mother in this. After the wedding, when the curse is broken and you're escorting your wealthy new bride away, no one will think to question it." She clasped her hands over her heart. "Your love will have tamed the beast, broken the curse. The bards will be falling all over themselves to sing about it. Who doesn't enjoy a good love story, hmm?"

Latimer didn't look convinced. "And what does Father say?"

The woman flicked her hand at him. "Your father does as he's told. Any other objections?" Her tone said clearly that she didn't want to hear them. That it would be best if Latimer buried them deep and did as he was told, like his father.

For a second, Latimer considered arguing. It would do no good. "No, Mother."

"Excellent." She smoothed her skirts. "It will all work out. You'll see." Somewhere deep in the keep, a bell tolled. "Is that the time? Lady Zarla will arrive any minute. I better get ready." She cleared her throat meaningfully. Latimer bent to kiss her cheeks, and then she left without another word.

Today, for the first time, Latimer knew that if he looked into a mirror, he wouldn't like what he saw reflected. Mother was happy. This morning she'd been *singing*. His father was *laughing*. Latimer should be dancing down the hallway. Soon their coffers would be replenished, and everything would go back to normal. Their way of life restored. All he had to do was nothing.

Nothing should be easy to do. He could think all he wanted, but as long as he didn't act, everything would be perfect.

He was usually very good at doing nothing. With Cedric, he'd paid the godling's fee, then stepped out of the way. With Freddie, he'd put one of the chemist's powders that his mother had provided into a tea flask. He hadn't meant for him to fall into the river; the powder was supposed to make him dizzy and sick, so everyone thought he was still drunk. If Cedric was an ostrich and Merit thought Freddie had made an ass out of himself, suddenly Latimer was the best choice.

All he'd had to do was give one little push to get things going, and then step back and let the boulder roll down the hill. Then do nothing as it careened into the village below. It was his only job, and he wasn't sure he could do it anymore.

He *liked* Merit—that was the problem. He'd liked talking to her. No one really *talked* to him. His parents talked at him, like he was a trained puppy. Servants did his bidding. Prince was good at listening. But he was a horse. It wasn't the same.

If he married Merit, she wouldn't see the lake in springtime. She'd never see the flowers. His mother had a plan, and if all went perfectly, Merit wouldn't live to see the spring.

The beast coughed, spitting up a wad of chewed-up blanket. Something in the corner of the cage caught Latimer's eye—a glint of silver. Keeping an eye on the beast, he slowly leaned over and picked it up. The chain was broken, the locket scratched, but when he opened it, the mirror was still intact. He cupped it in his hand.

He couldn't stand against his parents. They were too strong. But he could give a different boulder a push, couldn't he? Then it wouldn't be his fault, just gravity.

He tucked the locket and the broken chain into his pocket and left the beast to her blanket. He'd promised Merit she could call Tevin, and he wouldn't break his promise. It was the best he could do.

CHAPTER 28

HEY, HE CAN BE CHARMING, TOO

It was dark when they stepped off the street and onto the walkway up to the house, the weak mage light sconces by the door bathing the steps in yellow glow. The door opened, revealing Kate for a moment before she picked up her skirts, ran down the steps, and flew onto the path. He barely had time to open his arms to catch her in a hug.

Kate leaned back, smiling up at him. "I want to hear *everything*."

Tevin looked past her to see his parents in the doorway.

He let go of Kate. "Later. I promise."

They made their way up the stairs, stopping on the porch, since Florencia and Brouchard blocked the entrance. For a long moment, no one spoke, the night full of crickets and the clop of horseshoes from the street. Brouchard sighed and stepped back. "Welcome home."

"Wipe your boots." Florencia folded her arms and followed her husband inside.

Kate hugged Amaury and Val. "I missed you all so much." She said the words quietly, making sure their parents didn't hear them.

Since Tevin had come back empty-handed, his parents put him and Amaury to work around the house. They wanted to make sure Tevin and Amaury knew their place, and their place was mucking out stalls and scrubbing floors. At least they were together, even if Val spent her days moping and Amaury was back to his tight-lipped ways.

Besides, if Tevin worked, he didn't think, and thinking right now was not going in his favor. His brain seemed to delight in pulling up memories of Merit, connecting her to the most trivial things. He couldn't eat cake anymore. The beeswax polish they used on the furniture almost brought him to his knees because it smelled like the stuff she used to shine her horns. He was miserable, and it was exacerbated by the everyday tension of living with his parents. Residing in the DuMont house was an exercise in waiting for the other shoe to drop.

Sleeping was the worst. He dreamed of Merit constantly.

Basically, his brain was a diabolical villain, trying to destroy him from the inside.

A week after they came home, Val found Tevin sitting outside in the grass near the stables, scrubbing the horse tack.

"How goes your moping?" Val asked, flopping onto the grass.

"Excellent. It's some excellent moping. Top-notch. Yours?"

"I tried writing a love letter."

Tevin, who'd taken the saddle out into the sun so he could see the seam better to brush the dirt away, paused, squinting through the bright sunlight at his cousin. "You're not much of a wordsmith, Val. Was it any good?"

"No. I burned it."

"That's for the best, then." He went back to the saddle.

"I was thinking of using the mirror to call Cedric, you know, for help with my writing."

Tevin looked up from the saddle again. "Why would you do that? I mean, if you can't think of yourself, think of Kaiya."

Val rolled to the side so she could prop herself up with an elbow. "The point I'm trying to make is that I've hit some pretty desperate levels."

"Apparently."

"What are we going to do, Tevin?" Val asked. "You're not just going to sit here, are you?"

Tevin shrugged. "What do you want me to do, Val?" He glared at the saddle, throwing down his brush in disgust. "She's made her choice."

"Tell her she's making a mistake. That *you* made a mistake." Val huffed in annoyance. "I figured you'd come to your senses if I gave you a few days to mull things over, but now I'm concerned that you have the brain of a pudding."

"What are you talking about?" He left the saddle, deciding to go to the woodpile. He had the sudden urge to hit something very hard.

"You love her, you big lummox," Val said, giving him a shove.

"Why won't you leave it alone?" Tevin's lip curled up in a snarl.

"Because I'm your cousin, but I'm also your friend, and as such it is my job to tell you when your head is so far up your ass that I'm surprised you're still talking."

Tevin picked up the ax and grabbed a log, placing it on the flat stump they used for splitting wood. "Why don't you get it? It doesn't matter how I feel if she doesn't feel the same way. She'd only be trading one unhappy marriage for another."

Val crossed her arms and stared at him while he swung, splitting the wood with a loud crack. "It isn't the same at all, you donkey."

"Latimer is the superior choice. He's *her* choice."

"Give her a chance to make a better choice!" Val threw up her arms. "So you're not respectable. So you're a con man. So you snore sometimes and it makes a weird whistling noise that's really annoying."

"He's a pickpocket, too," Kate offered as she walked up, her arm around Amaury's waist.

"But a snappy dresser," Amaury said solemnly. "Never let them take that away."

Val put her hand on her hip. "Fine, so you're not perfect. Does that mean you don't get to be happy? Or find love?"

"Yes." Tevin cleared the split logs with his foot, grabbing a piece that was still too big and righting it so he could take another swing.

Val was so irritated she was almost vibrating. Amaury put a hand on her shoulder, shaking his head as he stepped up. "Do you love her, brother?"

Tevin held the ax loosely in one hand. He should tell them no. But that wouldn't stop them, because they'd know he was lying through his teeth. "Yes. The underworld take me for it, but I love her something fierce."

Amaury shrugged. "Then nothing else really matters, does it?"

Tevin looked forlornly at his brother. "She deserves better."

Amaury snorted. "Dear night, they all do, Tevin. Every single one of them. But that's the way the world works, and who are we to argue?"

Tevin blinked at him. "You're saying that even though I know I'm not good enough and my past is highly suspect, I should go after her anyway?"

Amaury pulled Val to him with one arm, linking her to him and Kate. "Absolutely. We steal all kinds of things that are too good for us. Why not a wife?"

"Stop thinking so much about your past, cousin," Val said, leaning into Amaury. "It takes time from considering your future."

Tevin stared at them, thinking about what they said. Imagining, for a moment. If he got down on his knees, confessed all to Merit, then what? Would his love be enough to break the curse? What were the odds that she would pick him over the others? Would it hurt to at least talk to her? To try?

"You're all cracked." He tossed the ax onto the grass. "I'll mirror her. Just to see if she's okay and to apologize."

Kate squealed, her dimples flashing as she jigged in place. "Yay!"

He pointed a finger at her. "Don't get too excited. If she looks happy, that's all I'm doing."

As a group, they jammed themselves into the small, cramped mirror room. A gold velvet couch was pushed against the new green pin-striped wallpaper. It was the only room they'd paid to repaper. Tevin's parents wanted to look good when people called.

The mirror, when they got to it, was flashing.

"Oooh," Kate said, "a message." She frowned. "It's probably a creditor. I'll erase it." She reached for the mirror.

"Kate," Tevin said, "we should at least see who it's from."

She nodded. "You're right. If we don't know who it is, we won't know which creditor to dodge. Wise." She tapped the mirror, stepping back so everyone could see the mage glass.

The image was sideways, so they turned their heads to make sense of it. Tevin could see what looked like a cell. Lady Zarla stood next to it, holding a handkerchief to her face. The skin around her eyes was red, like she'd been crying. Next to her stood an ethereal-looking blond fairyborn woman, obviously Latimer's mother. Latimer stood beside her, his face somber.

"She's quite safe," Latimer's mother said, her voice sounding oddly tinny. Either the mirror was flawed or it was set far from her.

Something in the cell growled, swiping a claw at the bars.

Lady Zarla stepped back, the handkerchief gripped tightly in her fist. "I don't know what happened. It's not her birthday yet. She hasn't come out of the beast at all? Even with tincture?"

The other woman patted her shoulder sympathetically. "We had a healer look at her. She assured us that as long as we go through with the ceremony, Merit's curse will be lifted." Another pat. "You'll have your daughter back soon enough. Two days will fly by."

Lady Zarla didn't look convinced by that last part. "I hate to see her like this. She must be miserable."

The blond woman tutted. "I know. We would do anything for our children, would we not?" She gently began to guide

Lady Zarla out of the room as the beast watched, her orange eyes tracking her mother's movements.

Lady Zarla sniffled, pausing to touch the bars of the cage before leaving. Latimer and his mother stayed. She continued to smile until the door shut with a heavy thud.

The smile dropped as she regarded her son. "Take her one of my calming potions, would you? Wouldn't want her to get too upset." She beamed at him. "I'll take care of the rest. All you have to do is show up at the altar and say 'I do.'"

Latimer nodded and stalked out of the room, Merit howling behind him.

The screen shone and then went blank. The message was over.

"What just happened?" Kate asked, reaching out to grasp Amaury's shoulder.

"That," Val said, "is a very good question. An even better question is what are we going to do now?"

"Willa and Diadora," Amaury interrupted. "They'll know what's going on, and I think they'll be more likely to talk to us than anyone at the Cravan House." The mirror chimed a few times before someone answered and went to fetch the sisters. Willa appeared after a few minutes, her cheeks flushed and her hair in disarray. Diadora followed, wiggling her fingers in greeting as they collapsed onto the gilded settee. Their mirror room was decorated in golds and creams, with a large vase of flowers. Diadora smiled at them while Willa wrote feverishly on her chalkboard.

It's so good to see you all! Veritess has been a bore since you left. Who's that?

"Our sister, Kate," Amaury said. "Kate, this is Willa and Diadora."

"Pleased to make your acquaintance." Kate dropped a curtsey as gracefully as she could manage with all of them packed tightly into the room.

"Have you talked to Merit recently? Or her mother?" Tevin said, cutting to the chase. "Have you heard anything about Merit's wedding?"

Willa's face took on a concerned cast, and she turned to her sister.

Diadora looked suddenly serious. "We went to see Ellery at Cravan House," she said, spitting out a sprig of lilac. "I've been having some problems with my curse. We got to chatting."

"Wait, Ellery isn't with Merit?" Val asked. The sisters shook their heads.

"She went to Huldre alone." Diadora stopped to fish an obscenely large pearl out of her cheek. "No one has spoken to her since she left. Latimer's people haven't let us talk to Merit. Say she's too busy or doesn't wish to speak to anyone. Lots of excuses." She coughed, pausing to spit up several daisies and an emerald. "Ellery is worried, Tevin."

"We're all worried," Willa said. A golden snake slithered out of her lips and hit her lap. She pursed her lips and picked up her slate and chalk. *Why do you ask?*

Tevin told them quickly about the mirror message, and by the end, they were both frowning.

Willa erased the slate, started to write, got annoyed, and threw the slate down. She grabbed a teapot, found it empty, and held it in her hands. "Who sent the message?" Willa maneuvered the teapot, catching several newts as they fell. "According to Ellery, the whole place is on lockdown until the wedding. No guests in or out."

"It's a good question," Val said. "I can't see either Latimer or Lady Zarla sending it. Obviously, it wasn't Merit. One of the staff, maybe?"

"You can't even get through to Lady Zarla?" Tevin asked, forcing himself to be patient. He didn't want to talk, he wanted to *do*. It would be foolhardy to attempt anything before he knew what was happening, but he was feeling excessively foolhardy.

"No," Willa said. "When we tried to put in a general mirror message to the castle, we reached a happy blocking message about the wedding."

Val took her hat in her hands, worrying the rim. "We can't just leave her, right?"

Tevin rubbed a hand over his neck. "She needs her curse broken, Val." He raised a hand to stop her from arguing. "I know I promised to give her a choice, but it's not like I can mirror the beast and talk to her."

"We go there. Let her choose. Beast doesn't want you?" She jammed her hat on her head. "We'll give her another option. Bring Cedric with us. What can it hurt to give her one more chance to choose?"

"A beast and an ostrich would make for an interesting wedding," Amaury said.

"We'll catch the next train to Veritess—" Tevin stopped. He didn't have any money. Except the money he'd stashed away. His parents had taken the coins in his trunk but had missed his second stash under the floorboard. Would that even be enough?

352

If they took Kate and used her savvy and his charm, maybe. He looked at Kate. "The only money I have for tickets—"

"You're getting on that train," Kate said firmly. Amaury nodded.

"Before you start to argue," Val said, her voice uncharacteristically flinty, "I want you to consider the fact that we *all* want you on that train. That we are your family and can be pigheaded when the mood strikes, as it is striking now. So I can hog-tie you and drag you onto that train, or you can walk on under your own free will."

Tevin's jaw clicked shut.

Diadora clasped her hands. "Are we crashing a wedding? How romantic." Flower petals drifted out of her mouth on a sigh.

"Yes." Amaury's eyes had a twinkle to them. "It'll be fun."

"What do you know of fun?" Val scoffed. "You hide at parties and read grocery bills."

"I'm always fun," Amaury said, deadpan. "Look at me now. I am a ball of laughs and jollity. A human construct of giddy social merriment."

"Of course you are." Kate hugged him.

"We're not crashing the wedding." Tevin tried to sound authoritative, putting his hands on his hips. He didn't think it worked. "We're going to find where they're keeping the beast and *discreetly* see if she needs help." They all stared at him, and he sighed. "Fine, and if that doesn't work, then *and only then* are we going to crash the wedding."

Diadora grabbed Willa's hand. "I've always wanted to crash a wedding."

Val rested her hands on her holster. "We'll let you know what train we catch. Can you call everyone together—Glendon, Ellery, Cedric, and Kaiya? We're going to need help, I think."

Willa grabbed the slate, writing another note. *We'll mirror everyone. And, Tevin? Every second helps, so don't feel the need to change or anything. Come exactly as you are.*

Tevin looked down. Due to the heat and the work, he'd taken off his shirt. He'd forgotten about it. He didn't even have his undershirt on, just trousers and his suspenders hanging down off his hips.

"What did you write?" Diadora yanked the chalkboard away, brushing away the diamond and two peony buds that fell from her lips. "Willa! You are not allowed to objectify him! He is asking us for help!" A carnation and three violets fell in quick succession.

Wilhelmina shrugged. "I can multitask." She grimaced as an orange tree frog hopped from her lower lip.

Diadora rolled her eyes, erased the board, and wrote a new note. *You earned that frog. Sorry, Tevin. You have time to put on a shirt. Let us know what train you're on, and we'll send a hack to fetch you.*

• • •

Tevin cleaned himself up quickly before putting on a fresh shirt. After that, he threw a few things into his satchel. Wondering who the beast would choose, or if she was even capable at this point. What would he do if she didn't pick him? What if they were too late and she couldn't choose anyone? Fear cascaded through him, and he let it. Yes, he was scared. He didn't have much to lose, not really, but when you only have a little, it seems important. He wouldn't lose Val. He'd still have Amaury and Kate. It was enough.

Once he had his stuff packed, he grabbed the rest of his money, practically running down the steps before halting at the bottom.

Brouchard blocked his passage, carefully removing his gloves and hat. He must have just come in the door.

Florencia stood next to him, easing out of her coat. "Where do you think you're going?"

Tevin didn't answer, but he figured he didn't need to.

Brouchard's eyebrow rose slowly. "Going after the girl? Good for you. A DuMont should never admit defeat."

"I'm not going for her fortune," Tevin said. "If she picks me, you won't see a single coin."

"Of course not." Brouchard clasped his hands behind his back, his tone mocking.

The words were a well-placed shot, echoing in the chamber of his body. He squared his shoulders and stared his father down. Tevin hadn't realized he was taller than him until now. Brouchard had always been lean—Amaury favored his build. At some point, Tevin had surpassed his father. He was wider. Stronger. "I promise you, Father. This is it. The end of the road."

Brouchard's expression became quizzical, affecting an air of innocence. "Amaury will be an adult soon enough, but what of your sister? You would leave her here? To struggle in a life of uncertain finances while you live a life of prosperity?"

355

"What if our next ship doesn't come in?" Florencia removed her hat carefully and hung it up. "Would you abandon us, after all we've done for you?"

Tevin felt something in him waver. Could he sacrifice Kate for his own happiness? A momentary look of triumph flashed across Brouchard's face.

Kate stepped onto the stairs. "Yes, he will."

Tevin turned to her. "Kate—"

His little sister lifted her chin. "Oh, no, brother. You're not sacrificing for me this time. Don't make me sic Val on you— you're getting on the train. I can take care of myself." She turned hard eyes on their father. "Tevin isn't my parent. It's not his job to provide."

Tevin was shaking his head. As her brother, he did share some responsibility.

"I don't have to go." He dropped his bag to the floor. "Val can take Cedric to Merit." Then she'd still have an option, if she'd changed her mind. His heart lurched, thinking of her pacing in that cell. Something was wrong, but maybe he didn't have to be the one to fix it. Kate might need him more.

"That's right." Brouchard reached for the handle of Tevin's bag. "Send your harridan of a cousin away."

"Father—"

Brouchard picked up the bag, rolling his eyes. "I'm only teasing, Tevin. Learn to take a joke."

Kate snatched the handle from her father, a thunderous expression on her face. "Oh, no." She jammed the bag at her brother. "I'm not a baby anymore, Tev. You're going."

Tevin accepted the bag out of reflex.

Florencia frowned at them both. "Kate."

Kate ignored her. "It's okay, Tevin. I can take care of myself. I promise. Have faith in me for once." She put her hands on her hips. "If I needed you, if I called, would you come?"

Tevin hesitated. "Always, but—"

"Then you're hardly abandoning me." She stared at him, the rest of her message clear. *No matter what they say.* "No. Go, Tevin. I'll be okay." She grinned, revealing her dimples. "Promise to get me something nice when you get back from the honeymoon."

"You assume a lot, sister, but thank you." Tevin enfolded his sister in a hug. He squeezed her tight. "If you ever need me."

"I know," Kate whispered. "Don't you worry about me. I'll handle Mama and Papa. Things are going to change in this house, just you wait."

Tevin laughed, letting her go with a final squeeze. Then he swept past his parents, without so much as a by-your-leave, and went to find Amaury and Val. Brouchard tried to follow him.

"We only want what's best for you." He quickened his pace to match Tevin's. "You're our child. We've clothed and fed you, given you everything, but of course if you feel comfortable leaving, I can only give you my best wishes." Brouchard took out his handkerchief, covering his mouth as he started coughing, a great hacking noise. "I'm sure we'll be okay."

"You'll be fine," Tevin said. "Aren't you always saying Du-Monts land on their feet?" Val and Amaury were already outside, their satchels full and ready to go.

Florencia leaned against the doorway but didn't go any farther. Brouchard followed him down the porch steps, Kate drifting behind him. "Tevin." His father straightened to his full height. "Tevin DuMont, I am your *father*, and you will listen. If you walk away from me, you'll not be welcomed back."

Tevin waited while Kate hugged Val and Amaury, all of them ignoring Brouchard.

"I mean it. Not even to visit."

"You keep walking," Kate said in a fierce whisper. "For once in your life, do something for *yourself*. You don't need to come back. We'll come to you."

He gave a final hug. "My door will always be open, even if I'm not sure where that door might be." He let her go, hitched his satchel over his shoulder, turned, and walked down the paving stones that led to the main street.

Brouchard kept spewing threats while Florencia stood a silent watch from the door. Tevin, Val, and Amaury ignored them both, then waved at Kate right before they turned and lost sight of her.

CHAPTER 29

ACKNOWLEDGING THE CORN

They caught the train to Veritess, then climbed into the hack Willa and Diadora had promised and went straight to their house. Val gave a low whistle as they arrived—Willa and her sister lived in an elaborate home of white brick and wrought iron that could comfortably sleep half the city. The staff let them in without question, showing them to a sitting room, where everyone had gathered. Glendon was talking quietly with Kaiya. Ellery fidgeted with their watch, a determined look on their drawn face. Willa and Diadora greeted them warmly, welcoming them all to their home. Someone in the corner squawked, and Tevin saw Cedric, looking much better than the last time he'd seen him, but still an ostrich.

"He agreed to help?" Tevin asked.

The ostrich lifted his chin and ruffled his feathers. "I cannot turn away from a maiden in distress."

"We need to speak with Merit," Tevin said without any preamble. "Glendon, Cedric—we could use your help."

"We heard about the mirror message," Glendon said, his fingers tapping on the arm of the couch. "Kaiya was already concerned about the lack of communication. I've tried getting

359

through to Lady Zarla as well, and haven't had any luck. However, I'm unsure what helping you three crash a wedding will accomplish."

"Hopefully it won't get to that point. We just want to talk to her. But it wasn't an accident that we saw that message. Someone reached out to us for help." Tevin leaned against the wall. He'd been sick on the train, and his stomach still didn't feel quite right. "I'm not sure what state she'll be in when we get there. But if she's back to herself and still wants to marry Latimer by the time we get there? Fine. I—" He suddenly felt twice the fool, surrounded by Merit's friends, in this grand house. Who was he to offer for their friend?

"Would she marry Cedric, then, if she didn't want Latimer?" Ellery said, adjusting their spectacles to take a good look at the fairyborn in question. "Because—and I don't mean this unkindly—he's still an ostrich."

"Only for a few months," Kaiya pointed out. "It's not like he's going to be a giant bird forever."

"Anything milady needs," Cedric said, his head held high. "Merit's a dear friend. I will happily offer myself as an alternative." He made that weird *hrrmm* noise with his throat.

"Pretty sure Tevin meant *he* would be the alternative," Amaury said, sprawling in his chair.

"Tevin?" Glendon looked at him carefully. "How will that help? I thought the whole point of this escapade was to make sure she still wants Latimer to break her curse. Or Cedric. Tevin can't do that."

"Unless he loves her," Kaiya said, a slow smile spreading across her face.

Everyone in the room turned to Tevin. He shuffled his feet, uncomfortable under the scrutiny. "That's why we're here."

Diadora hugged her sister. "So romantic!"

"He didn't actually admit anything," Ellery said.

Kaiya pushed her friend with her boot. "Don't be stubborn, Ellery. It's clear what he meant."

Ellery crossed their arms. "That may be, but if we're going to do this crazy thing, I want to hear it from his lips. There's no way I'm going to help possibly bust up my best friend's wedding just to toss her a groom who hems and haws and then pulls a Jasper. Even if we have Cedric as a backup to break the actual curse. It would be cruel. Merit doesn't need more heartbreak."

Kaiya dropped her foot back onto the floor. "Ellery does have a point."

Tevin had a feeling that they both believed him, but they wanted him to work for it, which was fair enough. He stepped away from the wall. "You get me there, and she says yes, I will marry Merit. I'll sign a wedding contract that will give you peace of mind—none of her money, her lands, anything, will come to me. Everything will stay hers. I love her." He stared right into Ellery's face when he said it, because he knew the spriggan was the one who needed convincing.

Ellery remained stony. "And if she says no?"

"I won't leave her cursed," Tevin said. "She can marry Latimer if she wants. We'll have Cedric with us on standby. Or you can bring Freddie. I'll fight for her, but if she says no, I won't stand in the way of her freedom."

"I would be honored to care for your lady love." The ostrich nodded solemnly.

361

"We might need someone to get Lady Zarla on board once we get there. Assuming Merit has changed her mind about Huldre." Amaury's eyes lit up as a maid brought in a tray of food. They all looked at Glendon.

"She might not listen." Glendon rubbed a hand over his face. "But I will do my best."

"Please," Kaiya said, rolling her eyes. "You're an ambassador. Talking people into things is one of your gifts. If that doesn't work, play kissy face with her."

Glendon didn't move. "Lady Zarla is a baroness and an intelligent woman. I don't like the implication that playing 'kissy face' will sway her mind. We share a mutual respect and—"

"I've seen you," Kaiya said, her tone deadpan. "Lady Zarla. You." She held her hands in front of her, like puppets. She slowly brought them together in a kiss, staring at her uncle. *"Canoodling."*

"What?" Glendon blinked at her. "When? How?"

Kaiya dropped her hands. "It's my job to know things."

"We know all, we see all," Amaury said. "And what I saw was you smooching Lady Zarla in the garden."

"And the stables," Val said.

"The pantry," Kaiya said.

Glendon's tan face was red to the roots of his hair. "Yes, I understand."

"That explains why Lady Zarla wasn't interfering with Merit more." Ellery affectionately punched the man's shoulder. "I'm a little in awe, really."

Glendon buried his face in his hands. "I don't feel comfortable discussing this with any of you. Can we stop talking about

362

it, please?" He held up a hand. "I will do my best to sway her around to Tevin's side if Merit chooses him."

"Excellent," Willa said, her fingers steepled. "Let's talk about the wedding, then, and how we're going to sneak in."

• • •

"How did I get talked into this?" Glendon asked the roof of the train his question, not aiming it at anyone in particular. Together they entirely filled the private train car Willa and Diadora had rented. Except for Cedric—despite his title and status, he'd been made to ride in the cattle car. No matter how well dressed or genteel the ostrich, it still couldn't ride in a first-class passenger cabin. Tevin didn't think that was an actual rule, but the conductor insisted that it was.

"We're very persuasive," Val said, leaning against the plush leather of her seat. "And we grow on you."

"Like fungus," Amaury said, as the train swayed around a slow curve. Countryside flew by, smears of blue, green, and brown.

"I want to die." Tevin hung his head between his legs. Diadora rubbed small, soothing circles on his back.

"That's not very heroic." Kaiya squinted at him. "Heroes on their way to rescue someone shouldn't cast up their accounts."

"Airin' the paunch," Val said solemnly, her hands folded in her lap. "You best acknowledge the corn, Kaiya—even heroes get motion sick."

Acknowledge the corn? Willa wrote on her slate. *What does that even mean?*

"It means to accept an obvious truth or to stop lying," Val said.

"We could all do with a little acknowledging the corn," Ellery said, rubbing a cloth over the lenses of their glasses.

"My head hurts." Glendon cradled his head in his hands and shut his eyes.

"I have a powder for that." Ellery stood up to grab their leather satchel from the rack above their head. "Have you been drinking enough water? Headaches can often come from mild dehydration."

"I think this headache has *DuMont* written all over it in giant letters." Glendon rubbed his temples.

Ellery opened up the medicine bag. "Either way, I have a powder to help." They handed a packet to Glendon. "Tip it back into your throat. I suggest with water to wash it down. The taste is dreadful. Tevin, you get a ginger chew."

"No, thank you," Tevin groaned.

Ellery tossed the small wrapped candy to Val, who caught it one-handed. Ellery grabbed Tevin's forehead and pulled him back in the seat, while Val unwrapped the candy and popped it in his mouth. His eyes watered.

"It's strong," he said through the hand Val still had clamped on his mouth.

"It will help," Ellery said.

Tevin chewed, because arguing with the combined force of Val and Ellery was useless.

"Maybe I should go back and sit with Cedric," Tevin mumbled through Val's hand. Diadora kindly patted his hand, though Willa rolled her eyes and mouthed, "Baby," at him.

Val removed her hand from Tevin's mouth. "Cedric is fine. If anyone tries anything, he can kick them."

"Glendon, what can you tell us about the Huldre kingdom?" Amaury asked.

"Precious little, really. The family isn't very friendly, and they very much see themselves as a cut above. I was there for a party they held a few years back celebrating an anniversary. It was theatrical and excessive. There were fireworks and dancers, bards, trained bears, and a dinner that went on for hours. They like to hit you over the head with their wealth. Everything is a spectacle. They will also have excellent security. Large palisade around the whole palace."

"The nearest village is Dalliance," Amaury said. "I looked at a map earlier."

Kaiya dug around in her pack, pulling out a leather tube. She unrolled it, revealing several small maps. She sifted through them until she found the one she was looking for and then spread it out. "Dalliance is the closest, yes."

"I know," Amaury said dryly.

Ellery leaned over the map. "What an odd name for a village."

Tevin leaned back into his chair, his eyes closed, pleased that his stomach was settling.

"I'm told it helps if you keep your eye on the horizon," Kaiya said. "But that might only work on ships."

"It will be a huge event." Glendon traced his finger along the edge of the map. "They'll be checking invitations closely."

"How are you going to get in, then?" Ellery asked.

Amaury snorted. "You're adorable. Don't you worry about the how. We just need to get to Dalliance. Once we're there, we'll handle the rest."

"Do you have everything you need?" Tevin asked Amaury.

His brother wobbled his hand back and forth. "I'll need to see an actual invitation before I can say for sure. Likely I have most of it." He hefted his travel bag. "I can get the rest. Easy."

Tevin felt his stomach roll at Amaury's words, hoping it was the motion of the train and not a sense of foreboding over the word *easy*.

CHAPTER 30

ENTER THE FOREST

Though the train ride wasn't a long one, they had short stop-overs at several stations along the way. At the last one before they crossed the border into Huldre, the train would be docked long enough to change out mages and also check crossing papers. Tevin hadn't been concerned about that—everyone had them except for Amaury and himself. They had forgeries, but since Amaury had made them, they were identical to the real thing. The problem occurred when they all clambered out at the station to stretch their legs. Amongst a wall of schedules, notices, and general signs was a large picture of Tevin. Val quickly swapped their hats, jamming hers onto his head and tipping the brim down while Amaury went to read it.

"They don't say what you did," Amaury said when he came back. "Just that you can't cross into Huldre. Mandate of the king and queen."

"If there are signs here, that means they'll be checking the roads, too." Ellery took out their pocket watch. "We don't have a lot of time. What are we going to do?"

Tevin thought back to Kaiya's map. There was a way to get to Dalliance that didn't involve the train or the roads, but it was a terrible idea. Unfortunately, it was the only one he could think of unless he suddenly sprouted wings. "You're going to get back on the train. I'll meet you in Dalliance."

"What's your plan?" Amaury asked.

"I'm going to cut through the forest." Tevin kept his hat low, but not enough to block his line of sight completely. He wanted to keep an eye on the crowd.

Glendon, Willa, and Diadora tried to argue. Val's face scrunched up, expressing her skepticism. Only Kaiya and Amaury appeared to be considering it.

"Does anyone have a better plan?"

Glendon rubbed a hand over his jaw. "No."

Willa and Diadora shook their heads.

"It could work." Like him, Amaury's gaze was restless, examining the train station bustle for danger.

"I'm coming with you," Val said. "No argument. The forest is dangerous, and last I checked, I had the pistols."

"I'll come, too," Kaiya said. "That way there's a small chance you will both live."

Given more time, Tevin would have talked them out of it, but at that moment, the train blew a warning whistle and people started to reboard. "Fine. We can cash in the rest of our tickets. We'll need horses or we'll never make it in time. Does anyone have coin we could borrow?"

They ran back on board, pausing in the cabin to grab their bags and pool funds. Everyone gave up what coins they could. He hugged everyone in thanks, saying quick goodbyes as he did.

Amaury grabbed his arm as he was about to leave. "I'll see you in Dalliance."

Tevin nodded, knowing that was Amaury's way of saying *be careful*. "Watch over everyone for me." His brother nodded and then Tevin was out the door behind Val and Kaiya, hoping they were making the best decision.

They used a few coppers to catch a hack to the closest town. After asking a few of the locals, they were able to find people willing to part with three horses, saddles, and tack, and that was only because Tevin leaned heavily on his charm. They only had a few coins left to buy food and canteens for the ride, something Kaiya wisely insisted they take the time to do.

Night was falling by the time they were done. Out of coin and not wanting to stay in town any longer for fear of drawing attention to Tevin, they rode their horses to the edge of the forest. There they paid a farmer to let them picket their horses and sleep in the hayloft. It wasn't smart to enter the forest tired, or at night. They would have to wait until first light.

• • •

The Enchanted Forest, for all that Tevin could see, looked exactly like a regular forest. It was large and full of trees, creating a wall of greenery that stretched off into the distance. Thick undergrowth nestled underfoot. Birds chirped, and something hooted. It didn't even look ominous. Looks, however, were deceiving, as Tevin knew well, and every instinct in him was running around and banging cymbals, yelling, *Danger! Danger!* and then making siren noises.

They'd pulled the horses up to the forest's edge and were currently in a loose line, staring at the trees.

"At this point I think we should remember that there are

giant cats in there," Val said, her head tipped up as she looked at the canopy.

"Merit just added another one, too," Tevin said, thinking of the marar from the carnival. "Best avoided, I think."

"Someone else told me that there's apparently a magical orchard in there where the fruits are all gems and the leaves are coins, but if we touch any of them, we die," Val said.

"How would we die?" Kaiya asked.

Val shrugged. "That point was unclear. When I went to the farmhouse this morning to buy us breakfast, the farmer said there was a dragon who will chew us up, bones and all, and his husband said to not eat anything because everything is poison."

"According to one of the ladies we bought horses from, I'm supposed to avoid all beautiful maidens, but I'm not sure if that means all of us or just me." Tevin shifted in his saddle. "Either way, be careful, Val. Don't go off chasing mysterious forest ladies."

Val leaned over and punched him in the arm.

"I think, then, based on what I know and what everyone is saying, we should assume that everything in the forest is trying to kill us." Kaiya's face was serene, her eyes untroubled as she gazed out at the forest.

"Yes," Val said. "That, exactly."

"I think the point is that we're supposed to kill the things first," Tevin said. "Before they eat us."

Val eyed his saddle. "You don't even have a rifle. How are you supposed to do that?"

"By standing behind you," Tevin said. "I'm a terrible shot, and no one wants me armed. I think my primary role is bait."

"I think it makes more sense to avoid what we can instead of chasing and killing everything we see," Kaiya said, pulling her hair into a ponytail.

Val tipped her hat back and looked out at the expanse of trees. "How big do you reckon it is, anyway?"

"Here's the thing—I checked the maps this morning, and the map the farmer had. The Enchanted Forest is vast, but the actual sizing seems . . . inconsistent." Kaiya shielded her eyes with one hand as she gazed along the tree line.

"Maybe they're bad mapmakers?" Val didn't take her eyes off the forest.

Kaiya shook her head. "Everything else matched. The only problem was the scale of the forest. Could be magic. May also be that the cartographers don't get paid enough to go in there."

"Well, we might as well get a move on," Tevin said, nudging his horse. "It's not going to get any less deadly or enchanted. But as the self-proclaimed bait, I'd like to ride in the middle."

• • •

The first thing Tevin noticed was the change in light. Since the tree cover was so dense, the bright light of morning became watered down and dark, like the sun had taken one look at the world, decided it wasn't worth it, and gone back to bed. At first they were met with an eerie silence: The only sound was the breaking of twigs as their horses pushed through the dense underbrush. But as they made their way in farther, the forest came back to life, and Tevin couldn't tell which was worse, silence or noise. Birds—at least he hoped they were birds—screeched and hooted. Occasionally the scratchy boom of an animal vocalizing cut through the racket, but Tevin couldn't for the life of him figure out what it was.

Kaiya pitched her head to the side. "Marar. Very large, from the sound of it." She moved on, unconcerned. Tevin and Val urged their horses to follow close behind her and pulled their limbs in a little tighter.

"It's okay," Kaiya said. "I suspect it's far off, and as long as we don't enter the creature's territory, we should be fine."

"Of course, we don't know where its territory is," Val pointed out.

"Please tell me you're armed," Tevin whispered to Kaiya.

She nodded. "Crossbow."

Tevin moved his horse carefully between them. He wasn't stupid—if anything attacked, Val and Kaiya were both experts with their weapons. The marar wouldn't care if his face was handsome; it would just eat it.

After an hour riding in near silence, they saw several pheasants and a few of the strangest rabbits Tevin had ever encountered—they were about twice the size of normal rabbits and had antlers. He didn't like the way they stared at him as he rode past.

The forest grew dense, and they began to follow a narrow game trail. Tevin kept his reins loose, trusting his horse to stay close as he kept an eye on the bushes around them. Val suddenly cursed behind him, and Tevin twisted in his saddle to find her rubbing at her face with the sleeve of her jacket. "Leaned in too close to a flower back there. Hanging off some sort of vine. Blasted thing opened up and poofed at me."

Tevin tried to get a good look at the flowers, only to find the blossoms closed up into pods.

"You've got pollen on your sleeve," Kaiya said. "So now you're just rubbing it around. Use your canteen and handkerchief. Rinse out your eyes, mouth, and nostrils. We don't know what's in that pollen."

They paused in a small glade, giving Val the opportunity to take out her canteen and rinse her face, taking swigs of water and spitting it out onto the forest floor. "Did any get on my horse?"

Tevin looked as close as he could from his saddle. The horse returned his stare, calm and clear-eyed. No bright yellow dust that Tevin could see. He shook his head. He left Val to her rinsing and sipped from his own canteen, checking out the clearing as he did. A murky pond lay off to the side, surrounded by cattails and boulders. It wasn't much of a pond, really. More of a glorified puddle. Small red mushrooms with white spotted caps nestled next to the largest boulder. The groundcover was mostly moss, the sun almost completely blocked by the forest canopy.

Kaiya took out her compass, checking their bearings to make sure they were going the right way. "We need to go *there*." Kaiya pointed. "I don't see a trail, so we'll have to cut through the forest as best we can."

Tevin nodded and glanced at Val, who had been staring off into the trees, her eyes wide.

"Val?" Tevin said her name slowly, making it into a question. "Are you okay?"

Val snapped to attention, finally seeming to hear Tevin. "What?" Her eyes suddenly went wide, and she screamed, her voice shrill, startling them and the horses.

Kaiya reached out and grabbed the reins to Val's horse, making sure it didn't bolt.

"Well, that was unexpected." Tevin drew his horse up to Val, who was currently hyperventilating. "Val?"

"Spider," she hissed. "Giant spider. It was in the air. I saw it."

"Val, you like spiders," Tevin said. "You found one in the privy at home and named it Gus. Wouldn't let any of us put it outside."

Kaiya reached out and touched Val's arm. Instead of the touch calming her, it seemed to make things worse. She slid from her horse, running as soon as her feet hit the ground. They were so surprised they didn't move for a second. Then Val threw off her jacket and vest, her fingers fumbling with the buttons of her shirt. "Spiiiiddddeeeerrsssssss!"

Kaiya sprang from her horse, hitting the ground at a dead run. Luckily, she was fast and Val was slowed down by her focus on her buttons. Kaiya tackled her from behind, both of them hitting the ground with an *oof*. They wrestled briefly, but Kaiya's skills in that arena far outmatched Val's.

"Rope," Kaiya said calmly, her arms and legs wrapped around Val's, pinning her. "Bring me rope. Shhhhh, Val. You're safe."

Val shook her head wildly. "Spidersspiderspidersspiders spiders."

"No spiders," Tevin said, digging through Val's pack, finding a length of rope.

"No spiders?" Val pressed the side of her face into the moss.

"They're all gone, Val. Promise." His cousin seemed to believe him, as she relaxed in Kaiya's hold. Tevin handed the rope to Kaiya, who quickly tied Val's hands and feet. Then Kaiya sat back on her heels, taking a moment to examine Val's blown pupils and hammering pulse. "Did you see the flower?"

Tevin shook his head. "Not open. They hung almost like pods on a large vine encircling a tree."

Kaiya frowned. "I wish Ellery were here. I've never heard of such a thing. We'll have to tie her to her horse and hope it wears off soon." Kaiya wiped the hand that had been touching Val on the grass. "We need to make sure there's no more pollen on her. Grab my canteen, will you? And better wipe down the saddlebags before you touch them. I don't need two people off their gourds on pollen."

After they rinsed Val's face again, Kaiya went to double-check the horses while Tevin carefully removed Val's shirt and replaced it with a clean one from her bags.

They carried Val, her mouth slack as she hallucinated, back over to her horse. Tevin untied her, Kaiya ready in case Val bolted again. Once they got Val up onto her mount, Kaiya tied her to the saddle. Val was upright now, but not fully coherent. After a short discussion, they used handkerchiefs to tie her wrists to the pommel. Tevin handed off the reins to Kaiya, then picked up Val's jacket, vest, and hat. Val wouldn't care about the shirt and vest, but she'd be unhappy if she lost her hat.

Tevin carried all of it over to the pond, needing to wash whatever pollen residue was left on the clothes as well as his hands. He rolled up his sleeves past the elbow and hunched down close to the water. The water held a touch of swamp, the air around it rich with the breakdown of vegetation. Not particularly something Tevin wanted to bathe in, but he had little choice. He dunked the hat and clothes in short order and set them aside. He was in the middle of rinsing his hands when something large and green shot up out of the pond. Tevin stumbled back, getting the impression of a set of large jagged teeth and reptilian yellow eyes. Only his reflexes saved him as he scuttled madly away from the pond. He spun and righted himself, grabbed Val's hat, and sprinted toward the horses. The creature didn't follow, instead lowering itself back into the water.

"Don't go near the pond," Tevin said, bending over, his hands on his knees while he caught his breath. "Something tried to eat me." Val's shirt and vest were still by the water's edge. He decided they would stay there.

"You two need to pace yourselves." Kaiya swung up into her saddle, her bay horse dancing to the side as she adjusted the reins. "It's not even lunch yet."

CHAPTER 31

NUISANCES FROM ABOVE

They were back in single file, Kaiya in the lead, Tevin bringing up the rear. He'd taken Val's pistols, tying the holster to his saddle, not that he could do much with them. He just didn't want Val to have them until she stopped hallucinating. In the meantime, he'd keep them with him.

Kaiya twisted in her saddle. "How are you feeling, Val?"

Val, in turn, twisted as best she could to look at Tevin. "Did you say that?"

"No," Tevin said.

Val seemed relieved. "Good, because I don't talk to pinecones."

"She's fine," Tevin told her evenly. "But I'm a pinecone."

"I wonder why a pinecone," Kaiya said.

Tevin shrugged.

This part of the forest seemed darker than it had been, the tree cover particularly dense. It gave the air a strangely still quality. In forests, there's always something to hear. Squawking of birds, chirping of insects, the rustle of undergrowth as something moves through the bushes. But the forest around them had gone eerily quiet, and the only time that happened was if there was a predator nearby. He was fairly certain it wasn't because of them. The forest had been making plenty of noise up until now.

Kaiya halted her horse, her eyes on the trees. Tevin did the same.

In the hush of the forest, the air became tense with expectation. They were being hunted.

"Run!" Kaiya shouted, pressing her heels into the sides of her own horse and leaning forward; Val's horse followed suit. Tevin urged his own mount to follow. Val, thankfully, decided this was a fun game, and hunched over her saddle. He leaned forward, ignoring the adrenaline coursing through him, making his palms sweat against the reins. He couldn't tell his heartbeat from the pounding of the horse's hooves as they tore through the forest.

Something behind them gave a low growl that Tevin felt more than heard. He sat up and turned to look, missing the chance to duck away from a branch. Pain lanced through his shoulder as the branch knocked him from the back of his horse. He fell, rolling along the moss and dead leaves that lined this part of the forest floor.

When he opened his eyes, it was to the sight of a large black jungle cat. The size of the creature made his mind stutter. Tevin estimated that the cat was at least three feet tall and about a foot longer than his horse. No feline should be that big. Or that close to him. Tevin's horse, riderless and scared, kept galloping. Tevin could only hope that Kaiya would catch it, and that he lived long enough to get back in the saddle. Kaiya shouted, but he couldn't make out what she said, and he didn't dare look away from the cat. Tevin lay on the ground, bruised, dirty, his eyes wide as he stared the cat down. He didn't have many options. He couldn't run—the cat was too close, too big, too fast. It would pounce before he made it two feet. Val's pistols were in her holsters, hanging from his saddle, making them exactly useless.

Tevin did the only thing he could think of—he started talking. "Hey there, big fella. Aren't you the pretty kitty?" He kept talking, the words a jumble of soothing nonsense, while slowly raising one hand, his palm flat. The giant cat sat on its haunches, leaning forward. Light caught the tufts of dark gray fur fluffed out from its face, along with long whiskers. A thin, familiar scar sliced across its nose. Everything about the creature's design was pure, sleek power, and still Tevin held out his hand.

The cat sniffed it, opening its jaw enough to let Tevin's scent wash over its tongue. It sneezed. Tevin wiped spit from his face.

"Thanks for that." He reached his hand back out, and the creature brushed the side of its face against it, scent marking him. The cat purred, again a sound he could feel more than actually hear. He kept talking to the cat, a low murmur, as the marar rubbed against his palm, its green eyes hooded.

Tevin pulled his hand away, getting up slowly, making no quick or sharp movements. The cat watched, staying on its own haunches, its ears tipped forward. Nothing about it said *aggressive*, just curious. Tevin used both hands to scratch the cat around its face. The feline closed its eyes and stretched out its neck to give Tevin greater access. He blanched a little as the cat yawned, exposing very large, very sharp teeth. "I would appreciate it if you didn't do that again. You have a large mouth, sir." The stuffed one at the Cravan House had been smaller and didn't have the ruff. "What does that mean, eh? Are the females the small ones, or the males?" The cat didn't answer, but he was pretty sure it was male.

Tevin crooned at the marar. It head-butted him in the gut. With its head raised, it would look at Tevin's rib cage, and yet it was nudging him like a kitten. Tevin looked up at the trees. "You're supposed to sleep during the day, did you know that? Perhaps we presented too tempting a target?"

He heard a crackling noise and looked up to see Kaiya, the two other horses tied behind her.

She pulled up on the reins, stopping the horse. "I thought for sure I was coming back for the pieces."

When Tevin didn't tense or change what he was doing, the cat seemed content to watch her. "I think we're friends now." Tevin ran his fingers through the big cat's cheek fluff. "Who's a good, giant carnivorous boy? You are!" The cat bumped him again, and he grunted.

"Do you think he'll let you leave?"

"Only one way to find out." Tevin gave the cat a final scratch. "Let's part as friends, okay, buddy? We don't chew on our friends." The cat huffed.

Tevin took a step back, and the cat tilted his head but didn't move. Tevin took another, edging his way to his steed. The marar continued to watch as Tevin took a moment to soothe the horses, who were justifiably scared of the giant cat. Once they were calm, he pulled himself onto his horse's saddle. After a long stretch, the marar stood, his body language telling Tevin that he was waiting for them to go.

"Either he's playing with his food and wants to chase," Tevin said, gathering up his reins, "or he's coming with us."

"Like you said, only one way to find out." Kaiya edged her horse around, clucking at it until it started walking along the trail.

"I think he's the one Merit freed from the carnival. Same scar on his nose." Tevin followed behind Kaiya, and as soon as he'd gone a few feet, the cat padded behind him.

Kaiya looked over her shoulder to make sure they were following. "Then you know who to thank for your new friend."

• • •

They traveled like that for two hours before Val started to come out of her pollen haze.

"Why am I tied to my saddle?" Val asked, her voice raspy.

"For so many reasons. How are you feeling?" Tevin brought his horse up to hers.

"Fine?"

"Are you covered in spiders?" Kaiya asked, not turning around. "Is Tevin a pinecone? Do you feel like you're made of light?"

"No," Val said. "Should I?" Then she blinked slowly. "I do see a giant cat, though. Like the stuffed one you got at the fair."

"He's really here," Kaiya said, "so that's fine." They stopped so Kaiya could check her pupils and ask a few more questions. When she declared Val to be on the mend, she untied her, and Tevin reluctantly handed back her pistols.

"They're stunning rounds," Val reassured him. "The mages make a lot of nonlethal options."

They rode into another small clearing, this one completely

open to the sky. Even with the cloud cover, it was brighter without the thick forest to filter the light. A stream cut through the land here, and they paused to let the horses drink and fill their canteens. The marar took that opportunity to wade into the river and scare away some minnows.

"Leave those baby fish alone, you hobgoblin," Tevin said, chastising the giant cat, who didn't look repentant at all. He chuffed at Tevin, shaking and spraying him with water. "Well, thank you for that." Canteen refilled, he climbed back into the saddle. "Come on then, Hob."

"Did you just name the giant man-eating cat Hob?" Kaiya asked.

Tevin shrugged. "I have to call him something. And he's mischievous, like a hobgoblin."

"Pretty sure hobgoblins are small." Val scrutinized the cat as he climbed out of the stream, shaking more water off his coat.

"The next time one of you gets a giant cat, you can name them whatever you want." He waved at Kaiya to get moving. "Come on, we're wasting daylight."

They were only a few feet away from the stream when Tevin heard a sort of churring noise. Hob's head snapped up, his whiskers twitching.

"What was that?" Val placed one hand on the butt of her pistol.

"It sounded like a fladger," Kaiya said, her face scrunched up in a scowl. "But we shouldn't have to worry about those. They're generally pretty skittish. One of the stable lads used to keep one as a pet."

A shadow fell over them, and Tevin looked up. The sky was

filled with fladgers—at least thirty of them. They were hissing and obviously ticked off, and they descended on their party with an unholy glee.

Tevin wondered for a second if he had inhaled some of the pollen earlier and not realized it.

The marar leapt, tearing into one of the fladgers while it was still in the air. A fine mist of blood sprayed, and the fladger squealed, and then they hit the ground rolling. They all ducked as the fladgers flew at them, their great big gray and black wings extended. Tevin's horse wheeled, and he tried to calm it, but that was the exact moment Tevin was knocked off his horse by a giant, flying, angry fladger.

Tevin hit the ground, the air slammed out of him from the fall and by forty pounds of snarling fur and wings. The fladger sneezed, covering Tevin's face in snot.

Suddenly the creature was gone, Kaiya having kicked it off him. She stood over Tevin, her hand held out. He grabbed it, sucking in breaths as his lungs surged back to life. Val stood in front of them, both her pistols raised, the sharp crack of shot after shot ringing through the clearing. Kaiya handed Tevin the reins of the horses as she grabbed the crossbow. They kept their horses behind them, Tevin kicking out at any of the fladgers that came toward them, trying to discourage the frenzied creatures. Kaiya kept the crossbow ready in case any of the fladgers got too close.

"Do you think they would actually eat us?" Tevin shouted, trying to shake a particularly tenacious fladger off his boot, the wings smacking his legs.

"I have no idea. I've never seen them frenzy like this." Kaiya grabbed Tevin's attacker by the scruff and threw it, almost getting bitten in the process. "They're a lot heavier than they look." She kicked another one away. The next fladger jumped at Tevin, aiming for his trouser buttons. He dodged while Kaiya yanked its wings and awkwardly tossed it away.

"Why do they keep going for my crotch?"

"Perhaps that's their way of showing affection," Val yelled, trying to make herself heard over the melee. Her pistol clicked, her rounds spent. "Kaiya, switch!"

Kaiya moved in front of her, bringing up the crossbow and loosing bolt after bolt on the creatures while Val reloaded.

Tevin could see Hob batting another fladger out of the air with his paw. Val was grinning as she snapped her pistols shut.

"I think you're enjoying this," Tevin said, holding the reins in a death grip.

"I'm not *not* enjoying it." She stepped forward, flanking Kaiya. For several minutes, they kicked, shot, and punched their attackers away. When Kaiya ran out of crossbow bolts, she pulled out a dagger and dropped into a crouch. By then the madness had mostly stopped, the fladgers either dead or fleeing. They watched warily, but the remaining creatures seemed to be ignoring them now. After a few more minutes, the last of the fladgers waddled away, having decided that their quarry wasn't worth it. They were left in a trampled clearing, the only noise coming from the marar as he settled down to eat one of the fladgers he'd caught.

"Is it over?" Tevin asked. "Kaiya, I thought you said they weren't aggressive."

"Maybe it's rutting season?" Kaiya wiped her dagger in the

grass, checking the blade carefully before sheathing it. "Or per-haps they got into the same flower as Val." She walked over to the nearest slain fladger, put her boot on it, and pulled out one of her crossbow bolts. She sighed. "It's cracked." Kaiya threw it on the ground. "Val, help me get the bolts. Only keep the ones that seem to be intact." They quickly gathered up the bolts while Tevin managed the horses.

"I hate having to kill so many," Kaiya said. "Maybe they were sick, I don't know."

"It was us or them," Val said. "But that doesn't make me feel good about it, either. At least Hob will be well fed."

• • •

They exited the forest, weary and travel-worn, and made their way into Dalliance—a small town nestled between brilliant green foothills. Tevin waited with Hob on the outskirts until Val could figure out where everyone else was staying. Luckily, Dalliance's size meant that people had a limited number of options.

Kaiya pointed at a slender road that snaked up into the mountains. "That's where we have to go tomorrow morning. Those are the Nobbles."

"That's a terrible name for mountains," Tevin said, following where she pointed.

"Yes, well, they aren't really mountains, more like really large hills. The one to the right there, it doesn't have a proper peak, but a flat top, like a plateau. That's where Huldre's castle is."

The Nobbles were heavily wooded, the occasional thin road snaking across the sides. "Single road entrance?"

Kaiya nodded.

"We're definitely going to have to bluff our way in, then." Tevin stared at the Nobbles, not liking all of that land between him and Merit. They seemed so close now; he wanted to urge his horse into a canter and go straight to her.

Val arrived then and led them to the small set of rooms that Glendon had managed to rent. There was a shared sitting room, which boasted a love seat and a round table with four mismatched chairs. Two bedrooms, each with two beds. It was a room usually used for family visitors, and they were going to have to share beds, not that anyone was complaining. They had to sneak Hob in through the back stairs in the same way they'd apparently used for Cedric, as they didn't think it was a good idea for the big cat to sleep in the stables. Tevin told Hob firmly that Cedric was a friend and he wasn't allowed to eat him, which only seemed to alarm the ostrich more.

Everyone had been busy in their absence.

"We're going to sneak in as performers," Amaury said. "Glendon and everyone else can go in with their invitations. I figured since we had an ostrich, it was our best bet, and it meant we could wear costumes to disguise ourselves."

"The only problem is that the performers received different invitations." Glendon eyed Hob as he sniffed the ambassador's shoes. "Ellery went out with Willa and Diadora earlier to see if they could get their hands on one."

"How was the forest?" Amaury asked, pulling out a slim wooden case. Tevin knew from experience that it was full of pens, pigments, and other tools of the forgery trade.

"It feels like I played a round of poule and I was the chicken."

"Poule?" Glendon asked.

"It's a game. People throw things at a chicken. Whoever hits the chicken wins." Tevin loosened his tie. "It's a fairly simple game."

"What do they win?" Glendon rested his chin in his hand and watched Amaury set up.

"The chicken." Tevin leaned back in his chair. "It's a popular game in the poorer districts."

The door rattled, and the rest of their group piled in.

"All hail the conquering heroes," Willa said, drawing a tube of paper out of a hidden pocket in her skirts. She unrolled it, displaying the rough sketch of what appeared to be Huldre's castle. "All Diadora had to do was bat her eyes and smile, and people told her all kinds of stuff."

"The powers of asking people nicely," Diadora said, pushing her curls back out of her face. "We have a rough outline of Huldre's palace based on the information we were able to gather. It's not complete, but I'm hoping Glendon can fill some of it out."

Ellery swayed, collapsing next to Glendon. "I got the grooms drunk. For such skinny little things, they sure packed away a great deal of moonshine." They tried to unbutton their vest and missed a button, frowning at it. "Respectable."

"Did you learn anything from the grooms, besides the fact that they're respectable drinkers?" Tevin asked.

"Support staff is supposed to stay in the village, so we can't sneak in as grooms or maids or anything like that. Amaury was right." Ellery blinked, fumbling another button. "Did you see that? Damn things keep disappearing. Some mage magicked my blinkin' vest."

Kaiya took pity on Ellery and helped with their buttons. "Ellery, do you have anything for the assuredly wicked hangover you're going to have? We won't have time to coddle you in the morning."

Ellery's head lolled in a vague approximation of a nod. "Bring me my thingie."

"Anything else?" Tevin asked as Val fetched the healer's bag.

"Rumor going around that a jilted lover wants to protest the union, so guards will be keeping him out." Ellery looked at Tevin blearily. "That's you. The upside is that you're so damn pretty that people are stealing your wanted posters. There's an actual underground market on them." They dug into their back pocket, missed, tried again, and managed to pull out a stained and folded piece of paper. Ellery tossed it to Tevin. He unfolded it and found a fair likeness of his face.

"Nothing we didn't anticipate after the train station," Glendon said, looking over Tevin's shoulder. "You'll need to stay in the rooms until we're ready to go. It might be best if we all keep out of sight until we head to the castle."

"Try to get a seat up front," Tevin said. "In case something goes wrong or we don't get to Merit in time. We might need you three to stop the wedding somehow."

"We'll handle it," Willa said.

"Ellery, did you manage to get ahold of an entertainer's invite?" Amaury asked. He had all of his pigments and odds and ends out and ready.

Ellery had just finished tipping back some sort of powder into their throat and was sipping from a cup of water Kaiya had handed them.

"I really hope you're not poisoning yourself." Kaiya watched her friend with gentle amusement.

Ellery shook their head. "Everything's in abbible . . . appa-piiple . . . apple pie order." The healer reached into their shirt and pulled out a rumpled piece of paper. "Borrowed this. Have to get it back. Don't want to leave the boy atwixt a rock and a hard place. Not a bamboozler like you lot. Gave him my word."

"Gave who your word?" Tevin asked, taking the paper. "Oh, good, this is damp."

"Spilled my drink," Ellery slurred.

"I certainly hope so." Tevin handed the paper to Amaury.

The faintest whisper of a smile lit Amaury's face. "Brilliant, Ellery."

Tevin leaned over his shoulder. The (slightly) damp paper in Amaury's hand was a signed contract for a group of fire-eaters. Now that Amaury knew what the entertainment was going to be carrying, their chances had become infinitely better.

Tevin clapped the healer on the shoulder. "Amaury's right. You're brilliant. Thank you."

"As sharp as a tack in a barefoot hootenanny," Val said with a grin.

"I didn't understand most of what you just said," Ellery admitted, "and I can't tell if that's the drink or you, but either way it's time for bed."

Ellery was snoring before they hit the mattress.

CHAPTER 32

BACK BEHIND BARS

The guard at the gate examined their invitation carefully before looking back at Amaury. Glendon, Willa, and Diadora, of course, had gone separately. Ellery and Kaiya had decided to join Tevin's team, just in case the guards were looking for a group of three. After a quick discussion, they decided to be something called the Mythical Monte Calvos, a traveling performance group.

Since Amaury had spent the least time in contact with Latimer, he was to be the head of the troupe. Ellery expressed some skepticism about this—Amaury was more of the type to blend into shadows than act the flamboyant showman. Tevin and Val promised them that Amaury was a DuMont and had therefore mastered enough skills and personas to help them now.

The guard stared at Amaury, dressed in ostentatious silks, the bright colors shifting as he moved, the jewels sewn into them catching the light. He'd applied a thick line of kohl and color paints to his eyes.

"Did he have that with him in his bag?" Ellery said in a low voice, their lips barely moving. Ellery was similarly garbed in vibrant colors, the bright gold of a gown borrowed from Diadora, and golden face paint. Ellery had looked decidedly uncomfortable while they were getting dressed. They were used to wearing trousers, but no one had trousers that were flashy enough for Ellery to use as a costume.

"Probably," Tevin said, pretending not to watch the guards as he assessed them. His siblings usually had a few such items with them. Ellery and Val had to do their best with clothing pooled from the group, and Tevin's and Amaury's skills with makeup.

"Very few people could pull an outfit like that off, and I wouldn't have thought your brother would be one of them. But he is stunning." Ellery's head tilted. "Are there any ugly people in your family?"

"We're just ugly on the inside," Tevin said. "It's protective coloring, like those brightly colored poisonous frogs."

Ellery stifled a laugh.

The guard stepped closer to Amaury. "What kind of troupe are you?"

Amaury puffed himself up like a strutting rooster. "You've never heard of the Mythical Monte Calvos? We're magic! We're mysterious!" He sniffed, his nose high. "You're lucky we are here."

Kaiya, her dress a striking scarlet, her face painted like Amaury's, guided Cedric forward. The horse she'd been riding was currently being used as a packhorse, since riding an ostrich made them look more like a troupe of entertainers, and would also explain Cedric's presence. They'd managed to fashion him a jeweled collar in matching scarlet, painting the rest of him in bright swirls of color. He'd been uncomfortable about going

391

anywhere naked, but they reminded him that he wasn't *technically* naked because he was covered in feathers.

Tevin wasn't sure which one of them had been more uncomfortable: Ellery and Val in borrowed dresses, or Cedric. Hob, for his part, had patiently accepted the jeweled collar they'd assembled for him. Diadora had, kindly, waited to take her tincture this morning until after she'd talked enough for them to gather the jewels for their costumes.

"We dance, we juggle, we ride." Kaiya lifted one hand grandly, her fingers pointing up like a dancer. "There is nothing we cannot do."

Tevin didn't look at the guard, but instead stared ahead, his face a calm mask. He'd shaved this morning and slicked his hair back, covering it with a long blond wig. His face was painted like his brother's, a sweeping rainbow of colors, kohl darkening the rims of his eyelids, framing eyes that were now a deep blue. Some costumes obscured features, and some, like the ones they wore, didn't bother but instead distracted the eye. It was hard to pay attention to facial features when they were covered in rainbow makeup.

The guard, not taking his eyes off Kaiya or, more specifically, her formfitting dress, finally handed back their invite and let them pass.

Tevin urged his horse through the gate nestled in the tall palisades surrounding Huldre's castle and gave a sigh of relief. Between the worry over Merit and his brain helpfully kicking up every single thing that could go wrong today, he'd barely slept. As a result, his nerves were on edge.

"Try not to look so relieved," Val said, her lips tipped up in a smile. "We still have a long way to go."

Tevin mimicked the haughty gaze and bearing of his brother and followed them deeper into the grounds. There was already quite a mass of people. The wedding had brought out the crowds in droves. Jugglers, fire-eaters, and tumblers, all lit by the giant bonfires that dotted the area. A group of musicians sat in a ring around one fire. Guitars, banjos, fiddles, and even a mandolin played together, making music as couples danced and twirled. The air was thick with music, laughter, and the smell of roasting meat, corn, and a dozen other foods that Tevin couldn't even name. His stomach growled, but he ignored it as they chose their camping spot and dismounted. Tevin left the rest of them to set up camp and settle the horses while he went with Val to get a better idea of the layout of the grounds. Hob grumbled about being left behind, making several people move away from them.

Close now, he was so close. Only Huldre castle's thick oak doors kept him from Merit. Doubt snaked its way into Tevin's thoughts. Latimer's home was so grand. So were Cedric's and Freddie's. Generations of good breeding and land—Tevin had a leather satchel full of clothes and a face full of rainbow makeup. That wasn't much to offer a person. He wondered if he should bother with his offer, or if he should just step aside and let Cedric marry Merit.

They finally broke into the outer ring of the crowd, moving closer to the castle doors. Tevin followed Val as she moved around, taking them to the side of the building to see if any of the back entrances were open. He glanced behind them while turning the corner and smacked right into Val . . . who had walked right into Latimer. Though Tevin's costume was good enough for strangers, it did nothing to hide him from Latimer or the guards who were with him.

The guards grabbed Tevin's arms and spun him around. The metal of the cuffs was cold as they slapped them onto his wrists. Val met a similar fate.

"I was hoping you'd be smart enough to—" Latimer hesitated, glancing quickly at the guards, who hadn't seemed to notice the prince's hesitation. "Stay away."

"Let me talk to Merit. See that she's okay. Then we'll go."

Latimer laughed. "I could send you to the moon more easily." He nodded to the guards. "I'm sorry, I really am. They're going to take you to the dungeons now. It's the safest place for you."

"Should we search the grounds, milord?" one of the guards asked.

Latimer leaned close to Tevin and said the words slowly. "Did anyone else come with you?"

"No," Tevin lied. "My brother stayed home."

Latimer's lips curled up into a hint of a smile. "No, you don't need to search." He straightened.

The guard seemed unsure. Latimer drew himself up. "I've met the brother. He's a liability. I know I would have left him behind if I had the chance. You're welcome to look about the place, but then you would need to explain to the queen why you weren't at your post."

Both of the guards paled. Latimer nodded. "That's what I

thought." He turned to walk away and then stopped. "What you can do is spread the word that you captured two prisoners and put them in the dungeon. Let people know exactly what happens to people who go against us."

"Yes, milord."

Then the guards dragged Tevin and Val away while Latimer vanished back into the castle.

CHAPTER 33

PLAN B

This seems familiar," Val said, slumping onto the hard bench that lined the cell.

Tevin slumped next to her. "We went through all of this only to end up back in the pokey. We didn't even get to talk to Merit."

Val bumped him with her shoulder. "At least it's a different cell, yeah? Progress!"

Tevin rubbed his wrists. They'd taken the handcuffs off when they'd thrown him in with Val. The dungeon, as Latimer called it, was indeed under the castle. It was wet and dank and fitting of the moniker, though it was fairly clean. A handful of cells lined one wall facing a table and four chairs for the guards.

Tevin and Val had been searched, and their stuff, such as it was, currently sat on that table, waiting for the guards to decide what to do with it. He could see Val's pistols and her holster, Tevin's wig, and various odds and ends from their pockets. Two guards sat in the chairs, playing cards and grumbling about missing the party tonight as well as the feast that would follow. One of them, a large oafish man, his skin so pale you could see the blue tracery of veins underneath, was most certainly cheating. Tevin hadn't caught him switching out the cards yet, but he could see the man's hand, and it changed too much for the draw to be the reason. His cohort, a woman a good two inches taller than Tevin, shouldn't have been playing at all. She chewed her lip when she was nervous, and Tevin could see a fine sheen of sweat beading the deep brown skin of her brow. She had a terrible poker face, her tells blatant.

Tevin settled his back against the solid stone wall. They'd come so far and done so much just to fall short right at the end. His chest tightened, the hopelessness of the situation suddenly overwhelming him. They weren't going to win. Merit would be stuck married to Latimer. Who knew what would happen to him and Val. He closed his eyes, unwilling to break down in front of the guards. Willing or not, the tight feeling in his chest increased, and he felt the tears as they went down his cheeks.

"Hey, hey," Val said. Tevin opened his eyes as she used her cuff to pat at his cheeks. "None of that. I mean, I'm one for a good cry. It's not healthy to keep that stuff in, but I don't think it's as bad as all that. Besides, you're going to smear your makeup, and Amaury did a really good job."

He laughed then, the sound wet and thick from breaking through his tight chest. "It's okay, Val. It is as bad as all that. We did our best." He squeezed his friend tight to him. "I suppose it was foolish to think—" Tevin stopped himself, but it didn't matter. Val knew him too well.

"Foolish to think we might win? Foolish to think you might actually be the hero in all this?" She scraped her fingers through his hair, like he was a dog needing a good scratch. "Silly boy, you're a hero to me. You're my best friend." She gave a final scratch, shoving his head away playfully.

He grabbed her hand. "You're my best friend, too."

"So trust me." Her eyes glittered as she moved her face close. "And if you think this is our best? Then maybe you are a fool."

"What are we going to do, Val? We're locked up."

She nodded, an absolutely vicious grin blooming on her face. "That we are. But our friends aren't."

"Friends who by now know exactly where we are," Tevin said slowly. "Did you think that was weird? All that stuff with—" He checked to make sure the guards weren't listening but dropped his voice anyway. "With Latimer?"

Val rested her head against the wall. "Yeah, I did." They watched the female guard lose another hand, the pasty guy taking the pot. "It was almost like he was trying to help us."

• • •

They didn't have much to do after that but wait. Waiting, as most folks know, does a strange thing to time. Minutes stretch like taffy, becoming protracted and mutable, seeming to go on far longer than they should. Waiting as doom sneaked closer and closer only made it worse. Tevin had no idea how much time passed as they sat there, but after a while, there was a knock at the outer door.

One of the guards, the card sharp, stood up to let in a liveried servant holding a large tray.

The woman eyed the newcomer setting the edge of the tray on the table. But the servant didn't seem to notice, quickly divesting the tray of several elegant dishes. Tevin and Val kept their faces blank, not wanting to tip off the guards to the fact that they knew the servant. Where Ellery had managed to get their hands on a retainer's uniform, Tevin had no idea.

Ellery quickly explained each dish, ending with a flourish as they poured each guard a small glass of wine. "I know it isn't much, but it's compliments of the wedding party. This way you won't entirely miss the festivities."

The guards sat down to their meal, clearly pleased with the offering.

"Might I recommend the lamb? It's been roasted with peppers—quite spicy, though I'm sure not anything you two couldn't handle. I'm told the meat melts on your tongue." Ellery lifted thin slices of lamb onto their plates. With a roguish wink, they grabbed a sliver of the meat off the serving plate and popped it into their mouth, eyes rolling back in bliss. The guards immediately dug in, responding to Ellery's challenge. After all, if a servant could handle the spicy lamb, so could they. Tevin watched as the guards chewed. The man's face flushed, and they both broke out into a sweat. They weren't quite crying, but they looked uncomfortable.

The guards grabbed for their wine, gulping it like water. The wine quickly gone, Ellery tutted in sympathy, grasping the metal pitcher of water the guards had with them. Ellery refilled their glasses with water twice before they finally slowed down.

"Perhaps the risotto?" Ellery spooned the creamy rice onto their plates. "No peppers in this one, promise."

Which was precisely the moment the female guard collapsed forward, her cheek barely missing the risotto. The male guard stared at her for a moment, weaving slightly before he joined her, but he didn't miss. Instead, his meaty head hit the plate with a muted squish. Ellery swiftly opened the door and gave a soft whistle. Kaiya and Amaury darted through the door, Ellery shutting it behind them. Their flamboyant outfits were gone, replaced by clothing fit for wedding guests. Ellery went to the guards and checked their pulses.

"I'm not sure how long they'll be out," the healer said. "I had to guess on the dosing, not knowing their precise weights. We should put them in a cell, just in case." Amaury and Kaiya grabbed the man first, dragging him to one of the empty cells. Meanwhile, Ellery took the keys off the belt of the other guard, quickly flipping through them and trying each in the lock until one finally turned with a distinct click.

Tevin picked Ellery up, squeezed, and kissed them on the cheek.

"You're not my type," Ellery said dryly as they slid from Tevin's grasp. "But I appreciate the enthusiasm. Better clean yourself up. We have a wedding to crash."

Tevin quickly stripped out of his outfit, putting on the clothes brought for him and Val by Amaury. Kaiya dipped a cloth in the water pitcher, using it to wipe off Tevin's makeup as best she could. "I won't be able to get all of the kohl from around your eyes, but at least I can get the colorful stuff off. I wish we'd thought to bring some cold cream or something."

Val had her weapons well in place by the time Tevin was back to his normal self. He eyed the group carefully. Everyone on the grounds knew what Tevin and Val looked like. The guards might be less vigilant now that they'd been captured, but they couldn't count on that. What they needed was a disguise, but he couldn't imagine one that would transform them enough to pass through.

Tevin looked at Amaury, who didn't look worried in the least. "Oh no, we're not doing plan B, are we?"

Amaury's eyes lit. "We sure are." He dug around in the pockets of his coat, fishing for something. "Your rescue took too long—don't have time for anything else. We have to go straight to the ceremony."

"What's plan B?" Kaiya asked.

"*B* stands for Brazen," Tevin said.

"Bold as Brass." Val's eyes were alight with a wicked gleam, and she practically rubbed her hands together in glee.

"Basically," Tevin said, handing Val her hat, "we're going to bluff our way in as best we can. I would argue, but I can't think of anything else." Either they'd save Merit, or interrupt the wedding she really *did* want, angering everyone involved and likely getting themselves thrown back into the dungeon. He could stand being in the dungeon; he could even stand Merit being mad at him, as long as she got what she wanted.

Val spread her arms, wiggling her fingers and rolling her head. "This is going to be fun."

Amaury pulled a stack of paper from his pocket with a flourish. "Voilà!" He handed them out to the group. "We're all wedding guests now."

Tevin held his arms out for inspection so Ellery could check his finery and make sure he could pass for a guest, while Kaiya checked Val.

401

"Take out your lenses," Amaury said, waving at Tevin's face. "The guards have only seen you blond and blue-eyed. This will make them take at least a second to place you."

"I've always wanted to go to a big posh wedding," Val said, examining her invitation. "And this one is going to be even better, because we get to wreck it."

Ellery stopped fussing with Tevin's vest and looked at Val. They looked carefully at the excitement on everyone's faces, shaking their head in dismay. "That's it, they've ruined us. We're all DuMonts now."

Tevin reached out and tugged on Ellery's hat brim. "I'm seeing that as a good thing."

Amaury nodded. "DuMonts always win."

"Always," Tevin said firmly.

Val looked around, a frown on her face. "Hey, what happened to Hob and the ostrich?"

"The ostrich has been strategically placed," Kaiya said, escorting Tevin confidentially down the hallway. "We couldn't exactly move about with him unnoticed."

"Strategic ostrich." Amaury walked next to them, his stride telling everyone they passed that he belonged here and was every inch a fairy-blessed guest. "Probably the first time in his life that Cedric has been useful."

Ellery, still in livery, held off to the side. They'd left the tray and dishes with the guards, but had stolen some flowers from one of the many vases they'd passed. The healer didn't look at them, staring straight ahead as if they were on an important errand. That was the nice thing about livery—it made one practically invisible.

402

"And Hob?" Val asked.

"We don't precisely know what happened to Hob," Kaiya said, apparently completely unconcerned that a giant cat was wandering around the grounds.

"Couldn't exactly tell the guards he was missing," Amaury said. "That would draw attention. We decided that it was a problem for later." Tevin wanted to argue with him, but his brother was right—there wasn't anything they could do. They didn't have much time as it was.

Amaury had memorized the map of Latimer's castle, so had no problem taking them to the grand room where the wedding was taking place. As they got closer, they were joined by other guests, stragglers making it to the festivities at the last minute. They'd passed several guard checkpoints, making it past with a quick flash of the invitation. Kaiya was frowning at the lax security, but Tevin was grateful for it.

The last checkpoint was right outside the door, and those guards were of a different ilk. They were examining each invitation carefully. They were also scrutinizing faces.

Kaiya casually took Amaury's arm. Tevin took Val's, pretending not to know Kaiya or Amaury as they approached the guards. Amaury handed over his invitation—one that he'd purposely botched.

"This is a fake!" the guard said, her eyes wide.

Amaury stammered. "It is *not*. Don't you know who I am?" Kaiya started wailing, which made Amaury yell louder. The lead guard wasn't having any of it. She flicked her hand, and two of the guards departed, leaving her and a squat bald man with arms the size of hams. The two guards escorted Kaiya and Amaury away, both of them causing a maximum amount of fuss. The lead guard took their invitation right as Ellery stumbled and flowers went everywhere.

"I'm so sorry!" Ellery dropped down, grabbing for flowers, a constant stream of apologies flowing from their lips. They were dropping almost as many flowers as they picked up and kept knocking into waiting guests. The lead guard barely looked at Tevin as Val thrust the invitation at him while the ham-armed guard bent down to help Ellery with their flowers.

They were in.

• • •

In a mostly empty room in a different part of the castle, a beast paced in a gilded cage. Unhappy, the beast threw itself against the bars. It gnawed on the lock. Nothing happened except sore gums and a bruised side. The beast howled and howled, but no one came.

The door opened, and the beast looked up, expecting the people who had put it in the cage. Instead, the beast's hackles rose, its lip curled back, and it snarled. Another predator sauntered in like it owned the place. The large cat, for his part, seemed disinterested in fighting. He ignored her growls and snarls. He flopped in front of the cage, as cats are wont to do, his tail slowly flicking back and forth. *Oh, it's you.*

The beast whined.

The cat chuffed in response, the feline equivalent of, *Well, what do you want me to do about it? I have my own curse to worry about.*

The beast chirped.

The cat stared at the beast for a long, drawn-out moment before heaving itself up off the floor and sauntering over to the general area the beast had chirped at. His pace was slow—he was a cat, after all, and it wouldn't do to hurry to do anyone's bidding. It was bad enough to be doing it in the first place.

On the wall, on a hook above his head, hung a ring of keys. The cat stood and grabbed the ring with his teeth before dropping back down on all fours. He walked the ring over to the cage. The beast whined and clawed at the lock. It still had mind enough to know that it needed the keys to be free, but couldn't quite remember how to use them.

It clawed at the key ring in the cat's mouth, confused and trying to grasp the heavy ring, only to knock it free and onto the floor. It landed with a clang. The beast snarled in frustration.

The cat chuffed, bending down to scoop up the key ring with his teeth. *This isn't working, but I know someone who can help.* The cat's eyes narrowed. *But this makes us even.*

• • •

The room was mostly full already. Almost two hundred people in their best finery milled about, taking seats and chatting. It was so full it was already getting stuffy, so the guards were going along the tall windows and opening them up to let in a breeze. The hall itself was festooned with white silk garlands and white flowers. In the middle of the great rows of chairs, there was an aisle, a rich golden runner cutting up the middle. Every so often a golden birdcage hung off a wrought-iron holder, each one filled with white doves. Merit was nowhere in sight, though Tevin did see Willa, Diadora, and Glendon in one of the front rows.

"Now what?" Val said quietly as she smiled and nodded to a woman passing by.

"I honestly have no idea." Tevin waved a greeting, pretending to recognize someone. "I didn't think we'd get this far."

Tevin quickly ushered Val to some open seats in a back row. "We'll have to wait until they bring Merit out. I don't think there's any way to sneak around and find her before the ceremony—too easy to get lost or caught. But they'll have to bring her out sometime, and then we'll act." He examined the room. "There are a lot of people in here. I'm glad we're not trying to do this the sneaky way."

"You think Amaury and Kaiya will have any trouble?" Val asked.

Tevin shook his head. "Only two guards? Please. We just have to be patient."

"I hate being patient," Val mumbled.

Finally a few trumpets blared and the king and queen strolled in, resplendent in their finery, her hand resting gently on his arm.

"They match the décor," Val murmured. "Not very original." The king wore a white suit, and his tie was made of a shimmery golden material. Angelique wore a puffy golden gown with a train so long that an attendant had to carry it for her. She looked like something out of a children's book, a long strand of white pearls wrapped around her neck. Next came Lady Zarla, her dress a froth of creamy white lace and slim, elegant lines. Lady Zarla's face was drawn, but she held her head high.

Once they were seated, everyone quieted, and the ceremony began. A choir sang some songs that Tevin didn't really listen to. Then a bard sang a ballad that Tevin listened to very closely, mostly because it was full of overblown horse puckey about Latimer and how amazing he was to try to save Merit from her curse.

"I can hear you grinding your teeth," Val whispered. "Relax."

Other people spoke after that.

There were blessings.

He didn't really hear any of them.

Tevin basically ignored everything until four men in white wheeled the cage up onto the dais. All in all, it was probably seven feet by six. The delicate bars were filigreed and beautiful—something fit for a queen, really. But it was still a cage, and inside it, the beast paced. Any trace of Merit was gone. She padded about on all fours, snarling, her tail lashing back and forth. A low growl rumbled out as she spotted the crowd.

The cage was parked at the bottom of the dais, below the king and queen. The choir sang softly, a few of their voices wobbling when the beast snarled at them. A man in the front fainted and slid to the ground. A guard detached himself from the wall, grabbed the man's shoulders, and dragged him off to the side. Light streamed through the large windows as if the heavens themselves blessed this charade.

Val placed a hand on his. "Not yet."

The choir's song grew louder, turning into an exultation. Everyone swiveled to gawk as the doors in the back flew open. Latimer strode in, several attendants following. He was so polished that he absolutely gleamed. Every inch of him looked like a fairy-tale prince, the savior of the beast the bard's song talked about. Latimer's gaze swept the crowd, his eyes catching for a second on Tevin, but he kept striding to the front.

"Pretty." Val shook her head. "But sad. He has no friends to walk with him. No one to meet him at the end but a cursed bride and two toads for parents."

"He saw us," Tevin whispered.

"What?" Val's eyes were round.

"He saw me and kept walking," Tevin said.

"What does that mean, I wonder?" Val asked.

Tevin felt a surge of hope go through him. "I think he wants us to stop the wedding."

"That's crazy," Val said.

Tevin watched as heads turned to follow the progress of the prince. "I don't think we can trust him for help, but I don't think he'll get in our way, either."

Latimer reached the dais, positioning himself across from the beast. The bard strummed his guitar, ready to start the next part of the story.

Unnoticed by the crowd and off to the side, three liveried servants walked in quietly, two of them holding what appeared to be a tablecloth. They held it taut between them, so the top was flat, but the sides of the fabric draped down and touched the floor. The one in front, Ellery, glanced at Tevin.

Tevin nodded.

Ellery made some sign with their hand, and Amaury and Kaiya whisked their cloth to the side, revealing Cedric. He was still painted every shade of the rainbow. The ostrich put his wings out and hissed, then started running up and down the aisles. The bard stopped mid-strum. Cedric hit things with his wings, knocking them over. People screeched, finally starting to move.

"It bit me!" a man yelled. "That giant bird bit me!"

"We have our diversion," Tevin said, ushering Val out to the aisle.

In the confusion, Kaiya pulled a slim blade out of her boot and dashed to the nearest birdcage, releasing the doves. Amaury and Ellery joined her, opening cage after cage, releasing doves by the dozens. The attendants exploded into action, all of them attempting to catch the wayward birds, close the cages, or at least capture the people setting them free. Ellery, Kaiya, and Amaury did their best to hamper them.

Cedric snatched up hats, stole a wig, and dropped it onto the surprised face of the priest. One of the guards tried to corner him, lunging to grab the giant bird. Cedric squawked indignantly, biting the man in the face until he let go. It was absolute chaos. Tevin caught sight of Glendon taking hold of Lady Zarla and dragging her out of the madness. Willa was laughing so hard she was leaning over, snakes pouring from her lips. Diadora appeared to be tickling her sister. People started screaming as the snakes slithered over feet and ankles.

"Go." Val pushed him. "We got this."

Everyone was screaming now—or laughing—the crowd in disarray. Tevin attempted to weave through them, but it was slow going. He saw a dark streak running along the side of the room right below the windows. Hob was dodging the screaming crowd, bounding right for Tevin. People screeched and tried to skitter out of the marar's way.

Up on the dais, the king bellowed for the guards while the queen screeched at the officiant to get on with the ceremony. Latimer stepped back away from the hubbub, but didn't do anything else.

People climbed over chairs or shoved each other down, everyone trying to make it to an exit. At least two men were following Cedric around, trying to catch him. They had achieved mass chaos. Unfortunately, mass chaos was also making it difficult for Tevin to get to the front.

He passed the bard, who had climbed up onto a chair out of the way, holding his mandolin.

Tevin grabbed his sleeve. "Can I borrow your instrument for a minute?"

The bard handed it over to him reluctantly. Tevin strummed experimentally. He wasn't the best musician. Not that it mattered. He played some basic chords, humming along to get people's attention. The people next to him calmed, turning toward his voice. Tevin opened his mouth and sang. People froze, their eyes on him, gently swaying with his song, the effect rippling out until everyone in the room quieted. Hob padded up next to him, and Tevin looked down, realizing the cat had a set of keys in his mouth. His hands were full, and the cat seemed content to carry his burden for now, so Tevin kept playing.

"Once upon a time, I heard a wedding tune," he sang, his voice clear. He picked his way around the crowd, carefully stepping over fallen hats and dented birdcages. "And once upon a time was this afternoon." His hands were shaking—he was almost to the front now. He could see Merit pacing in her cage. "Seeing you this way, Merit, breaks my heart." His words rang out through the room as everyone quieted to listen. He wished he could come up with better lyrics, but the thing about charm was that the words didn't matter, just that he was saying them. "I wish I could give you a better song."

Tevin stepped onto the dais. "I wish I could give you a better person." He stopped playing, the mandolin dangling from his fingers. The beast's cage was in front of him; he only had to stride a few feet. "But whatever I am, Merit, I'm yours." He stopped singing, his attention on the beast in the cage. She stared at him, her head tilted. The beast chirped, and Hob dropped the keys by Tevin's feet with a chuff.

He had completely forgotten about the queen until she shouted, "You! Those are mine!" She charged at him, only to be met by Val and Kaiya.

"I wouldn't if I were you." Val raised her pistols. Kaiya stood next to her, her slim dagger in hand and a wicked gleam in her eye.

"No!" Lady Angelique yelled. She threw her shoulders back and held her head high. "You can't have her. Guards! Someone!" But everyone, including the king, had been swayed by the song. No one stepped forward to help. "Lady Zarla, we had an agreement!"

Merit's mother stood off against the wall, Glendon's arms around her. Lady Zarla regarded the queen. She looked at her daughter, pacing in the cage. Finally, she turned her head to Tevin. "An agreement my daughter couldn't sign." She dipped her chin once decisively at Tevin. "See if you can break the curse."

Lady Angelique hissed through her teeth. "How dare you!"

Lady Zarla's lips curled in a smile.

The queen snarled, lunging toward Tevin, only to be confronted by a large, angry marar. The cat paced forward, slowly herding Lady Angelique back.

"Don't move," Val warned, her pistols still up. Tevin could see Latimer off to the side, his eyes wide, his face bloodless.

"Mother," Latimer croaked. "Please."

She didn't seem to hear him; her eyes were on the keys by Tevin's feet. She lunged to the side, attempting to get past the cat, but he was faster. She stumbled back, trying to catch herself from falling, only to get tangled up in the long train of her gown. Her hands windmilling to regain balance, she started to go down. There was a flash of color as the king came, grabbing for his wife. She scrabbled onto him, only to tangle him up into her dress. As one, they tumbled to the side, their legs hitting the sill before they tipped out the window. For a moment, they seemed to hang in the air. Then, with a golden blur, they fell to the ground.

Latimer fell to his knees, his voice ragged and wordless as he screamed.

"Ellery," Tevin yelled to get the healer's attention. "See to him, will you?"

"I got this," Willa said, holding up her skirts and picking around the debris on the floor. She ignored the bright green lizard that ran along her shoulder as she dropped down and put her arms around Eric Latimer, the new king of Huldre, as his world fell apart.

"Thank you," Tevin said to her. He picked up the keys and went to Merit's cage.

"Wait." Latimer's voice was a thready croak, the room going silent except for the cooing of the doves. "Mother gave her an overdose of bloom." He held his hand out, indicating the room. "If you open that cage, she could tear into everyone here. She's not herself."

Tevin paused. He looked into the cage. The beast snarled back, drool dripping from her jaws. "Val?"

"Yes?" She still had her pistols out and ready.

"Perhaps we best evacuate the room?"

"You heard the man," Ellery said, standing tall in their palace finery. They clapped their hands. "Everyone out! Guards! Guards! Clear the room!"

A flurry of activity then as everyone left except for Tevin's friends, Latimer, Lady Zarla, and Glendon. Amaury corralled their group into the far corner for safety's sake. Val and Kaiya stood in front of them all, weapons out, in case of the worst. Cedric hid in the middle, giving a plaintive chirp. Amaury and Diadora put their arms around the ostrich, comforting him. Hob, somewhat disdainful of the whole affair, sprawled in a sunbeam.

Tevin dropped down and back onto his heels, his eyes meeting the beast. "Merit?"

She growled.

He saw no sign of her in the beast's eyes. Tevin swallowed. He sorted through the keys, inserting them into the lock until he found one that fit. "Merit Cravan, I have come for you, though I have nothing to offer but myself. I'm not a good man, but I'm trying. My heart is nothing special, but it's all yours." He heard the click of the lock opening. "I love you beyond

413

reason. Let's hope that's enough." Tevin yanked the door open and stepped back. The beast leaned on its haunches, ready to spring. He shook with adrenaline and fear but kept his eyes on hers. If this was to be his end, he'd meet it head-on.

"Will you have me?"

The beast sprang.

CHAPTER 34

A FAIRY-TALE ENDING

Merit knew rage. That was what the beast understood, and they were one. It was all-encompassing. She was tinder, and the frenzy burned through her. There was no room for anything else except the want, and what the beast wanted was freedom. Instead it got the cage.

She paced and paced and *pacedpacedpaced*, the rage growing, breathing, becoming alive.

Then a man.

Noises she no longer understood.

A door opening.

Freedom.

She leapt for it.

• • •

Later she heard there was a golden light. Bards insisted that the doves all sang together and everything in the kingdom, even the dishes, came to life and danced with joy. None of that was true, though it sounded lovely. Merit thought it might be a little difficult to eat with a dancing fork, but that was the difference between a fairy tale and reality. In a fairy tale, you never have to think about the practicalities of such things. You don't have to wonder how the beast changed or how Latimer would manage now that he was suddenly thrust into the leadership of a large kingdom, his family dead, scandal hanging like a pall. No one has to think past the happily-ever-after, really. That's where the pain of day-to-day living lies. Who wants to think about that?

Merit wanted it.

All of it.

Buried deep in all the pain and mess of everyday life, well, that's where joy can be found, too. She would get to wake up every day and deal with the good and the bad of living, but with her friends and Tevin at her side. That was the real happily-ever-after—not that there was no adversity to ever be dealt with, but that you had people to share and ease the burden of it.

If asked, what anyone in the ballroom could have told you was that the beast hit Tevin head-on. They rolled, Tevin landing on his back. The beast reared up, her claws extended, and stopped. He held his hands out, palms open, his face calm. The beast paused, her eyes confused. She sniffed. She hiccupped. No one blinked, and yet no one saw the change. One minute, there was a beast, and the next, there was Merit.

She was, unfortunately, suddenly quite naked in a room with several elaborately dressed people and a lot of cooing doves. Merit squeaked and tried to cover herself as she looked down at Tevin, her friends, then back to Tevin. She blinked down at him. "Tevin?"

"Yes, Merit?"

"I think . . ." She frowned at the utter destruction of the room. Gilded birdcages hung drunkenly from hooks, chairs were knocked over, flowers were trampled into the carpets. "Did I do this?"

"No. It was mostly us," Tevin said. "Amaury, can we have your jacket?" Tevin's brother shrugged off his jacket, ran over to drape it around Merit, and stepped away as if he didn't want to intrude. Merit slipped her arms into it.

"I don't . . ." She trailed off, her face pinched in thought. "Where are we? The last I remember, I was in the library."

"You're always in the library." Tevin grasped one of her hands gently, leaving the other to hold Amaury's jacket shut. "Merit, look."

Merit glanced at her hand, looked back at the mess, and then her head whipped back as she stared at her hand again. She made a fist before spreading her fingers wide. She touched her lips, her cheeks, her nose. Then Merit scrambled up, staring at her legs.

"The curse is gone." The words were quiet and reverent as they left her lips. She whooped, dancing around in a circle. "My curse is gone! Why is my curse gone?" She frowned at him. "Did I get married?"

"No, Merit." He eased himself up and dusted himself off.

"Then why is the beast gone?"

"Because I came for you," Tevin said. "Not for your title, or your wealth." He pulled her into his arms. "Not for your pointy ears, or your blood, but just for you."

Merit looked up at him. "You came for me?"

"Yes," he said. "And I would do it again, too. I love you,

Merit. Who else is going to yell at me and throw cake when I'm terrible?"

She grinned at him then, stood up on her toes, and kissed him.

Whatever had been holding her friends back burst, and all of them ran forward to cry and hold Merit as she sobbed and laughed in relief. It was over. It was all over.

• • •

There was a moment, after much hugging and rejoicing, that Merit looked up to see her mother. Merit stared at her from the safety of Tevin's arms, bracing herself for the argument she knew was coming. Lady Zarla stepped forward hesitantly. She reached out, touching Merit's hair, her cheek, her chin. Lady Zarla gasped out a short cry, her eyes filling. "My daughter." She pulled her close, her eyes shut, one arm around Merit, the other around Tevin. She held them to her.

"Thank you. Oh, thank you."

Merit held her back and wept.

• • •

Ellery eventually went to fetch Merit some proper clothing. She couldn't waltz about the place in Amaury's jacket forever. Once she was dressed, they adjourned to the dining hall. A huge feast was laid out, covered in gleaming silver domes, just waiting for someone to lift the lids. Bottles of wine breathed at every table, and though everything looked very fine, Merit missed her own dining room. This one was very pretty, but cold, and had no magic of home to it. Still, they liberated one of the bottles, poured everyone a glass, and told Merit everything. Val and Ellery did most of the talking while Merit hung on every word.

Tevin stayed quiet, rolling the empty wineglass between his hands. Merit could see the tense set of his shoulders, and though he smiled during the story, he seemed to be waiting for the other shoe to drop.

Once the tale was finished, Merit took her friends aside, giving them instructions—all except for Tevin. She left him sitting to the side, waiting. Everyone scurried off, leaving them alone in the room.

"It's rather lovely, don't you think?" Merit asked, her fingers tracing along the spine of a napkin folded into the shape of a swan. "So much work, gone to waste."

"I suppose it's pretty in a way," Tevin said, "but I'm glad it's not being used. Unless—" He swallowed hard, looking back down at the glass in his hands. "Your curse is broken now. You can do anything you want. You don't even have to get married."

She strode over to him then, each step purposeful. When she got close enough, she waited until he raised his head and looked up at her. "No, I don't *have* to do anything now. I don't have to marry Latimer. Or Cedric. Or Freddie." She took his face in her hands. "This is much better. I get to be me. Because of you and our friends, I got myself back."

Tevin wrapped his arms around her and waited for her to pull away. When she didn't, his grip tightened, and he buried his face against her stomach.

She pushed her fingers through his hair. "What are you going to do now?"

"I don't know." His words came out muffled. "We didn't plan this far."

Merit nodded. "Then how about I tell you what I have in mind, and you tell me if you agree with my plan?" She didn't wait for him to respond. "I suggest we not let this feast go to the dogs."

Tevin looked up at her sharply.

"I suggest we gather our friends close and give everyone here something to celebrate. Then I highly recommend that we go back to *our* home, together, and never come here again. Would you like that?"

Tevin laced his fingers through hers. "I'm right certain that I saw an officiant around here somewhere."

"You think we can convince him to try again?" she asked, her grin cheeky.

"I can convince him to dance a jig if you want." His gaze turned speculative. "They probably already paid him. Let's make him earn his coin."

• • •

Merit and Tevin decided to be married outside. It didn't seem right to use the hall where she was supposed to marry Latimer. Plus it was an absolute mess. They found Latimer out on a balcony overlooking his orchards, his tail twitching slowly, a half-empty bottle held loosely in one fist.

"It was my mother's plan," Latimer said, his voice hoarse. "Our coffers were almost empty. She wanted your crops, your land." He turned, sliding down against the rock half wall, sitting on the ground. Only then did he look at them. "We were close to losing everything." He set the bottle down beside him and closed his eyes, tipping his face back. "I needed to marry you, and quickly." His smile was faint and bitter. "Never could tell her no. And now my family name is properly ruined, and my parents are dead." His expression crumpled. "What am I going to do?"

Despite everything, Merit felt a little sorry for Latimer. She was still angry at him, but he'd paid dearly for his crimes; the king and queen had paid with their lives. They were rotten and terrible, but they were still his parents, and it would hurt.

"I'm sure you'll think of something," Merit said gently.

A broken laugh erupted from Latimer. "What we did to you was the worst kind of violation, Merit. The fact that I regret it, that I doubted it, doesn't matter." He shook his head slowly. "I can never make it up to you." He expelled a breath. "I paid Godling Price to curse Cedric. I gave Freddie something to make him dizzy. I didn't mean for him to fall, but that didn't matter." He turned to Tevin. "I did my best to turn Merit and her mother against you."

Merit leaned down and kissed his cheek. "You have made this mess, and now you must deal with it, but I think in the end, you're going to be okay."

Another head shake. "After all we did to you, you're reassuring me?" He gave her a weak smile. "You're too good for all of us, milady." He rested his head against the balcony wall. "I owe you. I will die in your debt, that's how much. Name it, and it's yours if I can give it."

She glanced at Tevin, and though he wasn't looking at her, he squeezed her hand. "I'll need to think about it. Let the problem rest for a while. I'll make my demands when I'm ready."

"As you see fit, milady."

Merit straightened. "In the meantime, I'd like to borrow your lands, your feast, and your priest, not necessarily in that order."

He pulled his large frame up from the ground, taking the bottle with him. "I will see it done. My home is yours." And then he walked off deeper into the castle.

● ● ●

Ellery found the priest. They had to hold him up during part of the ceremony, as he'd holed up in the king's study and steadied his nerves with several glasses of brandy. Some of the words he said didn't make any sense, but the gist of the ceremony was there. The groom looked a mess, and the bride had no shoes, but they beamed with happiness, and everyone agreed it was the most beautiful wedding they had ever seen. Merit's mother, Ellery, and Kaiya stood on her side; Amaury and Val stood on his. When they couldn't decide where the rest of the friends should go, they made a half circle around them both, Hob lying down in the middle of it and making a general nuisance of himself. The musicians played well into the night; food and joy and laughter were shared by everyone.

Even Lady Zarla looked happy, hugging and kissing her daughter on the cheek at every opportunity.

Merit held on to Tevin's hand firmly. "You're really not angry?"

Lady Zarla stepped back, her hands still on Merit's shoulders. "Today has me rethinking my approach. Clearly blood isn't the only factor I should have looked for." She studied Merit's face. "Are you happy?"

Merit practically glowed. "So happy."

"Then that's all that matters." She eyed Tevin. "Babies. I want lots of babies."

Merit and Tevin choked.

When it looked like Merit's mother was going to settle in for a longer discussion of this, Glendon, may the fairies bless him, wrapped an arm around her. "Lady Zarla, have I mentioned that my daughter was recently married?" He drew her away from the newlyweds, winking at them as he did. "I'm told she's already expecting. Twins."

"Really?"

"Yes, really. Of course it's a pity they have no grandmother to spoil them."

Lady Zarla looked up at him. "Is that so?"

He nodded. "A shame, really."

Lady Zarla didn't dip her chin, or blush, or look coy in any way. Instead, she looked him straight in the eye. "I would love to hear more about your family. Shall we dance?"

Glendon bowed over her hand. "Nothing would please me more."

Tevin pressed a kiss to Merit's temple.

"Thank the fairies for that," she said.

He nodded. "May his daughter be blessed with many children so your mother will leave us alone."

Merit snorted. "They won't distract her forever. I give her a year." She tipped her face to his. "What about your mother?"

"She gets no say. She'll be lucky if we let her visit. And if she does, you'll need to hide the silver."

• • •

As the night wore on, Tevin bowed to Val, asking her to dance. The fiddles played a bouncy tune, one that he knew Val would enjoy.

"You seem happy," she said as Tevin twirled her around.

"I am." He pulled her close. "Thank you for this. I wouldn't be here if it wasn't for you."

Val hit his shoulder. "Don't get all sappy on me now, Tev."

"Just giving credit where it's owed," he said with a grin. He leaned in close. "And now it's your turn." Then he spun her around, directly into a surprised Kaiya.

"Kaiya, would you mind taking a turn with Val? I have a wife to find." He didn't wait for an answer but left the two of them to figure things out while he went in search of Merit.

He found her chatting happily with Willa and Diadora. "What happened to Cedric?"

Diadora pointed across the dancing circle, where Merit caught sight of Amaury, his arm slung around the ostrich's neck. The large bird was definitely weaving. Hob sat next to them. Someone had made him a paper crown, and it rested crookedly on his head.

"Did he get the ostrich drunk?" Merit asked.

"Of course he did." Tevin cocked his head while he watched his brother laugh, lean across the back of the giant bird, and steal someone's drink. "You know they're going to follow us home, right?"

"He's grown on me." Merit put an arm around Tevin simply because she could. "Do you think Hob will go back to the forest?"

"He seems disinclined," Tevin said, his arm wrapping around her shoulder. "I owe my sister a present, though. She always wanted a kitten."

"You're evil," Merit said. "I like it."

"He's going to make Cedric sick." Diadora stood, shaking her head. "I better go keep an eye on them." Willa sighed and went with her.

Merit touched Tevin's chin with her fingertips. "May I steal the next dance?"

He led her closer to the fire, the music slowing as he pulled her close, her arms going around his neck. "You don't have to steal it. All of my dances are yours."

"I'll try to not stomp on your feet."

He slid his hands down, grabbing her waist. "If you do, I know an excellent dance instructor." He twirled her out, then pulled her back close, like he couldn't stand even an inch between them. "Can I ask you a question?"

"Of course." Merit curled her fingers around the hair at the nape of his neck, letting it filter through her fingers.

"You miss your tail, don't you?" he asked.

Merit thought for a minute, letting him guide her around the makeshift dance floor. "You know, I kind of do?" She sighed. "I keep trying to grab things with it, only nothing happens. It's going to take some getting used to. At least things will go back to normal now."

He let go of her waist, drawing his hands up until he cupped her face. Couples continued to dance and eddy around them, as if they were a boulder in a river—timeless, steady, and unmovable. "You gave up normal when you married me," Tevin said. "Marriage to a DuMont—it's a curse, but you'll never be bored."

Merit gave him a lopsided grin, the one that made his chest tight. "That's the funny thing about curses," she said. "From the right perspective, they look an awful lot like gifts."

"I think you've had too much champagne," Tevin said. "It's made you giddy."

"I think I've had just the right amount," Merit said, standing up on her toes. She grabbed his face. "I love you, Tevin DuMont."

"Way too much champagne," Tevin said. And then he kissed her, pouring into it all the things that people say but are hard to believe. Telling her that she was his home, his heart, and all the things that go into forever.

And she kissed him back, for once in complete agreement.

ACKNOWLEDGMENTS

Not to start with a pun, but this book was a beast to write. A big thanks to all of the people who helped me shove it into a ball gown and teach it to waltz. First to my agent, Jason Anthony, and the team at Massie & McQuilkin, for sticking with me through this whole process—I owe you a dapper ostrich. Lots of love to Jill and Sylvia at WME for all of their hard work over the years—you have been the best fairy gift (with zero side effects). To Ari Lewin for taking a chance on a charming con man and an awkward beast. And of course, to the entire team at Putnam for putting this beauty together. (Okay, the puns stop . . . now.)

To all of my author friends, beta readers, and cheer section who helped me stick with it: Martha Brockenbrough, Jolie Stekly, Leigh Bardugo, Gretchen McNeil, Jessica Brody, Melissa Marr, Marissa Meyer, Niki Marion, Kendare Blake, Andi Tosch, Mel Barnes, Anna Eklund, Anna Banks, S. A. Patel, Jennifer Wolfe, Avery Peregrine, Ryfie Schafer, everyone in my Third Place Books writing group, Will Ritter, Kat Santoro, Vlad Verano, Sarah Hull, Brenda Winter Hansen, and Colleen Conway Ramos. Big thanks to Molly Harper and Jeanette Batista for help with the Enchanted Forest, care packages, and general support (and to J for reading this book eight times), as well as to Olivia Waite for the carnival scene—fladgers for all. So many people were here for me during this process—I hope I didn't forget anyone. (If I did, please know that it's not that I'm ungrateful, but this book took forever to write, and I have a poor memory for anything besides movie quotes.)

Of course, huge thanks and all of my love to my friends and family, who put up with a lot. Most of all to every bookseller, librarian, book blogger, and reader who has supported my silly books and waited patiently for this one, thank you to the end and back.